THE NEXT BIG THING

When Tierney's gorgeous boss offers to promote her, she is ecstatic! Finally Matt's noticed her.

Then comes the catch – she must find the Next Big Thing, a girl for the sexiest ad campaign *ever. And she has one week to do it!*

But a rival wants both Matt and the promotion. Meet Vanita, with her designer broomstick and killer cleavage.

Now it's a race to see who'll find the Next Big Thing and succeed in the tough but trendy world of Cool Hunting.

And life is about to pull a fast one . . .

'A sassy, up-to-the-minute take on media manipulation and the cult of celebrity . . . insightful and lighthearted' – *Heat*

Sexier than last year's Earl Jeans and funnier than a grown man on a scooter, Sara Caspian's inside view on Cool Hunting is so bright you'll need a pair of Cazals to read it' – Chris Manby

About the author

Sara Caspian is a former Cosmopolitan Young Journalist of the Year. *The Next Big Thing* is her first novel.

THE NEXT BIG THING

Sara Caspian

CORONET BOOKS
Hodder & Stoughton

First published in Great Britain in 2000 by Hodder and Stoughton
First published in paperback in 2001 by Hodder and Stoughton
A division of Hodder Headline

A Coronet Paperback

10 9 8 7 6 5 4 3

British Library Cataloguing in Publication Data

Caspian, Sara
The next big thing
1.Love stories
I.Title
823.9'2 [F]

ISBN 0 340 76955 6

Typeset by Phoenix Typesetting, Ilkley, West Yorkshire
Printed and bound in Great Britain by
Mackays of Chatham, plc, Chatham, Kent

Hodder and Stoughton
A division of Hodder Headline
338 Euston Road
London NW1 3BH

This book is dedicated to my mother
– the bravest person I know

THANKS TO

A MASSIVE thank you to my brilliant brother John, for taking me seriously when I decided to write a book, and for then introducing me to the idea of Cool Hunting; for always insisting we would see the *NBT* on the shelves; for his unflagging optimism and gorgeous sense of humour over the last two years; finally for being both a wonderful brother and a true friend.

My one-in-a-million mother, for redefining the word 'brave' and proving that miracles do happen. I cannot convey in words the incredible level of support you have shown me, not to mention such unconditional love, kindness and generosity over the years. Thank you for never losing your smashing sense of fun and being an inspiration to all who know you. Mostly, thank you for having faith in me during those times when I didn't. Mum, this one's for you!

Grandpa, for the little green book, all the stories, and for looking over my shoulder.

My father, for still being the wittiest person I know and for his ongoing love and support; big-time thanks also to Betty for all her kindness to me over the years; also to my lovely

Nana, for the constant supply of chocolate and TLC!

To the very special Pat Jacobs – you must have had a word with Him upstairs again!

A heartfelt thank you to Philip 'Saint' Saunders, whose wise words, sense of humour, and super-staunch friendship have meant a great deal. Thanks for putting up with me during my more demented moments, for coming to the rescue when the demon-computer rebelled, and for being e-mail guardian when technophobia took over completely!

The wonderful, witty Tammy Klee, for making me laugh till I cry on a regular basis, for being such a great friend and for always understanding me; finally for being a true kindred spirit and for sharing in the bad hair days and Japanese food obsession!

The one and only Phil Stein, for not letting the miles make a difference, for knowing me too well, and for *always* being right!

Annie Fine – you are quite simply fantastic! Cheers for always telling it like it is, for being there with a pep talk whenever I needed one, and for being one of the most loyal people I have ever met.

The totally lovely Lorraine Kaye, whose infectious laugh never fails to make me feel good and who was so understanding when I kept disappearing to work on the *NBT*; thanks for being there and being you!

Jo Mendel, for being a fabulous friend and for putting up with my constant cancellations and vanishing acts while writing this book.

As a first-time writer I was lucky to have the support of an agent who is very kind, extremely clever and eternally patient.

Special thanks go to Simon Trewin – you truly were an invaluable help in getting the *NBT* right, and in being so encouraging every step of the way, especially when the book went out. Finally, thank you for retaining a wicked sense of humour and making me laugh so much throughout!

Steve Mathieson, for the *Varsity* days and for being so enthusiastic over my early journalistic efforts; also for his continued friendship.

To Tristan 'KTF' Marshall; Huy Nguyen, Adam Lamb, Maryam Gouple, Hagit Ben-Artzi and Emma Fletcher, for being such good mates and always being so positive; for his expertise on ice sculpture, Jamie Hamilton of 'Duncan Hamilton Ice Sculptor'; Mick and Ros Abrahams for their help and kindness with the photos.

Debra Fisher, who for so many years told me I should, could and one day would write a book, and whose support and friendship during the writing of the *NBT* meant a lot.

Finally, thank you so much to Philippa Pride and all at Hodder & Stoughton, for believing in the *Next Big Thing* and making it happen.

THE NEXT
BIG
THING

1

Cool Hunting

'*She's back* – Satan's Sister is in the building!' Tierney shuddered. 'I can *feel* it!' Jumping up, she lurched out of the bustling office, across the hall and into the kitchen. By the time Liz caught her up, she was busy lighting a cigarette with trembling fingers.

'Tier! What are you talking about? Vanita won't be back for another hour at least!'

'Trust me. Any second now she'll strut in like a peacock on Prozac.' Tierney glanced out of the window; sure enough the sky had darkened, sunlight fleeing.

Even the weather was scared.

'But she'll be with the clients right up until it's your turn to meet them.' Liz tapped her watch. 'And that's not until two.'

'Unless they really love Vanita's pitch and decide to go with her!' Tierney's blue eyes widened with horror as she collapsed into a chair. 'I bet they do! I bet they won't even turn up this afternoon! The sods are probably e-mailing me right now to cancel!' She let out a wail of pure despair.

'Stop stressing!' Liz sat down beside her at the tiny chrome table. 'You're the best Cool Hunter around – even better than me! They'll adore you.'

'Can I have that in writing? 'Cause if they don't, and Vanita clinches the contract, she'll get promoted. *We'll be working for the Valkyrie . . .*'

Both girls winced.

'I feel dizzy . . .' Tierney slumped forward, blonde hair falling over her face. 'Think I'm going to pass out . . .'

Liz looked at her in alarm. 'Take deep breaths . . . that's it . . . and again . . . it's just a panic attack.'

'Or this flipping Wonderbra – it's so tight it's cutting off the blood supply to my brain! Lizzy, how do I look?'

'You look nice, relax.'

'*Nice!*' Tierney scowled. 'What d'you mean, *nice*? I need to look more than *nice*! I need to look *great*! I need to look confident! Calm!' She flung the cigarette over her shoulder at the bin; it hit a stack of newspapers which instantly burst into flame. '*I NEED TO LOOK LIKE I'M IN CONTROL!!!*'

Jumping up, Liz chucked a mug of cold water over the burning bundle, her eyes watering from the smoke. Tierney, gazing glumly into space, didn't even notice.

Then they heard it: the lift hissing open, followed by the snap of killer heels against the parquet floor.

'Told you,' muttered Tierney.

'It might not be her . . .' Liz protested weakly.

They both fidgeted and looked at the door.

A moment later Vanita swept into the room, her thin lips curving in a smile cold enough to cause frostbite.

Tierney watched her nervously. A buxom brunette, Vanita Slater was known for wearing plunging tops and wielding her cleavage like a weapon. Her blood-red fingernails were long enough to ski off, and her raven ringlets snaked round her face and to her waist. She looked like Rapunzel gone wrong, and Tierney often imagined her being throttled by all that hair while asleep. No harm in hoping . . .

Vanita and Tierney had joined Prophets Inc. at the same time, and it was a case of loathing at first sight. The older woman enjoyed calling the shots and resented Tierney's ambition. Worse, Matt Lucas, a colleague, was keen to go out with Tierney, and Vanita was emerald with envy.

Now, as Tierney waited tensely for her rival to speak, Vanita's smile became a smirk. 'My pitch went brilliantly! They *loved* me!' she declared, flicking back an ebony curl. Tierney's face fell, and, satisfied, Vanita turned and marched back into the corridor.

'Fuck.' Tierney felt sick.

'And they'll like *you*! Come on!' Liz pulled Tierney out of the kitchen. 'Remember: it's not over till it's over.'

'Yeah, well, the fat lady may not be singing, but she's clearing her throat, I can hear it!' Tierney pasted a bright beam on her face as she followed Liz into the huge main office. Its walls were smothered in a shade of migraine yellow so painful the Marquis de Sade would have winced. Joel, their MD, insisted the colour was cool and that as trend-spotters, they must lead the way. Prophets Inc., which had their headquarters in the States, were leaders in the field of trend prediction. The London office also advised Channel Five's style programme, *The Next Big Thing*. Right now its presenter, American journalist Jake Sheridan, was filming the Prophets Inc. team for a documentary on trend analysis.

Curling up on the lilac inflatable *chaise longue* by the window, Tierney surveyed the room. As usual it was organised chaos, looking and certainly sounding like a playground. People were standing on chairs, screaming into phones, jumping up and down with excitement as they rushed around, showing off their latest finds. Several girls were exclaiming over a range of mobile phones covered in snake-skin, currently all the rage in Paris. Playing at full volume was the latest CD by Deadly Nightshade, the hippest group around; Tierney thought they sounded like cats being castrated, but music critics and teenage girls begged to differ.

And in the midst of all this activity, grey eyes narrowed, Jake Sheridan paced up and down, preparing the intro for his documentary. 'It's the trendiest career *ever* – **Cool Hunting!** We're talking hip, happening, twenty-somethings whose job is to zoom in on the zeitgeist and find out what *you* want! They get paid to hang out and tune in, because being cool is serious business for the heads of companies like Virgin, Sony, IBM, Coca-Cola, Reebok and Nike. They offer big bucks for trend-spotters to scour the streets for the fads, fashions and faces that will excite Generation Y. Everyone's looking for the Next Big Thing. Of course, to be really cool, you'll need to watch it too . . .'

His blatant plug for the show made Tierney groan.

'That bad?' Jake gave her a challenging smile, his eyes flitting over her in appreciation, and Tierney blushed. He was very attractive.

'The last bit is! Apart from that . . . it'll do. You might want to look at this.' Going over to her desk, she rummaged around before locating a slim, electric-blue binder. It was Prophets

Inc.'s latest report, the company's name and logo racing across the cover: 'PROPHETS WE ARE, PROFITS WE MAKE!'

Jake began flicking through it. 'What is this?'

'This' – Tierney grinned – 'is the Cool Bible.'

Prophets Inc. specialised in consumer trends. From clothes to cars, shoes to sounds, cosmetics to cuisine, it was all here: what people would want, need and buy. Their client companies would be itching to get hold of this report.

Jake studied it for a few minutes before turning back to her. 'It's great. Cheers.' But she was staring past him. For sauntering through the door, wearing the kind of confidence other men envied and most women fell for, was Matt Lucas.

Tierney's hormones started cheering.

He didn't walk so much as *prowl*. And something in the way he moved said here was a man who knew what he was doing between the sheets, who knew what you wanted, even those special, *secret* things you'd never, ever say . . .

Now he sent Tierney a smile so disarming it could be an anti-terrorist device; she responded with a bold wink, and Matt chuckled. Lately he'd been pursuing Tierney with a passion, keen to wine, dine and undermine her vow never to have an office fling. Why bother? They only ended in tears. And for reasons she tried not to think about, at twenty-five Tierney had already known enough heartache to last this lifetime and well into the next.

She watched Matt chat and charm his way round the office. He was six foot tall with a body so fit it should be illegal, dark hair flopping forward over those wonderful, warm brown eyes . . . Drop-dead gorgeous with a body to *die* for; truly a Fatal Attraction. Now every woman present was obeying the clarion call of escalating oestrogen: chests were thrown out, skirts hitched up and tops yanked down, the room sighing with the sound of fluttering lashes and flicking hair.

Matt started describing his recent trip to the Seychelles and Tierney made a face; no doubt he'd enjoyed studying the lesser-known mating habits of *Nubilius Babeus*.

'Lusting after Matt again?' Liz's face was wistful. 'If he was chasing me I'd be—'

'Flat on your back in his bed, you tart!' Tierney looked at her sternly. 'Well, *I* won't jeopardise my job for a bloke, especially not Matt. He's after anything with blonde hair and matching chromosomes!'

'So why are you always flirting with him?' Liz accused her. 'Talk about verbal foreplay! Poor guy doesn't know whether he's coming or going . . .'

'No harm in a bit of fun. Do him good to learn he can't have every woman within a ten-mile radius falling at his feet. In fact' – Tierney glanced over at Matt, her face mischievous – 'it's my feminist duty to teach him "No" doesn't mean "Not Yet". So, it would be positively remiss of me *not* to flirt, right?'

Liz wished she had the luxury of leading Matt on. She looked enviously at her friend: Tierney was sleek-sexy in a black T-shirt, dark denim jeans and Nike Air trainers. Her make-up was light, but she'd pencilled in some fake freckles over her nose; very hip. But then, Tierney always was, being a 'Scenester', a term coined by American-Japanese schoolgirls for someone who was ultra-cool.

'Why not just put the poor sod out of his misery and go out with him?' Liz flipped a paperclip at her.

Tierney made a face. 'But you know what I've always said about dating guys from work – oh God, remember that Christmas party?'

The girls burst out laughing. Soon after Tierney had joined Prophets Inc., a colleague, Stuart, had slipped up behind her at the Christmas bash and begun mauling her under the mistletoe. Livid, she'd pulled no punches, proving she hadn't learned karate just for kicks. Jaw and pride both bruised, Stuart had beaten a retreat so rapid sparks flew off his feet. And the word had gone round: any bloke trying it on with the new blonde bird would get laid all right – flat out on the floor faster than he could *blink*.

'At least you get asked out. Look at me!' Liz sighed. 'In the Lottery of Love, *I'm* always the rollover! And there's you, with the divine Matt Lucas ready to fall at your feet! I really think—'

'Hear those footsteps, real fast ones? That's the sound of my patience – ***running out***!' Tierney jumped out of her seat.

'Where are you going now?' Liz looked exasperated as Tierney dashed for the door.

'I've scheduled a nervous breakdown for one o'clock. If anyone wants me, I'll be in the loos!'

In the ladies', Tierney tried to tame her crowning glory; she'd washed it twice that morning, using three anti-frizz products so toxic she'd almost asphyxiated herself and caused a mini ozone hole to appear. Now she managed to squirt a stream of MaxiHold, SuperCurl, UltraLift hairspray straight into her left eye. It stung like *crazy*. Splashing icy water over her throbbing orb, Tierney hopped round the room, screeching in pain, until she stumbled into the door and tripped over the person strutting through it.

Vanita.

The temperature seemed to plummet.

Taking in Tierney's dishevelled appearance, the brunette arched one perfectly plucked eyebrow. 'God, you look a *state*! Isn't your pitch in fifteen minutes?'

'It is.' Tierney returned to the mirror and began applying blusher. Her hand shook.

Vanita saw, her beady black eyes glinting. 'You realise that even if by some miracle you get this promotion, people will think it's because of you and Matt?'

Tierney froze. 'Excuse me?'

'Oh, come on! Everyone knows he's gagging to get into your knickers, and he has the final say on who gets the job. Hardly fair, is it?'

Shoving her make-up back into her bag, Tierney tried to sound calm and failed miserably. 'I've been slogging my guts out for this promotion! If I get it, it'll be because I've *earned* it!'

'But that isn't what people will say.'

''Cause you'll make sure of that, right?'

Vanita shrugged. 'You know how it is. People gossip. Not that there's much danger of you getting the contract. Barnaby, Julian and I go way back.'

Barnaby and Julian were the clients, and were about to launch a girly beer filled with herbs and supplements especially good for women. Tierney knew she had to convince them she could make it the coolest thing around, or she could kiss goodbye to the contract. Now her butterflies began doing backflips. Olympic style.

'Known them for years,' continued Vanita cheerfully. 'Barnaby and my father play polo together. Can't wait to work with them.'

'*If* you get the contract,' Tierney reminded her through gritted teeth.

The Valkyrie gave her a pitying smile. '*When*, darling, *when* . . .'

'It's strange, Vanita, but whenever you're around I break out in this godawful *rash*! Must be allergic to you!'

Slamming the door behind her, Tierney stormed back down the hallway. Behind her, she could hear Vanita laughing coldly.

As Tierney marched back to her desk, Matt Lucas watched with interest. He couldn't work her out and it bothered him. Physically she was a definite type; if he met her at a club he'd dismiss her as just another good-looking blonde. But, he frowned, this babe had *bite*.

He felt hopeful. Matt wanted to want a serious relationship, but in his mind they were like motorway pile-ups: messy, dangerous, easily avoided by skilful manoeuvring, reading the signs, knowing when to hit the brakes. He tried to commit, but the road to his bed was like the road to hell – paved with good intentions. He was just too easily seduced. There he'd be, out with a girlfriend, when he'd see an attractive woman and start wondering mentally how it would be with her. Soon he'd be wandering physically to find out. And there was always someone prettier, wittier, *better*. So now, thinking about Tierney, Matt resolved to ask her out again. She was different, and maybe with her, *he* could be different . . .

'She your latest conquest?' An edge slipped into Jake Sheridan's voice as he watched Matt watching Tierney.

'Let's say I'm working on it. Know her?'

'I've seen her around.' Jake shrugged. 'She's . . . cute.'

Matt looked at him in surprise. The only woman Jake ever mentioned was Lisa, his fiancée, currently back in the States, waiting patiently for his six-month contract to end.

'Hey, you're spoken for, remember?' Matt teased, amused to see the journalist looking guilty.

'Just meant Tierney seems sweet, that's all.' Though Jake might flirt, he was a one-woman man, and Lisa was that woman. Except lately . . . Nothing was wrong, something just wasn't . . . *right.*

He turned to the report Matt had given him for that week's programme, chuckling at some of the trends mentioned, and deciding to lead with Kyudo, a medieval form of Japanese archery that was the latest fitness fad in LA.

Glancing back at Matt, he found his friend watching Tierney again. A vivid image of them together in bed flashed into Jake's mind, and suddenly he was stiffer than a Brit's upper lip. A jolt of jealousy towards Matt made him frown; how could he, why would he, feel possessive over a girl he didn't even *know*?

*

'It's almost two o'clock.' Tierney gulped. 'Right, well, here goes nothing . . .'

Liz held up crossed fingers. 'Best of luck, Tier. I know you can do it.' She clutched her friend's hand. 'You've got to – *I can't work for Vanita*!'

Despite herself, Tierney laughed as she headed out of the office.

As she passed Matt he blew her a kiss, eyes sliding over her. 'Tierney, don't worry. They'll adore you.' His tone softened. 'How could they not?'

That *voice.*

Her legs turned to blancmange.

Fear took over again as she entered the reception area, this month decorated in Star Wars chic. It resembled the inside of a spaceship, all gleaming silver and futuristic fabrics.

The clients, Julian Parry and Barnaby Hamilton, both had sandy hair that flopped forward, and bland if chiselled features. As Tierney approached, they glanced up, eyes ricocheting off her.

The fairer one nodded curtly. 'Two coffees, both with sugar. One black.'

He sounded like he should be teaching elocution at Eton, and Tierney's polite smile dithered on her face before deserting her totally. Nervously she extended her hand. 'Hi, I'm Tier—'

'We don't need your name, doll, just the drinks would be nice. So that's two coffees, one black, both with sugar.' As she stood there, bemused, he gave his companion an incredulous look. 'Good God, must I actually write it *down*?'

'That won't be necessary!' Tierney blushed. These jumped-up twits had assumed she was the secretary! 'I'm Tierney Marshall, Joel may have mentioned me?' She waited for a response, but both men continued staring. It was like being in Madame Tussaud's, all glassy eyes and cold faces. 'Would you like to follow me?' she persevered, fixing a smile on her face as she tried to decide the best way forward.

Julian and Barnaby were ex-public schoolboys born with not silver spoons but entire canteens of cutlery in their mouths, plus Swiss bank accounts with more digits than the National Lottery. They already owned a nightclub where the glitterati went to party, and their latest project was Bar Eden, in Queens Park, an area tipped to become the next Notting Hill. Their new product, the girly beer, would be launched at the opening, following a massive advertising campaign.

Unhappy with what their creative team had suggested, Barnaby and Julian were searching for a theme, something cool yet quirky, and Tierney knew they were turning to Prophets Inc. as a last resort.

Now she led the men outside where, lighting cigarettes, they looked round impatiently.

'I thought you'd at least organise a car!' Julian snapped.

'Wouldn't help with what we're about to do,' Tierney replied calmly, starting to walk down the street.

'Which is?'

'We call it "cultural immersion".' Tierney forced herself to sound pleasant.

'Meaning?'

'Hanging out, basically. Watching people. You want your product to be cool; well, hopefully, today you'll get some inspiration.'

They walked along in silence. Around them tribes of American and Japanese tourists brandished guide books and cameras, looking like they were about to wage war over who deserved the most pavement space. Shopkeepers leaned against doors, whistling at career girls striding past with short skirts and bulging briefcases.

Tierney gestured at the girls. 'See them? Okay, keep looking, 'cause they're your customers. Women with money to burn and a point to prove – that they can drink the blokes under the table.' She paused, checking the men were still listening. 'But our research shows this trend will reverse itself. There'll be a backlash against the Ladette Lifestyle. Instead, "future-theming" will be cool – women will invest more in looking after their health and spend more time at the gym. Is your beer organic? It should be, with all the food scares, and the whole GM food debate.'

Still sullen-faced, the men walked on ahead, taking up all the pavement so Tierney was forced to walk behind like some second-rate citizen. Undeterred, she kept up a commentary on trends she spotted.

'When you design your product's image, note how retro is in. See those women over there?' The men followed her gaze to where three brunettes were buying ice-creams. 'Look at their feet. Those canvas, flat-heeled shoes were first sold back in the 1930s, as a tennis shoe. Lots of designers and manufacturers are dipping into the archives and mixing old with new.'

Again the men digested her comments in silence. Tierney's temper was fraying at the edges but she continued talking.

'Now, see those guys? Look at what they're wearing, the cropped trousers and boxy shirts. Sort of sporty-looking, right? They're from a label called Flynow, set to be the Next Big Thing in men's fashion. You see, and this relates to your product, people want things to be functional *and* fun. Now, if you have a drink which is healthy and holistic, as well as tasting good, you're there!'

A moment later she pointed further down the street. 'This is big in Soho, but it's a trend that will spread: rickshaws. Loads of people use them, especially at night. They're cheap, environmentally friendly, and part of a wider craze including three-wheeled cars and prams.'

Leading them down a narrow alleyway, she stopped outside a frosted door on which was a sign: 'PLUG INN'. As Tierney touched it the glass cleared, becoming transparent.

The men gaped.

'What is this place?' Barnaby pushed the doors open.

'A twenty-four-hour café dedicated to escapism.' Tierney stood back while the men looked round. The walls and ceiling were mirrored, making the room look bigger than it actually was. Baleri egg seats were dotted throughout, in which people reclined, wearing headsets, staring into space, while on low wooden tables in front of them, little black boxes flashed and flickered at various speeds.

Julian stared. 'What on earth are they doing?'

'Using mind machines, or Light Technology Devices. It's a hip thing to do in the States right now; there was a rumour Kurt Cobain used to use one.' Seeing that both Barnaby and Julian were listening intently, Tierney explained further. 'Basically, bright light flashed at specific frequencies stimulates the right side of the brain and increases creativity.'

Lounging on a circle of chairs in the centre of the room, a group of teenagers sat quietly, holding slender blue canisters up to their faces. Tierney grinned. 'They're inhaling pure oxygen. Another new fad is laughing gas.'

Barnaby walked slowly round the room, examining the tables on which lay Sony PlayStations instead of magazines or papers.

Tierney led the men back to the door. 'The Plug Inn also has a woman-friendly policy; lots of places are doing this now. There's a freephone over there for girls to call cabs, women are given priority when it comes to getting tables, and they've even hired all-female bar staff.'

Outside, Tierney walked on ahead, listening to the men mumbling irritably. She could feel panic setting in, and promotion passing her by, since it was clear their minds were locked tighter than Fort Knox. 'Might as well stand on my head and start speaking in sodding Swahili for all the difference it would make to these *schmucks*!' she muttered angrily.

Seeing Julian's eyes darting her way as he said something to his colleague, Tierney strained to hear.

'*Barbie* goes to work! Surprised she's not melting in all this sunshine!'

'Yeah, more cleavage than brains, that one!'

Tierney's hands itched to bang their stupid, sexist heads together. Good-looking guys were always assumed to be equally blessed in the brains department – why didn't the same apply to women?

I've got an IQ of 168! she wanted to yell. *How's **that** for an impressive vital statistic?*

'And what is it you planned on showing us next?' Julian glanced at his Rolex.

'Guess we may as well, since we're here.' Crossing to the far side of the tiny courtyard they were now in, her shoes clattering on the cobbled floor, Tierney rapped loudly on a long, concertina-like door. 'Jamie? *JAMIE?*'

A few minutes later the door was pulled back with a loud whinge to reveal an amiable-looking guy with dishevelled brown hair. 'About time!' Grinning at Tierney, he beckoned them inside and introduced himself.

Exchanging a look, Barnaby and Julian brushed past Tierney, walking into a large studio. In the middle were seven huge blocks of ice.

Barnaby shivered. 'It's freezing in here!'

Tierney turned to Jamie. 'Can we have a look in the cold store?'

He nodded and led them further back into the studio, opening a huge metal door and showing them into a smaller, even colder room.

Inside were several works in progress, including a series of intricately carved Gothic chairs, the ice smooth and rounded. Nearby was a line of slender trees, also made totally of ice, and simply beautiful, as they shimmered and sparkled under the soft lighting.

Seeing the men's faces, Tierney smiled. 'The ultimate in Cool – *ice sculpture*! A natural extension of the clean lines and restrained design of the chrome and glass being used in homes and offices. Ice is the Next Big Thing; organic, pure, chic. Right, Jamie?'

The sculptor nodded. 'We've noticed a big increase in commissions lately. More and more television adverts feature ice, for example. It has that lack of permanence you've probably seen in other areas, like inflatable furniture. That same element of flexibility.'

Barnaby and Julian started chattering quickly.

'Could you sculpt a person?' Barnaby demanded. 'I mean, if we provided the model, could you reproduce her in ice? Life-sized?'

'Sure.' Jamie wiped his hands on his apron. 'You'd lose some of the surface detail by doing it that way, but they can be pretty striking. I've done them before.' Closing the metal door again, Jamie led them back into the main studio.

'Jules, are you thinking what I'm thinking?' Barnaby asked slowly.

'It's perfect!' Julian laughed. 'Just what we wanted! Cool but quirky . . . let's do it!' He turned back to Jamie, who was watching closely. 'How much notice do you need?'

'About three weeks.' Digging in his pocket he produced a crumpled business card. 'I start work early at the moment because of the heat. You can get me here any time before midday.'

Bemused, Tierney followed Barnaby and Julian out into the tiny courtyard again.

Julian cleared his throat. 'I guess we owe you an apology. We did think you were rather, well, off track, but this latest thing, it's ideal.' He managed a chilly smile.

'You haven't actually told me much about your product,' Tierney pointed out.

Julian slipped on Calvin Klein sunglasses. 'It's a girly beer: low alcohol, full of herbs and fruits traditionally good for women, like cranberry and raspberry. We're also adding mead, and we'll take your advice and look into making it organic.'

'Do you have a gimmick, a USP?' Seeing their frowns, she

laughed. 'Unique Selling Point. Mind you, aiming it at women is that, I guess.'

'The biggest problem is that we don't have a name for it yet.' Barnaby shrugged. 'I tell you, our usual creative team came up with umpteen ideas: none of them worked. It's a nightmare.'

Tierney thought for a moment. 'You need something cute . . . something women will identify with instantly . . .' Suddenly her face lit up and she clapped her hands in delight. 'How about – **EVE'S BREW** . . . ? After all, it's being launched at Bar Eden, right?'

Barnaby and Julian stared at her, their eyes widening. 'That's it . . .' Barnaby whispered, clutching Julian's arm and nodding emphatically. '**EVE'S BREW!** Oh, my God, I *love* it!'

Even Julian was smiling.

Tierney felt herself starting to get excited about the promotion again. Surely she was close to clinching this contract?

'So . . .' She stared down at the kerb, scared her hopes and fears would be evident in her eyes. 'So what happens now?'

'Right, well.' Again Barnaby glanced at Julian. 'We'll tell you what we told Vanita. Your pitches have both been excellent. It's hard to choose between you. So, we think the fairest way to proceed is this: whoever finds what we're looking for gets the contract.'

'What you're looking for?' Tierney echoed, puzzled.

'The right face to front our product. We've tried every model agency in the country and still drawn a blank. It's crucial we get it right, because, trust me, she's going to be the most talked-about girl in the country.'

Tierney frowned. Cool Hunting for people was the toughest type of all, since it was so hard to define the right look, and it was so much more than just regular features and good bone structure.

'So you want me to find a girl for the Eve's Brew ads?'

'Not *a* girl – *the* girl!' Barnaby smiled. '***We want you to find us the* Next Big Thing . . .'**

2

The Principles Of Lust

Chaos with walls. That was their home, Tierney decided, dumping her bag in the hall. She could hear Carin and Andy, her housemates, watching television in the living room. About to join them, she caught movement from the stairs, ducking as Genghis, Carin's beloved Shitsu, flung himself at her head with a frantic gnashing of teeth. He'd been jealous of Tierney since the day she moved in, and Carin was now taking him to an animal shrink for canine counselling. Tierney sighed – Genghis was still a psychotic mothball, but Carin was calmer . . .

Slinging her coat over the banisters, she fought her way through the hall, which, filled with triffid-like rubber plants, looked more like the Amazon than a semi-detached in suburbia. Once in the kitchen, she lunged for the ghetto-blaster, desperate to reduce the volume; Carin insisted the plants needed music, and this week was treating them to Gregorian chanting, morose-sounding monks lamenting in Latin.

Glancing round, Tierney winced. 'Oh my God, *look* at this

place, it's a *tip* . . .' The tiny kitchen was overflowing with wine bottles and beer cans, which rolled around and sounded like out-of-key windchimes. The sink overflowed with cups, plates and bowls, all sporting impressive clusters of what resembled botulism. Clearly her housemates had a fatal allergy to Fairy Liquid. Well, no way was she tidying up, not again. This was *Char Wars*.

'Tierney, doll, you don't mind if Gina crashes here this week, do you?' Carin breezed into the kitchen, munching a KitKat and licking the chocolate daintily from her fingers. Gina was Carin's latest girlfriend and a one-woman demolition squad.

'Why? She finished wrecking her own place?' Tierney looked at her housemate suspiciously. 'You've already told her she can stay, haven't you?'

Carin laughed. 'You know me too well.'

Their eyes locked and Tierney blushed.

She watched Carin grab some cold drinks and head back into the living room. Her housemate was striking, with olive skin, a lush red mouth, and legs so long she probably suffered permanent vertigo up there. After two years, Tierney was still bemused by the effect Carin had on both sexes. Even girls who were sincerely straight and happily heterosexual responded to the promise of pleasure in her siren-sweet voice. Male and female alike, they saw, succumbed and suffered, being swiftly replaced. Tierney suspected that for Carin, sex was mostly about having her ego stroked; still, her charm was a seductive, slippery spell enveloping everyone.

Even Tierney.

Once.

Retrieving a tub of Häagen-Dazs from the freezer where she'd buried it beneath a packet of peas, she headed for her bedroom, aka the Black Hole. Flopping on to the bed she tried to think about Eve's Brew, but all she could see in her mind's eye was Matt Lucas, and the slow, smile he'd sent her earlier today.

'He knows!' she sighed.

She's right, of course. Matt is perfectly aware he only has to look at her and Tierney falls into a fantasy more risqué than romantic. Gorgeous, graphic images of limbs entwined in Kama-Sutra-style sex . . . positions so voluptuous, pleasures so *violent* . . .

True, she's seen him seduce secretaries, ravish researchers, and tease temps keen to excel at more than just touch-typing, but never mind. Lust is running the show, and Logic not getting a look in. And Tierney knows she's never felt this way about anyone.

Not even Ben?

'Not even' – she hangs her head – 'about him.'

Ben. They'd met at university, and been together four years. Simple, special, storybook Love. Until a teenage brat who lived nearby took Daddy's gleaming new Porsche out for a spin. Like most men, he believed speed limits were for wimps and women only, and, turning a corner too fast, ended up smearing Ben all over the pavement.

Now Tierney buried her face in a pillow. She wanted to cry, but it was impossible to shed a tear, and had been since the day Ben died.

Something had frozen inside.

'Two years . . .' she whispered. Two whole years since it

happened. Twenty-four months. One hundred and four weeks. How many hours, how many minutes? So many seconds that must have elapsed, and all of them coated with the dull, gaping grey of grief. All of them empty and pain-filled.

So time healed all wounds, did it?

'Yeah, *right* . . .'

Trying to distract herself, she opened her bag and pulled out her copy of the Cool Bible, eagerly scanning the neat pages of text. Prophets Inc. employed fifteen fulltime researchers; this was market research elevated to an art form. Tierney spent a lot of time, when not actually out Cool Hunting, speaking to 'creative visionaries': artists and designers who were good at identifying underlying shifts and patterns.

She flicked through the glossy pages. Trends tipped to be big included . . . ultra-light leathers . . . futuristic fabrics . . . cotton blended with NASA-developed synthetics . . . smart clothes with in-built electric circuits to power wearable computers including laptops and mobile phones . . . denim was making a comeback . . . retro futurism with its space-age imagery and fibreglass furniture . . . kilim slippers . . . names to look out for were Japanese label Geisha . . . other names to watch were Silas . . . Maharisihi . . . Ibechick . . . Boyd . . . Blaak . . . Maggie May . . . Triple O . . . hip designers included Zakee Shariff . . . Luella Bartley . . . John Body . . . Shami Senthi and Masahid M Yasin . . . the coolest shops were Koh Samui . . . The Cross . . . The Pineal Eye . . . The Foundation . . . the Hoxton Boutique . . . Kokon To Zai . . . the buzz word was 'authenticity'; people wanted clothes that were functional but with a fun, fantasy twist . . . the Next Big Thing in dance was Capoeira, an exotic mixture of Brazilian music and martial arts . . . Russian food was set to be all the rage . . . inflatable furniture was a must-have . . . the latest craze among celebs was having exotic pets like chameleons . . . Green would be the 'in' shade for interiors . . .

Smiling, Tierney snapped the report shut and settled down to her notes for Eve's Brew. She *had* to find the right girl for this ad campaign. Work for Vanita the Valkyrie?

'I don't *think* so!'

*

The sound of his conscience screaming followed Matt as he sauntered into Titanic. Pausing at the bottom of the stairs, he considered turning round and walking right out again, because he really shouldn't be here meeting Vanita to talk about this promotion. After all, there was nothing to say. Whoever found Eve, got the contract, and the job. End of story.

However, he and Vanita were old flames, and she'd pleaded with him to meet her, so now Matt followed the waiter past the bar, his conscience still nudging him. He was uneasy, and everything seemed dark and distorted. At the next table, someone had ordered a salad, and to Matt the slices of shiny black olive lurked like giant beetles in the lettuce. Beside him, the radiator hissed angrily, and though it was a warm evening, he felt chilly.

Glancing round, he watched Vanita sashaying towards him as though on an invisible catwalk. She met several admiring looks with a slight tilt of her dark head, like a deity descending Mount Olympus. Matt smiled wryly; the woman had moves

Machiavelli would marvel at, plus she was such a shit-hot lay she practically set the sheets on fire.

'Hi . . .' Kissing him lightly on the mouth she slid into the seat opposite his, wasting no time before launching straight into her pitch. 'Matt . . . darling, you know how long I've waited for a shot at being made creative director. This position's perfect for me!' Her smile was suggestive. 'And I really *want* it.'

'Oh, I'll just bet you do . . .' Matt drawled, looking her up and down, 'but so does Tierney.'

'But can she handle it? The job, that is.' Her eyes snared his. 'I don't think she's got enough experience.'

Matt got the message: Tierney was no threat to Vanita, in bed or out of it. Well, he'd just have to check that out for himself, wouldn't he?

And in that moment he knew working for Vanita would be as much fun for Tierney as having a tooth ripped out *sans* anaesthetic. Once Vanita clawed her way through the glass ceiling, she'd slot it firmly back into place under her elegant Miu Miu heels. Hell, she'd probably have it done over in reinforced concrete!

'I've got something Tierney hasn't.' Vanita's smile was smug.

'Really?' Again Matt's eyes flicked over her. 'And what would that be?'

Just then the waiter arrived with coffee and cakes. Matt waited impatiently for Vanita to continue, but she simply stirred Sweetex into her drink, face impassive.

'So? What have you got?' he pushed.

'Adonis.' She took a delicate bite into the cake and Matt's

stare strayed to the sugar now glistening on her plum-coloured lips.

'Adonis . . .' He struggled to steady his voice as his thoughts went racing ahead. Adonis was a men's fashion house, the most exclusive in the country. There were rumours that Haden Charles, the MD, was looking to branch out into men's cosmetics and health products, a real growth area, and that he was determined to make it the trendiest range around.

Matt whistled. 'That contract must be worth . . .'

'And the rest!' Vanita's smile was droll.

'So how do you figure you could reel them in?' He poured more coffee for them both.

'Oh, long story.'

Matt gave her a look. 'Vanita . . .'

She laughed. 'All right! Haden plays golf with my father. Daddy told me, in confidence, about how Adonis are working with the Trend Factory. But the thing is' – lowering her voice, she leaned in close – 'Haden and his lot are obsessed about keeping their connection with the Trend Factory private. Daddy says the man's paranoid!'

Matt nodded his understanding. Cool Hunting was still a relatively new area and some companies remained wary.

'Anyway, the Trend Factory's MD, David, is pushing for publicity. He and Haden clash every five minutes. Now, I've got lots of contacts in the media. I can easily leak the story and keep my own name out. Haden will assume it's David and he'll go *ballistic*! They can't stand each other; word has it they're *this* close to a major showdown. All they need is an excuse. I can easily pitch Haden and persuade him to give us a shot. But I need my name kept out because Daddy would really lose it if he found out. So you'd get all the credit. And Matt, don't tell me you're not tempted, because I *know* you.'

Matt smiled. If he brought in a client like Adonis, Joel would probably make him a partner!

'But darling' – Vanita placed a hand lightly on his arm – 'this is strictly *quid pro quo*. I'll deliver Adonis, if you get me this promotion.'

As their eyes met again, Matt heard his conscience, like a voice calling in the distance. He should tell her that this was out of order, that he wouldn't let Tierney down.

But under the table, Vanita has slipped one shoe off, and the tip of her slender foot is caressing his crotch until it's hard for him to think straight. 'Feel like mixing all this business with some pleasure . . . ?' Her voice is silk-soft.

He hesitates. Last time they met here they ended up back at her place. Vanita obviously wants a repeat performance, and so, Matt realises, does he. Throwing some change down on the table and following her outside, he shrugs.

The guilt will pass.

It always does.

*

'Andy! Do you *have* to leave these here?' Waiting for him to glance up from the television, Tierney glowered at the muddy football trainers on the living-room table. When Andy didn't respond, she grabbed the shoes and lobbed them into the utility room, glaring at the trio sprawled on the sofa. Though he was only twenty-six, Andy's shock of white-blond hair was already flecked with silver, making him look a lot older. Along with Carin, he was the closest thing Tierney had to family in London, since her relatives were all in Dublin. Currently working in the City, Andy was about to go travelling round the Far East, a longtime ambition.

Also on the sofa were Carin and Gina, a lanky brunette with all the curves of a toothpick, both giggling and whispering. Gina gave Carin a playful push and she tumbled back, falling against Andy who instantly tensed.

'On a collision course with heartbreak . . .' Tierney murmured.

Andy had been obsessed with Carin Wheeler since the day they'd met, and Carin loved it. She dangled his heart like a yo-yo, toying with him, hinting he stood a chance, implying they were more than mates, even while she paraded her partners before him. Tierney figured eventually they'd stop flirting and start fucking, and it made her uneasy, for Carin's idea of commitment was wearing the same shade of lipstick two days running. She just wanted to add another heart to her collection.

Glancing up, Andy caught her staring, and with a wry look at the girls got up and came over, slipping an arm round her waist, smiling affectionately at her earnest face. 'You all right, Tier?'

'Fine. Question is, are you?' Her eyes returned to the sofa where Gina and Carin now reclined, legs entwined. 'What gives?'

'Nothing.' Andy laughed at the sceptical slant of her eyebrows. 'Don't miss much, do you?' His gaze drifted back to Carin. 'It's madness, knowing all I do about her, but what can I tell you? The girl *gets* to me! Stupid, right?' His tone was as blue as his eyes.

Tierney understood all right. Two years ago, when she'd first moved in, she hadn't known Carin swung both ways.

She soon found out.

It was a hot August afternoon. The heat was sticky and sweet and slow, making her limbs heavy and her hair cling in damp tendrils to the back of her neck. The air was thin and still, flattened by the summer storm everyone knew was on the way.

After sunbathing in the garden, the girls had collapsed on Carin's bed, a large futon under the window, scattered with brightly coloured cushions. Thunder heaved in the distance, and the sky had been a strange, smoky violet, reminding Tierney of a huge amethyst covered in dust.

Lightning flared like a brilliant camera flash at the edge of her vision as the storm stalked through the sky. A bumblebee hurled itself kamikaze-style against the window, buzzing indignantly, and barely having the energy to speak, the girls had just lazed there, too hot even in bikini briefs and thin summer tops.

Tierney's back was badly sunburned, sore and prickly, and seeing her wince, Carin had rummaged through the bedside table, finding some aftersun lotion. Casually, she'd shifted position so she was kneeling behind Tierney on the bed, her bare thighs warm and firm as they pressed against Tierney's legs. Drowsy, Tierney hadn't thought anything of it when Carin began rubbing the cream in, just enjoying the cool lotion bathing her thirsty skin.

As Carin's fingers gently massaged it into her neck and shoulders, Tierney's eyes became heavy, and by the time she realised Carin's fingers seemed to be lingering, she was too comfortable and confused to move, so just sat there, wondering if she was imagining it or if there was the slightest, softest suggestion in the way Carin's hands were now slipping under her top, brushing gently over the hollow of her back. She'd told herself not to be stupid, it was the heat toying with her brain.

But as Tierney knew, a person's voice and even their eyes could lie, but not their touch. Skin to skin was true.

Carin's soft, slender fingers were trailing along her shoulders, swirling lightly over her spine, stroking and swaying against her skin until Tierney had felt need rippling through her body, until she couldn't help wondering what those hands would feel like sliding over the quivering plane of her stomach, easing along the inside of her thighs . . .

The storm had gathered momentum and it grew hotter, the air seemed to smoulder, and things had taken on a dreamlike quality as Carin started teasing and tempting Tierney's breasts through her flimsy top. Around them, lightning swiped through the sky like a huge electric claw, thunder slammed, and storm clouds looking like singed cotton wool loomed, swelling and shape-shifting as they closed in. Carin's hand became more insistent, slipping inside Tierney's top and caressing her breasts, and for a few moments, Tierney felt like she was drowning in waves of confusion and pleasure. Then Carin had slowly unbuttoned Tierney's top, sliding it over her shoulders, before leaning forward, her long dark hair brushing against Tierney's bare back, her warm thighs hugging Tierney's hips, her lips stealing over Tierney's spine in tiny, tantalising butterfly kisses.

She sighed as Carin began kissing her on the mouth, drawing her lips into honeyed, heavenly, forever-kisses, while her fingers were still stroking Tierney's breasts until she felt her nipples hardening. Around them the storm was seething, the sky convulsing, lightning lunging through it in blinding white spasms.

Then Carin was slipping her fingers inside Tierney's bikini briefs, over the base of her spine and the tight curve of her buttocks. Carin's hand was trailing over her hips, her fingers sliding round and down as she began finger-fucking her, and Tierney heard herself cry out, but her voice was lost as the thunder began stamping, getting louder by the minute, the sky flickering furious and fast like a giant strobe light under the window.

A part of Tierney's mind had done a double-take. If she'd been back home in Dublin, she'd have pulled away, pulled back. But she was here, alone, in London. Ben was gone, and no one knew her yet, not really. No one to speak of shoulds and shouldn'ts, to tell her what she was or wasn't.

It was like being in freefall.

The next day she'd panicked. What did this make her – straight but – *flexible*? Was she about to plunge headfirst into an identity crisis?

Over the next few weeks, Tierney had tested herself constantly, scrutinising women she passed in the street, appraising models in magazines, scanning her emotions and body for the faintest flicker of desire in response to a pretty face or fantastic figure. To her relief, she never felt it. It wasn't Carin she wanted: she had just been vulnerable, would have responded to anyone offering to fill the sad, solitary space within her, the legacy of Ben's death. Maybe, she'd mused, being with a woman didn't make her feel as disloyal to Ben as being with a man might.

For a while she'd been awkward with Carin, but her housemate guessed what was wrong and told Tierney not to worry, she wasn't really her type. Then they were laughing and, to Tierney's delight, became the best of mates. When Andy had moved in, things were even better. And if occasionally the two girls' eyes met and Tierney knew they were both thinking of that night, it didn't matter, for it was a door that had been firmly closed.

Now, remembering, she blushed again and Andy gave her a quizzical smile. Suddenly Tierney was uneasy. For didn't every experience make its mark? And just as losing Ben had left a glint of grief in her eyes even when she smiled, might there now be a trace of a pleasure once shared?

Some slight, subtle, indelible sign; a keepsake of the skin.

'Look, I know you're crazy about Carin, but it *will* fade.' She tried to reassure Andy, who was still looking miserable. 'You'll see, it'll burn itself out . . .'

'Sure, like a forest fire!' He sighed, watching Carin and Gina again. Then, face still morose, he sat down and started flicking through one of his many travel guides.

Back in her bedroom, Tierney started thinking about Matt again. Then she began jotting down ideas for the Eve's Brew project. Tomorrow she'd start Cool Hunting for the right face, and when she found that, promotion would be hers.

The promotion she wanted so badly it hurt.

3

Who's That Girl . . . ?

'Amazing Vanita's little finger isn't swollen, the way she's been twisting Joel round it!' Tierney frowned as she watched the two of them, standing out in the hall, talking quietly. It seemed each time she looked up, there they were, huddled together, deep in discussion.

Brushing a load of sweet wrappers off her desk, Liz smiled sympathetically. 'From your less than sunny mood, I take it Project Eve isn't going well?'

Tierney sighed. 'I tell you, Lizzy, I've *never* had this much trouble finding the right face. It's a *nightmare*!'

Over the past month she'd run herself ragged Cool Hunting for the Next Big Thing. A current trend was to use students as models, and since Manchester was the hippest university, Tierney had spent three days there, scouring the city. No joy. Barnaby and Julian had graduated from Cambridge, so she'd tried there. Ditto. It was the same story in Leeds, Hull, Leicester and Liverpool.

In London, she'd tried all the usual haunts, hanging around for hours outside Top Shop in Oxford Circus, a favourite with model-agency scouts because of the teenage girls who swarmed there. Still no luck. She'd tried clubs and pubs, bars and schools, but every face she found lacked *edge*. All Tierney knew was that she'd recognise the right look, if and when she saw it.

She'd also tried every modelling agency in the country, looking at thousands of photographs until her vision blurred. Nothing. Each night after work she went straight home and sat up until the early hours, flicking frantically through every magazine she could get her hands on. To stay awake she knocked back enough black coffee to fill a reservoir, and the caffeine was making her jittery. Right now her skull felt like it was rattling with tension.

All her colleagues knew she and Vanita were competing, and Tierney knew her quest to find Eve was a standing joke. Her competitive streak was taking over: she couldn't *bear* the idea of losing her precious promotion to the Valkyrie.

Tierney was a woman obsessed, and everyone knew it.

'I haven't heard any whispers that Vanita's having better luck.' Liz patted her arm, trying to console her.

'I know, but it's weird, she doesn't seem worried, does she?' Tierney didn't get it. Vanita seemed strangely smug, and Joel and Matt were treating her like she was made of finest porcelain. Something was going on, but what?

Now her eyes widened at Vanita's outfit: a skimpy grey dress-cum-gymslip which she'd teamed with knee-high black socks and black lace-up boots. Her raven hair was in two long plaits and her lips dripped with baby-pink lipgloss.

'Jesus *wept* – and he would if he saw her!' Liz shook her head in disbelief. 'Okay, School is Cool right now, but what does she *look* like? Welcome to St Trinian's – the Twilight Years!'

'And I know just where she can shove her sodding hockey stick . . .' Tierney snapped the end off her Biro. In actual fact, Vanita looked younger than her thirty-two years.

The phone rang and she jumped, not wanting to answer it. Julian and Barnaby called every day for progress reports, piling on the pressure, reminding her – like she didn't know – that they needed Eve, and fast. Tierney reckoned if she didn't come up with results soon, they'd turn to another company or choose Vanita just because she was more on their wavelength. She felt queasy at the thought.

Ignoring the phone, she switched on her computer and tried to focus on listing the trends she'd found lately. The first was Pretty in Punk, a revival trend: teenage girls ramming their bodies into rib-cracking black leather and painting their faces until they resembled long-lost members of the Addams Family. More scary than sexy really, but Tierney knew several fashion houses would jump on the look. The next trend made her laugh despite her bad mood. A label called Après Noir had started producing silky, frilly lingerie – for blokes. Hyped as being for guys man enough to reveal their feminine side, it was seriously cool.

'Tierney!' Joel materialised beside her, his round blue eyes twinkling away at her behind his glasses. 'How's the flat coming on?'

'Not bad, actually.' Her face brightened. Prophets Inc. was working on a project with *The Next Big Thing* team: together they were designing the hippest home in Britain. In three months the programme's viewers would name the person who epitomised Cool, and first prize was the flat. Everyone was excited and the tabloids were giving it lots of publicity, to Joel's delight. Though she'd never admit it, sometimes Tierney felt a flicker of envy for the winner.

Now she grinned at her boss. 'I met up with Sebastian Carmichael for a drink, and guess what? He's agreed to come up with something for the project.'

'Good girl.' Joel beamed. 'This should be interesting.'

'Lethal, more like . . .' muttered Tierney, as Joel wandered off, polishing his glasses absentmindedly.

Sebastian was the artist *du jour*. His first exhibition, **'Femme Fatale'**, featured a glass case containing a naked woman, lying totally still on a sheet of red silk. The press went mad, waxing lyrical about the 'sheer simplicity and beauty' of the statement, about how the model's amazing ability to lie still for hours was an 'inspired testament' to women's 'intrinsic serenity and inner calm'. On day one, reviewers raved, queues formed and Sebastian was hailed as the coolest creative in the capital. Then a teenage boy meekly pointed out that since the lone air-hole in the glass was too small, the model was actually unconscious. Since the press weren't about to admit they were wrong, they proceeded to hype Sebastian even more.

'So, Ms Marshall, moment of truth!' With a confident grin, Matt Lucas cleared a space for himself on her desk, pushing papers aside and making himself comfortable, before leaning towards her until their heads almost touched. 'Saturday night. Dinner. I'll cook.' When Tierney looked blank, he laughed. 'Come on, even you can't refuse an offer like that. My culinary skills are impressive, so I'm told. Addictive, even. I promise, you won't go hungry . . .'

Attempting a smile which emerged more as a grimace, Tierney prepared to decline. But – she scowled at Liz making swooning motions in the background – her will felt weak and her body was begging her to pleasepleasepleaseohwon't-you*please* just *go – for – it*!!! Clinging on to her willpower, she lurched out of her seat, grabbing her coat and bag. 'I can't, sorry.'

'Where are you going?' Bemused, Matt stood up too, frowning as she went flying towards the door.

Tierney tapped her watch. 'Lunchtime. I'm going shopping! Retail therapy!' She was desperate to get away before she agreed to something she'd probably regret.

Whizzing round the corner, she collided with Jake Sheridan, and laughing, he reached out to steady her as she pitched forward. 'Going somewhere important?'

Tierney made a face. 'Not really.'

Noting her dejected expression, Jake squeezed her shoulder, his eyes softening. 'Hey, you okay? Don't look your usual cheerful self . . .'

For a moment, seeing the genuine interest in his face, Tierney felt strangely tempted to pour out her tale of lost promotion and career angst. Then she chided herself; she barely knew the bloke, for God's sake! 'I'm fine. Just in a rush, that's all.'

Jake nodded, and as she looked at him, he realised he was still holding her. He quickly let go. 'See you, then.'

Tierney smiled briskly. 'Sure. 'Bye.'

Then she was racing off down the corridor; turning the corner, she glanced back to where Jake was still standing, staring after her. They both smiled, shyly, and went their separate ways.

*

'*Bugger!* My bank balance could rival the Dead Sea for the title of Lowest Point On Earth!' Tierney glared at the glowing cash-point screen as behind her the queue shifted impatiently. 'Oh well, time to give my overdraft some exercise . . .'

In the road drivers locked horns and wills as they fought for space. The sudden screeching of brakes as two cars almost crashed made Tierney jump. A yell from behind caused her to turn sharply and she hopped out of the way as a bicycle went whizzing past, its rider shaking a furious fist in her face. Stumbling backwards, she just avoided bashing into a toddler, swiftly snatched from her path by a glaring mother who scolded Tierney loudly.

Suddenly she was scared to move; it seemed there was no tiny space on this street belonging to her. Tierney felt a flutter of panic. She was out of sync with herself and with the world. So much for shopping the stress out her system. 'I *am* going to enjoy this!' she vowed fiercely, crossing the road. 'This *is* going to be fun . . .'

*

Two hours later she was glaring heavenwards at which-ever mischievous fate was lounging round with nothing better to do than irritate the hell out of her. 'It's working!' she informed it.

First she'd headed for Claire's, the trendiest shop for girly accessories, to buy some make-up and cheer herself up. Impatient, Tierney had tried to push her way through a crowded aisle; next thing she knew, her basket caught the corner of a stand and a mountain of hairclips came tumbling down. A woman skidded on one, grabbed on to her friend for support and pulled her over as they both went sprawling into a display case which promptly collapsed. Chaos ensued.

Tierney had legged it into the next aisle, trying lipsticks in bright pink and deep brown along the back of her wrists and arms. Then she realised three were fluorescent and apparently there to stay. 'Oh great, now I'll glow in the dark to boot! Bloody *brilliant* . . .'

Now suffering from the mother of all migraines, she'd headed for the nearest chemist, desperate to find a packet of the only pills that ever helped. Already, red-hot needles of pain were boring their way into her brain; anxiously she waited for her turn, noting that the pharmacist was young and determined to do things by the book. Dangling the box of pills before her eyes, he swung them back and forth like a demented hypnotist, reading the instructions out loud to himself, slowly, while Tierney leaned on the counter and massaged her throbbing temples.

'Look, I don't mean to be rude, but would you please just give me the tablets?'

Giving her an officious frown, he'd clasped the pills to his chest like they were made of gold. 'Not so fast. Have you taken these before?'

'Yes, and I *really* need them—'

'You mustn't take them without water, and always with food!' He wagged a finger earnestly in her face.

'I know!' Stars were exploding before her eyes, her brain enjoying its own fireworks display. 'Please – just give me the pills!'

'They're very strong and contra-indicated if—'

'I really do need them *now*!' In desperation she shoved the money forward.

Flicking a piece of lint from his shirt, the man gave her a patronising smile. 'And are you aware that if you're taking any other medication, like the Pill, for ex—'

'Just give me the sodding tablets!!!' Tierney had screeched, prising the packet from the hapless chemist's fingers and throwing the money at him.

Now, gathering up all her bags, filled with clothes, CDs and cosmetics, she headed for the station. Around her, people brandished designer carrier bags as they barged in and out of shops, squealing over purchases and having fist-fights over taxis. Tierney sighed as she got caught up in a knot of snap-happy Americans determined to take photos of every shop, street and road sign in sight.

After trying to slip past them and finding herself blocked, she gave up, shuffling along behind the chattering convoy. Her skin felt unbearably hot and sticky under all the make-up, and the new top she was wearing was scratchy and sore against the back of her neck.

And all the while, she was still looking for the Face, her eyes skimming hopefully over every girl who passed, searching for that elusive . . . what, exactly? Character? Charisma? Factor X? That certain something which made someone stand out. She was surrounded by women, but they were all wrong. Too pretty. Too bland. Too young, and not merely in years.

Frustrated, Tierney swung her Koh Samui bag so violently she almost knocked the person behind her unconscious.

Surely there must be *one* girl, somewhere, who would capture the mood? Like when Sarah Doukas, head of Storm, glimpsed Kate Moss lounging round an American airport, and just knew the girl had 'it'. That, Tierney smiled wryly, was what she needed now, a bit of luck.

A face.

A face with a bit of edge.

A face with a hint of humour or hunger or anger or *something.*

Maybe she'd never find it.

The thought sent panic hurtling through her body, and gasping, she stopped, trying to catch her breath. Anxiety fluttered like some giant insect trapped in her chest. And it was at that moment Life kindly decided to cut her some slack, for as she collapsed against the wall, swamped by fear and fatigue and a sudden sense of failure, Tierney saw her.

The Next Big Thing.

She was scared to look away in case the girl vanished like a mirage, so she stayed where she was, leaning against a shop front, legs unsteady, and watched her standing in the middle of the crowded pavement, holding out copies of the *Big Issue* to the people brushing past. Tierney blinked. This could *not* be happening. Life didn't work this way. Or did it? Because it was as though someone had reached into her head and plucked out a blueprint of how Eve should look, then fashioned her into a living, breathing woman right before her eyes. Or rather, girl, since she didn't look more than seventeen.

Her mouth and jaw were taut, like she'd swallowed too much pride and it had lodged in her throat like a peach stone.

She had sandy hair, cropped short, and she was tall, with a lithe, lanky body. Her movements were deliberate, careful, as though she lost a little more energy each time she moved, as though one more knock and she'd be down for the count. Tierney recognised that look, because after Ben died she'd seen it in the mirror.

She edged closer, pretending to look in shop windows. The girl had tawny eyes, slanted like a cat's, and way too large in her small face. Her cheekbones were so sharply defined they were like ledges jutting out of her skin, and her mouth was wide, but lovely.

Feeling like a spy, and a bad one at that, Tierney inched closer still, until she was standing opposite the girl. Her eyes weren't just one shade of brown, but a mosaic of tiny golden flecks. She wore faded jeans which hung loosely over her slender hips, and a thin white T-shirt.

Tierney laughed with sheer delight. There was no one thing which made this girl stand out. She wasn't the most beautiful or stunning woman around, but she was attractive in a way that was raw. Edgy. *Cool.*

Taking a deep breath, she walked over, nodding at the magazines and pulling out her purse. The girl held one out but Tierney stopped her. 'Thanks, but I don't want one. I want them all.'

'They're a pound each. And I've got over fifty here.'

Tierney pulled out some ten-pound notes.

'Suit yourself.' Shrugging, the girl handed over the bundle, pocketing the money quickly and glancing round warily as if expecting to see a television camera lurking nearby.

Tierney stuffed the magazines in her bag and held out her

business card which was ignored. 'Okay, I know this is a cliché' – Tierney smiled sheepishly – 'but has anyone ever suggested you try modelling?'

'Yeah, but they're usually blokes and I tell them to fuck off!' White-faced, the girl began backing away, looking at Tierney like she was some figure from her worst nightmare.

Tierney stayed calm. No way was she about to let this chance slip through her fingers. 'Calm down.' She pressed her card into the girl's hand. 'This is kosher, promise! I'm looking for a face, and I think you're it. How would you like fifteen minutes of fame and a whole lot more?'

The girl examined the card for a minute before glaring at Tierney again. 'And in plain English, what you're saying is . . . ?'

'I'm what's known as a Cool Hunter. One of my clients wants a face to front their product. I think you could be it. At least let me give you the details.' Tierney looked at the girl pointedly, knowing her next remark was brutal, but, frankly, past caring. 'What have you got to lose?'

It worked. Weariness flickered in the girl's eyes, and quickly Tierney guided her towards a tiny Italian café nearby, asking as many questions as she thought she could get away with, and learning that Zoë Mason was seventeen and currently staying at a shelter for the homeless in London.

'What's it like there?' Tierney was intrigued.

Shaking her head, Zoë tried a laugh but couldn't quite pull it off. 'You don't want to know.'

'Because . . .' Tierney prompted as they entered the café.

'Load of psychos there,' Zoë mumbled.

Over coffee Tierney explained the Eve's Brew project and

Zoë listened carefully, interrupting once or twice. Tierney tried to get some information about the girl, but she deflected the questions as easily as Superman dodging bullets. Not that Tierney was bothered; let Julian and Barnaby sweat the details. They'd wanted the right face, and she'd found it for them.

As they left, she gave Zoë the address of the photographic studio Barnaby had mentioned. 'Can you be here at nine sharp tomorrow morning? We need to get some pictures of you, and I want to set up a meeting with the clients in the afternoon.'

Zoë's smile was shaky. 'It's all happening a bit fast . . .'

'No point in wasting time.' Tierney ushered the girl back out into the street. She was busy picturing Vanita's face when it was announced that she, Tierney, had won the promotion. They said goodbye and she began walking quickly back down Oxford Street.

Glancing back she saw Zoë still standing outside the café. There was a controlled tension to her body, as though at any second she could break into a run or a jump. She looked like she'd discovered she could reach up and pull down the stars. People hurried past her, heading back to cosy homes and crowded lives, but in that moment, it struck Tierney that of everyone she could see, though there was nothing remotely like a smile on her face, Zoë somehow looked the happiest of them all.

*

Tierney sauntered along, feeling like she was perched on top of the world. Excitement fizzed through her as she brushed impatiently past the tourists clustered in groups and hogging the pavement. The sky was a clear, baby blue, clouds like giant icebergs sliding through it.

Her face was a grin.

She was Tierney Marshall, Cool Hunter, *and she'd just found the NEXT BIG THING*!

Her promotion was in the bag, her career was on the fast track, and after this, there would be no stopping her! As she marched along the street, Tierney beamed – it was fate that she'd happened to be here today.

Her steps slowed again as she neared Selfridges and was swallowed up by a mob of people outside the department store, clustered around two traders setting up their stalls. Glancing round, Tierney noticed a man and a young girl standing arguing on the edge of the pavement. Behind them, the traffic was gridlocked, drivers like petulant children faced with broken toys as they pounded their dashboards in frustration. Car radios spluttered, and in the distance a fire engine howled its way slowly along the street.

Shifting the weight of her bags to her other hand, Tierney watched the traders' sharp eyes scanning the crowd for a likely sale as they set out their wares. Her glance returned to the man and the girl, who was in school uniform, a slight figure with shiny brown hair. The man was trying to placate her, wrapping his arms tightly around her as she tried to pull away. He shouted something about her being late back for school as he hustled the girl towards a car. The crowd shifted and Tierney edged forward, watching the traders bantering lightly with the crowd now swarming round the stalls like flies lured by food.

Drawing level with the man and schoolgirl, she got a better

look at them; he was about five foot five, stocky, with a pasty face. Tierney smiled sympathetically at the row they were having: the man must be a brother or father and the girl was clearly playing up. It looked like he'd caught her playing truant. Then someone in front of Tierney moved; for the first time she caught a glimpse of the child's expression, and her smile vanished.

The girl looked *scared*.

Feeling foolish, Tierney stopped walking, and tried to dodge out of the way of the people shoving impatiently past her. The man was still shouting and urging the girl over to the car, ranting and raving about their always being late, while she tried again to jerk out of his grasp.

Uneasy, Tierney looked round to see if others had noticed. The traders' stalls obscured the couple's faces, but a few people were glancing quickly at them before averting their gazes.

This was London, and no one wanted to get involved.

This was a domestic, and families had them all the time.

This wasn't their problem, and they wanted it to stay that way.

Shrugging, Tierney walked on, relieved that the crowd was thinning out and she could move more quickly. All she could think about was getting back to work and telling everyone her news. She couldn't help glancing back, though, couldn't shake the feeling that something was wrong, a feeling now weighing her down as heavily as the bags she was still struggling with.

And what if . . . a horrible thought occurred to her and she tensed, craning her neck to see past the people still blocking her way. *What if that man* **wasn't** *a relative?*

What if he was just contriving to make it seem that way?

'Oh, Jesus . . .' Tierney chuckled at her vivid imagination. 'I've really lost the plot this time.' Shaking her head, she carried on walking. Bond Street Tube station was two minutes away.

But the horrible thought wouldn't leave her alone.

It sat in her mind, and *wriggled*.

Finally, Tierney sighed and, stopping again, ignored people's irritated looks as she waded back through the oncoming troop of shoppers. Now feeling totally absurd, she stood still, watching the man and girl. Something just didn't look right.

Around her, the world was turned up to full volume. Children yelled, mothers shouted, music blared, the throbbing bass from a car stereo seemed to shake the ground, while the plaintive cry of a dozen mobile phones all in slightly different keys faded in and out.

And in the midst of it all, Tierney tried desperately to make sense of what she was seeing. She only had her intuition to go on, and that had never, ever let her down. Still . . .

The man was bustling the girl towards the car, the girl was still pulling away. Tierney stood there, face scrunched up with indecision.

What if she was wrong and went barging in like an idiot?

What if she was right and did nothing?

After all, girls were assaulted all the time, it was in the papers day in, day out. But in the middle of a busy street, in broad daylight? Tierney agonised. She'd read about such cases. Was she, could she, be seeing one now? 'But how can I be the *only* one seeing it?' she wondered aloud. She had to do something.

'Excuse me . . .' She stopped a middle-aged woman clutching a large bag. 'There's a girl over there and I think she's in trou—'

The woman waved her away without even breaking stride.

Blushing, Tierney tried again, turning to one of the men watching the traders. 'Please, can you help me? I think that girl—'

He began jabbering away in a language she'd never heard before.

Tierney looked for the schoolgirl again, panicking when she couldn't see her. Then she caught sight of the couple: the man was struggling to get the car door open while still holding the girl, who was trying to wrench free. When Tierney saw her face, her heart swerved violently inside her ribcage. She was still hyped up from finding Zoë; now adrenaline went skidding through her system. The carrier bags slid from her hands. Everything around her became a pale blur, sounds strangely muffled as she marched over to the couple.

'Leave her alone!'

'Fuck off!' the man hissed, gripping the girl's arm. Tierney looked into his muddy-brown eyes. Eyes dark and blank as the windows of an empty house. Dead eyes.

The girl tried to pull away again, wincing.

And Tierney saw red. Brightest scarlet, in fact.

'Let *go* of her!' She hadn't done karate for a few years, but her body remembered the moves. Bringing her right leg back, she snapped it forward in a quick kick to the man's shin.

'*Bitch* . . .' Face warped with rage, he loosened his hold on the girl, lunging forward and grabbing Tierney's arm, twisting it up sharply behind her back.

The air around her tightened, like elastic pulled fast.

Everything merged, faces and sounds running together until the world was just an aching gash of colour and noise. Mentally Tierney groped for a rational thought: this couldn't be happening in such a public place; this couldn't be happening so fast; and it couldn't be happening to her. What was wrong with everyone; why didn't anyone *see*?

The man twisted her arm again, and she felt her throat filling with pain until she could hardly breathe. Frantic, she tried to turn slightly, bringing her other hand up and delivering a short sharp karate chop to the windpipe. Clutching his neck, he staggered back, gasping.

Tierney's legs buckled and she stumbled into a stall, tripping over some cardboard boxes and sending a load of purses and wallets tumbling to the floor as she fought to steady herself.

Incredible as it seemed both then and later, those nearby still didn't realise anything was wrong, a few of them gaping and even giggling at the sight of this lipstick-covered blonde going berserk in the middle of the street. The schoolgirl was standing nearby, hand over her mouth, looking dazed.

As the attacker backed away, Tierney grabbed his arm, but he was too strong for her and she knew she couldn't hold him, not the way he was twisting and turning. Glaring at the crowd, she managed to choke out a few words: '*Do something . . .*'

The man gave her a violent shove and she fell, landing on her backside and grazing her hands which instantly started stinging, her palms bloody and flecked with dirt. Tierney watched helplessly as the man melted into the crowd while everyone stood, staring. People began turning to each other, talking in hushed voices, shaking their heads in confusion.

Slowly Tierney stood up. The edge of her vision blurred, black wavy lines crawling like slugs across her eyes. There was a terrible pounding, like drums in her brain; it felt like all the synapses had stopped firing and started fighting each other.

The schoolgirl, meanwhile, was edging away, glancing round furtively even while she was still trembling with fear. Tierney figured she'd been playing truant and was now scared the police would be called. As she watched, the girl suddenly turned and dashed off down the street, while onlookers stared after her, not sure what to do.

In shock and not realising it, all Tierney could think about was getting away, and going back to work, making sure Barnaby and Julian and Joel knew she'd done it. She'd found Eve.

That was what mattered.

That was all that mattered.

She blanked out the events of the last fifteen minutes and, grabbing her bags, limped away towards the station, hurrying down the dirty grey steps into the Underground.

'Hey, wait up! Blondie, hang on . . .'

The beautiful oriental girl who had witnessed the whole attack from across the street was hurrying after Tierney, dashing down the steps two at a time, cursing when she realised she'd lost her quarry. Glancing at the row of shiny silver payphones, she debated whether to call in the story now.

Lian patted her camera. Better to wait. She'd got some *unreal* photos; all she needed was the identity of the mystery girl and she'd have a front-page splash on her hands. Because unlike Tierney, unlike everyone else there, Lian had recognised the schoolgirl, and knew exactly what a shit-hot story this was. Now, delicate face tight with resolve, she played a hunch and hurried back up the stairs to where people were still clustered in groups.

Lian glanced round, her dark eyes narrowed.

Then she saw it. It had to be the blonde's, it just had to be. Bending down, she picked up the carrier bag and, stepping back into a shop entrance, rummaged through it, smiling as her fingers closed round a crumpled piece of paper.

A credit card receipt.

Lian punched the air with excitement. All she had to do was call in a few favours, get a police contact to persuade the bank to release a few details.

Just a name.

She had a few stories she was trying to stand up, but they could wait. Because now the only thing she wanted to do was hunt down the blonde babe with the feisty fists.

Lian beamed. Today, she'd died and gone to tabloid heaven.

*

'My God, what happened to you?' Liz looked up in surprise as Tierney staggered into the ladies' room and thrust her bloody palms under the cold tap.

'Just tripped, that's all.' Tierney smiled wanly. She didn't have the energy to tell her friend about her Oxford Street escapade. All she cared about was finding Matt and giving him her news. Hurrying back into the buzzing office to call Julian and Barnaby and set up a meeting, Tierney caught Vanita's eyes, and sent her a slow, knowing smile, savouring every second. Now it was her rival's turn to worry. But the brunette merely shrugged and looked amused. After leaving a message for the clients, Tierney hurried down the corridor, bumping into colleagues in her excitement, and rapped impatiently on Matt's door. When there was no response her face fell, excitement waning already. Then suddenly he was there behind her and, startled, Tierney jumped, banging her head on the doorframe.

Matt smiled. Attraction was written all over her face and she didn't know what to do about it, did she? But not to worry, because soon, he was going to show her.

'So, how's it going?'

Tierney beamed. 'I've found her! I've done it – *I've found Eve*! Oh, Matt, seriously, she's bloody *perfect*!'

'Is she now . . .' Matt felt strangely moved by the sheer happiness on her face. 'Well, you'd better set up a meeting with the clients, then. And you also need to cancel any plans you had for tonight. We're having dinner. Eight o'clock at the Ivy.'

She tensed. 'I told you, the answer's no. I can't go out with you!'

'Who said I was asking?' said Matt quietly as, mortified, Tierney clamped a hand over her mouth.

'Oh, God, *sorry*! I just assumed . . . I mean I thought you . . .'

'Forget it. Maybe you're right and this is a date in disguise. Maybe it's purely business. Only one way to find out. See you at eight . . .' Giving her another slow grin, he strolled past her into his office.

*

Once inside, Matt stood very still, frowning. He had mixed feelings about tonight. Joel had loved the idea of getting Adonis on board, but was worried. 'We need to handle this carefully,' he'd warned. 'It would be a disaster to upset Tierney too much. We don't want her to walk.'

So they'd hatched a plan. Promoting Vanita was a done deal, but Tierney would never know. At the end of their little meeting, Joel and Matt found they couldn't quite look at each other, now co-conspirators who didn't like themselves very much. Tierney deserved better.

This was wrong.

This was callous.

This was *business*.

And it was, they'd rationalised, going on in every company, at every level.

Now Matt nodded. Vanita was going to be happy and so was he. Tierney would get over it; after all, there were worse things in life than losing a promotion, and this was something he'd explain to her. Oh yeah, there were lots of things he wanted to teach that girl. His smile widened. And Matt had a hunch she'd prove a real fast learner . . .

*

Tierney stared at Matt's closed office door.

Dinner.

At the Ivy.

This *had* to be about her promotion.

Then again . . .

Suddenly she let out a shriek of horror. 'Fuck – what am I going to *wear*?'

4

Fast Love

'Talk about being dressed to kill – this outfit's *murder*!' Tierney tottered out of her bedroom, tripped over the ironing board and almost hurtled headfirst down the stairs. Getting through tonight without straining, smashing, breaking or bashing something would be a minor miracle. In a moment of total madness and sheer masochism, she'd dashed out and splurged on Manolo Blahniks: they had cost an arm and a leg, with stilt-like heels capable of crippling a girl for good if she put a foot wrong. 'God, no wonder Cinderella left her shoe behind, it must have been a blinking Blahnik!'

Glancing at the clock, she gasped. 'Shit! I have to get *out* of here!' Her exit was hampered by Genghis, who was determined to shag her left leg. Tierney lurched for the front door, howling with pain as he sank his sharp little teeth into her shin.

'Get *off* me, you oversized rat!' She tried to grab his collar but he just clung on harder. 'Carin! Do something with this mad mutt or I swear I'll poison the little bugger!'

Giggling, Andy and Carin hurried out of the living room.

'Where are you two off to?' Tierney watched as Carin handed Andy her coat and dragged the seething Shitsu away.

'Gina couldn't make it to the play we'd booked, so Andy's filling in for her, as it were . . .' Carin winked at Andy, who instantly turned dreamy-eyed.

Feeling uneasy again, Tierney slammed the front door and stumbled down the street to the station, feet hurting all the way.

*

She arrived at the Ivy fifteen minutes early and was already seated when Matt turned up.

'Tierney,' – his voice was soft as he slid into the seat opposite – 'you look even lovelier than usual.' He checked his watch. 'One day Joel'll be on time for something and I'll pass out with shock!'

Joel was coming! So this *was* to do with her promotion!

'Don't look so relieved! Is being alone with me so terrible?' Matt teased.

She grinned. 'Ask me again in an hour!'

Matt laughed, and unsure what to say next, Tierney sat back and studied her fellow diners. The conversation was hushed, punctuated by silvery peals of laughter from the women, and she smiled, wondering at the stories, successes and secrets being shared. Trends might wax and wane, fads might come and go, but the Ivy was always in vogue.

'So' – Matt closed the wine list – 'guess we were destined to have dinner after all. Maybe next time it'll be just the two of us.'

'You don't give up, do you?'

Matt ignored her anxious expression. 'And you don't want me to, or you'd be angry by now.'

'What makes you so sure I'm not?' Tierney sipped her water.

'Intuition. And mine says that with you, I need to take a more hands-on approach . . .'

Next thing she knew, he was reaching over, pulling her wrist across the table towards him, his fingers closing over her hand, his touch sending tiny shocks of pleasure rushing through her body.

'Did you know' – Matt's tone was chatty – 'that doctors in India still use palmistry for diagnosing medical problems?'

Tierney tried to extricate her hand without making it obvious and attracting attention.

'Ah, now, see those? Look, those sort of bands around your wrist?'

Glowering at him, she looked down and indeed saw three faint, chained lines running round the base of her hand.

'See? The more visible those are, the more trauma you've had in your life.' Gently, Matt brushed a fingertip over the lines, the lightest, slightest of touches, but enough to make Tierney shiver. Matt felt her skin warm under his; good, she was nice and sensitive. 'Now for the most important one, your heart line . . .' He leaned forward, staring intently at her palm. 'Interesting . . . it has a break at the end, see how it splits into two smaller lines?'

Tierney's mouth went dry. 'What does that mean, if anything?'

Frowning, Matt looked at it again. 'Usually that there's been a parting of the ways, some sort of ending.'

She jerked her hand back. 'Most people have had at least

one major break-up by the time they're my age! What total, utter *crap*!'

Matt noted the flushed cheeks and tightly clasped hands as she sat there rigidly in her seat. 'Why are you so upset?'

Tierney just stared into her glass, wishing she could shrink in size and dive into the warm red wine, feeling it lapping over her twisted nerves. 'Let's change the subject.'

Matt poured her another glass of wine. 'Why aren't you with anyone?'

'You mean . . . ?'

Matt nodded.

Tierney avoided his eyes. 'No reason.'

He caught the tightness in her voice and asked cautiously, 'I suppose you're waiting for Mr Right?'

To Matt's surprise, she tensed again. 'Perhaps.'

'You don't sound too sure. Don't you believe in the idea of soulmates?' he pushed.

'Why, do you?' Tierney challenged.

He paused, watching a couple saunter past to a nearby table. 'I want to.'

'Well, best of luck, I'm sure she's out there somewhere.'

Matt's smile was flirtatious. 'Maybe closer than I thought.'

'Blind optimism on your part!' Tierney could hear her voice was scratchy with tension but couldn't help it.

'Apologies, all!' Joel came scurrying over. 'Parking's a *nightmare* around here!' Flashing them a cheery smile, he picked up a menu. 'Right then, we need to have a bit of a chat about changes at work, and Tierney, of course you want to know about the latest on that promotion.' He paused to taste the wine and she held her breath.

Finally . . .

'Though I have to say' – picking up a napkin Joel folded it neatly over his lap – 'I always think it so much more civilised to eat first, talk shop later, don't you agree?'

Tierney gritted her teeth. 'Oh, *absolutely* . . .' The words almost choked her.

As the two men launched into an animated discussion about Matt's new car, Tierney stifled a yawn. While she tucked into a delicious *hors d'oeuvre* they debated the pros and cons of turbo-charged engines. She smiled every five minutes and downed one more glass of wine plus the entire bread basket.

By the time the next course arrived, Tierney was searching for matchsticks with which to prop her eyelids open. Joel was delivering a long lecture on the superiority of British cars over their German counterparts. Tierney downed another three glasses of wine.

During dessert the topic tackled was the value of personalised licence plates, and Tierney came up with a few choice ones of her own which she kept to herself. By the time coffee was served she was past caring what they talked about.

Joel was now addressing her; she tried to focus but it was hard since she was now seeing two of him. The only thing that did penetrate her booze-laden brain was the mention of Vanita.

'***VANITA THE VALKYRIE!***' With a bloodcurdling shriek, Tierney held up two fingers in the shape of a cross. 'My God, that woman's *evil*! Never goes out in daylight!' She howled with laughter. 'Probably sleeps hanging upside down, like a giant killer ***BAT***!'

The pause that followed was so pregnant Tierney could **hear** water breaking.

Her giggle became a gasp and her cackle a cringe as she realised she'd committed a *faux pas par excellence*. Joel's lips winced into a small smile, but his eyes were two tiny slits of disdain, his face blank and tight as a mask.

Tierney groaned. And *what* was that godawful, throbbing pain in her jaw?

Oh, of course. The pressure of her foot jammed up against the roof of her mouth.

Joel's voice was an icicle. 'As I was saying, given her experience, I've decided to offer Vanita the position of assistant creative director.'

'*What?*' Stunned, Tierney looked wildly from Joel to Matt and back to Joel again, wondering why he was speaking gibberish.

'But that's mi— I mean, *I* found the face for Eve's Brew! That was the deal! You can't just . . .'

Voice trailing off, she managed a shaky smile.

Obviously, this was just a misunderstanding.

Crossed wires.

A hallucination?

Or was Life pulling a fast one?

'Tierney, I invited you to dinner because I wanted you to hear this from me, away from the office.' Joel sighed and rubbed his chin thoughtfully. 'Now look, I realise you must be bitterly disappointed, but Vanita really does have the requisite experience, and when you calm down and think this through, you'll see how much you'll gain from working with her.' Holding up a hand sternly, he pre-empted her outburst. 'Of course I know you've found a possible face for Eve's Brew, but this deal was never set in stone. The clients aren't meeting the girl until tomorrow, and they may not even like her. But if they do, you'll continue working on the account, okay? In six months you're up for a review; no reason why you won't be eligible for promotion then, is there? Don't give up.'

'Fine!' Tierney met his eyes, chin tilting defiantly. She wasn't buying any of this, not for one minute. That job had been as good as hers; something had happened, something they weren't telling her. God, she could kill Vanita, with her well-connected father and bulging contacts book.

Recalling Matt's promises and assurances of support, her eyes narrowed in accusation, but he merely shook his head, apparently bemused, and she sighed; no point in blaming him. Joel was speaking again, and somehow she managed to make it through coffee with her smile intact and tongue in check.

Her mind clung on to the tiniest details: the shiny black shoes worn by all the waiters, the fact that the small ice cubes in the water jug melted more slowly than the larger ones, the way that Joel took three sugars in his coffee but never actually stirred it.

Finally, shortly before midnight, she followed the men out of the restaurant in a daze, even smiling brightly at the *maître d'* as he helped her on with her coat.

Outside in the street, Joel muttered a swift goodbye before dashing off.

She hoped he'd get decapitated on the way home.

'How're you doing?' Matt squeezed her shoulder gently.

Tierney opened her mouth to tell him she was fine, then closed it again. She wasn't.

'Tierney?' Matt slipped his arm round her shoulders and she didn't have the energy to shrug him off. Over the past few weeks she'd been living on her nerves, so excited about her promotion, and now an avalanche of adrenaline was crashing down around her.

'You poor thing, you're shivering! Come on, my flat's not far, let me at least make you a hot drink, then I'll run you home.' Matt's arm slipped from her shoulder to her waist.

The night has taken on a strange sense of inevitability. It's like she's acting out a script someone else has written. Her part has no lines, she just has to be there, just has to show up, and everything slots neatly into place for those around her.

She's merely a prop.

The car is quiet and smooth and comfortable. Matt turns on the engine and expertly manoeuvres out of the cramped space.

'Be there in about twenty minutes, okay?'

In the darkness his profile is all hard lines and angles. Suddenly Tierney doesn't recognise his face; he's a stranger to her and she feels afraid.

Then the moment passes.

She catches him glancing at her now and then as though trying to gauge her mood, but she keeps her face averted, staring out of the window, watching the lights twinkling in the distance, no doubt mocking her and all her naive ambitions.

Matt decides Tierney is more lovely here in the darkness than ever. She doesn't meet his stare and he's glad, for it means he can admire the shadows gliding over her milky skin as she sits there so still and silent beside him.

And now he wonders if tonight will end the way he's been planning, with Tierney in his bed, or whether he will surprise himself and this once – perhaps only, ever, this once – follow his conscience.

Then Matt sighs, knowing as usual it will depend on which is harder – his resolve or his dick.

*

Lian gazed at the photographs she'd taken of the Oxford Street attack. They were her best ever, for sure. And now she had a name for the karate kid: Tierney Marshall. She'd proved surprisingly photogenic, even in mid kick, and now Lian hugged herself, knowing these pictures were going to look brilliant splashed across every tabloid in the country. And after this, getting shifts on a national would be within her grasp, finally. As she looked at the stack of papers she'd bought that day, imagining her by-line in them all, Lian smiled. She was on her way to becoming the Next Big Thing in tabloid journalism.

*

Matt's flat was on the second floor of a building with a spacious lobby and a night doorman who smiled haughtily. Tierney wondered if he kept count – how many other women had Matt ushered in this way, quick and quiet in the middle of the night?

Standing in the lift, though, she couldn't help feeling sorry for Matt, stuck with this silent, sulky girl now crumbling the moment things didn't go her way.

Unlocking the door, Matt switched on some lights and

vanished, leaving her standing in the middle of the den. From further down the hall she heard the clink of china and the sound of cupboards closing.

Vaguely, Tierney noted the room was large with soft white carpet and a black leather, semi-circular sofa. One whole wall was taken up with sliding patio doors leading out on to a tiny balcony. The far corner of the room was dominated by a sound system so sophisticated it looked more like a miniature spaceship that had crash-landed than a stereo.

'I'm starting to feel like the guy in the Gold Blend ad!' Matt reappeared, carrying two mugs of steaming coffee. 'Here you go, a hot sweet drink, good for shock.' He fed a cassette into the stereo and Tierney recognised it as the same music he'd played in the car.

Matt patted the cushion beside him, waiting for her to join him on the sofa. Instead, she chose a chair in front of the patio doors, perching on the edge of the seat.

Matt was studying her, his face inscrutable. 'You know, I don't think you're the way you seem.'

'Who is?' Tierney countered swiftly.

'Some people are. With some people, what you see is what you get. They're transparent' – he gestured to the glass wall behind her – 'like that. But you're not. You're sort of . . .' He paused, frowning 'In *layers*.'

'God, what is this – psychoanalysis?' She slammed her mug down on the coffee table. 'I thought I was coming back for a drink, not therapy!'

Unfazed by her outburst, Matt smiled. 'What, I hit a nerve?'

'No, but you're getting on them!' Tierney glared.

The emotional temperature in the room had rocketed and

Matt liked it. 'Look, Tier, I know you're upset about that stunt Joel pulled, and I don't blame you. Why don't you just give in to it and have a good cry? You'll feel better.'

'Offering me a shoulder to cry on – how *original*! Bet you'd just love that, wouldn't you? Another pathetic female breaking down in tears so you can rescue her!'

Jumping up, Tierney marched over to the glass doors and glared at the lone star which had ventured out. Walking over to her, Matt put a hand on her arm to pacify her, but she shook him off. 'I'm going home.'

She started to push past him, but he was too fast for her, grabbing her firmly by both shoulders.

'You're not dashing off in this state! Get as angry as you like, I don't care!' Matt watched the implacable line of her mouth quiver. 'You women, you bang on and on about how we blokes should be more like you, more in touch with our feelings, but look at you now! Trying to pretend everything's fine, when you feel like shit, only you're too stubborn to admit it!'

Tierney lowered her head as disappointment and desire and anger and confusion and a hundred more emotions plucked at her heartstrings until she feared they might break.

'Tierney . . . come here, you fool . . .' Matt pulled her towards him until her head was resting on his shoulder. She could feel his heart beating, and behind her, hear the rain, falling faster, drumming against the window like fingers tapping urgently against the glass. Somewhere outside, a car door slammed, a woman shouted. Then it was quiet again but for the rain scolding the glass and the music flowing softly.

For a few minutes they just stood there, hips touching,

Matt's hand resting lightly on Tierney's back, his fingers warm through the thin dress. She sighed as he began stroking her hair, soothing the sadness, easing the anger. She felt all the tension ebbing away, a wonderful, terrible restlessness sweeping through her. Then Matt was tilting her head back, winding his fingers more tightly through her hair. She caught the hint of control in the caress and trembled as his hand cupped the slender curve of her throat, increasing the pressure of his fingers until he heard her sharp intake of breath and made it melt into a sigh of pleasure by touching his lips to her neck, trailing kisses along the gentle slope of her shoulder, kissing the delicate ridge of her collarbone and along her neck to her mouth. Tierney felt weak as the kiss deepened, such a long, luxurious kiss, as though every molecule in her body was being stroked by softest silk.

She pulled away. 'I'm sorry . . . I can't . . .'

Matt noted the flushed cheeks and heavy-lidded blue eyes. Who was she trying to kid?

'Hey, take it easy . . .' He moved towards her again. 'I won't do anything you don't want me to . . .'

Tierney tried to rouse her willpower. Matt Lucas was heartache waiting to happen; everyone knew what he was like. *She* knew what he was like.

And she wanted Ben.

Always and only.

She looked at Matt. Almost two years since she'd been with anyone. Tonight she could kickstart time and speed her life up. Move forward, move on. Now or never, she thought.

So maybe now. Or never.

Glancing up, Tierney nodded. An almost imperceptible

movement, but Matt saw, closing the space between them, pushing her back until she was wedged between his body and the cold, rain-washed glass wall. Gently he traced the line of her mouth and Tierney's lips parted. His touch was different to Ben's: surer, cooler.

shouldn't wouldn't mustn't compare

'. . . think we can lose this . . .' Reaching behind Tierney, Matt unzipped her dress so that it slithered to the floor, leaving her in two scraps of pale peach lace, her nipples hard and swollen against the flimsy bra which he deftly unfastened and tossed carelessly to one side. Tierney shivered as these hands that weren't Ben's began stroking her breasts, running lightly over her body before Matt lowered his head, taking first one then the other nipple in his mouth, circling them with his tongue until she was moaning with pleasure.

Ben kissing her eyelashes

Seeing her head thrown back, perfect features contorted with wanting, Matt slipped a finger inside her knickers and slid them down over her knees so she could step out of them, his mouth brushing over the curve of her hips, heat rippling under her skin as his tongue flicked over her stomach and along her inner thigh. Tierney felt her groin tighten with lust.

Matt's arm was circling her back, pulling her to him; eagerly she reached out but he smiled and held her wrists firmly in one hand so her arms were pinned behind her back, breasts thrust up against his chest, pain, scissor sharp, jarring through her arms. Tierney squirmed, a feeble effort at trying to loosen his hold.

Ben so gentle Ben too gentle?

Feeling deliciously, dangerously helpless, she wriggled

again as Matt's other hand started sliding insistently up and down her thigh, trailing lazy circles over the soft skin of her stomach. The edge of pain blurred as he started stroking her between the legs, need so violent it sharpened into pain making her cry out.

Then she was trembling as pain and pleasure merged, like a thousand ice-hot tongues lapping at her body, and she started sobbing openly from wanting it, biting down on her lip so hard she tasted the sweet-slick of blood.

'*Now* . . .' Tierney urged, pressing herself against him.

Still Matt teased her, his tongue loitering over her skin until she was so wracked with need she could hardly stand. Then he was sliding his fingers inside her, feeling her tight and hot and wet clenching around them, and he heard her cry out again as he caressed the hidden knot of heat until finally she shuddered, falling against him, her breathing ragged.

Matt pushed her away from him slightly. 'What happened to "I can't", Tierney?' he murmured as she stood there before him, naked and trembling. 'Want more?'

Unable to look at him, she nodded.

'Prove it.' He placed a hand firmly on the back of her head, pushing her down until she was kneeling in front of him, eyes dark with wanting, fingers fumbling with the button on his trousers.

Matt knew that after this, he was going to fuck Tierney to within an inch of her life. As he watched her kneeling there, the moonlight playing over her glistening skin, Matt felt guilt tugging at him again, and for a mad, mad moment debated coming clean, telling her of his part in wrecking her promotion, telling her and doing the right thing. Then he felt the sweet relief of her tongue. *This* was right, this was more than right, this was perfect. Better to keep quiet. Because ignorance was bliss and so, he closed his eyes as Tierney took him deep in her throat, *was she . . .*

5

About Last Night

'Mmm . . . always thought a *Swooping Shakti* was a cocktail . . .' Tierney yawned, wishing she could sleep for oh, say another hundred years – this Tantric sex could sure wear a girl out . . .

Matt was still asleep, a lock of dark hair falling over one eye. Tentatively, she brushed it back, shy suddenly. Then she sank back against the pillows, listening to the faint murmur of traffic outside, watching a beam of sunlight slope across the ceiling, and basking in the rosy cosy afterglow of sensational sex.

The only thing ruled out last night was inhibition.

But now, oh dear. She sits up straighter in the bed, clutching the sheets round her naked body and feeling a sudden flicker of fear. Even the sunlight seems to retreat slightly. In a flat above, a baby wails and for a moment she feels like joining in. For two years her world has been a simple if stark black and white: Tierney Marshall, single. No flings, no flirtations, nothing. But now she's woken to find her universe redecorated in shades of grey, and it scares her.

Ben . . .

She remembers waking in the night, eyes snapping open, staring at Matt. Confused, she'd panicked; where was she and who was he? The moonlight was streaming through the curtains, bathing the room in a silvery sheen. As she lay there, watching Matt, so still in the darkness, Tierney thought she'd finally be able to cry.

But the tears refused to fall, and she'd blinked as the men's faces had merged, like two photographs superimposed on top of each other, their features fusing until she wasn't sure who she was seeing any more.

She was moving on, and it felt right.

And it felt wrong.

Now Tierney trails trembling fingers over Matt's shoulder, over his warm skin.

She shouldn't be feeling this way.

Because this is just a physical attraction, a chemical reaction.

Just her genes taking a shine to his.

Pulling the sheet around her body, she slides off the bed, padding down the hall, the carpet like warm snow beneath her feet. As she shuts the bathroom door sunshine filters in through the stained-glass window, scattering colour like jewels over the spotless white tiles.

Peering into the mirror, Tierney grimaces at her dishevelled hair, her eyes heavy with lack of sleep and the remnants of kohl eyeliner which has smudged down one cheek in a sooty black streak.

'Oh God, I look like an extra from a bad porn flick!'

And there, garish against her throat, is a throbbing red love bite.

A token of Matt's affection, or is it more like his *signature*?

Suddenly, cynically, Tierney wonders if he always leaves this love bite in this particular spot?

Mark of Matt.

Has she been *branded*?

And as what, exactly?

*

Matt awoke to the sound of his ego applauding. Smiling lazily, he reached over to the bedside table for his watch, before sitting up slowly and staring at the space beside him for a few moments. Then he pulled on boxer shorts and crossed the room to his desk, quickly typing out a brief e-mail apprising Vanita of last night's dinner then switching off the computer, and trying to ignore a sudden attack of guilt.

'Oh, you're awake!' Towel sarong-like round her slender body, Tierney stopped just inside the door, tiny beads of water clinging to her neck and shoulders. Her fair hair was damp at the ends, her eyes wary as she hovered there.

'Good *morning*...' Matt grinned, brown eyes moving appreciatively over her scantily clad figure. She looked like a water spirit with her long hair flowing loose around her bare shoulders and gleaming wet skin. Tierney smiled shyly, blue eyes warming as he sauntered over and pulled her to him, covering her face with kisses, laughing when she wriggled and giggled against him as his lips teased her with the promise of what was to come.

'Shit!' Matt cursed as the phone started ringing. 'Who the hell . . . ?'

Tierney watched the muscles rippling across his back as he stalked over to the bed and snatched the phone up.

'Yes?'

Wondering if she should leave the room but too curious to do so, she listened. Matt's voice softened as, back still towards her, he spoke quietly for a while before falling silent. Suspicion swiped at her; *who was on the other end of that phone?* It must be a woman, judging by Matt's tone and the distracted, almost self-conscious way he ran a hand through his tousled hair.

But what right did she have to be jealous, she reminded herself fiercely, dumping her clothes on the bed and sitting down next to them, staring morosely at the wall. He'd promised her nothing.

Tierney felt insecurity clawing at her heart like fingernails scraping down a blackboard. Hearing Matt say goodbye and replace the receiver, she waited for him to reach for her again. Instead, he just gazed into space. Body cold with tension, she started dressing, feeling more awkward with every moment and wishing she was at home.

Matt felt sick. Vanita had called to say things were in motion, and though he knew this was going to happen, still he felt like a bastard. Worse, turning round and seeing Tierney just sitting there, seeing the dejected slump of her shoulders, Matt felt like calling Vanita right back and telling her to forget it. Again he tried to convince himself last night had just been about sex. It wasn't like he was falling for Tierney.

He watched as she dressed swiftly, wondering how he could at least help her through the next few days. Today or tomorrow, the story about Adonis which Vanita was going to plant in the press would appear, and if the plan worked, things would start moving quickly.

'So, Tier, isn't it today the Eve's Brew guys meet Zoë?' He was amazed at how relaxed he sounded.

She glanced up, then nodded.

'How about I cook dinner for us tonight? I'd love to hear about the meeting. Say about nine? We can meet at my local for a quick drink, then come back here?'

'Fine. That's fine.' Tierney carried on towelling her hair dry.

He waited for a moment but she didn't look round. 'Anyway, look, I've got an early meeting, better get moving.' His grin was weak. 'I'm just gonna grab a shower. Help yourself to breakfast, and there are some cab numbers in the hall by the phone. You're going home before work, right?'

Again she nodded, and when she spoke, her voice was distant. 'Yeah, just to get changed.' As she finally turned to face him, Tierney felt hurt trickling through her blood like ice water.

By the bedroom door Matt paused and looked at her again. Tierney's fair hair glinted in the pale sunlight as she leaned back on the bed, clear blue eyes locked on his, lips pressed together in that slight natural pout. He was struck by how the purity of her face was strangely at odds with the sinuous line of her body, her grave eyes a rebuke to the suggestive set of her mouth.

'Hey,' he spoke softly, 'I'll miss you today.' She regarded him seriously, as though trying to gauge his sincerity, then her face relaxed into a smile. Relieved, Matt blew her a kiss and headed for the bathroom. If she ever found out how he'd doublecrossed her over this promotion, she'd go berserk. And, Matt reminded himself as he turned on the shower, hell had no fury like a woman scorned. But then, he smiled as the water pounded his muscles like a red-hot boxing glove, heaven had no pleasure quite like Tierney Marshall . . .

*

Sliding down in the back of the cab, Tierney strapped the seat-belt firmly over her chest. The beige leather seats were cold against her skin; the radio was too loud, and she was out of sorts. She was *homesick*. Suddenly Tierney felt very alone and vulnerable here in London, though usually she loved it. But right now she felt a sudden desire to be with her family and her old friends back in Dublin. Yet she also wanted to be with Matt. Conflicting emotions tumbled around inside her and she had a horrible suspicion that between them, she and Matt had more baggage than passes through Heathrow in the height of summer.

6

Dangerous Liaisons

The tension was so thick she could have cut it with a knife and served it up for tea.

Tierney was a little blonde bundle of angst; Julian had spent the past hour grilling Zoë, with a face that would make the Grim Reaper look friendly by comparison. Talk about interrogating someone – he and Barnaby had done all bar rugby-tackling her to the floor and injecting her with sodium pentathol!

Zoë must have been exhausted, after spending the morning posing for photographs now spread before them in a glossy pile. Her eyes were guarded, her answers polite, if brusque. Tierney figured she was nervous, who wouldn't be? Getting this job would change her life, and Zoë knew it.

Tierney herself was shattered. Her arm was still hurting from where the assailant had twisted it; she'd waited anxiously to see if anything appeared on the news about the attack, but so far there was nothing. Not that she cared: she'd been so busy thinking about Matt, and organising Zoë's photo-shoot, she'd had no time to worry about anything else.

Now, hearing Julian clear his throat, Tierney looked at him and knew exactly what he was about to ask the girl.

'So . . . tell us, how is it you ended up being . . . well . . . being—'

'I think "homeless" is the word you want!' Zoë was angry, and Tierney's heart went out to her.

'So why are you?' Julian demanded impatiently.

There was another tense silence as Zoë stared down at her hands, which looked very small and pale clasped together on the polished wooden table. Her face was closed, sealed tight as any vault.

The silence dragged on.

Tierney felt her stomach knotting with tension again; no way was Zoë going to tell these two anything. And who could blame her? Anxiously she glanced at her watch. The meeting had started late, and it was already gone six. She was supposed to be meeting Matt at nine, but she had a nasty feeling she wasn't going to make it on time, not at this rate.

'Do *you* know?' Julian looked at Tierney, who shook her head before turning to Zoë.

'I promise' – she smiled warmly – 'nothing you tell us goes out of this room. Whatever it is. But we do need to know something about you before we make a final decision.'

Inside, Zoë was quaking. She'd been up half the night thinking this through and she knew she couldn't tell them the truth. Now she spoke quickly, hating to lie to Tierney, especially. 'It's nothing new. I'm from a tiny village in Suffolk, so small it's not even on the map. Stay there long enough and it'd bore you into a coma. Anyway, my mate and I swore that as soon as we turned sixteen, we'd come to London. Guess we believed all that crap about the streets being paved with gold, or something. So,' her smile was defiant, 'here I am.'

'But what about your parents?' Tierney was suspicious.

'Oh, they think I'm staying with my sister and her husband.'

'Why aren't you? Must be better than wherever you *are* staying!' Barnaby also seemed uneasy.

Zoë looked bored. 'I was, for a while. Until my brother-in-law started giving me a hard time, if you get my drift . . .'

Feeling naive, Tierney frowned. 'You mean . . . ?'

'Waited until my sister was out at her weekly girls' night and then shoved his hand up my skirt.' Zoë's voice was bland but her tawny eyes were angry. 'I left that night; they're too embarrassed to tell my parents that I'm not there, so we all carry on this pathetic little charade. Works quite well, actually. Jo, that's my sister, slips me guilt money now and then, which helps. And it's not like I'll be staying in this hostel for ever. It's not that bad there.' Her voice quivered.

'But why don't you just go home?' Tierney was worried; the story sounded weird. Contrived.

'And admit everyone was right when they told me not to leave? Yeah, *sure*.' Zoë's face tightened. 'I said something good would happen for me in London.' Her eyes skimmed over Barnaby and Julian. 'Looks like I was right, doesn't it?'

Tierney was confused. She couldn't figure Zoë out; when they'd first met, she'd seemed fragile, but today she seemed tougher, more confident. And was her story true, or was she lying for fear of losing this chance? The whole tale seemed flimsy.

Suddenly another worry occurred to Tierney. 'You're

seventeen, right? So before we can sign you up, we'll need permission from your parents. Or some other guardian. Will that be a problem?'

Zoë smiled slightly. 'I'll be eighteen in a month.'

Tierney frowned. How convenient.

'So what happened to your friend?' she challenged.

Zoë shook her head. 'You don't want to know, trust me.'

Julian looked unimpressed, but Barnaby was still staring at the photographs, and Tierney knew he thought Zoë was perfect for the ad campaign. Closing her eyes briefly, she issued a frantic prayer to every deity known to mankind plus some she invented for good measure. If the men rejected Zoë she could kiss goodbye to this contract for sure, and in six months, she'd lose out on promotion again.

Lost in thought, Tierney jumped as a chair scraped sharply; looking up, she realised Barnaby had asked Zoë to wait outside. She managed to send the girl a reassuring smile as she left, her head held high.

Julian's handsome face was disdainful. 'Well, not the most convincing story. Can't say I'm mad about her, but she's certainly got the right look. Congratulations on finding anyone at all. I didn't think you would.'

Tierney acknowledged the backhanded compliment with a dry smile. 'You're too kind.'

'And she's got a certain' – Julian frowned – 'attitude. Just what we need for this ad campaign. It's just that, I don't know, something about her story doesn't ring true . . .'

'I believe her.' Tierney spoke firmly.

She was lying through her teeth.

Julian looked at her coldly. 'Because?'

'I don't know, just a gut feeling, I guess.'

'Women's intuition?' Julian smirked. '*Please* . . .'

'Intuition told me she was the right face in the first place!' Tierney turned to Barnaby, her eyes pleading with him.

He looked at the photos thoughtfully. 'I'm inclined to agree. I mean, she could have come up with a hundred better reasons for being homeless. But she didn't.' He sighed. 'Even so, it's hardly ideal, is it?'

Tierney smiled, feeling more confident. She was going to sell Zoë to them if it killed her. 'Actually, in terms of "cool", it's perfect.'

'How so?'

'Because the market you're aiming at, the under thirties, is a seriously clued-up group. They're not naive, and nor is Zoë. How could she be, in her situation? She's tough. *Streetwise*. Just what you wanted. And people will get that about her, it shows in her face.' Tierney paused. 'Plus, with her, you have a readymade marketing ploy: girl goes from selling the *Big Issue* to being the Next Big Thing. It's cynical, I know, but true.'

Barnaby nodded. 'It would be great publicity.'

Julian slapped the photos back on the table. 'Her hair's too short. Eve needs long hair.' He glanced at Tierney. 'Like yours.'

'So we'll get Zoë hair extensions! It's not difficult.' Tierney wondered if it was possible to dislike Julian more than she already did. Probably not.

For a few minutes, there was silence as the men stared at the photographs again. Then Barnaby shrugged. 'I say we go with her. She's the best we've seen and we don't have much time left. The launch is in a few months.' He looked at Julian who was still staring at the photos. 'Jules?' Barnaby raised an eyebrow. 'What do you say?'

'Okay . . . okay. She'll have to do.'

'Are you both sure?' Tierney looked at them nervously. 'I'd hate to get her hopes up.'

'She's it.' Barnaby spoke firmly. 'Now, I want to show you some mock-ups of the ads we're planning to run.'

'Sure, but first, I must tell Zoë!'

Tierney hurried out into the hall where Zoë was perched on the edge of a chair. Gone was the confidence, and once again she looked fragile as she sat there, staring into space.

As Tierney approached she looked up, her face slumping. 'I didn't get it, did I?'

'They loved you – you're Eve!'

'Oh my *God*! Really? I *really* got it?' Jumping up, Zoë started shaking, golden eyes huge in her pale face. 'You mean it? They really want me?' Shaking her head in wonder, she began dancing down the corridor.

'Congratulations. Can you wait until our meeting's over? Barnaby and Julian will want to talk to you properly.'

Through the tears now sliding down her pale cheeks, Zoë nodded happily. 'I don't know what to say!'

Tierney smiled, still bemused by the girl's quicksilver mood changes.

Back in the boardroom, mock-ups for the ad campaign were spread out on the table, and she studied them with interest. They were good, but nothing special.

'Er, they're a bit . . . well . . .' Stuck for words, she looked up to find the men watching her intently. 'They're all right, but I can't help thinking you need something a bit more . . . I don't know, "cheeky". Something a bit more sexy.'

'Such as?' challenged Julian icily.

Tierney bit her lip, staring into space as a plan started taking shape. She tapped one of the proofs. 'You really want this drink to be the Next Big Thing, right?'

'Obviously.' Julian rolled his eyes.

'Okay, so here's what I think the theme of the ads should be . . .' With rising excitement she tried to convey the image that was coming together in her head, pleased to see Barnaby nodding and smiling slightly.

'And why not take this campaign one step further? Make it the Next Big Thing – *literally*!' Tierney couldn't help giggling as she outlined her idea, rewarded with admiring smiles from both men this time.

'Another thing' – Tierney was glad to see Barnaby scribbling notes – 'you should make Eve's Brew LE – limited edition. Best way to achieve large sales and commercial success, while keeping your product exclusive. Think Levi's K-1s, a remake of the 1932 original. They produced 1,932 pairs, all numbered. People were desperate to get their hands on them, it was *frantic*. It's the way to make something instantly cool.'

Julian looked confused. 'But how would that work for us?'

Tierney thought for a moment. 'Well, for the first month or so, Eve's Brew should only be on sale in Bar Eden, and also your nightclub. See, the idea is to get everyone talking about it, but to make it exclusive, at least to start with. A product or brand that's ubiquitous can't reflect the individual; *ergo*, it's not cool. Eventually, Eve's Brew will be available everywhere, but by then it won't matter. Why do you think that in the

States, Studio 54 was the coolest place to be? Because you couldn't just walk in. You had to be on the list. It's human nature, right? *We always want what we can't have.*'

'I'm impressed. No, really, I am.' Barnaby smiled warmly, and even Julian looked like he was thawing.

Tierney tried to look relaxed, gathering her papers together and standing up. 'Okay, well, those are my proposals. I'm sure Joel will want to discuss the contract with you further.' She turned to go.

'It's yours.' Barnaby laughed at her delighted face, reaching out to shake her hand. 'I'll tell Joel today, and Vanita, of course. And don't worry about Zoë, I'll organise a hotel room for her and anything else she needs. We'll take good care of her.'

Tierney wondered if maybe she'd misjudged Barnaby. 'Okay, well, great!'

'So, let's go and celebrate!' Not giving her a chance to respond, Barnaby beamed again and began ushering Tierney out of the door, even as she glanced frantically at the time again.

Almost seven.

*

It was a nightmare in blonde.

Matt was surrounded by girls with golden hair; the pub was packed with them. Normally this would be heaven, but tonight he felt like he'd taken a wrong turning into hell, because though from a distance any of them could be Tierney, none of them was.

She'd stood him up.

And that didn't happen to Matt Lucas.

End Of.

Lungs protesting at the cigarette smoke, he pushed his way through the crowd, anxiously scanning the room again. Suddenly he saw a girl with tumbling fair hair and slender build standing by the door with her back to him, wearing a long, gypsy-style red skirt he recognised as Tierney's. Even as he stared, she pushed a blonde curl out of her eyes, and Matt grinned at the impatient gesture he'd seen so often.

Fighting the urge to yell with relief, he hurried over. 'About time! I was worr—' His hand touched her shoulder and the girl turned quickly. 'Sorry,' he mumbled, 'thought you were someone else.'

'Wish I was . . .' She gave him an impish grin, and, bemused, Matt stared into her wideset blue eyes.

He was tempted. Tierney hadn't bothered showing, and a part of him couldn't believe he was still here. Meanwhile the girl was smiling at him, waiting, and Matt knew how tonight could end.

Old habits were hard to break.

He started to smile back, but his lips let him down and Matt shook his head, amused at himself. He couldn't do this any more.

'Sorry,' he apologised again, and the girl shrugged as he headed back to the bar.

At the front of the pub the weekly karaoke contest was under way, four women sounding like dying parrots as they massacred a Mariah Carey song, clutching on to each other for support and looking as though they were about to swallow the microphones.

Hearing raised voices, Matt turned, watching as over at the dartboard two blokes argued; a third man tried to mediate, and was now in danger of being thumped by both. Matt sighed. The entire room was flirting and fighting, posing and preening, and here he was, miserable as sin.

Another singer took the stage, easing into a simple, sweet rendition of 10CC's 'I'm Not In Love'. Hearing the words, Matt smiled wryly. Was this it, then, was this what being in love meant? Panicking when she was late. Scared when he couldn't find her. Jealous of anyone with her right now. ***Would it always be this way?***

*

Back at home, Tierney tore round like a human cyclone. 'Forget El Niño, I'm *El Agro* . . .' The celebratory drinks had gone on for ages and been great fun; Zoë was beside herself with excitement and even Julian had smiled. Now it was just gone nine and Tierney was hoping Matt had waited. Hopping out of the shower, she grabbed a big blue towel and sprinted down the hall.

Passing Carin's door, she caught a low, throaty laugh and assumed her housemate was with Gina. They must have come in while she was in the shower. Tierney's steps slowed. She could hear a man's voice and it sounded like . . . *Andy* . . . ?

Feeling like a voyeur, she stood outside the room, clutching the towel around her body, straining to hear the voices talking in hushed, teasing tones.

It *was* Andy.

Tierney felt like a gatecrasher in her own world. How long had it been going on? They'd thought she was going straight out after work, so they'd obviously waited until they had the place to themselves.

She padded back to her own room, feeling tense. Tierney

had seen Carin stamp on so many hearts, she couldn't bear to watch it happen to Andy. But she knew it would. 'Bye 'bye friendship. Nothing would ever be the same again, not for any of them, and she felt resentful.

Then she blushed at her own hypocrisy, for hadn't she enjoyed herself with Carin when it had suited her? Snatching up her keys, Tierney hurried back downstairs. She was glad she was seeing Matt tonight. Right now, he seemed like the most solid thing in her world.

*

Vanita flashed the night porter a smile so angelic he could hear harps playing in the silence of the lobby.

'I'm here to surprise my boyfriend, so he can't sign me in. That's not a problem, is it? He's in flat thirty-six, the name's Lucas. Matt Lucas.' She leaned forward ever so slightly, just enough for her thin summer coat to fall open and reveal lacy red lingerie.

'Well, I don't know . . .' he stammered, 'we're really not supposed to let anyone into the building this late at night unless accompanied by a resident . . .'

Vanita winked. 'I won't tell if you don't! Please, I *really* want to surprise him!'

The porter prayed her coat would slip open again and give him another glimpse of heaven. 'I really can't . . .' His voice wavered.

'Sure, of course. I understand.' Vanita smiled meekly, tone sympathetic. 'I can't expect you to take responsibility for a decision like that. What was I thinking? I should have checked with your boss, or someone with that kind of authority. Not to worry. Sorry to have troubled you.'

Watching as he visibly swelled with self-importance, Vanita thanked God for the male ego: fat, fragile and a girl's best friend.

Sure enough, the porter was now squaring his shoulders and giving her a proud smile. 'Well now, luv, *I'm* in charge of this building until seven a.m., an' *I* reckon it's okay to let you in. Can't have you disappointing your boyfriend now, can we? Just sign there for me . . .'

Emerging on the fourth floor, Vanita rummaged through her coat pocket, producing a key to Matt's flat which he'd given her ages ago and neglected to retrieve. After knocking loudly and waiting for a few minutes, she let herself in, face gleeful as she slipped off her shoes. Here she was, alone, where she shouldn't be, when she shouldn't be.

And after tonight, everything would be perfect, for this was a surefire way to rekindle waning interest or remove a threat. Not – Vanita almost laughed out loud – that Tierney Marshall was much of one.

Still . . .

For though she'd sooner suffer a bad hair day than admit it, Vanita had always planned on ending up with Matt. Sure, she'd played it cool, allowing him to be an emotional lodger in her life, coming and going as he pleased. And, she unfastened her bra, musical beds could be fun. But now she was thirty-two, and it was time to play for keeps. Matt was twenty-eight; old enough to get serious.

Slipping into the bed, she draped the silk sheet loosely over her naked body. Matt was hers, and tonight she would prove it to him, in a way that left no room for doubt, and certainly not for Tierney Marshall. Oh yeah, she was going to give him one big treat all right . . .

*

Matt waited for the first round of the karaoke contest to finish, then headed for the door. Time to go home, Tierney wasn't coming. Starting the engine, he paused; he had a bad feeling about tonight, and much like the music spilling out of the pub, it was getting worse by the minute.

As his car sped off up the hill, Matt leaned forward to shove a tape into the stereo.

If instead he'd glanced into the rearview mirror, he'd have seen Tierney, hurrying around the corner into the road he was just leaving, and dashing up the pub steps, glancing anxiously at her watch.

She practically fell into the pub, stopping suddenly as she tried to catch her breath, glancing round and hoping Matt had waited. She was thirty-five minutes late and her shoulders sagged; he'd clearly given up.

'Oh great, now what?' she muttered, fighting her way to the other side of the room just in case, ignoring the row of guys propping up the bar and the way their heads swivelled as she approached.

'Hey, sweetheart, boyfriend stood you up, then, 'as he?'

Turning, she saw the group of lager louts she'd passed on her way into the pub, and who had half swaggered, half staggered in behind her. Now one of them stood before her, barring her way, his heavy-lidded brown eyes sweeping lazily over her body.

'Excuse me.' Tierney tried to move past him, but he quickly

stepped with her, blocking her escape, as his mates moved in and closed round, cutting her off from everyone else.

'Don't look very friendly now, does she, lads? She must be *shy* . . .' The ringleader winked at his mates and they began edging forward, forcing Tierney to step back, pushing her towards the dimly lit corridor from the pub to the cloakrooms. 'Reckon we just need to get to know her a bit better . . .'

He reached out to grab Tierney round the waist and her eyes narrowed.

'*Don't even* go *there* . . .'

Startled by the venom in her voice, he paused, and quickly, Tierney pushed past him, banging her hip on a table and feeling pain slice through her as the men jeered and called out while she rushed towards the exit.

Outside, she paused, wondering what to do next. Was Matt at home? His flat was only ten minutes away, she might as well try. It would be easier to phone, but, she glanced back at the pub, she couldn't face going back in there and being hassled.

Suddenly Tierney realised how badly she wanted to see Matt. Finding out about Carin and Andy had unsettled her; all she wanted now was Matt's arms around her, and so, crossing her fingers he'd be home, Tierney began walking quickly up the hill.

*

'What the *fuck* . . .' Matt gaped at the sight of Vanita lounging in his bed. 'What the hell are you playing at?' He looked at her suspiciously. 'Did Tierney turn up here? What did you say to her?'

Vanita stretched, back arching, the bedsheet sliding down

over her naked torso. 'Lost your girlfriend already?' She tutted. 'My, how careless of you . . . but then, maybe you couldn't. Care less, that is.'

Trying not to look at her, Matt scooped up her underwear, flinging it on to the bed. 'Get dressed.'

Ignoring him, she reclined on the pillows, and despite himself, he couldn't help the way his eyes lingered on her bare breasts.

'I'll try again: *have you seen Tierney*?'

Vanita shook her head. 'What's the panic? She's a big girl, she can take care of herself.' Her face was coy. 'So why don't you start taking care of *me* . . .'

Weary suddenly, Matt sank into a chair. The intensity of the feelings he'd been experiencing lately was getting to him. He remembered the dinner he'd prepared for Tierney; now it would be nothing but charred remains, and he wondered if that was some kind of metaphor, because burned out was exactly how he felt.

'For crying out loud, would you get dressed?' He tossed Vanita a bathrobe.

'Usually you can't wait to get my clothes off!' she teased, pulling on the robe and sitting cross-legged on the edge of the bed. 'So what's up?'

Matt sighed. 'You wouldn't understand.'

'Try me . . .' Vanita smiled suggestively. '*Please* . . .'

He couldn't help it, he chuckled. 'You're too much, you know that?'

'But you can handle me. Any time . . .' Vanita winked. 'So what's going on? Why so stressed, darling?'

The need to confide in someone was overwhelming, even

if it was Vanita. 'Tierney was supposed to meet me but she didn't turn up.' Matt smiled shakily.

She realised he was genuinely worried. 'Not like you to get this worked up over a woman.'

'Yeah, well, this is different.'

'How?'

Matt hesitated. He felt uneasy discussing this, but figured she'd find out soon anyway. 'Different as in . . . serious.'

She shifted position, recrossing her legs. 'How do you know?'

Irritated, he scowled. 'How do you think I know? I can feel it!'

Vanita frowned. 'It must have come on pretty fast, then.' She gasped in mock surprise. 'Surely you weren't in *lurve* with her when you were in bed with *me*?'

'It wasn't like that. I didn't feel this way then.'

She nodded. 'So you've felt this way for, what, a week? Two?' Seeing his face tighten, Vanita knew she'd hit him where it hurt. 'You know what they say, Matt: easy come, easy go.'

Sliding forward on the bed again, she leaned in close, voice soft and sure. Oh, this was good, sort of like . . . therapy in reverse. Emotional acupressure.

And the trick was knowing just when, just where, to *push* . . .

'I mean, Matt, come on . . . what makes you so sure this time is different? Look me in the eye . . . tell me she can trust you . . . *really* trust you . . . that you'll never let her down again . . . What are you waiting for? Come on . . . *tell me* . . .'

He swallowed nervously, closing his eyes against her words.

'Think about it . . .' Her voice faded to a whisper, and to Matt it seemed as though the words were coming from inside his own head. 'Why not do the right thing and leave Tierney alone before you hurt her again? Because you will, Matt . . . Oh, maybe not now, not today, but you will . . . and she can't take it . . . she's not like you . . . or me . . . she's not like *us* . . .'

'Perhaps that's why I like her!' Matt snapped.

Vanita simply smiled. 'Novelty value. This, what you're feeling now' – light shrug – 'it's just a guilt trip gone wrong. Wait. Watch. In a few weeks you'll be bored out your brain, and poor Tierney, she won't know what's hit her! You'll see, I'm right . . . this girl can't hold you, Matt. It can't work, not with her.'

Matt walked over to the window and stared out at the moon, a shimmering crescent, like a huge fish scale hanging there in the darkness. He remembered reading that lunar phases could affect people's moods, sway their emotions. Perhaps that's what he was feeling for Tierney.

A celestial kiss.

Was Vanita right? he agonised, leaning on the windowsill, head bowed. Could Tierney trust him? Gazing out into the night again, Matt shook his head sadly.

It was the wrong question.

What he needed to ask, what he needed to *know*, was if he could trust himself . . .

Vanita watched him. It was working. She wasn't surprised: if you sounded confident enough, you could convince a person of anything, turn their lives upside down and back to front, given enough time. And, she walked over to Matt, she had plenty of that.

She had all the time in the world.

*

'Jesus, I look a wreck!' Tierney peered at herself in the lift mirror, shaking her head in dismay. Hitting the stop button before the elevator reached Matt's floor, she pulled out her make-up case. Her eyeliner had smudged and her face was pale; no way could she let him see her in this state. Swiftly she applied blusher and a new lipstick in a darker, more sultry shade than she usually wore. Smiling, she hit the button and the lift went jolting upwards.

*

'I've told you, I can't *do* this any more!' Agitated, Matt ran a hand through his dark hair, trying to ignore the fact that Vanita was standing so close. He forced himself to meet her eyes. 'It's over. I'm sorry.'

'I see.' Her tone was cool. 'And if I hadn't shown up here tonight? When were you planning on telling me?'

Matt shrugged. 'You know how it's always been with us: casual. I didn't think it was a case of having to tell you we were officially "over". We were never officially "together".'

She placed a hand lightly on his arm and he tensed. 'Why so nervy, Matt?' she murmured, taking a step closer until their bodies were touching. 'Perhaps you're not as sure as you think. You don't sound it.' Vanita tilted her head back slightly, lips close to his. 'Aren't you, Matt? Aren't you *sure*? Better be . . .'

'I'm with Tierney now!' Matt's voice was rough with impatience. 'Why can't you just accept it?'

'Because we're here together and she's . . . well, we don't know, do we?'

Gently Vanita traced the line of his mouth with her finger, and Matt knew his willpower was about to do a runner.

'Oh, I know you think you love her, and I agree, you're close, closer than you've ever been before, but it's still not quite *enough*, is it, Matt . . . ?'

Trembling with anger and something else he didn't want to feel, Matt pushed her away. 'You stupid bitch! Can't you get it through your thick head? *It's over!* Now get dressed and get out, before I really lose it!'

Vanita flinched. For a moment she looked like a vulnerable young girl, and it was strange; her expression seemed to blur, as though two people were staring out from one face. Then her features realigned themselves into their usual mask of icy assurance.

She picked up her underwear and pulled it on, then her coat, grabbing her shoes and walking quickly down the hall to the front door where she turned and faced him again. 'You'd better hope Tierney doesn't get to hear about our little pact over Adonis, hadn't you? I mean, you know what offices are like, so many people working so closely, so many secrets, so easy to let one of those secrets just . . . *slip* . . .'

Matt gave her a pitying look. 'Funny, I never had you down as a bad loser, Vanita. You won't say anything. You're *bluffing*.'

Hand on the door, she frowned. 'Maybe. But you know, Matt, that's the thing about secrets. They're like love. They don't last.'

She sent him one final taunt of a look and left.

Somewhere inside, Vanita could feel a scream starting.

Matt stared at his half-open front door. The flat was empty but he wasn't alone, because for company he had Vanita's words and his doubts, could feel himself bumping up against them everywhere he turned, like invisible furniture. And suddenly his oh-so-spacious flat felt like the smallest space on earth.

*

Tierney hugged herself with excitement as the lift arrived on the fourth floor; impatiently she waited as the doors slid open slowly, only to reveal Vanita standing there.

In silence they appraised one another.

'Tierney. Here to see Matt? Ah, how sweet . . .' Vanita allowed her coat to fall open and reveal the lingerie.

Tierney glanced at Matt's door, feeling panicky but determined not to show it.

'Better luck next time,' Vanita drawled.

'With what, avoiding you?' snapped Tierney, starting towards Matt's flat.

'With promotion. I'm sure you'll get another shot at it. Meanwhile' – the look Vanita gave her was about as sensitive as a serial killer – 'you'll learn a lot working for me.'

Tierney felt her mouth turning down at the corners and looked down at her feet. 'As Joel pointed out, you have got more experience than me – I'm not surprised you got the promotion. I would say congrats, but hey, I'm not that hypocritical.'

Vanita leaned against the lift door. 'You really don't know, do you? My God, do you have to practise being this naive or does it come naturally?'

Tierney sighed. 'God, you could redefine the word "boring", you know that? If you've got something to say, just *say it*!'

Vanita spoke slowly. 'It was a done deal, Tierney; nothing to do with my having more experience. I promised to deliver Adonis, if Matt got me the job. He's been in on it the whole time. Go ask him now if you don't believe me.'

Tierney's mind winced.

'You're lying . . .' she whispered, even as images began clicking logically, horribly, perfectly into place.

The Ivy. Joel suddenly going back on his word.

The phone call Matt took the next morning.

She shook her head. 'Matt wouldn't . . . he—'

'Cares about you?' Vanita looked thoughtful. 'Yes, in his own way, and for what it's worth, I'd say he does. But he still fucked you over. Oh' – she laughed – 'and me too, by the way. We really should get together and compare notes one day.'

Seeing Tierney pale, she sighed. 'Do yourself a favour – *grow up*! You're making a fool of yourself.' She glanced back at Matt's door. 'With some help from him, of course. Anyway, must dash. *Ciao*, darling!'

She swept past Tierney into the lift, and as the doors hissed shut Tierney could hear her laughing again.

It couldn't be true; Matt couldn't, *no one* could be that two-faced.

She had to tell him what Vanita was saying.

Matt would sort it out.

Matt would shut her up.

Matt would make all this go away.

'Oh!' Turning round, she jumped at the sight of him standing there in the doorway to his flat. Smiling shakily,

Tierney started to walk towards him, then stopped, her stomach giving a rollercoaster-like lurch.

Matt's face was *crawling* with guilt.

Tierney tried to speak, but it was impossible, it felt like her throat was crammed with knives. All she could do was stand there, drunk with shock.

Vaguely, she was aware of Matt speaking. Explaining. Justifying. Rationalising.

Impatiently she cut him off. *'Is it true?'*

'It's not the way it sounds; please, Tierney, please just let me explain . . .' Now he was holding her tightly, his arms grasping her shoulders.

'The other night . . . at the Ivy . . . when we first . . . when we . . . had you already decided to help Vanita?'

His grasp tightened. 'Please, you don't understand, you have to let me—'

'Had you already decided?' Her voice trembled.

Matt hung his head.

'You *bastard* . . .' Tierney slumped back against the wall. All the time, he'd been the reason *why* she'd lost the job . . . all the time, he'd been there in the background . . . watching her, tricking her, using her . . . that night . . . *all the things she'd let him do* . . . 'How . . . how *could* you?' She felt sick as she looked at him. Her hand went to her mouth and she gagged. *'Why . . . ?'*

Matt grabbed Tierney's arm, desperate to make her understand he was different now, but she pushed him away.

'What's happening to me? I can't stop *shaking* . . .' Even her teeth were chattering, spasms of shock wracking her body.

Wrapping his arms around her, Matt pulled Tierney to him,

hugging her so tightly she could hardly breathe. She twisted out of his grasp, pushing him away and collapsing back against the wall again while Matt stood there helplessly.

'Tierney, I'm in love with you . . . and I was going to tell you everything . . . I was going to tell you *tonight* . . . we can work through this, I *know* we can . . . if you'll just listen, I can explain . . . *please* . . .'

She just looked at him.

And if looks could kill, Matt Lucas knew at that precise moment he'd be six foot under, still plummeting, eating a dirt sandwich.

He shrank back.

Tierney staggered into the lift, before her legs collapsed under the weight of her heavy, hurting heart.

7

Fame

'Fuck *me*! I don't believe this . . .' With a piercing shriek that would wake the dead but not Tierney, Carin burst into the darkened room, pouncing on her friend's bed. 'IT'S *YOU*! On the front page! Every front page of every paper! ***YOU!'***

'. . . g'way . . .' Tierney shoved her head under a large turquoise pillow. At nine o'clock she should be leaving for work, but had lain awake half the night picturing Matt and Vanita together. As a result, for the first time ever, she'd slept clean through the alarm.

Carin jerked the sheets back. 'I can't believe you didn't *say* anything!' She slapped down the bundle of newspapers. 'For crying out loud, will you *wake up*!'

Tierney shot bolt upright in bed, blonde hair a wild mass of static-stiff ringlets leaping away from her head, as though she'd spent the night plugged into a light socket. 'You're *evil*! Sod off and let me sleep or I'll make your life *a living hell*!' With an indignant yelp she vanished under the covers again.

Marching over to the window, Carin yanked back the curtains. A slice of sunshine darted through the room. There was a muffled scream as above the bedsheets one large, blue eye appeared and gave her a baleful look.

Carin held up a copy of *Metro*.

The large blue eye widened, closed tightly for a long minute, opened slowly, and was joined by its twin as, gasping, Tierney sat up. 'But that's . . . it's . . .' She pointed to the paper with a shaking hand. 'That's . . . *me* . . . ?!'

And indeed it was. Mad-eyed and in mid karate chop. In the background she could just make out the bemused face of a trader and part of Selfridges.

'Jesus bloody Christ . . .' Clutching the sheets under her chin, she slid down in the bed, glancing round with a hunted look, as if expecting a pack of reporters to come bursting out of the wardrobe. 'But how did they . . . when was . . . I don't *understand* . . .'

Carin patted one of the papers with a gleeful smile before curling up on the end of the bed. 'Some freelance hack saw the whole thing. She sold the pictures on to the papers through one of those agencies they all use.'

Tierney paled. '*What?* You mean some journalist stood there taking *photos* while the whole thing was happening? I don't believe it . . .'

'Believe it!' Carin nodded with delight. 'You, my love, are *famous* . . .'

Hands trembling, Tierney grabbed the paper and began reading.

Have-A-Go Heroine Saves Girl From West End Rapist

When Lucy Midas played truant from school on Tuesday she got more than she bargained for. The granddaughter of media mogul Richard Midas was attacked in the middle of Oxford Street when a man tried to drag her into his car. The assailant, whom police now want to question about four brutal rapes across the capital, tried to snatch the schoolgirl in what is being described as a 'brazen' assault.

The man duped members of the public into thinking he was a relative, a ruse police say he has used before. Onlookers only realised something was wrong when Tierney Marshall, pictured, rushed to the victim's aid, kicking and hitting the attacker, who fled minutes before police arrived.

Detective Inspector Kaye, leading the investigation, said, 'This man is extremely violent. He has now struck five times in full view of others and we have no reason to think he will stop.'

The incident is sure to reignite the debate over whether members of the public should intervene during assaults. The argument flared up in May 1999 when a female commuter was attacked on the Underground in front of numerous witnesses, none of whom responded to her pleas for help.

Leader comment p.17: Bystander Apathy - a British disease?

Tierney stared at the paper, unsure whether to be angry or amused. Her emotions were sliding around inside her like water rolling over the deck of a ship, unable to settle. She tried to reconcile the way she felt inside to the person in the papers.

That girl looked so confident, so in control, so *together*. Who said the camera never lied? Unless she had a *doppelganger*! A fiery, fearless, *feisty* double even now gallivanting around, running riot, causing chaos!

Tierney's mind clung to this idea. Maybe it hadn't been her in Oxford Street at all . . .

'Oh my God!' Carin gasped. 'Look at the *Sun*!'

She's A Knockout!

Karate Kid Keeps Her Cool

And Foils Sex Attacker

The first four pages were devoted to the story, including more pictures. An angry editorial demanded, 'ARE WE A NATION OF WIMPS?' and blasted the British for turning a blind eye even while a child was being attacked.

> If any of the blokes who were there had more balls, that rapist would be where he belongs right now: behind bars! Shame on you – and you all know who you are . . .

'Here you go, read 'em and weep!' Carin extracted the relevant pages from the other papers and Tierney scanned them nervously. According to the *Mirror* she was a 'Brave Blonde Bombshell', but the *Telegraph* issued a stern warning against vigilantism, scolding Tierney for placing both herself and the victim in more danger, a sentiment echoed by *The Times*.

Carin tore those two papers into shreds and stuffed them into the bin. 'Are they *insane*? If it wasn't for you, that girl would have been raped and God knows what else! Probably chopped into tiny bits! She'd have turned up in a suitcase somewhere with half her vital organs *rip—*'

'I get the idea, thanks!' Tierney grimaced. Again her eyes returned to the papers spread out on the bed.

'I can't believe what you did. That took real guts, Tier!' Carin stared at her friend in admiration. 'Come on, I want to know *exactly* what happened!'

Shrugging, Tierney drew her knees up to her chest, resting her chin on her hands. 'There's not much to tell . . .'

'But weren't you frightened? I would have been!'

'I was more worried about getting it wrong and making a prat of myself! I didn't really think about getting hurt.' Tierney's smile was self-deprecating as she rubbed her shoulder, which still hurt from where the assailant had twisted it. 'Pretty stupid of me, right?'

Carin patted her hand. 'Pretty cool, I'd say. We'd better look at the rest of the papers. God, no wonder there's so much about it. I mean, you didn't just rescue anyone! We're talking about the granddaughter of *Richard Midas* . . .'

Midas was a self-made millionaire who owned several newspapers, a shipping line, a chain of restaurants, and also dabbled in various other ventures. His autobiography, *The Midas Touch*, had been number one on the bestseller list for several months, and he'd openly stated that at some point he planned to enter politics.

Now there was silence as the girls read. The *Mail* surmised the rapist was becoming reckless, that it was merely a matter of time before he murdered someone. A forensic psychologist, commenting in the *Independent*, stated that victims snatched and taken to a second location, as would have been the case with Lucy Midas, usually wound up in the morgue. Several of the papers suggested Tierney had saved the girl's life.

Now she felt queasy, recalling how close she'd come to doing nothing, walking on, giving in to whatever stopped others from acting. Closing her eyes, she pictured Oxford Street, but this time there was a black silhouette where she should have been standing, as she watched what could have happened had she been a fraction weaker, in more of a hurry, had she been two minutes later, five minutes earlier, looking the other way.

It seemed so random.

Such a delicate, dangerous balance of fluke and fate, luck and chance.

Andy appeared in the doorway, his tie hanging loosely round his collar as he knocked back a cup of tea. 'I don't want to worry anyone, but half of Fleet Street appears to be camped out on our doorstep.' His eyes rested fondly on Carin, who instantly fidgeted and looked irritable.

Tierney watched them uneasily. She knew the warning signs: Carin was getting bored with her latest plaything. Any minute now, Andy would find himself dumped.

Then she realised what he'd said. *Fleet Street.*

Jumping out of bed, she bolted from the room while Carin shoved a newspaper at Andy, pushing past him and following Tierney, who was now bounding down the stairs two at a time. The girls dashed into the living room and peered out of the window, their mouths falling open in shock.

A media circus had landed outside their house, the driveway swarming with journalists. Armed with laptops, designer sunglasses perched jauntily on their heads, they strutted around talking earnestly into mobile phones, voices fat with urgency, as though the world would end if they didn't get their story. Most of them were smoking, and already the ground was littered with cigarette butts. Feeling weak, Tierney leaned on the windowsill. The air outside glimmered with heat, quivering into faint, wavy lines as though bowing under the weight of the reporters' angst.

'Blimey! Remind me never to go shopping with *you*!' Andy finished reading one of the papers. 'Don't think I could take the excitement!'

Carin muttered something and Tierney saw him give her a sharp glance.

Suddenly a jubilant shout from just outside the window made her jump.

'There she is! Tierney! *Tierney!* Come out and talk to us, then, luv!'

The reporters flocked to the window, cupping their hands around their eyes, pressing their faces up against the glass, squinting as they caught movement from behind the curtains.

Tierney stumbled backwards. 'What do I *do*?'

The three friends looked at each other helplessly.

The hacks started pounding on the door, rapping sharply on the window, still calling out.

'Tierney! *Tierney!* Look, we know you're in there, luv! Why don't you just come out and give us a few minutes? TIERNEY!'

'You might as well talk to them!' Andy started towards the door.

'NO!!!' The girls pulled him back.

'Why not?' he demanded, looking at them like they were insane. 'You can't just *ignore* them, for fuck's sake!'

Carin rolled her eyes. 'She can hardly go out there looking like that, can she?'

Andy glanced at Tierney; she was wearing a tiny black négligée which grazed the tops of her thighs and left little to the imagination. Her hair was in disarray and the remains of yesterday's make-up was smeared down her face.

He gave her a gentle push in the direction of the stairs. 'Go on, get ready. And hurry up! I have to go to work, and I don't fancy vaulting next door's fence to get out of here!'

Tierney hurried into the bathroom, slamming the door and staring at herself in the mirror. As always, her face was serene. Only she could see the hint of thrill in her eyes. She recalled feeling this way as a child, when she'd watched scary films, clutching a cushion to her face, feeling the tiny feet of fear scuttling down her spine.

The journalists' voices floated up towards her.

She wanted this.

She was scared of this.

She was scared *because* she wanted this.

Badly.

Turning on the shower and waiting for the water to warm up, she perched on the edge of the bath. Trying to exert control over her life was like trying to clasp a snowflake: it kept slipping and sliding from her grasp, and it seemed the harder she tried, the more sanity and security dissolved.

So perhaps she should just give in, and go with the flow.

Just go with the flow, and see where it took her . . .

*

Jake Sheridan almost dropped his coffee mug as he stared at the newspaper spread out on the table before him, and the picture of Tierney Marshall kicking a man. As he scanned the text, some gossip he'd heard about her tugged at his memory: hadn't she decked some poor bloke at a Christmas party?

Now he looked thoughtfully at the paper. Sure, Goldilocks had done a good deed, but he could just imagine what would happen next: she'd carve out a whole new career on the basis of this one incident. Jake knew how things worked, and someone, somewhere, was going to pick this girl up and turn her into the next five-minute wonder.

'The next thing *you* do, sweetheart, will be . . . let's see now . . . yeah, it'll be the cover of a men's mag.' He could see it now, see her gazing out from the cover of *Arena* or *Maxim* wearing little more than an inane grin.

Still . . . he picked up a notepad and pen and began scribbling quickly. Tierney was a natural for his programme because this was gonna be a trend all right. Girl Power, *street style*.

He had to have her on his show.

*

'Right . . .' Carin looked up as Tierney padded into the bedroom swathed in a huge yellow towel. 'Here you go . . .'

Tierney nodded in approval at the clothes laid out on the bed: a denim mini-skirt and a Gina Wall T-shirt.

'Oh, and make sure those hacks know you're up for writing a celebrity column or anything like that!' teased Carin.

'Ever thought of going into PR?'

'Actually' – Carin's face was serious as she began tidying up the mountain of clothes on the bed – 'we probably should see about getting you an agent.'

'Really? What for, though?' Tierney was dubious.

Carin gave her a pitying look. 'Because, you naive creature, you're going to be in demand! While you were in the shower, offers were already coming through the door and the phone's going mad! You're the girl who tackled a serial rapist – everyone wants your story! Reckon you need someone who knows what they're doing, to make sure you're not exploited, and all that.'

'Oh . . . so where do we get one, then?' Tierney tugged on her friend's sleeve. 'Sounds cool, doesn't it? "Sorry, you'll have to speak to my agent!"' She giggled.

Laughing, the girls hurried downstairs.

'*TIER*-NEY! *TIER*-NEY! *WE WANT TIERNEY! TIER*-NEY! *TIER*-NEY! *WE WANT TIERNEY!!!*'

Carin ignored the racket going on outside, looking suspiciously at the breakfast tray Andy had set out.

'It's for you,' he explained shyly. 'I know how you always rush out in the morning without eating and I thought . . .' His voice trailed off.

'You're sweet.' Carin spoke briskly, shoving the tray away and darting a quick look at Tierney, who clearly wasn't supposed to notice. 'But I don't even expect that from boyfriends, let alone mates!' She paused, to underscore what she'd said. 'Cheers, though.'

Angry, Andy started to protest, but fed up with being treated like a fool, Tierney cut in. 'I realise you two have stuff to sort out, but can it wait? Only, in case you hadn't noticed' – an edge crept into her voice – 'we do have a *slight* problem to deal with here . . .'

Neither Carin nor Andy seemed to hear her as they stood there, both bathed in the harsh white sunlight streaming in, like a giant spotlight exposing all the cracks in their relationship, whatever that might be now.

'You really don't give a shit, do you?' Tierney slammed the hairbrush she was still holding down. 'I'm in the middle of something I have *no* idea how to handle, and all you can do is fight! If you want to sleep together, *fine*! Just don't take it out on me when it doesn't work out!'

Seeing their surprised faces, she laughed bitterly. 'Yeah, I know, it's supposed to be like this big secret! Thanks a lot!'

Carin looked searchingly at her. 'How did you . . . I mean, how long have you—'

'What difference?' Tierney cut her off sharply. 'Look, I don't care if you two want to have a total *shagfest* from dusk till dawn every day of the week! But you must have known it would change things! You don't seem to give a shit how it'll affect us!'

'You bloody *hypocrite*!' gasped Carin, staring at her in amazement. Knowing she was referring to their fling of two years ago, Tierney felt sick with embarrassment as Andy's eyes widened.

'What am I missing here?' he asked slowly, taking a step back, away from them, and shaking his head as though to clear it, before looking at them again, his face pale.

A few of the hacks had picked up dustbin lids and were now clashing them together in a rusty-sounding thunder. Around them, the chanting was building in energy, climbing in volume like some primitive, panicked war cry.

'*TIER*-NEY!!! *TIER*-NEY!!! *WE – WANT – TIERNEY!!! TIER*-NEY! *TIER*-NEY!!!'

'Well?' Suspicion was stamped on Andy's features as he looked from Carin to Tierney and back to Carin again. '*What did you mean?*'

'Nothing. I just meant that Tierney had a thing with a bloke from work and didn't seem too bothered about ethics then!' Carin spoke glibly, smiling warmly at Andy, whose face instantly relaxed.

At the reference to Matt, Tierney felt hurt slicing through her and quickly shoved the image of his face from her mind.

'Look, you guys, I'm sorry, really.' She slipped one arm through Carin's, the other through Andy's. 'I'm just all shaken up. And now all this . . . I could use a bit of support from my two best mates!' She looked at them hopefully. 'Friends?'

Subdued, they all walked slowly into the hall.

'Ready?' Andy glanced at Tierney, who took a deep breath.

'As I'll ever be . . .'

He started to open the door.

*

Vanita lowered her lashes, coaxed her lips into a pout any woman would be proud of and most men would fall for, then watched the eager-eyed builder do just that as he staggered into a pile of wooden planks. His mates cackled and Vanita smiled. The fool had been staring at her ever since she got out of her car. Now, while he was doubled over in pain, she was doubled up in delight. It was just too, *too* easy!

As she sauntered across the car park towards the main entrance, she knew the other builders had downed their tools and were watching her. And why not? She looked good and she knew it: this summer gingham was in, and today she wore a long, checked skirt with a slit so high it should be illegal. Now Vanita laughed out loud, tilting her face up, enjoying the feel of the sun flowing over her skin like warm honey. Today was the first time she really felt like *herself* again. After her run-in with Tierney she'd been panicky, before she'd taken herself in hand, persuaded herself all was not lost.

Just misplaced.

Temporarily.

Because Matt *would* come round. Matt would come *back*.

She'd got the job she wanted. And she'd get the man too, because making Matt hers was now a matter of principle. It wasn't just about love, it was about *losing* – something Vanita never did and wasn't about to start doing now.

Strolling into the spacious, air-conditioned lobby, she stopped short, staring. Employees were huddled in small groups, eyes glued to newspapers, all wearing bemused smiles. And those had to be journalists clustered round the wide-screen television in the corner.

Noting most of them were in their twenties, she deduced, correctly, that they were from the tabloids, hotshot hacks desperate to prove themselves. Offer this lot a juicy story and they'd say 'so long' to their scruples quicker than you could say 'by-line'. Offer them a front-page splash, and they'd reach inside their bodies and tear out their own souls.

And that was why Vanita liked journalists.

They understood ambition.

In the background, the same French dance music CD they'd been playing all week was thumping away, an edgy combination of electro pop with rock guitars. It was a group called Phoenix, tipped to become the coolest sound on the club scene that summer.

Making her way over to the reception desk, Vanita placed her hand firmly over the phone that the temp, Stacey, was just reaching for. 'What's going on?'

'They're all here about Tierney Marshall.' Stacey gestured to the hacks.

Vanita's good mood evaporated like the early morning mist.

Her smile snapped back into place as she caught sight of Lian among the reporters. She'd known her from years back when they'd both worked in PR, and she liked the oriental girl. Lian wasn't merely tough, she was *hard*, and, like Vanita, she'd do anything for her career.

'Lian, darling! What a *gorgeous* surprise . . .'

The women kissed each other twice, then Vanita linked her arm through the journalist's, steering her away from her colleagues.

'So, what's the story? Do tell . . .'

Lian's black eyes widened. 'Haven't you seen the papers?' Seeing the other woman's blank face, she shook her head, ebony hair falling forward in a shiny curtain. 'Vanita, you are *seriously* out of the loop . . .' Quickly she passed her one of the tabloids, and Vanita read it in stony-faced silence.

She wanted to vomit. Letting the paper slip from her fingers, she sat very still, oblivious to Lian's scrutiny. At every stage of the game, Tierney Marshall managed to get the better of her, half the time without even trying. She'd be on Matt's mind for sure now.

She'd be on everyone's mind.

'Think this story could run for a while, then?' she asked casually.

'Do I ever! That's why I broke it in the first place . . .' Lian grinned at Vanita's shocked face.

'This is *your* story?'

'You bet! And now everybody's talking about your friend here. I mean, let's face it, she's got it all: the looks, the trendy career.' Lian paused. 'I take it you know her pretty well, working together and all?'

'You could say that.' Vanita's voice was pure acid.

So Tierney was all set to become a media babe, was she? Glancing across the crowded lobby, she saw Matt gazing at Tierney's picture with a lovelorn smile on his handsome face.

And Vanita felt rivalry harden into hatred.

*

Tierney was trapped in a tangle of light and noise. Cameras flashed constantly, the afterburn searing her eyes. Reporters were lined up on the front steps, all shoving and pushing one another to reach her, their voices gritty with impatience as they bellowed out commands and compliments, comments and criticisms.

'Tierney, turn to your left, big smile for us now! And again . . .'

'Tierney, were you scared? Did the West End Rapist hurt you? Did he say anything?'

'Aren't you worried he might come after *you* now?'

'Turn a bit to your right, luv . . . no, not that much . . . better, hold it . . . I said *hold it* . . .'

'Is it true you have a black belt in karate?'

'What does your boyfriend think about all this? Who *is* your boyfriend, Tierney?'

'What was the West End Rapist *like*?'

Tierney wanted to answer all their questions but it was impossible. She tried to move back, to edge back into the house, but two of the journalists were jammed up against the front door, right beside her.

'Do you *mind*?' she asked icily, expecting them to move. Unfazed, they simply stared back at her, faces impassive, eyes cold. Disconcerted, and starting to realise just how far out of her depth she was, Tierney looked away. The voices were becoming garbled and the heat was stifling.

Then, suddenly, there was silence. The reporters all turned, staring at a sleek grey limo pulling up outside the house. The door opened and a man jumped out, his fair hair gleaming in the sunlight, his shorts, T-shirt and running shoes all bright blue.

Tierney gasped. She'd seen him countless times in the women's glossies. It was Damien D'Ville, agent *extraordinaire* and PR guru to the stars. But what was he doing *here*? She stared as he began jogging up the steps towards the house, cutting through the hacks like a modern-day Moses parting the Red Sea.

When he reached Tierney he slowed, running on the spot for a few minutes. 'Want me to take care of this lot?' he asked cheerfully, his good-natured round face breaking into a grin as he gestured at the reporters.

Flummoxed, Tierney just nodded.

Winking at her, Damien turned to the assembled media. 'Come on now, people! *Move those butts!* I'm sure you've got stars to stalk, homes to wreck! I'm representing Ms Marshall – you want to speak to her, you come through *me*!' Turning back to Tierney, he pointed at the limo. 'Your chariot awaits!'

And suddenly, Tierney knew she'd got it all wrong.

This was about more than fifteen minutes of fame.

8

Wannabe

Reality had ripped, Tierney decided. Ripped and left a whopping great hole through which she'd now fallen.

Someone really should have warned her.

Mind The Gap.

Damien had jogged briskly back down the steps and was now busy arranging interviews with various papers. As Tierney followed him, the hacks shared wry smiles and witty asides, but she caught sour stares from the women; catty, clawing comments about her being another bubbly blonde set to join the great Peroxide Parade, and become a fully-fledged TV Tart.

In the sunlight the limousine shimmered like a mirage which might suddenly vanish. Tierney glanced back at the house. Carin and Andy stood in the doorway, watching her, their hands by their sides, nearly but not quite touching. They looked a long way off, somehow, and Tierney felt like running back to them.

Then she was stepping into the limo, sinking into the soft, cerise leather. The car slid along like some sleek, silent creature as it slipped into the early-morning traffic. Tierney twisted around in her seat and stared until she could no longer see her friends.

'Want one?' Damien held out a white container full of candied pink slices. 'Siberian ginseng – swear by the stuff! Keeps your energy levels up, go on, eat!' He popped a few into his mouth just as his mobile rang; with an apologetic smile he flipped it open, listening for a moment before cooing, 'Caprice! *Angel-face* . . .'

Damien ran the UK's trendiest celebrity management company, called simply WANNABES. Damien didn't 'manage', however, he 'empowered'. Facilitated. Enabled. Rivals swore he was a control freak, fans insisted he was pure genius. Now Tierney glanced at him chattering away and wondered.

*

Barnaby Hamilton smiled.

God did indeed move in mysterious ways, and right now, the Almighty One's timing was rather impressive.

On the other side of his plush office he was vaguely aware of the new cappuccino machine gurgling away, but it could have exploded for all he cared. Because there was only one thing holding his interest right now, and that was the newspaper spread out before him.

Quickly he dialled Julian's number, his fingers drumming impatiently on the desk. 'Jules? I take it you've seen the papers? Good. Now, are you thinking what I'm thinking?'

At the other end Julian smiled lazily. 'Of course. She's perfect. This is all perfect, the added publicity would be a *dream* . . .'

Barnaby chuckled at the enthusiasm in his colleague's voice. 'Thank the Lord we didn't start using the pictures of Zoë yet. Better cancel that press release about her. And when had you arranged for Jamie to start on the ice sculpture?'

'Not for ages, so no problem there.' Now Julian sounded anxious. 'But do you think Tierney will go for it?'

'Why not? Eve's Brew is going to be the coolest thing around, and she's the perfect person to front the ad campaign!' He laughed. 'We can even add another slogan just for her – The Beer With Real **Kick**! And you can bet whoever ends up representing her will make sure she does it!'

Julian still sounded worried. 'But how do we get rid of Zoë? We'll have to pay her off.'

'Hardly.' Barnaby sneered. 'We're talking about some kid off the streets, what does she know? We just say the contract's being cancelled.'

'I really think we should slip her some mon—'

'Leave it to me. You always worry too much.' Barnaby tapped the newspapers. 'I'll sort it out. I'm telling you, with Tierney Marshall, Eve's Brew will be a success, guaranteed.'

Julian was still dubious. 'And what do we tell Tierney? That Zoë did a runner or something?'

'Precisely. Problem solved.' Barnaby grinned. 'Jules, stop worrying. Tierney's going to be Eve – she just doesn't know it yet . . .'

*

The limo stopped outside a large white townhouse covered in lush green ivy clinging fiercely to the walls, as though protecting those within. Tierney followed Damien through the half-open front door, into a circular hall with a polished wooden floor. On the wall was a large photograph of the three pouty, pretty nineteen-year-olds who were *Paprika*!, the latest girl band to make it big.

On another wall, a baby-faced brunette smiled down, and Tierney realised it was Candy Floss, a sixteen-year-old model who was currently the cutest thing on the catwalk. She recognised the next picture also: it was Telepathic Tamara, a forty-nine-year-old tarot reader whose book, *Release The Witch Within*, was being hailed as a radical feminist text.

Seeing these high-profile clients unnerved her; they were famous because of their looks or skills, but what was *she* doing here, what was *her* claim? She'd just acted on impulse and helped a girl in trouble. Hardly any special talent required there, she thought miserably, as she followed Damien down the long hall. Somewhere upstairs a radio was blaring and phones rang constantly.

'This,' Damien said as he threw open a polished mahogany door, 'is the Sanctuary.'

Tierney found herself in a spacious, white-walled room, empty bar two Japanese rice mats either side of a low table, and a shiny red exercise bike in the corner. She bit back a giggle; the room was so minimalist it was in danger of disappearing entirely.

'So . . .' Damien sank to the floor and looked at her expectantly.

Awkwardly Tierney lowered herself on to the other mat, hard to do gracefully in a denim mini-skirt soft as cardboard.

The agent gave her a blinding beam. 'I have to say, I'm excited. I have a good feeling about this.'

'But I haven't *done* anything!' Tierney stared at him in

confusion. 'I thought you only took on celebrities!'

'Which you're halfway to becoming.' Damien poured a jug of bright green liquid into two frosted glasses. 'Jalapeño juice. All the rage in health spas. Drink up!'

Tierney knocked back a generous gulp, gasping as a mini volcano erupted in her mouth. 'Oh-my-God!' She clutched her throat, eyes streaming. 'What did I ever do to *you*?'

Damien's smile was serene. 'You'll get used to it, all my clients do. It's good for you.'

'So is arsenic in small doses . . .' muttered Tierney.

Abruptly Damien clapped his hands and she jumped. 'Stand up!' he ordered, and bemused, Tierney scrambled to her feet. Damien walked round her in a counter-clockwise circle, studying her through narrowed eyes. 'Hmmm . . . your aura's rather *spiky*, isn't it?'

'No complaints so far!' giggled Tierney, hopping nervously from one foot to another while Damien continued pacing, his face dark with concentration and a tan she figured was fake.

'It is, it's spiky! In fact' – he shook a finger at her – 'your energy, young lady, is lopsided! Too much yang and not enough ying.' He placed a hand on the small of her back. 'Yes . . . thought so . . . your kundalini is sluggish and your chakras, good heavens, they're spinning *far* too fast . . .'

'That's nothing – my astral body's close to detaching itself completely! And as for my biorhythms, well, complete chaos . . .' quipped Tierney, waiting for Damien to smile.

Instead he nodded earnestly. 'Nothing a fruit fast won't fix. For the next month I want you to eat only kiwis and kumquats.'

'I can still have chocolate though, right?' Tierney joked.

Damien winced. 'Absolutely *not*! Caffeine is an evil, *evil* substance! Should be banned as a Class A drug!'

Tierney stared at him in dismay. Not only was he a fruit-cake, he was a fruitcake *sans* a sense of humour.

Damien gestured to her mat and Tierney sat down, waiting for him to do the same. Instead he went over to the exercise bike and gazed fondly at it. 'So, Tierney, let's focus on PM – profile management. Right now, everyone's talking about you, but it won't last. Your image is cute but controversial, and if we don't capitalise on it, you'll be a five-minute wonder. I take it you don't want that to happen?'

Tierney shook her head, rewarded with an approving smile as Damien ran his hand lovingly over the bike's front wheel.

'Good girl. Now, you'll be invited on to loads of shows to take part in debates about people being more community-minded, intervening in crimes, etc. *TFI Friday, Esther, Trisha, Richard and Judy, It Happened To Me,* and so on. People look at you and see *real* girl power.

Damien leapt on to the bike so energetically he almost fell off the other side, 'We need to present you as being fun too. Your job will help – *I'm going to turn you into the Coolest Girl in the country!* Having your own column would be a good start . . . I'll have to give it some thought . . . plus I can think of several clothes and cosmetics companies that will jump at the chance to sponsor you.' He started pedalling. 'But we *really* need you to become associated with one particular product, something young and hip. Leave it with me.'

Damien fiddled with something on the bike. 'Rule one of profile management: Less Is More. If you do too much too soon, people will get bored. It's quality, not quantity, for now. What we must do is *build* your image, and if we do it properly, it'll take on its own momentum.'

The red and white wheels whizzed round while Damien sat hunched over the handlebars, pedalling frantically, eyes locked on an imaginary finishing line. Soon he was going so fast his feet were tiny flashes of colour and Tierney yawned just watching.

Cycling seemed to be taking it out of the agent, his words coming in short, sharp bursts. 'Guess what you're doing exactly three weeks today!' he rasped.

'What?' Tierney rubbed her knees which were now red and sore from the scratchy mat.

'You're posing for the August issue of ***Sorted!***. The cover!!!'

Tierney paled. *'Me?!!!* You're joking! You *are*, aren't you . . . ?'

'Hardly.' Damien frowned as the bike began shaking. 'The editor's a mate of mine. I spoke to him on the way over to you this morning.'

Over the faint rattling sound the bike was now making, Tierney could hear something else. It was Reality, splintering apart again. Wide, *wide* apart . . .

Only this wasn't a hole, it was a *chasm* . . .

Sorted! was the hippest men's mag on the market. More laddish than *Loaded*, it was a showcase for the sassiest writers and the most controversial, candid, not to mention chauvinistic commentary on men's culture. Any staff writer who bowed to political correctness was sacked instantly, and any starlet who wanted exposure dreamed of finding it on the magazine's cover.

'A-front-cover-automatically-bestows-celebrity!' Damien

gripped the bike as it began lurching violently from side to side.

Tierney had a horrible feeling that any second now he would be flung headfirst across the room. She'd hoped they'd get off to a flying start, but this was ridiculous . . .

'Once you appear in ***Sorted!*** the papers and television companies will all want you, and companies will pay more for product endorsement. It's your ticket on to the A-list.'

Face contorted with pain, Damien clambered off the bike, which was still rocking with a vengeance. 'God, I feel good . . .' he wheezed, collapsing on to his mat. From under the table he pulled out a sports bag, removing some sort of device which he attached to his right arm.

Tierney gaped. 'Er, sorry, but what are you doing?'

'What do you *think*?' Damien rolled his eyes. 'Checking my blood pressure, of course!' He pumped up the thick black band until his arm swelled to three times its normal size. '*You little bugger, don't talk crap!*' Glaring at the small electronic monitor, Damien slapped it hard a few times before nodding. 'Perfect.' Seeing Tierney's bemused face he beamed. 'I'm in training. Got a big run coming up.'

'London Marathon?' she ventured.

Damien looked offended. 'Please! I said a *run* . . .' His eyes glazed over, his voice an awed whisper. 'A hundred and forty-one miles across the Sahara . . . sun . . . sand . . .'

'*Certifiable*,' mumbled Tierney, fast concluding her career was in the clutches of a crackpot.

Wriggling on the mat, she twiddled a lock of hair around her index finger. All she could see was that magazine cover. 'And they really, like really, want *me*?'

'Absolutely! They're going to tie the cover in with a contest: readers have to design a computer game, like Tomb Raider, but starring *you*! You're a real-life kick-ass Lara Croft!' Damien grinned. 'Oh, how I *love this*! A week after that cover shot is the première of Honey Trapp's new movie. You're going.'

Honey Trapp, so named because her father's hobby was bee-keeping, and because she had a smile so sweet it was dangerous for diabetics, was the hottest singing sensation in the States, and had been in London for the last few months, making her first movie, *Beauty And The Feast*, a romantic comedy about a famous musician who fell in love with a humble sushi chef, predicted to smash all previous box office records.

Damien was still talking. 'It's the ideal place for you to be seen. I've been talking to another client of mine, and I'm going to pair you up with him. The two of you will be a celebrity couple: wherever one of you goes, the other follows. Double the exposure!'

'Who is it?' Tierney asked nervously.

'Jake Sheridan. Focus groups are going mad over his TV appearances; I think there could even be a movie opportunity for him further down the line.'

'Oh. Jake . . . okay . . . actually, we've met.' Tierney smiled, relieved she wasn't going to be lumbered with some brat of an actor. 'Hang on, though, isn't he engaged?'

'So?' Damien shrugged. 'Adds another angle. The eternal triangle . . . he can clear it with his fiancée, I'm sure she'll understand it's for the good of his career. And, this is important, nothing must actually happen between you and Jake.'

'As if!' Tierney coloured. 'But isn't the whole idea that something *does*?'

'God, no!' Damien shook his head emphatically. 'It's one of those "will they, won't they" scenarios. Everyone will see you together, looking like you can't wait to rip each other's clothes off. But no one will be *sure*. If you really did get together, it would be a disaster! You'd break up, slag each other off! No, what we want is a bit of . . . *mystery*.'

Suddenly he leaned forward, fixing her with an unblinking blue stare. 'Ground rules: I need you to be straight with me. The press will put you up there on a pedestal, but there'll come a time when they'll get bored, and want to knock you right off it again.' He paused. 'Everybody has their skeletons. So, Tierney, what I want to know is this: *What's rattling around in your closet?*'

'Shoes, mostly . . .' Tierney smiled but Damien looked stern.

Defensive, she glared at him. 'Nothing!'

'Really?'

'Really!' Tierney insisted.

Damien threw his hands up in exasperation. 'You're saying there's *nothing*? No so-called friends to dish the dirt? No old boyfriends to come crawling out the woodwork for a wad of cash?'

'That's *exactly* what I'm saying!' she retorted, offended.

'Ever done drugs?' Damien shot back, ignoring her irritation. 'Naughty photos? Threesomes? Been in trouble with the police? Lesbian romp?'

The room dimmed.

She was back with Carin.

Thunder pounding.

Heat cloying.

She and Carin, limbs entwined, kissing, touching.

Doing other things.

Tierney shook her head to clear it, felt the colour climbing into her cheeks as Damien sat quietly, watching her. For a horrible moment she panicked, opened her mouth to tell him, because what if he found out? She felt paranoia taking hold, felt a slow, sickening churning in her stomach. She would *die* if people ever found out. Then she took a deep breath, told herself to get a grip. How could Damien find out, how could anyone? She sure as hell wasn't telling, and Carin never would.

No need to mention it at all.

She, Tierney, wasn't public property, not yet.

It meant nothing.

It was in the past.

It was *private*.

'None of the above, sorry! Just call me Saint Tierney!' she laughed.

'Okay. Guess I have to take your word for it, don't I?' Damien looked bemused. 'But you'll be the first, the *only* client I've ever had with no deep, dark secret waiting to be revealed. I'm tempted to invent one, spice up your image a bit. We don't want you being labelled as a Pollyanna.'

Tierney grinned. 'I promise not to wear my halo in public!'

'Come with me . . .' Damien rose gracefully to his feet and was already out of the door and halfway down the hall by the time Tierney was standing again. Feeling like Alice through the Looking Glass, she followed him into a narrow room at the back of the house, full of people sitting at computer screens. Seven televisions were all on at full volume and Tierney flinched at the resulting din.

Damien handed her a sheet of paper. 'These are the places you're to be seen at over the next month. Anything else is out of bounds until I tell you otherwise.'

She scanned the list, recognising the clubs and restaurants on it. 'I don't understand, what do you mean, out of bounds?'

He beckoned her over to a computer screen on which was a map of London covered in brightly coloured stars. 'Each star represents a client. I call it "Celebrity Circuits",' announced Damien proudly. 'Every client has a set list, or grid, of places they can be seen at, and I make sure there's no overlap between you all. That way, when I tip off the paparazzi about where they can get a photo opportunity, there's no danger of you having to share the limelight. Then every four or five weeks I swap the networks around.'

Tierney blinked. Was this guy for real?

'And what about my job? My *career*?' she queried anxiously. 'I mean, your plans sound very exciting and all that, but I'm serious about Cool Hunting. There's loads of projects coming up at Prophets Inc. that I want to work on over the next few months. My career comes first, okay?'

'Absolutely!' Damien nodded before abruptly turning and scooting out of the room.

Silently, she followed Damien back into the Sanctuary, feeling like someone had picked up her orbit and started shaking it. Nothing was logical any more. She'd stepped into some parallel dimension and now she kept slipping between that and the real world, one foot in each, belonging to neither.

'Ah, now before I forget . . .' Damien slid a sheet of paper across the table to her and handed her a pen. 'It's just an agency agreement.' He smiled smoothly. 'Makes everything official, that's all.'

Tierney stared at the paper. If she signed this, what was she letting herself in for? Biting her lip, she stared at the words, but they were starting to merge and didn't make any sense.

'I'm not sure . . .' Putting the pen down, she looked at Damien, who sat there patiently.

He nodded. 'We have to establish you. Otherwise it'll be like I said before, you'll fade in the public's mind. Sure, you saved someone's life. But any moment now, another story, another girl, will come along and topple you from those headlines! More and more people are becoming "famous", you know, for shorter periods of time.' Damien paused. 'But you've got the spotlight now, Tierney! Why not stay there? Why not have fun with it? *Enjoy it* . . .' He shrugged. 'Chances like this, they come along once in a lifetime.'

Then he did his usual close.

The one that always clinched the deal.

That one that worked, every time, with every wide-eyed wannabe who sat here.

'Tierney, *imagine* it . . .' his smile was conspiratorial, 'imagine yourself on the cover of that magazine, on *all* the magazines! Every bloke in Britain wishing you were his girlfriend – bet you've got an ex or two out there and you'd like them to see that happen, right?' When she blushed, Damien continued. 'It's up to you. You can walk out of here now, go back to your job, hoping for a break . . . and you'll look back, and you'll wonder, but you'll never, ever know what might have been . . .

'Or you can walk out of here, and later today, it'll be you

Jake Sheridan's interviewing on his show. Just think of all those people watching *you*, hearing *you*, admiring *you*.' Seeing the wistful look in her eyes, he smiled. 'It's all there for you. I promise, you won't look back.'

Tierney stared at the contract again.

Damien stood up. 'Come on, I want to show you something.' Puzzled, she followed him out into the hall and over to a door by the stairs. Damien stopped. 'Close your eyes.'

She complied and heard him opening the door, then he was pushing her through it, still talking softly. 'Tierney, all this time you've been out there searching for the Next Big Thing! Well, now you've found it . . .'

Tierney opened her eyes and stared into the mirror.

9

Friends

Tierney's ego was about to launch a takeover bid for her personality. It started innocently; there she was, in the busy, bustling green room, waiting to be called for her slot on Jake's show. She was curled up in the corner of the sofa, trying not to take up *too* much space, since she felt she was trespassing, and shouldn't really be there.

The atmosphere was two parts nicotine to one part nerves, every other person clutching a cigarette, the room draped with smoke. Production staff and crew members scuttled around, bellowing into heavy black headsets, while make-up girls and wardrobe assistants flew in and out, fussing and fixing, fiddling and fretting. Along one wall ran a long wooden trestle table, groaning under the weight of huge plates of cakes, cookies and crisp chocolate croissants.

Tierney looked with interest at the other guests lounging around, all looking so confident. Unlike her.

And was she imagining it, or was the girl sitting on the sofa opposite *staring* at her? The culprit looked familiar, in a candy-pink summer dress and strappy sandals, her gaze now locked longingly on a plate of cream cakes. Tierney gasped as she realised who the girl was: *Honey Trapp*. She recognised the long, syrup-smooth hair, and those huge amber eyes.

Tierney blushed as Honey caught her staring. To her surprise the actress hesitated before leaning forward. 'Excuse me, but aren't you that girl from the news? The one who saved Lucy Midas?'

'Er, yes, that's me . . .' Tierney smiled nervously. The starlet's smile was even more captivating than the pictures of her suggested.

'I *knew* it!' Beaming, the singer jumped up, dumping Tierney's bag unceremoniously on the floor so she could sit beside her.

'You must be sick of hearing this, but I think what you did was *unreal*! That poor kid, it must have been terrifying!'

'Oh, well, you know.' Tierney shrugged modestly, trying to sound suitably blasé.

'That's the trouble with this country!' Honey made a face, looking quite put out. 'Everybody's worried about being *polite*! They'd rather have someone murdered in front of them than – God forbid – be rude and interrupt!'

'I know what you mean, it does my head in!' Tierney agreed, and soon the two girls were chattering away, voices getting louder and louder until a group of guests and staff formed around them and an intense debate about the Bashful Brits was under way. Tierney looked at the animated faces around her and gasped inwardly; these were the people she read about in the gossip columns, and they were listening to *her*!

One of the make-up girls, hovering nervously while trying

to dust powder over Honey's perfect features, nodded at Tierney. 'Shame there aren't more like *you* around, that's what I say!'

Everyone joined in, weaving a cocoon of compliments around Tierney. She was Gutsy. Great. Brave. Ballsy. Brilliant. She smiled her way shyly through all this adulation, not sure how to handle it. Suddenly, she was *somebody*, and Tierney liked it. She imagined herself looking like the child in the old Readybrek advert, surrounded by a warm orange glow. Word was spreading about Damien's involvement, and now, realised Tierney, people had her marked out as someone to watch; people wanted to be near her, as though she was some kind of talisman and her good fortune would rub off on them if only they could get close enough.

The Honeymoon Phase of her love affair with fame had started.

Glancing up, she saw Jake Sheridan watching her. Embarrassed now she knew they were to be paired off in the press, she grinned, waiting for him to respond. Her smile was met with a cool look. Hurt, she bit her lip and turned back to Honey Trapp, who was insisting they 'do lunch' later in the week.

*

Seeing Tierney's face fall, Jake felt a twinge of regret, and busied himself pouring a cup of coffee. He was ambivalent about escorting her to events; he recognised it as a shrewd career move and would sell it to his fiancée as such, but for some reason spending time with Tierney Marshall didn't feel like a good idea.

Glancing over at her again, his face darkened. Jesus, look at the girl, holding court over there like she was some A-list celeb as opposed to a five-minute wonder! Jake shook his head in disgust; she was just a girl who got lucky, happened to be in the right place at the right time, that was all. But she was already busy networking; look how quickly she'd roped Honey Trapp into conversation. Oh yeah, he had to hand it to her, she was a fast worker all right.

Jake frowned. If she thought *he* was going to be massaging her precious ego like the rest of these groupies, she was *way* off . . .

*

Tierney stood at the back of the studio, watching the first segment of the show. Jake was interviewing Honey Trapp, his gentle questioning revealing a side of the actress which all the magazine profiles had missed, including details of her interests which included criminology, a hobby of Andy's, Tierney noted.

The American girl came across as being bemused by her own success. 'I mean, I love singing, but I've got so much money I don't know what to do with it! What I'd really like to do is put it into something worth while, maybe also set up my own production company. I'm looking for the right project at the moment, in fact.'

'Okay, now if you'll wait here, someone will call you over in a few minutes!' Marsha, the assistant producer, appeared beside Tierney. 'We'll be ready for you soon.'

Tierney returned her smile and glanced round while Jake thanked Honey Trapp for coming on the show.

The studio resembled a large, empty, grey-walled warehouse. In one brightly lit corner was a small sofa, and a glass-topped table with two goblets filled with iced water. A gaggle of cameras stood in a semi-circle, wires slithering across the wooden floor like shiny black snakes.

And suddenly it hit Tierney for the first time that she was about to appear live on national television. A wave of panic sent her heart rushing into her ribcage.

She couldn't do this.

Turning to Marsha, she screwed her face up in what she hoped was a good impression of agony. 'Er, I don't feel well. Quite queasy, in fact.' Taking a step towards the door, she smiled wanly. 'Sorry. Going. *Now*.'

'Oh, I'm sure it's just a bad attack of nerves, nothing to worry about,' remarked a dry voice from behind her, and spinning round, Tierney found herself staring into a pair of smoky-grey eyes as Jake smiled mockingly.

Again her heart collided violently with her ribcage.

'No, really.' Tierney sent a frantic mental command to her skin to go pale and back up her lie. 'Really, I think I'd better just go and lie down . . .'

Jake seemed amused. 'And I'll arrange it, personally, *after* the show . . .' Ignoring her protests, he steered her gently but firmly over to the set. 'This'll only take about ten minutes. Now' – he patted the sofa – 'you sit right there, sugar—'

'Er, hello, newsflash! My parents *did* name me at birth and it was *not* **sugar**!' snapped Tierney.

Jake raised an eyebrow. 'Feeling better already, I see?'

One of the crew waved at them. 'Hey! Ready when you are, kids!'

The studio went quiet. The cameras moved in closer and Tierney grimaced as she stared at herself in them. She looked pale, and began pinching her cheeks to bring back some colour until she caught Jake's grin. 'Relax, babe, you look fine . . .'

'I am not a *babe*!!!' hissed Tierney, gripping the sides of her chair.

Jake winked. 'Sure thing . . . *doll* . . .'

Then they were being counted down. Tierney swallowed nervously, feeling her pulse beating in her throat so hard and fast it hurt. The cameras swung in closer still and she was confronted with half a dozen reflections, all from slightly different angles. It was like being in a hall of mirrors, and she wriggled around in her chair, trying to avoid staring at herself, but it was impossible.

Jake smiled brightly. Catching sight of the autocue, Tierney watched with interest as he started reading from it, briefly recapping on the Oxford Street attack. Suddenly he turned away from it, looking at her as though troubled.

'Now the media has, for the most part, been full of praise for my guest, but I can't help wondering: are we going to see a trend for self-styled have-a-go vigilantes, taking the law into their own hands? A police spokesman has already expressed concern. What do you think, Tierney?'

She looked wildly at the autocue again. The bastard was ad-libbing, trying to provoke her. Now everyone was waiting for her to respond.

'What I *think*' – she gave him a sweet smile for the benefit of the cameras – 'is that you're exaggerating. And perhaps if we did have more so-called "vigilantes" we'd also have more criminals behind bars!'

Jake inclined his head slightly to acknowledge her point.

'But didn't you realise you might be aggravating the situation? That you might provoke the attacker further and put both the victim and yourself at risk?' He shrugged, suggesting confusion. 'I mean, why not just call the police? Then the West End Rapist might not have escaped!'

'And how exactly was I supposed to contact them – *by telepathy*?' Tierney shot back, as the crew burst out laughing. 'A girl was in trouble! I didn't have a mobile phone. I did the best I could, and that was more than anyone else!'

Jake regarded her steadily, wondering how far he could push her. So far, she was hanging on to her temper admirably. 'Some have suggested you in fact knew there was a journalist taking pictures and that you took advantage of the situation to further your own career.' His voice carried an edge.

Tierney's laugh was scornful. 'Make your mind up! First you suggest I placed myself in mortal danger by stepping in, now you're saying I'm an opportunist!' Her voice was crisp. 'What you should be asking is what sort of *sick* individual, upon seeing a girl being assaulted, stands there taking photos instead of helping!'

Jake looked at her sternly. 'And you're okay with the fact that a large number of young girls will now sign up for kick-boxing and karate classes, thinking it's the "cool" thing to do?' he demanded, grey eyes fixed on her angry face. 'Isn't it enough women are already drinking men under the table? Now you want them to start brawling like the blokes too?'

'I hardly thi—'

'So presumably you'd challenge the police's advice, which

is for people to call them and not intervene?' Jake cut in smoothly. 'I take it you'd advise others to ignore that advice too?'

'Now you're putting words in my mouth!' protested Tierney.

And so it continued.

*

Zoë put the phone down and retched. She managed to stagger into the pretty pink en suite bathroom before throwing up violently, gripping the sink to stop herself fainting. Then, sinking slowly to the floor, she covered her mouth with a trembling hand, hot tears trickling down her cheeks.

The call had been from Barnaby Hamilton's PA, a clipped voice informing her she was no longer needed for the Eve's Brew campaign. When Zoë had protested she'd already signed the contract, the woman had sighed.

'If you'd read the small print, you'd have seen there's a cooling-off period of one month. Legally, you don't have a leg to stand on.'

Zoë glanced round the hotel room where she'd been staying, the bill being picked up by Julian and Barnaby. Since meeting Tierney Marshall, she'd felt something she thought she'd never experience again. Hope. More than hope, *excitement.* Tierney had painted her a picture in bold, bright, beautiful colours, and Zoë had believed her.

Now the world seemed grey and cold.

Shivering, she rocked back and forwards, trying to make sense of what was going on. *Why* was this happening? Wiping her face, she stared bleakly at the luxurious room. Over the years, she'd coped with more than any girl her age should have to, and now she'd cope with this.

From her trouser pocket she pulled out Tierney's business card and noted the address, then stood up on shaky legs.

This wasn't over.

Tierney said she was perfect for the job.

Tierney said she'd be the Next Big Thing.

Tierney **owed** her.

And Zoë intended to collect.

*

Finally, after fifteen minutes of riling Tierney, Jake brought the interview to a close and the adverts rolled. 'See? That wasn't too painful, right?' He grinned.

'Compared with what – appendicitis?' Tierney turned to face him, no longer trying to hide her anger. 'You tried to blindside me!'

'Just doing my job, and you might as well get used to it!' Seeing anxiety flicker in her face, he felt bad. Tierney had an idealistic view of fame, and was loving every minute of all this. Why ruin it?

'What do you mean?' Her voice wavered.

'Nothing,' Jake said flatly, shaking his head, 'absolutely nothing.'

They stood there, staring past each other and into the distance, both aware the silence needed filling.

Finally Jake smiled hesitantly. 'So I guess we're going to Honey Trapp's première together later this month?'

'Can't *wait* . . .' Tierney muttered.

Jake felt his temper catch again. 'Yeah, well, spending the

night – I mean, the *evening* with you isn't exactly my idea of a good time!'

Picking up her bag from the sofa, Tierney frowned. 'Could you do me a favour? Please?' Her wide blue eyes were troubled as she looked at him.

Instantly Jake's face softened. 'Sure . . . what?'

'Take a vow of silence!' Her smile was brittle. 'Starting now!'

They scowled at each other until, despite himself, Jake felt his lips sliding into a grin. Tierney saw, and he watched with amusement as a smile fought its way on to her face and she turned away to hide it. Finally, giving him a wry look, she clamped a hand over her mouth and waved at him before turning and walking quickly out of the studio.

Jake stood, staring after her. One thing was for sure: the next few weeks weren't going to be boring.

*

'Tierney? Want a lift?' Honey Trapp came sprinting down the corridor, grabbing Tierney's arm.

'Oh, thanks.' Tierney felt awkward. 'But it'd be right out of your way.'

'No worries. Got nothing better to do.' Beaming, Honey led her out into the parking lot, pointing to a long, white limo. 'Rick, the driver, is great. He even let me drive the car yesterday when I got bored! I went the wrong way down a one-way street, it was chaos!'

She giggled and Tierney gaped at her in astonishment. 'Bored? You? But, I mean . . .'

'You don't believe me?' Honey's smile was weary. 'All I do is give interviews! The only people I know in the UK are the other people from the movie, and they're all off doing new projects now . . .' She shrugged, eyes sombre. 'I get homesick, y'know?'

Tierney smiled. 'Actually, I do . . .'

On the drive home she told Honey about her family back in Dublin, how homesick she felt sometimes, and how much she missed all her old friends. Honey understood perfectly and soon the two girls were swapping life-stories. Tierney couldn't believe how genuinely nice and down-to-earth the actress was, and they parted with promises to meet up later in the week.

*

'. . . and lead with the hips . . . shoulders slanting back . . .' Tierney sashayed through the front door, using the new walk Honey had started teaching her. Gliding into the kitchen she tripped over Genghis, mistimed a step, went sliding into the cooker, then almost dislocated a shoulder as she lurched forward to grab the ringing phone.

'Speak!' she ordered breathlessly, hoping it was *Hello!* magazine.

There was silence, but whoever it was stayed on the line; it sounded like they were phoning from an office, since she could hear phones ringing and muffled voices in the background.

'Hello? *Hello?*' Tierney was getting impatient.

Then, on the other end, one of the muffled voices came closer as somebody approached the caller, speaking loudly. 'Gina, have you got the report for—' The line went dead.

Tierney stared at the phone. *Gina.* She must have been trying to get Carin. Tierney groaned. Her friend was probably up to her old tricks, sleeping with both Andy and Gina. The question was, did Andy know?

Even as she stood there, the front door slammed and Carin came breezing into the kitchen, chestnut curls spilling over her shoulders as she opened the fridge and took out a bottle of beer.

Tierney looked at her coldly. 'There was a call for you. It was Gina.'

'Yeah? What did she say?' Carin was trying to sound casual, but Tierney knew her too well to be fooled by the bland tone.

'You're still seeing her, aren't you?' she accused her friend. 'Does Andy know? Well? Does he?'

Carin coloured and Tierney shook her head in disgust.

'I don't *believe* you! This is a friend we're talking about!'

'Tier,' Carin hurried into the hall after her, 'don't be like that! You don't understand!'

'Got that right!' Tierney turned to face her. 'You *know* how Andy feels about you! I mean Christ, Carin, the guy would probably marry you tomorrow if he thought you'd say yes!'

Carin looked at her miserably. 'I'm really screwed up right now, I need some time to sort my head out . . . Please, Tier, don't say anything to Andy, not yet! It should come from me. If you're really my friend, you'll do this for me. Please?'

'Don't ask that of me!' Tierney couldn't believe she was being put in this position. 'I can't just stand by and watch you walk all over him!'

'But I care about him, I just need time to work out what

I really want, and it could be him! It could be . . . *Please,* Tierney, *please* don't make things end when they might not have to! I *swear,* I just need a bit of time to end things properly with Gina, that's all. Please be a friend and understand I'm doing the best I can . . . oh fuck . . . I'm so *confused* . . .'

Tierney sighed. She found it so hard to say no to people, and Carin *did* seem genuinely troubled . . . Maybe she should leave her to work it out on her own, and not interfere. Who was she to play God with people's love lives, anyway?

She looked sternly at her friend. 'You promise you will talk to him? Soon?'

Carin nodded vigorously. 'Cross my heart and hope to die! I won't forget this, Tierney, this makes such a difference, you have no idea.'

'Yeah, well, can't say I'm happy about it, but you're right, it should come from you. Just don't string Andy along, okay?'

'Promise.' Hugging her, Carin smiled wanly and went back into the kitchen.

Subdued, Tierney sat down on the stairs, wondering if she'd done the right thing. Andy was holding his heart out to Carin, while she was turning playing the field into an olympic sport. And she, Tierney, was stuck slapbang in the middle. If she told Andy what was going on, she'd betray Carin. And if she didn't, she was letting Andy down.

The answer machine's winking red light caught her eye and wearily she hit the 'play' button. Damien was right: there were nine messages, all from the media. *Cosmopolitan* wanted to feature Tierney in a piece entitled 'Women Behind the Headlines'. *TFI Friday* wanted her to appear on next week's show and re-enact her karate moves using Chris Evans as the assailant. Richard and Judy wanted her on their programme to take part in a phone-in on bystander intervention. *The Big Breakfast* wanted to talk to her about possibly doing a ten-minute regular spot on London's coolest spots. And it went on. Trisha. Esther. Kilroy-Silk. Talk Radio. As instructed, Tierney duly made a note of them all, to pass on to her agent the next day. Then she smiled slightly as she listened to two messages from her parents, both full of concern for her.

There were also four messages from Matt, all long, rambling apologies, begging her to call him. Tierney gulped. Seeing him at work was going to be hell.

Now feeling thoroughly deflated, she trudged upstairs to her room, getting undressed without even bothering to turn on the light. Lying down on her bed, Tierney stared at the ceiling; right above her head was a thick black crack where the paint was peeling away. She imagined that on the other side of it was some other, brighter dimension where life made sense again, where people she loved didn't die, or hurt each other. The crack seemed to widen slightly as she stared and Tierney wished she could just float up and through it.

Each time she thought about Matt and how he'd played her, it was like her heart was turning black with rage. He could say sorry a million times, in a million different ways, and it wouldn't make any difference. As for Joel and Vanita . . . Tierney punched the pillow in disgust.

Sitting up again, she pulled open her bedside drawer, taking out a small black velvet case and opening it to reveal a chunk of crystal. Rose quartz. Palest pink with silver threads running through it. Rose quartz, for healing anger, calming hurt feelings. Tierney didn't go in for New Age nonsense, but growing up back in Ireland, her grandmother, who was either wonderfully fey or a raving fruitcake depending on your outlook, had instilled in her a love of crystals. Holding the quartz tightly, Tierney lay down, drifting off to sleep with her fingers still curled around the cool pink stone.

10

Indecent Proposal

'In the beginning was the Word' – Damien's beam was so blinding Tierney saw sunspots – 'and that word was *networking*!'

'Okay . . .' Tierney looked at her agent warily. They were in his office, discussing her first public appearance, later that day, at Richard Midas's birthday celebration.

'Now, you won't need to work the room too much. We'll focus on Cleopatra.'

'Who?' Tierney giggled.

'Editor of *Dado*.' *Dado* was the coolest lifestyle magazine going, snapped off the shelves the second it appeared, leaving *Wallpaper* standing.

'Hang on.' Tierney frowned. 'I could have sworn the editor was Caroline Fraser?'

'Ssh!' Damien looked nervous. 'Whatever you do, don't call her that!'

'Why not? It's her name!' Tierney protested.

'It *used* to be her name,' he corrected her sternly, 'then she went to one of those regression hypnotists, *fabulous* chap in

Harley Street. Thinking of popping along myself. Anyway, turns out that in a past life, Caroline was Cleopatra.'

'From Caro to Cairo . . .' Tierney started to smile again. 'You're winding me up, right?'

'No. She takes it seriously, too.'

'But she doesn't actually think she's . . .' Tierney's voice trailed off as Damien nodded.

'Refuses to bathe in anything but soya milk – closest you can get to ass's in terms of purity. Mind you, she drives the men at work mad, insisting they carry her round on one of those things, what are they called, you know, like sedan chairs?'

'You're joking. You *must* be . . .'

'Not at all. Though she gave up that idea when one of the sub-editors tripped and almost tipped her down three flights of stairs.'

Tierney shook her head in disbelief. 'More out than in. There are definitely more out than in. And is this woman . . . er . . . a good mate of yours?'

'Absolutely! She's lovely, really down-to-earth.' Damien said this without any trace of irony.

Tierney suppressed a giggle. 'So you want me to talk to the journalist formerly known as Fraser?'

'I'm hoping she'll offer you a column; we could call it . . . I know! "Tierney's Trends!" I've already had a word with her and paved the way, but she's very selective. Richard Midas owns the magazine, as you know, so anyone he approves of, Cleo will accept. Now, here's the thing: these parties of Midas's are always the same. *Deathly* boring affairs. He's teetotal, so the strongest drink you'll get is coffee.' Damien shuddered at the mere mention of caffeine. 'Anyway, he sits at the head table with his family and everyone sort of queues to get a few words with him. We need to make an impression. I don't want you to be just another face in the crowd. Now, how shall we do this . . .' He stared into space, blue eyes glazed. No doubt he was communing with his spirit guide, Tierney thought darkly.

'I think . . . yes . . . I think you should play the role of Humble Heroine. Ordinary girl who did something extraordinary.' Damien nodded slowly. 'I don't want to glam you up too much, not just yet . . . we'll leave that for when you do the ***Sorted!*** cover . . . Tell me, when you had your little fist-fight with that nasty rapist, did he hurt you at all?'

Touched by his concern, Tierney smiled at her agent. 'Well, he did twist my arm up behind my back and it hurt like hell for a—'

'Perfect!' Damien clapped his hands in delight. 'Love it to bits!!!'

She looked at him coldly. 'Excuse me?'

But he was staring intently at her arm. 'We'll need to bandage it, of course . . . yes, nice bit of crêpe should do the trick . . .'

'What are you *talking* about?' Tierney shook her arm around. 'It's fine, see? Doesn't hurt at all, in fact.'

Damien looked glum. 'Pity.' Then his face brightened. 'But no one needs to know it's better, do they? We want all the papers printing pictures of you, your good arm around Lucy Midas, bad arm lying limply by your side as you transcend the pain . . . maybe I'll hint that you've got a touch of post-traumatic stress disorder . . .'

'Or just stick me on a stretcher with an IV tube in my arm and a priest on call to read me my last rites!' Tierney snapped.

'Don't be silly!' Damien chided her, sarcasm lost on him as usual.

Seeing him looking at her shoulder again, she tried to distract him. 'So, tell me more about the party.'

'Well, Barnaby Hamilton and Julian Parry will be there. Had a rather interesting chat with them about you the other day, actually.'

He paused, smiling to himself, and Tierney waited for him to enlighten her. Instead he glanced at his watch before speaking briskly. 'God, we have to be there in two hours and I've still got twenty-six miles to run today! *Nightmare!*'

*

'I don't give a shit what she's doing! I need to speak to her – *now*!' Dumping her denim jacket on the reception desk at Prophets Inc., Zoë scowled.

Stacey, the temp, eyed the coat with distaste. 'As I've *already* explained, Tierney Marshall is unavailable. Perhaps someone else could help?'

'And as *I've* already told you, no!' Zoë insisted angrily. 'When will she be back?'

Stacey didn't bother with the polite smile supposed to be a permanent fixture at all times and with everyone. 'No idea. All I can suggest is you leave your number with me.' Turning her back, she began sorting through some files.

Impatiently, Zoë waited for her to look up again. Right now, she had no time for protocol, or this moron of a mannequin barring her way. Leaning forward, she grabbed the folder

Stacey was holding, slamming it down on the desk as the other girl gaped.

'I'll make this *real* clear.' Zoë's voice was tight with temper. 'I am not moving until you get Tierney Marshall down here! I don't care if I have to chain myself to this fucking desk – *I'll do it*!!!'

'What in God's name is going on?' Hearing the raised voices as she emerged from the lift, Vanita came storming over.

Relieved at being able to dump the dilemma on someone else, Stacey gestured ungraciously at Zoë. 'She's demanding to see Tierney. I keep explaining she's not in today, but I'm not getting anywhere.'

Vanita glanced at the angry-faced girl beside her. 'I work with Tierney Marshall.' She smiled warmly at the teenager. 'Why don't we have a little chat, maybe I can help you.' Not even giving her a chance to protest, she nodded at Stacey and all but frogmarched Zoë into a vacant office.

*

Richard Midas's house had a driveway longer than the M1 and more pillars than the Acropolis. Standing on the doorstep with Damien, Tierney fidgeted. Even though it was late spring, it was a blistering hot day and she felt like her skin was on fire. Behind them the circular driveway was filling up with cars as a steady stream of guests arrived.

'Yes . . . I think you'll do.' Damien nodded in approval at Tierney's outfit, a pale-blue summer dress from Geisha, a hip new Japanese label. He'd insisted she didn't wear too much make-up. 'Tasty but traumatised, that's how you need to look.'

To Tierney's alarm, he'd carried out his bizarre plan of

wrapping her arm up in miles of crêpe bandage, from the wrist to the shoulder, fastening it so tightly it was cutting off her circulation.

'Damien, my arm really does hurt now! Can't you loosen this thing a bit?' she whispered as they were shown into the house and led down a long, plushly carpeted corridor to one of several reception halls. The room was large, one wall taken up with french windows leading out to a long garden bordered by white roses.

As they slipped through the people milling around, another agent waved and headed their way. Damien smiled warmly at the man as he approached them. 'Git!' he whispered under his breath.

'What?' Tierney frowned.

'Sod stole one of my clients last year! Love to smash his skull in with one of those plates, the *wank*— Adam! *Fabulous* to see you!'

While the two men chatted, Tierney tugged irritably at her bandage, trying to loosen it, but it held fast.

'Look, there's Richard Midas.' Damien pushed her forward. 'Come on.'

She looked with interest at the entrepreneur as they approached. He was standing in the middle of a group, a spry man in his late fifties with sparkly blue eyes, craggy face, and grey hair worn long. He looked like Tony Curtis, she decided. As they joined the crowd of people around him, she noticed his tie was covered with tiny golden hands, and recalled reading that he took the Midas Touch logo seriously.

Suddenly she heard exclamations of anger and watched in disbelief as Damien began elbowing other guests out of the way, planting himself right in front of Midas and chatting away before turning and glaring at her. 'Richard, this is Tierney Marshall. I'm sure I don't need to say anything more.' He all but shoved her on to Midas's lap.

'Ah, Ms Marshall.' The blue eyes sparkled away at her. 'I've been looking forward to meeting you. How can I ever thank you for helping my granddaughter?' He smiled. 'You're an extremely brave young lady.' He frowned, gesturing at her arm. 'But I didn't realise you'd been hurt during the altercation?'

'Oh, no, I wasn't, really, my arm's absolutely fi—*OWWWW*!!!' Tierney hollered as behind her Damien suddenly whacked the bandaged shoulder.

Immediately Midas looked at her with concern. He beckoned one of the waiters over, 'Peter, fetch another two chairs for Ms Marshall and Mr D'Ville. They'll be sitting with me.'

Seeing Damien's serene little smile, Tierney realised he'd had this planned every step of the way.

*

Vanita listened with a sympathetic smile as Zoë poured out the whole story.

It was all the Valkyrie could do not to turn cartwheels.

Because this was a cosmic e-mail!

Fate faxing!

This was Destiny *shrieking*!!!

Now she just had to translate what it was saying.

Why, Vanita mused, had Zoë been dropped from the campaign so abruptly? It didn't make sense. She was definitely missing a piece of this puzzle.

But she'd find it.

And when she did, who knows what she might do with it?

'Give me your telephone number.' She handed Zoë a pen. 'I'll find out what's going on.'

'You'll help me? Why?' Zoë's tawny eyes were wary.

'Because I don't like the way you're being treated.' Vanita scribbled her own number for Zoë and they swapped bits of paper.

Getting up, Zoë slung her bag over her shoulder, following Vanita back through the spacious lobby. At the doors she paused, looking earnestly at the older woman. 'I've given you the number of the hostel, and also one for the hotel I'm at now. I'll be there until the day after tomorrow. Will you make sure Tierney knows I came by? I *really* need to speak to her. You will remember to tell her, right?'

'Of course!' Vanita smiled warmly as she crossed her fingers behind her back. 'That's a promise.'

*

Tierney was being treated like royalty. Midas heaped food on to her plate, introducing her to everyone, waxing lyrical about her bravery while Tierney smiled her way bashfully through all the attention.

Every ten minutes, just as she started to enjoy herself, Damien would kick her hard under the table, stare pointedly at her arm and hiss frantically, *'Look like you're in pain!'*

'I *am* – you just broke my sodding *shin*!' Tierney would glare back, wincing.

Midas would see, make even more of a fuss of her, and the whole charade would start over again.

By the time they'd been there an hour, her legs were black and blue, her left arm had gone numb, and her bladder was bursting from all the tea being poured down her throat. Each time she tried to excuse herself to go find the toilets, Damien would shove his own chair back to block her way.

'You can't. Cleopatra will only stay about fifteen minutes. I'm not having you wrecking everything by being busy powdering your nose when she gets here. Forget it.'

By the time Cleopatra actually arrived, Tierney was in agony, writhing around on the chair, face screwed up. The journalist gave her a strange look and Damien cut in quickly. 'Poor Tierney, she's on medication, for her arm.'

Cleopatra was in her late twenties, with charcoal-black hair worn in a blunt bob, and a brightly patterned, diaphanous gown which flowed out behind her and which kept tripping people up. Her kohl-covered eyes flickered over Tierney. 'So this is the Cool Hunter . . . Damien tells me you've put together an article for me to look at?'

'I have? I mean, I have!' Tierney nodded energetically, wondering what the hell Damien was playing at. She'd done no such thing and wouldn't even know where to start.

Cleopatra looked at her haughtily. 'We don't usually commission unknowns, they're terribly unreliable, you know . . .' Just then her eyes widened as Midas turned to Tierney to ask yet again if she was all right.

'But as I always say,' Cleopatra continued sweetly, 'there's a first time for everything. Why don't you fax me the column over later this week and I'll have a look? If I like it, well, who knows?'

'Consider it done!' Damien beamed. He and Cleopatra talked a little longer before she drifted off and he turned back to Tierney. 'Barnaby Hamilton and Julian Parry have just arrived. Come on.'

Tierney turned to Midas. 'It was nice meeting you, I look forward to seeing Lucy later.' She smiled as he covered her hand with his.

'The pleasure was all mine, I assure you. We must get some photos of you and Lucy together. I'll organise it. And I'm sure this isn't the last time we'll be speaking, Tierney.' Midas's blue eyes warmed. 'I'm working on a certain project and, though I can't say anything about it just yet, I think it's something we'll be discussing in the near future.'

'Oh . . . sure, fine.' Tierney smiled again before dashing off to join Damien who was waiting impatiently with Barnaby and Julian.

To her surprise they ushered her out of the room and back into the corridor.

Watching as the three men grinned at each other, Tierney frowned. 'What's going on?'

Barnaby's grin widened. 'It's about your involvement with Eve's Brew. We have a proposal for you.' He paused, glancing at Julian. 'We want *you* to be Eve!'

'Come again?' Tierney looked blankly at them.

'You. We want you to be Eve in the ad campaign.'

Stunned, she looked at Damien, who nodded and gave her the thumbs-up.

'I don't understand . . .' Tierney decided they were all suffering temporary insanity.

Julian took over. 'Look, you're cool, and you're well on the way to being famous. Damien's told us a bit about his plans for you, and we like them. You sum up the spirit of Eve's Brew:

colourful, controversial, cute. You're perfect. And we want you.'

Totally bewildered, Tierney took a step backwards to distance herself from this madness. 'It's the most ludicrous thing I've *ever* heard! I'm a consultant on the project, for God's sake! And anyway,' she looked at them accusingly, 'I found you the perfect person – Zoë!'

Turning her back on them, she stalked over to the window, gazing out with unseeing eyes. Barnaby and Julian looked at Damien, waiting for him to sort this out. Instead he just smiled calmly, sipping his organic wheatgerm drink and watching Tierney out of the corner of his eye.

She *was* going to do this.

He'd already issued the press release.

Finally Barnaby broke the impasse, joining Tierney at the window. 'If Zoë was still in the picture, I agree, she'd be ideal.'

'What do you mean, if she was still in the picture?' demanded Tierney, puzzled.

He turned, staring out of the window with a pensive expression, praying inwardly that Zoë was miles away. 'I hate to be the one to tell you this, I know you were fond of the girl, but, well,' he shrugged helplessly, 'the fact is, she's vanished on us!'

'What?' Tierney suddenly realised she hadn't heard from Zoë lately, but she'd been too busy to give it a second thought. 'Why would she do that? This job meant everything to her! There's no way she'd just go, not without saying anything! I know she wouldn't!'

Barnaby nodded sympathetically. 'It took me by surprise as well.' He lowered his voice slightly. 'I gather her family were putting out feelers. She panicked, and next thing we knew, she'd gone. It's very upsetting.'

'That's awful . . .' Tierney paled. It hurt to think of Zoë, out there scared and alone.

'I promise you, we're doing all we can to find her, but meanwhile' – Barnaby smiled wryly – 'we've got an ad campaign to sort out. We *must* have the right person to front it, and well, what can I say? We think it's you. We *know* it's you.'

Tierney rubbed her forehead, feeling overwhelmed. She'd found them the perfect Eve, and if the girl really had disappeared, it was up to her to solve the problem. But like *this*?

Again, she shook her head. 'No. I'm not doing it, I'm sorry.'

Without meeting anyone's eyes, she turned and hurried down the hallway, out of the front door, shoes crunching across the driveway as she headed for a tiny wooden seat set to one side. Sitting down and massaging her aching temples, Tierney sighed. They all thought she was crazy for knocking back this chance, and they were probably right.

For some reason, though, taking on the role of Eve felt wrong. Tierney didn't know if it was a whisper of intuition or an attack of nerves stopping her from saying yes, and she didn't care. Rummaging around in her bag she found a scrunchy, pulling her long hair back into a ponytail and instantly feeling cooler. The heat was clinging to her skin, slowing her thoughts. Closing her eyes, she imagined she was standing under a cold, clear, cascading waterfall . . .

'You know you're wrong, don't you?' Damien had followed her outside. Now he sat down at the other end of the bench and spoke quietly. 'It's a product aimed at women, and women *like* you, like the way you used your intuition and rescued Lucy Midas. Eve's Brew is just the sort of thing you should be associated with – something frothy and fruity and *fun*!' He fixed her with one of his steady blue stares. 'I suggest you reconsider.'

Seeing the stubborn look on her face, he gave Tierney a benevolent smile, as if she were a wayward child refusing to see reason. 'Tierney . . . there's no point in my representing you if you don't listen to me now, is there? It won't look good for me if word gets out you want to reject a deal most girls would kill for . . . What sort of agent would I be to let you turn down a chance like this? You're on your way to making it . . . now is when we have to work the hardest . . . if we let that momentum slip now . . .'

He gazed sadly at her. 'The public are fickle. Your relationship with them is still casual . . . a fling, really. You don't have commitment, not yet. But *this* . . . this could give it to you . . .'

Tierney felt her resolve weakening.

He sounded so **sure**, and she was so *unsure* . . .

And what if he was right? What if people lost interest in her? Anything, she'd do *anything* to stay in the spotlight. No one could understand what it was like, she thought miserably, no one who hadn't been there. Having fame, if only for the shortest time, changed you. It left you wanting more.

Now she felt panicky. She'd only been in the public eye for what, five minutes? And already, she knew she'd never be the same again.

She couldn't go back, not now.

It would be like trying to close Pandora's Box.

And, Tierney thought, looking at Damien resentfully, his words carried a veiled threat: if she didn't play the game by his rules, there was always another would-be waiting to step straight into her shoes and agree to whatever she'd refused. He'd issued the threat so lightly, so *nicely*, almost like he was doing her a favour, so Tierney could hardly call him on it.

'Okay.' She nodded, face subdued. 'I'll do it. I'll be Eve.' But she resolved to go and look for Zoë, try and track her down somehow.

'Good girl! Knew you'd see sense in the end!' Damien jumped up, grinning. 'Let's go and give the others the good news. And it's almost time for the photocalls with Lucy Midas.'

Not waiting for her to follow, he went skipping across the driveway and through the front door while Tierney walked slowly after him.

In the space of an hour, she'd agreed to write a column for which as yet she had no ideas, and front an ad campaign that would make her the most talked-about girl in the country.

Being steamrollered was becoming a way of life.

11

Überblonde

'You *clever* girl! I simply adore it!' Cleopatra began gushing more than Niagara Falls as Tierney clutched her mobile phone, beaming with relief. She'd faxed over her first column, 'Tierney's Trends', yesterday, then waited anxiously – would her ideas be cool enough?

The first product was a new lipstick which changed colour when the woman wearing it could expect PMS. Called *Banshee,* it came in a range of Miami-bright colours and Tierney had a feeling it could catch on big-time.

A new line of dresses had also caught her eye. Produced by the company **Easy Girl**, they were sheer and sexy and part of a major new trend – 'smart clothes'. Tiny, electrical sensors were woven into the material; if the wearer's temperature dipped below a certain point, special heating pads in the dress's lining kicked in.

The third product Tierney mentioned was hemp boots: huge, white and clumpy, they were all the rage in Scandinavia and she was sure they would catch on in the UK too.

Tierney had never worn any of these items herself, but all had the potential to be *way* cool. Damien was sure that once the column appeared the companies involved would want to sponsor Tierney to endorse the items, but she was leaving all that to him and hadn't given it a second thought.

'I'm so glad you like it!' Now Tierney slumped back in her chair as Cleopatra continued complimenting her.

Suddenly the journalist realised the time and gasped. 'Must dash! I'm off to Sebastian Carmichael's latest exhibition, he's doing something *terribly* chi-chi with bats and Lurex! Later, precious!'

And she was gone.

Tierney flopped back in her chair and looked around. It was ten o'clock on a Tuesday morning and she was at ***Sorted!*** waiting for the make-up artist and stylist to arrive. The dressing room resembled a padded cell, being white and round with no sharp edges or corners. The wall in front of her was one large mirror and she wasn't surprised to see faint shadows beneath her eyes. She wasn't sleeping well, guilty and confused over not telling Andy about Carin's two-timing him. She felt trapped, caught between her two best friends. It was horrible.

Tierney found she just couldn't think straight, partly because the last few weeks had been manic. Her life was on fast-forward, a colourful, chaotic blur, and though she was enjoying it, having time to herself was a luxury she missed. Now she felt guilty, realising she'd only seen Liz about twice socially in the past month.

Work was going fairly well, since she was now a real asset to Prophets Inc. Joel treated her like a princess and had insisted on making her a creative director; Tierney wasn't as happy as she thought she'd be, and was tempted to tell Joel where to go, but as usual she'd swallowed a sharp retort and just smiled. Cool Hunting was still her passion, and her career still came first, although public appearances and parties were taking up more and more of her time. At least, Tierney sighed, that meant less time around Matt. Thank God, because every time she looked at him Tierney felt upset again.

Best of all, the Eve's Brew project was going brilliantly, the ad campaign really starting to take shape. Tierney had seen some rough sketches and loved them. Vanita was totally off the venture, Joel having placated her with a business trip to the States.

Jake was still putting together his programme on trend-spotting, and given that he and Tierney were now a 'couple', Damien had insisted the American film her at work. After noticing a craze among teenage girls for belly dancing, Tierney suggested doing a live report from one of the classes.

Jake had rolled his eyes. 'Give me a break! That's so *girly* . . .'

But the programme went ahead and Tierney ended up joining in the session, having great fun donning a gorgeous red swirling skirt, red bra with beads and tassles, and silky, slinky veil. Sashaying across the room with the other women, she'd beamed into the camera, declaring with a wink and a wiggle, 'This is – literally – the *hippest* craze in the capital!'

Jake was unimpressed, but that episode of his show proved a hit. Ratings climbed, and the next day the *Mirror* ran a picture of Tierney under the caption 'LADY IN RED', her big blue eyes gazing out seductively from above the veil. All the men at work had raved about the photo, except Jake. He gave the paper a cursory glance, then gave Tierney a cool look and a wide berth for the rest of the day.

The next week, he'd suggested she look into quad biking, since blokes were taking to this in a big way. He then threw down the gauntlet, publicly daring Tierney to take part, a challenge she'd risen to but regretted, after spending most of the day face down in the mud while Jake gleefully ensured his camera crew captured everything.

'*Ugh!* Look at my *hair*!' she'd wailed, picking herself up for the umpteenth time and kicking the bike so hard she almost fractured her foot. 'Stupid thing! OW!!! That *hurt*!'

Jake had stared pointedly at her wedge-heeled shoes, shaking his head in sheer disbelief. 'Maybe if you'd worn trainers, like I *told* you to . . . typical woman!'

Scowling, Tierney had tried to scrape the mud off. '*Fine!* Next time I'll get your permission in writing before selecting my footwear, okay?'

Grinning, Jake had taken her hand and helped her stagger across the field to the clubhouse, where she'd collapsed in a heap on the floor, accused the bewildered instructor of being a raving sadist, then lurched back to the car.

Now Tierney yawned, shifting position so she was sitting cross-legged; according to Damien, this would kickstart her kundalini and recharge her chakras. God knows he'd been right about everything else, and Tierney had watched with excitement as her profile began taking shape. Following Midas's birthday, every single paper had run pictures of Tierney with her arm round Lucy, her other arm hanging limply by her side, a pained smile on her face. Two days later she was invited on to the programme *It Happened to Me*, and also learned she would receive the George Medal for bravery.

What Tierney enjoyed most, however, was finally being Taken Seriously. People listened to her views on everything from capital punishment to colour therapy.

Things were taking on a momentum of their own, Tierney could feel it. Someone nicknamed her the Golden Girl, and the name stuck. Honey Trapp had stayed on in the UK to work on her next project, and took Tierney to countless parties and events, introducing her to a steady stream of celebs and stars.

Still, though, Tierney knew she was a B-list name.

Now she jumped as two women with identical brown bobs and Colgate smiles materialised beside her, guiding her across the room to a high black chair which tilted back at a ninety-degree angle.

The first woman beamed. 'I'm Anastasia, call me Stasi. And this is Anushka.' Tierney blinked. This had to be the brunette version of *Stepford Wives*.

She fidgeted while one of the women covered her with a huge pink towel, securing it under her chin and draping it over her entire body until she couldn't even move her hands.

A peculiar sort of music was playing in the background, full of high-pitched squeaking and squealing.

'Dolphins mating,' Anushka informed her with a beatific smile.

'Brilliant,' mumbled Tierney, '*fish fucking*. Just what I want to hear for the next four hours . . .'

Moving round so they were both in front of her, the make-up artists leaned forward and scrutinised her face.

'Oh, now that's *bad.*' Stasi shook her head. 'That's *very* bad.' She and Anushka exchanged worried looks.

Tierney frowned. 'What's bad?'

Stasi folded her arms. 'Your pores, that's what. Worst I've ever seen.'

'My pores?' Tierney echoed, perplexed. 'What's wrong with them?'

'They're wide open, that's what!' Suddenly she reached over and pinched Tierney hard on the left cheek.

'Ouch!!!' Tierney wished she could move her hands so she could slug *Stasi* round the jaw.

Every gesture radiating disapproval, Anushka began dabbing something astringent on her skin. '*Someone's* been a naughty girl and washed her face with soap and water, hasn't she?'

Tierney repressed a grin. 'Actually, I usually don't remove my make-up at all, just sleep with it on, let it sort of *slide* off overnight, you know?'

There was a collective gasp as both women recoiled in horror.

Anushka rapped her across the knuckles. 'CTM!!!'

'You what?' Tierney looked blank.

'CTM – Cleanse, Tone, Moisturise!' Stasi repeated it several times like a mantra. 'Twice a day. Essential.'

By the time the make-up artists from hell had tamed her apparently rebellious epidermis, Tierney's face was throbbing from where it had been vigorously pushed, pummelled, prodded, pounded and pressed.

But, she managed a tight smile, at least her precious pores were now well and truly *shut*!

She was just trying to loosen the towel and get up when a hand shoved her firmly back into the seat.

'Oh no you don't! We haven't even started . . .' Anushka whipped out a pair of giant tweezers, a gleeful light in her eyes.

Tierney paled. 'What are they for?'

'Your eyebrows, silly!' The women cackled, and Tierney suddenly knew how alien abductees must feel.

'What, you're going to shape them a bit, are you . . . ?' she asked suspiciously.

'Oh, something like that . . .' murmured Stasi.

The next forty-five minutes were agony. Tierney wasn't good with pain at the best of times and couldn't even get through an episode of *ER* without throwing up or passing out, so being trapped under a fuchsia towel the size of Birmingham while her eyebrows were systematically ripped out of her forehead was not her idea of fun.

'*Jesus bloody Christ!!!!!!!!!*' she screeched. 'The UN has passed resolutions over things less painful than this! AAAAGGGHHHHH!!'

Stasi tutted and turned up the stereo to drown out Tierney's screams. The frantic howls and piercing wails of dolphins in the throes of orgasm filled the room.

Tierney decided she must be dreaming.

This was just too surreal.

Anushka handed her a small oval mirror and she upgraded it from a dream to a nightmare.

'What have you *done* to me? They're gone! I have no frigging eyebrows!'

'We're going to pencil you in some new ones.' Stasi patted her arm reassuringly. 'Now, look through this.' She handed

Tierney a book full of photos of famous females. 'Choose which eyebrows you want. The Paltrow is proving popular just now, though personally I think the Tyler, or even the Aniston, might suit you more . . .' She smiled. 'Don't fret. You'll love them.'

'I'd better!' Tierney's eyes widened as she caught sight of what Anushka was removing from a sterile container. 'Dear God, please tell me that isn't what I think it is . . . please?'

It was a hypodermic needle.

Anushka advanced slowly and Tierney struggled to throw off the towel and make a run for it.

'Damien says you're to have collagen in your upper lip!' announced Stasi.

'No way!' Tierney glared. 'You're not sticking that in my trap!'

Lurching out of the chair, forehead still red and smarting, one eyebrow drawn in and one absent, she bolted for the door and freedom. But it wouldn't open. Cursing, Tierney rattled the doorknob. It didn't budge.

Wild-eyed and trembling, she turned round, back jammed up right against the wall, hand clamped protectively over her quivering lips. 'This won't work! People know I'm here. Friends. Friends know I'm here. Lots of them. You won't get away with this!'

Anushka and Stasi each took an arm, prising Tierney away from the door and back to the chair.

'Poor thing, she's over-excited. *Bless*. Now look, Tierney.' Stasi's voice was soft and soothing. 'You just sit back and close your eyes.' She replaced the towel around Tierney's body and continued trying to placate her. 'Truly, you won't feel a thing, it's just the *tiniest* of pricks!'

'Sounds like my ex . . .' Anushka sighed.

'I'm not having it.' Tierney was becoming hysterical with panic. 'I'm not, I tell you!'

'But Damien says—'

'Sod Damien! I'm not having it! They're my lips, aren't they?' Tierney demanded shakily, wondering if she'd somehow managed to sign her body parts away without realising it.

'Of course . . . of course . . . and they're beautiful lips . . . and they could be even more beautiful, so much *fuller*, if you'd just let us give you this *tiny* bit of collagen . . .' Anushka spoke softly. 'All the cover girls have it . . . all the successful ones . . . you want a pout to be proud of, don't you? You do want to look stunning on the cover, don't you . . . ?'

She leaned in closer, voice warm with enthusiasm as if imparting some vital secret. 'Tierney . . . you'll have every magazine in the country clamouring to have you on its cover . . . so much *publicity* . . .'

At the magic word, Tierney's hand slipped from her mouth slightly as she slumped back in the chair, confused again.

Anushka continued. 'Just picture it . . . they'll *all* want you: *Loaded* . . . *GQ* . . . *Maxim* . . . *Esquire* . . . *Arena* . . . *Elle* . . . *Cosmo* . . . *Vogue* . . . all asking for you, Tierney, *you* . . .'

Tierney felt weary. It was just too tiring to keep on battling everyone all the time. And besides, what did she know? Who was *she* to argue?

'Collagen is safe, though, right?' she pushed. 'I mean,

there's no danger of me having a fatal allergic reaction to it, is there? I can't, like, stop breathing or anything, can I?' Her voice rose in panic. 'Or fall into a coma? You two *are* trained in first aid, right? You are, aren't you? Where's the nearest hospital to here anyway? What happens if you give me too much? Can you overdose on collagen?'

Laughing, Anushka tightened the towel under Tierney's chin. 'Relax. We do this all the time, promise. Now, I want you to just close your eyes and try to keep still, can you do that for me?'

Meekly, Tierney did as she was told.

Moments later a cold, sharp pain went shooting through her upper lip and she cried out. Stasi squeezed her hand, while Anushka finished the injections, one on either side of her mouth.

'Right, now your lips will be numb for a while, so just sit quietly.' Anushka spoke briskly. 'We'll get going on your make-up, and Steven here' – she gestured to the hairdresser who had slipped into the room without Tierney even noticing – 'will see to your hair.'

Steven, a sulky-looking bloke with a squint, stood behind Tierney and ran a hand through her crowning glory with something less than appreciation. 'Just as I suspected.' He gave her hair a sharp yank. 'You have *confused follicles*! But don't worry, the girls will see to your face, and I will take care of your hair and finish you off!'

'That's what I'm afraid of . . .' Tierney mumbled thickly.

*

Zoë decided she was either very brave or totally stupid, and she wasn't sure which. Dragging her feet down the tiny, tree-lined cul-de-sac, she felt her confidence running out with every second. At the end of this road was a large white mews house: Icons, the coolest modelling agency in the country.

She only had tonight left before she had to vacate her hotel room. She'd spent the last two days sitting on the bed, staring at the phone, picturing Tierney's face and telling herself she wasn't wrong to believe the girl would call.

Zoë never trusted *anyone*, but she'd trusted Tierney.

She'd replayed their meetings in her mind a thousand times over, remembering all the compliments Tierney had given her. Zoë didn't like her own looks much, but now she looked at herself with kinder eyes. Tierney had seen something special in her face; maybe someone else would too.

Among the pile of magazines in the hotel room was a recent issue of *Cosmo*, and Zoë had read an article about Icons in it, about how the agency was always searching for fresh young faces. So here she was, one last-ditch attempt, before she left London. After all, she shrugged, what did she have to lose?

She hadn't started with anything in the first place.

Now, as she stood there outside the agency, a line of lanky, designer-clad girls sauntered past her and into the lobby. Telling herself she was as good as any of them, and knowing it was a lie, Zoë followed them.

The lobby was opulent, with soft white carpet. Large white leather sofas with big pastel-coloured cushions beckoned to her. Behind each sofa was lush foliage, huge tropical plants, some over six feet tall. A striking arrangement of hot-pink orchids adorned a low glass coffee table covered with beauty magazines.

And on the walls were pictures of the agency's models. Zoë

stared. The most beautiful women in the world. Icons.

As she hovered nervously just inside the doors, other women, bookers, went gliding past. Zoë noted they were all carbon copies of each other, wearing black hipsters, black tops with the Icon logo on them, long hair pulled back in sleek ponytails, looking horribly efficient.

One of the women stopped beside her, her flawless face impassive. 'Can I . . . help you?' Her tone was perfectly pleasant, so why did Zoë feel like she'd already been judged and found wanting?

'Er, thanks . . . I hoped to speak to someone about, well . . . possibly doing some . . . modelling . . .'

She felt absurd even suggesting it.

Her voice faltered as the woman looked her up and down, taking in her faded jeans and tatty trainers.

'Where's your portfolio?' The booker held out a beautifully manicured hand.

Zoë frowned. 'My what?'

The woman looked faintly amused. 'Do you have any photos?'

Zoë shook her head.

'I see. Well, if you want to wait . . . someone will have a chat with you. Can't say how long it'll be, though.' She gestured to the line of girls all perched tensely on chairs and sofas, busy pouting and plucking. The woman's eyes softened slightly as she took in Zoë's nervous face. 'Are you here because of the article in *Cosmo*?'

Zoë nodded and the woman jerked the thumb at the girls. 'So are they! Take a seat and fill in this form, okay?'

Gratefully, and starting to feel just the tiniest bit excited,

Zoë took the bit of paper and hesitantly sat down on the nearest sofa, horribly aware that everyone was staring at her. But the booker hadn't told her she was wasting her time, had she? Hadn't laughed in her face, as she'd feared. Zoë felt hope flicker within her again, so sweet it hurt.

On the sofa opposite sat a young girl, she didn't look more than about fourteen, with glossy brown hair and perfect features. Her mother was beside her, scrutinising the form, and as she watched them sitting there together, Zoë felt more alone than ever.

But it didn't matter, not if she could do this. She'd show Tierney Marshall.

She'd show everyone.

*

When Tierney was allowed to look in a mirror again, she decided she needed a stiff drink before the photo-shoot. While Stasi, Steven and Anushka stood back, admiring their handiwork, Tierney stared and stared and stared some more.

Gone were her luxurious, wavy, honey-blonde tresses. In their place was an equally long but super-sleek mane of pale hair, streaks of ash and silver glimmering as Tierney turned her head this way and that. She looked like she'd overdosed on Peroxide.

The face also belonged to a stranger. Tierney's skin was nowhere to be seen, now buried somewhere beneath layers of fake tan and a foundation which looked and felt like industrial-strength cement, while two sweeps of tawny blusher gave her cheekbones so high they practically slid into her eye sockets. Her eyelashes had been mascarad until they were now long and thick enough to plait. And as for her mouth . . . Tierney winced. Her upper lip was now so large it would need its own passport.

Bemused, Tierney continued staring, looking at herself from different angles. It was her and yet it wasn't her. And it was the *weirdest* thing, but . . . She frowned, turning her head slightly again, and yes . . . she could see shades and elements of a host of other blonde celebs. Gail, Gaby, Ulrika . . . they were all there . . . she was a *composite* . . .

And suddenly Tierney felt sad. When she'd woken up this morning she'd been a good-looking, fresh-faced twenty-something.

Now she was an ***überblonde***.

*

Zoë wanted to cry. She gazed at the form, as if by doing so she could make the letters rearrange themselves. They wanted a thousand details she either couldn't or wouldn't provide, like her address. Yeah, like she was really going to tell them she was about to return to a hostel for the homeless; she'd *die* of embarrassment. Hearing a giggle, she glanced up to find the mother and daughter opposite watching her haughtily; now they averted their eyes, whispering, and Zoë realised they were talking about *her*. She dropped the form and the pen which fell with a clatter to the floor. The mother and daughter tittered loudly.

A sea of eyes, some pitying, some pleased, followed Zoë as she bolted for the door.

Outside, she walked in a daze to the nearest Tube station. She must have been mad. That booker had only given her the form because she felt sorry for her.

This, coming here, was a mistake. *She* was a mistake.

Zoë hugged herself, trying to crush the disappointment welling up inside. She was going back to the hostel, back to selling the *Big Issue*, back to the life she'd created before Tierney Marshall had appeared and shaken it all up.

Who needed to go chasing dreams anyway?

*

Tierney wondered what Jake would think of her new look. And, she felt a flutter of panic, why did she care? He was trespassing into her mind too often. Banishing thoughts of his sardonic smile, she started getting ready for the photo-shoot. The clothes had been chosen by the magazine's creative director, who had opted for biker chic, which, with its streamlined leather jackets and low-slung hipsters, was all the rage.

Tierney's outfit comprised a black leather jacket which, as instructed, she zipped up to halfway over her breasts to show plenty of cleavage, black lacy knickers, sheer black stockings and suspenders, and black leather knee-high boots.

'Gorgeous!' Stasi appeared behind her, showing Tierney down the hall and into the small studio which was empty but for a ghettoblaster and a pale-coloured screen at one end. 'Alex, the photographer, always likes to put music on,' explained Stasi. 'This'll be a great cover, you'll see! And Alex is the best, all the girls love him!' She squeezed Tierney's shoulder and left.

Tierney looked at her reflection again. She'd done several photo-shoots for the tabloids and women's mags, but this was her first men's mag, and the skimpiest outfit she'd had to wear yet. Peering more closely at herself she sighed; her new eyebrows were ridiculously thin, and she couldn't help giggling.

'Tierney. Good to meet you.'

Laughter dying on her lips, Tierney turned and tried not to do a double-take as Alex walked over and casually shook her hand. He was *seriously* fit. Sun-streaked blond hair worn long. Eyes as blue as hers. And, Tierney could have sworn the room suddenly got hotter, he was dressed in jeans and a brown suede waistcoat under which he wore . . . nothing. She watched the muscles rippling as he bent over to switch on the stereo. The soundtrack to *9½ Weeks* came thumping out, but to Tierney it seemed faint, probably eclipsed by the pounding of her pulse. This was a full-on Lust Attack.

'Normally my assistant would be keeping us company, but she's off sick today. So for now it's just the two of us; later we'll be getting John, a male model, in to pose with you for a few shots. Sound okay?' Alex's smile was slightly anxious.

Tierney nodded, aware of the warm black leather brushing against her bare breasts as she let him lead her by the hand to the middle of the studio.

'Now, I know you haven't done a men's mag before, but I don't want you to worry about a thing, all right?'

Right now, the only thing worrying Tierney was whether she possessed the willpower to keep from ripping this guy's clothes off. 'I'll do my best,' she replied gravely.

'Good girl. So, let's start by taking a few test shots and getting you warmed up!'

'*I wish* . . .' she mumbled.

'You just do exactly as I tell you.' Alex raised the camera. 'Move back a bit . . . now smile . . . and again . . . now turn your back . . . and glance over your shoulder at me . . . *nice* . . . give me another smile . . . just relax . . . better . . . better . . . and turn round again . . . good girl . . .' He started snapping away, moving around, the music still blaring in the background. 'And smile for me . . . come on, *enjoy* it . . . good . . . look up at me . . . no, keep your head angled *down* and sort of glance up at me through those lovely long lashes . . . yeah, better . . . relax . . .'

The fan is turned on full so that Tierney's new peroxide-pale bob is misbehaving, flowing out around her face. Laughing, she flicks it back from her eyes and Alex moves in closer.

'That was *great* . . . do that again . . . brush your hair back like you . . . yeah . . . and laugh again . . . lovely . . . you're doing fine, Tierney . . .'

Alex starts cracking dirty jokes he's got off the internet, and before long Tierney's laughing and telling him worse ones.

'. . . lovely . . . unzip the jacket for me a bit . . . I like it . . . now blow me a kiss . . . and again . . . *very* nice . . . cross your arms . . . and narrow your eyes . . . good . . . legs wider apart . . . a bit more . . . lovely . . . and tilt your head back a bit . . . come on, Tierney, *flirt with me* . . . I just need you to unzip the jacket a bit more . . . just a bit . . . that's great . . .'

And as she whirls and twirls, struts and smiles, Tierney can feel the gaping great Matt-made gaps in her self-confidence begin sealing over, Alex's praise acting like a sort of psychic Polyfilla.

More. At some indefinable, inevitable point, appearing before the camera like this stops being natural and starts being necessary. Positively addictive, in fact. It's the easiest thing in the world. Alex is beaming, moving closer all the time, laughing in delight as Tierney becomes more confident.

'. . . stunning . . . now I want to see you *pout* like I *know* you can . . . gorgeous . . . and undo the jacket just a bit more . . . good girl . . . brilliant . . . give me that look again . . . and again . . . *love* you . . . you're a natural . . . wink at me, Tierney . . . now show me shy . . . *adorable* . . .'

Suddenly Tierney realises her jacket is undone practically to the waist, now revealing more than it hides. She blushes. 'Jesus, I'm practically *topless* . . .'

Lowering his camera, Alex raises an eyebrow in challenge.

For a moment they just stare at each other.

'I couldn't.' Tierney shakes her head. 'No way.'

Alex shrugs. 'You could. But you won't. You're not the type. Besides, I know your agent, and he'd never let you.'

Tierney bristles. 'Damien doesn't *let* me do anything! I do what I want!'

Alex laughs. 'Sure. Whatever you say.' He fiddles with the camera. 'I mean, sometimes I suggest to a girl that she loses the top and lets me take a few snaps. Only when I know it would look really cool. It's something private, you never have to show it to anyone, not if you don't want to.'

And suddenly, Tierney feels *reckless*.

She's nearly naked now, for God's sake!

Something just for her . . .

Why the hell not?

'Maybe I could . . .'

Alex gives her a sceptical look. 'I don't think so. Like I said, you're not the type. And Damien would go ballistic.'

That does it.

Tierney smiles briskly. 'And like *I* said, it's up to *me*!'

Quickly, before she can change her mind, she shrugs off the jacket.

Grinning, Alex starts taking pictures again.

'Good . . . good . . . now turn to your right slightly . . . face me again . . . okay, now sort of stretch like you're in a real lazy mood and smile for me and . . . girl, you are *heaven* . . .'

Tierney loses count of how many photos he takes. When the music stops she puts the jacket back on, bemused at her own behaviour. Quite out of character, really.

Glancing at his watch, Alex gives her a regretful smile. 'I've got another shoot to get to, so I guess I'll have to make a move. You'll get an advance copy of the magazine before it's on sale. Oh' – he gives her a conspiratorial grin – 'and I'll send you those last few photos the minute they're developed.' He hands her a business card after scrawling a number on the back. 'Call me. Maybe we can meet up for a drink. Now, I'd better go and get John, get some shots of the two of you.'

Tierney nods, hugging herself as she watches Alex saunter out of the studio with one last regretful glance in her direction.

Feeling a bit nervy now she's alone, she reaches up to twist an unruly lock of blonde hair around her finger. Then she remembers her new haircut, her hand dropping limply to her side.

She'll get used to it.

She'll have to.

*

Zoë stopped outside the Tube station. Above her, night was chasing day out, blue fading to black, and all around her, people were spilling out of plush offices and into brightly lit cafés and packed restaurants. Couples sauntered by, their heads close and hands linked, teasing and testing and trying to know each other. People were screaming, horns bellowing, a cacophony of voices all demanding to be heard. Zoë knew that with each passing day, her own voice was fading, until soon it would be just a whisper.

As she joined the crowd of people pushing through the ticket barriers, she began wishing she'd never met Tierney Marshall. She was worse off than before, wasn't she? Because the only thing worse than having no hope, was having hope and losing it. Then she stuffed her hand in her pocket, and felt the crinkly bit of paper with Vanita's phone number on it.

Maybe it hadn't been a total waste of time after all.

Maybe one person was on her side.

12

Close Encounters

'So sorry to interrupt your out-of-body experience, Damien' Clutching the phone, Tierney spoke through gritted teeth, 'but I'm going Out Of My Mind! I CANNOT wear this dress tonight – I look like a total *tart*!'

Closing her eyes, she prayed her agent would descend from whichever astral plane he was inhabiting that week long enough to listen. 'Yes, Damien, I *know* I mentioned Easy Girl in my first *Dado* column . . . yes, Damien. I *know* they're sponsoring me, but the dress is aw— Yes, Damien, I *realise* it's a great deal, but I look like I should be standing outside King's Cross and charging by the hour!

'Yes, Damien—' Gripping the phone cord, she imagined wrapping it round his neck. Tightly. 'Yes, I *can* feel some negative vibes and – no, I don't think assuming the lotus position would help, but what would is if you'd just *listen*—' She threw up her hands in despair as Damien interrupted again.

As he rambled on, Tierney looked at herself in the hall mirror and shuddered. 'I look like a sodding carrier bag!' The dress was short, tight, white and plastic. It came with matching bra and briefs, both silver, the underwear shimmering through the flimsy material. Tiny electrical sensors built into the material were monitoring Tierney's temperature; if she got cold, the dress acted like an electric blanket, instantly heating up.

Now she sighed. 'With my luck I'll spontaneously combust halfway through the night – talk about being a hot date!' Combined with her bright blonde just-had-sex-so-*there*! hair and a fake tan, she knew exactly how she looked. *Cheap*.

Suddenly Tierney realised she wasn't wearing one thing she actually liked.

Her lipstick was from *Banshee*, also mentioned in her column. Oestrogen-activated, this shade was a garish, gleeful pink called *Laughing Flamingo*. And because her period was due, her mouth kept going a violent, vile purple before switching back to crimson.

Worse, she was in pain because of the hemp boots, the final product she'd written about. They were clumpy, clumsy, white, wedge-heeled and so *itchy* they were driving her mad. Plus they were huge. 'These aren't shoes, they're flipping *hovercrafts*!' Tierney stamped her foot in frustration and almost demolished the floor.

Now she stared at her reflection in despair. She was a walking, talking advertisement. And a hypocrite. These were all items she'd hyped in *Dado* – of *course* she had to be seen wearing them.

But right now, being *cool* was leaving Tierney **cold.**

Recognising from Damien's closed, controlled tone that she was getting nowhere, she said goodbye. They'd argued over this outfit for two days, and Tierney was proud of the way she'd stood her ground. But he was adamant: she had to wear something striking to tonight's première. The tabloids would pick up on it, and the sponsors would be happy. It was a means to an end, and Tierney didn't have to like it. She just had to do it. She'd tried to stand firm, but Damien wore her down with his usual ploy of fusing compliments and coercion. The Eve's Brew campaign started soon and Tierney knew it would bring massive exposure; she couldn't fall out with Damien, not now.

'Hey, what you doing?' She watched Andy go racing past and up the stairs. His smile was sheepish.

'Said I'd run a bath for Carin. She's had a bastard of a day.'

'You know, slavery *was* abolished . . .' Tierney joked, hoping he'd get the point. Seeing the plate he was carrying, she frowned. 'What on earth . . . ?'

On the plate, beautifully arranged, was a circle of plump green grapes. *Peeled.*

Tierney shook her head in disbelief, and, defensive, Andy scowled. 'No law against doing things for one's girlfriend, Tier! Carin likes them that way.'

'There's something to be said for playing it cool, though.' Tierney watched as Andy gave her another scornful look before bounding up the stairs.

She couldn't bear to watch much more of this. As far as she knew, Carin was still seeing Gina whenever she felt like it. What really worried her, though, was that Andy had stopped talking about travelling. Totally. Tierney had a nasty feeling he was thinking of cancelling his trip to the Far East because he couldn't bear to leave Carin.

Resolving to have words with one or both of them when she got the chance, she went outside, perching on the low brick wall separating their house from the next. It was a silver, star-freckled night, with the slightest of breezes, and under the streaming moonlight, her hair shone like a pale flame. Tierney knew she should be feeling happy and excited about going to Honey's première, but instead she felt sad. Her thoughts turned, as they often did, to Zoë. Over recent weeks she'd tried several times to find the girl, even paying a visit to the hostel where the teenager had been staying when they'd met. But the people there couldn't help her. Now Tierney wondered yet again where Zoë was, and how she was coping. If she was coping.

Hearing a car purring up the road, she stood up and dusted herself down as a limo pulled up smoothly.

Jake watched her slide into the seat opposite, and smiled calmly. 'Tierney. You look absurd.'

She winked. 'Jake . . . really . . . you say the *sweetest* things . . .'

'Someone has to tell you.'

Rummaging through the well-stocked mini-bar, Tierney's voice was rueful. 'And it always has to be you, right?'

Shrugging, Jake looked her over again, taking in the skimpy underwear and minuscule dress. One thing was for sure: the outfit left little to the imagination.

Catching his glance, she sighed. 'If you must know, I have to wear this. It's a sponsorship thing.'

Jake frowned. He hadn't realised she was being packaged to such an extent. 'But surely you have some say in what you promote? You do, don't you?' he pushed.

When she just stared at her drink, he felt uneasy.

'Tierney, do *you* like the way you look? Frankly, I think you're dressed like a superbimbo!' He ignored her outraged gasp. 'It's a shame, that's all. But hey' – he held up his hand in a conciliatory gesture – 'if you don't have a problem with it, just tell me, I won't say another word.'

Tierney glared. It was one thing to have doubts herself, but be slagged off by Jake? No way. 'Get this through your stupid skull: I do *not* need your stamp of approval on my sartorial selections!' With trembling hands she mixed herself a drink, knocking it back quickly. 'Christ, it's bad enough I have to spend time with you! Can't we at least do it in silence?'

'How about I gag you? That'll sure work for me!' Jake shot back, grey eyes stormy. 'In fact, here's an idea – we can turn it into a trend! Designer gags: "Silence is Golden". You can put it in your column, it's sure to sell then!'

Wincing at the derision in his voice, Tierney stared into her glass. Everyone loved her column, everyone thought she was a brilliant Cool Hunter. Except Jake. Not, she reminded herself sternly, that she cared what he thought.

Looking up to find him watching her, she leaned forward, placing a hand lightly on his knee, glancing up through lowered lashes. Instantly Jake tensed, his eyes very still, as Tierney said softly, 'You know, I really feel there could be something so much more . . . *satisfying* between us than all this tension . . . something I know *I'd* enjoy . . .'

Jake couldn't take his eyes off her, cursing himself for the way his pulse quickened the second Tierney touched him. 'Between us? Like what?'

'Oh, like' – she smiled flirtatiously – 'the ***ATLANTIC***!!!'

Jake kicked himself for letting her wrongfoot him. 'Believe me, if anyone could make me leave, it'd be you!'

Tierney slammed her glass down. 'You know, it's true what they say about you – you do look a bit like Heathcliff. So why don't you follow his example and get lost – permanently!'

Jake's grin was complacent. 'Come on, you'd pine away without me . . .'

Her laugh was scathing. 'In your *dreams*!'

'*That'd* be a nightmare!' he snapped.

Exchanging a final furious look, they both turned away, folding their arms and staring out of their respective windows for the rest of the journey.

*

A gang of journalists was clustered around the cinema entrance, some of the photographers balancing on little stepladders. Tierney watched the guests making their way into the brightly lit foyer, pleased to see they were strictly A-list. As she and Jake approached, the reporters began calling out and whistling at her outfit. Tierney gulped; she felt more naked now than when stripped down to the waist for Alex.

Pasting a bright smile on her face while she posed for pictures, she waited for Jake to finish doing the same, and was getting ready to go inside when one of the hacks grinned.

'Let's have one of you together, then! Come on!'

Jake and Tierney glanced at each other before he moved closer, putting his arm lightly around her slender shoulders, feeling her silky skin through the sheer material. The cameras flashed more frantically.

'Come on, you two – give us a kiss, then!' a photographer yelled, and the others joined in.

Horrified, Tierney stepped back, but with a wicked smile Jake turned quickly so he was facing her, placing his hands lightly on her hips. He was going to shut her up once and for all, and pay her back for that stunt she'd pulled in the car. 'This'll teach you . . .' he murmured, and the next thing she knew, he was kissing her.

For a split second she froze, before her lips parted and the kiss deepened. Jake's hands tightened slightly over the curve of her hips and Tierney felt her own response intensify. Vaguely she was aware of cheers breaking out around them before she and Jake broke apart, gazing at each other with bemused, bashful faces.

'You *bastard* . . .' Tierney raised a hand to slap him but Jake caught her wrist.

'Not in front of the cameras . . . wouldn't want them to get the wrong idea now, would we?' He watched defeat slide over her pale face.

Tierney yanked her hand away and stormed off towards the cinema.

Standing there alone, Jake shook his head, confused.

What was *wrong* with him?

He'd only meant for it to be a quick kiss. A wind-up. Publicity stunt. He'd just been trying to score a point, that was all. He tried to rationalise the impulse, then gave up. Because the second their lips touched, he'd felt it.

More than Lust, less than Love.

Now he groaned as he saw the reporters' knowing smiles. He'd gone and upped the stakes, because the press would never leave them alone, not now. Walking slowly after Tierney, he felt regret wash over him. Jake would give anything to cancel that kiss, to erase the moment, rewind his emotions. He smiled wryly; could you delete desire?

Probably not, but God knows he was going to try.

*

Approaching the cinema from the opposite direction, Vanita smiled at Matt, slipping her hand into his. She'd only returned from New York that morning, to find a message from him on her answer machine; finally, he was returning her calls. This was the first time he'd agreed to go out with her since Tierney finished with him; progress, she decided proudly.

Tonight should go well; Daddy had *promised* to pull strings and get her on to the guest list, which had impressed Matt, since like the rest of the Western world he was caught up in the hype over this movie.

Vanita smiled confidently as she gave her name to one of the bolshie-looking bouncers.

'I'm sorry,' he shrugged, 'we don't seem to have you down here.'

She fixed him with a look that could and often did reduce grown men to quivering wrecks. 'Then you'd better look *again*, hadn't you?'

Beside her, Matt was looking bored, dropping her hand and wandering off to look at posters for new releases.

Glancing at his colleague, the bouncer checked the list a second time, then put it down and moved forward, forcing Vanita back out into the street. 'Like I said the first time, your name's not on my list. Now, if you don't mind . . .'

She shook his hand off. Matt was clearly fed up, his eyes distant. More guests were arriving, looking with interest at their tense faces while the reporters, excited at the thought of a row breaking out, edged closer.

Then Vanita saw it: salvation.

Granted, in the unlikely form of Tierney Marshall, but still . . .

Anyone else would tell her where to go, but Tierney was so *nice* . . . Vanita smiled coldly at the bouncer and pointed at the blonde girl. 'I'm with *her*.'

He nodded, recognising Tierney at once. 'Ms Marshall, good evening. Ms Trapp says for you to go straight to the VIP lounge.' He gestured to Vanita. 'And this lady says she's with you . . . ?'

Tierney and Vanita faced each other in silence. It was like a replay of their showdown at Matt's flat, but this time, Tierney smiled, *she* was in control. Behind her, the foyer was filling up, the film's theme music filtering out into the street as guests milled around the chrome entrance.

Her eyes narrowed as she watched Vanita becoming more nervous by the moment. Her gut reaction was to do the right thing and help the other woman out; after all, two wrongs didn't make a right. She, Tierney, had everything now. No need to cling on to some petty feud.

But then it happened. The reckless, rebellious little sprite which had taken up residence inside Tierney's head began taunting her, *tempting* her, just like when she'd been in the studio with Alex.

After all, where had playing fair ever got her?

She turned back to the bouncer. '*Did* she? How strange – I've never seen her before in my life, sorry!' With a mischievous smile, she brushed past the Valkyrie, who was now cringing while the other guests looked on in amusement.

As the bouncer ushered them firmly back outside, Vanita hurried after Matt. 'Wait up! Where are you going? Matt!'

'Home. I'm not in the mood for company.' Matt waved but didn't turn round.

'But I thought we were . . .' Vanita's voice trailed off as he vanished around a corner.

'You okay?' Turning, she found Lian watching her, black eyes curious. 'What's the deal with you and Tierney Marshall?'

'Let's just say she's not my favourite person right now!' Vanita bent down to try and release her shoe which had become trapped in a grate. She scowled – brilliant, floored twice in as many minutes . . .

'You reckon she's getting too big for her boots now she's got the Eve's Brew contract and all?' Lian glanced back at the cinema to make sure she wasn't missing the arrival of anyone important.

'What? Say that again?' Shoe forgotten, Vanita stared at the journalist. *'Tierney Marshall's going to be Eve?'* It must have happened while she was away.

Startled by the look on her friend's face, Lian nodded.

'Oh, Tierney . . . you naughty, *naughty* girl . . .' Vanita murmured, nodding slowly as the missing piece of the puzzle slotted neatly into place. She could see just how it had happened: Tierney got bored watching from the wings, so she'd seized the moment and snatched the contract from Zoë. Vanita was almost impressed.

'Are you covering the opening of Bar Eden?' she demanded, as Lian was just about to rejoin the other reporters.

'Probably. Why?'

'Make sure you do. Could be . . . interesting.' Refusing to say more, Vanita waved a cheerful goodbye. Now she knew precisely how to get Tierney where and when it would hurt the most.

For there was only one thing the media loved more than making a Golden Girl.

And that was breaking *one.*

*

Sitting in the darkened cinema, Tierney and Jake chatted politely with the people on either side of them. On the screen swirling shapes in pretty pastel colours were shifting and sliding around while the audience whispered and giggled, waiting impatiently for the film to start. But Jake and Tierney weren't aware of anything going on around them, because they could both feel it. It was there, between them, and it was big. Bigger than it should be and swelling by the moment until it was far too large to talk about.

The Kiss.

Out of the corner of his eyes, Jake could see Tierney's legs. The dress, what there was of it, had ridden up as she'd sat down, revealing her shapely thighs. Jake fidgeted. He *never* noticed other women, never looked at women's legs. Tierney was doing this to him. He shook his head at his own paranoia. Maybe she'd put some sort of *sex hex* on him . . .

Tierney wriggled around in her seat, finally leaning her hand on the armrest and her head on her hand, blocking Jake from view. She would not let herself fall for a bloke with a fiancée tucked away back in the States! Irritably she tugged at her dress, trying to pull it down and succeeding only in showing more thigh. She caught Jake giving her an exasperated look.

In the film, a couple began kissing.

Jake and Tierney sat rigidly in their seats, staring grimly at the screen, both busy not thinking about each other.

*

'Oh my *God*!!!' Felix Lightfoot, London's most influential fashion journalist, turned away from Sophie Dahl and stared at Tierney over his little round glasses. '*That* is the Dress of Desire!'

Bemused, Tierney glanced round to see who he was talking about – surely he couldn't mean her? They were standing in a corner of the packed Soho wine bar where the post-première party was well under way. Tierney had never been to Alphabet before and was trying not to look overawed by the famous faces all around her. These were the people she saw in the women's glossies and newspapers; it was hard not to stare. Especially when Jude Law sauntered past. Tierney swooned; the man was *gorgeous* . . .

'So *clever* of you to create that look,' Felix continued, eyes welded to the silver bra and the curve of her breasts. 'Yes . . . I see how it works . . . futuristic yet trashy . . .'

'Yeah, that's it.' Sure he was winding her up, Tierney matched his sarcasm. 'I call it ***Space-Slut Chic***!'

Felix just shook his head in wonder. 'Positively inspired . . . reactionary in fact . . . I *must* mention you in my next column . . . I can see exactly what you've done, you *cool* creature, you! You've taken that silly trend for looking cheap that all the It Girls and celebs were following, and you're parodying it! I adore it . . . now do tell, what gave you the idea?'

Realising he was serious, Tierney bit her lip to keep from screeching with mirth. 'Oh, well, you know, I just wait for the Muse to start yelling . . .'

Felix nodded earnestly, and Tierney's eyes widened; where was Jake? He'd *die* laughing if he could hear this conversation!

'Felix is right, darling, you look sensational!' Cleopatra blew her a kiss from across the table where she was draped over Saul Klee, lead singer with Gits, the latest boy band to make it big. Everyone else chimed in with their comments, heaping compliments on her.

It was like sitting on top of the world, because here she was, the centre of attention, in a room full of celebs. And Tierney belonged. Totally. Felix wouldn't even let her get her own drinks: each time she finished one, he appeared at her side with the next. Now she could feel the absinthe starting to take effect, warming her entire body. Tierney beamed; she could stay here for ever.

*

Over by the bar, Jake had been cornered by a DJ he'd met a few times back in the States. She was vivacious, and usually he'd be enjoying the conversation, but it was weird, because tonight Jake felt like he'd developed a sixth sense.

A Tierney radar.

It didn't matter how crowded the room was, Jake always knew exactly where she was, even without looking. Now as the DJ chattered away, he glanced past her, instantly locating Tierney at the other end of the room.

Under the dim lighting her dress had taken on a pearly sheen, the silver underwear glimmering when she moved. A group of men had formed around her, and Jake was outraged at how they stared at her, as though Tierney was a juicy lamb chop they were dying to devour.

He was also worried about her knocking back endless glasses of absinthe like it was lemonade. Was he imagining it, or was she *swaying* slightly? He could hear her laughter above the other voices, becoming louder by the minute. Even as Jake watched, one of the men moved behind her, circling Tierney's tiny waist and winking at his companions.

Jake felt green, green envy gushing through him. Ordering another drink, he tried to look attentive as the woman beside him turned to him for a response. He was just watching out for Tierney, that was all; simply keeping an eye on her, the way he would a younger sister.

Or a friend.

Or a girlfriend.

The thought strolled into his mind and sort of lounged there, ambling around his imagination for a while, in no hurry to leave.

And Jake knew he was in trouble.

*

Someone was tapping her on the shoulder, and Tierney realised Cleopatra was speaking to her. Her thoughts felt slow, they wouldn't *move* properly. Finally Tierney realised her friend was talking about Saul.

'I think we might be making a move soon. God, isn't he stunning?'

Tierney glanced at Saul, who was trying to balance a champagne bottle on his head while counting to ten in Italian. 'Bit vapid . . .' She was starting to slur her words.

Cleopatra giggled. 'For what I have in mind, he doesn't need a degree in rocket science! So long as he doesn't run out of fuel too soon . . . if you get my meaning . . .' Glancing over at the door she beamed. 'A *very* good friend of mine's just arrived.' Her gaze flitted over Tierney. 'Feel like meeting the White Lady?'

'Who?' Intrigued, Tierney followed the journalist's stare, but since the entire room was now spinning, it was hard to focus.

Cleopatra grabbed her hand and pulled her through the crowds of people fighting to get to the bar.

Suddenly an arm shot out and barred Tierney's way, as Jake emerged from a group of people in front of her. 'Where are you going?' He noted her flushed face.

'Jakey . . .' Tierney giggled without knowing why. 'Come an' meet the White Lady . . . she's a friend of Cle . . . of Cle . . .' She made a face as her words got all knotted up. 'Of Cleopatry's an' she says I'll *really* love her . . .'

Jake's face changed. Grabbing her hand, he pulled her roughly from the room while Tierney continued giggling, stumbling forward, people laughing at her lack of co-ordination.

'Oh Jakey, you're no *fun* . . . don't wanna go . . . gonna meet the *Lady* . . .'

Ignoring her protests, Jake led her up the stairs at the far end of the room.

They were halfway up before Tierney realised they were no longer following Cleopatra. 'Where we going?' She pouted as he practically shoved her up the last few steps and into the street. 'Wanna stay . . .'

To Jake's relief the limo was parked on the corner. Still

mumbling away, Tierney gave him a reproachful look as he deposited her gently in the back and got in beside her. But as the car started to move, she clambered to her feet, banging on the glass partition separating them from the driver.

The car lurched to a stop and she toppled forwards. Jake tried to steady her, and the next thing he knew, Tierney landed in his lap, looping her arms around his neck, gazing earnestly at him.

'Jakey, who's the White Lady?'

He smiled fondly at the grave look in her wide blue eyes, putting an arm around her waist to stop her falling as the car started moving again. 'Not who, what.' Seeing her perplexed expression, Jake tried again. 'Charlie.'

Tierney nodded sagely. 'He also friendly with the White Lady, then?'

'Tierney, the White Lady is another name for cocaine.'

'Oh!' Tierney looked startled.

Then she passed out.

Carefully, Jake slid her across his lap and back on to the seat, covering her with his jacket, watching as she lay there, hair falling forward over her face, lashes fluttering against her cheekbones. Sprawled there on the back seat, slight frown on her face, she looked like a child sleeping peacefully.

Jake remembered that the Eve's Brew ad campaign would start soon. He didn't know the details, but he'd heard the usual whispers and rumours, and Tierney had let slip a few hints.

He didn't know why, but he was scared for her.

13

Hype

She was visual Viagra.

Sorted! hit the stands, and testosterone hit an all-time high. In bars and bedrooms, pubs and clubs, men who'd criticised Tierney for her 'violence' in Oxford Street had a sudden change of heart and rise in blood pressure. That issue was one of the fastest selling ever, the verdict unanimous: Tierney Marshall wasn't a babe.

She was a *goddess*.

The cover showed her standing, legs apart, leather jacket unzipped to reveal the tempting swell of her breasts, her pale hair streaming round her face. The skimpy black briefs and stockings enhanced her long legs and sleek hips, and one black, high-heeled leather boot rested lightly on the chest of a male model lying on the floor between her legs, gazing up at her with a knowing smile. Tierney's lips, painted metallic silver, formed a killer pout as she winked boldly at the camera.

The caption read:

DOWN **BOY . . .**

'No can do! Tierney Marshall doesn't pose naked.' Damien checked his horoscope, as on the other end of the phone *Playboy*'s features editor begged him to reconsider. Damien grinned; the guy was *gagging* to get Tierney on his cover.

His assistants, Natalie and Jon, sprinted past in opposite directions to answer phones going berserk as every men's mag in the country rang to try and book Tierney.

'No, sorry, it's not even an issue.' Damien's face was gleeful as the hapless hack on the other end doubled the amount being offered before finally giving up.

The agent sighed happily; this was the real fun, in creating a *buzz* about a client. He flicked open his contacts book, and a second later was back on the phone, leaking the story of how Tierney was the one, the only, *bona fide* media babe refusing to go all the way, reversing the trend her contemporaries had indulged.

Not for Tierney the antics of Gail and Denise.

Yet again, Damien reminded the women's mags, his client was leading the way.

Modesty was *in*.

He beamed as he spoke to a journalist friend at the *Guardian*, glancing at his copy of ***Sorted!*** and quipping, 'Tierney might tease, but she won't take her top off!'

Talking to his tabloid contacts he tried to come up with something catchy. 'She's . . . naughty but *nice*!' A beat. 'This girl says No to Naked Ambition!'

Then he sat back and watched as the reporters took those soundbites and ran with them.

It was an inspired bit of marketing. The women's mags were

already on the way to adopting Tierney as a hip, hot heroine; her refusal to strip only helped, and Damien negotiated an article in *Cosmopolitan*, the cover of *Elle*, and another regular column for Tierney, this time in *The Sunday Times*.

That week alone, Tierney appeared on *The Big Breakfast*, *TFI Friday*, and a *Woman's Hour* radio debate about media exploitation of women. Meanwhile, the papers all picked up on the story of the girl who knocked back *Playboy*.

The *Sun*, which had been hoping to get Tierney for page three, ran a piece about how she was depriving millions of men, imploring her to reconsider under the headline:

Tierney: You've Got It . . .
We Want It!

When he saw that, Damien patted himself on the back. It had worked, the media were starting to chase Tierney because now he had an angle for her: the good girl who just *might* strip . . . who was playing it cool . . .

The agent laughed as he spoke to a friend on the *Sun* who was driving him mad.

The hack tried to push him. 'Come on, all the girls do it. Is Tierney going to or not? I need to know.'

'What can I tell you?' Damien grinned. 'Some will, some won't, she *might* . . .'

Now every tabloid editor wanted to get Tierney's kit off.

Now there was competition.

Now there wasn't publicity, there was ***Hype***.

Keen to reinforce the impact of ***Sorted!***, Damien arranged for Tierney to appear on the covers of more men's magazines, but knowing the Eve's Brew campaign started soon, and keen to avoid overkill, he turned down everything bar *Loaded* and *GQ*.

Tierney also proved popular with younger women's magazines, which hailed her as being both trendsetter and role model. *Minx* ran a double-page spread on her, informing its readers: 'GIRLS – IT'S *COOL* TO KEEP YOUR CLOTHES ON!'

Media pundits agreed that Damien was managing Tierney brilliantly, packaging her so cleverly she appealed to everyone. She was a chameleon, her image changing when and as needed: a blank canvas ready, waiting and willing to be filled in.

Men saw her as a bombshell, which could have made her a threat to women, but because she'd rescued a young girl, and because of her No Nudity stance, women liked Tierney. And everyone was intrigued by her private life, owing to the rumours about her and Jake which Damien fed the press. Equally, there was never enough hard evidence to brand her as a girl stealing another woman's man. The fashion editors loved her since she was the one setting the trends, yet universal as everyone copied her.

Tierney was all things to everyone.

Or, as the more perceptive commentators noted but didn't say, nothing to anyone.

*

The first Jake knew of ***Sorted!*** was when he wandered into the smoking room for his daily drag, expecting to find it empty. Instead he strolled through the door, whistling, and stopped short at the sight of every guy who worked at Prophets Inc. lounging around, practically salivating over Tierney's picture.

Chris, one of the researchers, held it up, smirking. 'Reckon this'll give their rivals some *stiff* competition in the circulation area . . .' The men broke into raucous laughter. 'Here, Jake, mate, feast your eyes on that . . .'

Jake caught the magazine Chris lobbed over, sitting down and studying the cover in silence. Tierney looked sexy as sin; a bloke would have to be blind, gay or dead not to respond.

Then he peered more closely at the picture; it must have been doctored, retouched. Improved. Because Tierney's pupils were unnaturally large, the blue of her eyes too brilliant. She looked much older than usual, and worldly, like she'd been around, and he felt uneasy again. It was starting: Tierney's image would be manipulated and manoeuvred until she was all and *only* image. He shook his head in disgust. She'd had a chance to be taken seriously and she'd thrown it away, opted instead for the easy route. Jake felt disappointed; he'd really thought Tierney was different.

As for Damien . . . Jake could happily have punched his lights out. The way he was packaging Tierney was so cynical, so calculated, why couldn't she *see* it?

Or maybe she could, and she just didn't care.

'She scrubs up all right, don't you reckon?' Paul, one of the researchers, grinned at Jake, gesturing at the magazine. 'God, that girl is *built*! But then, you'd know all about that, wouldn't you? You lucky bastard!'

Jake shrugged. 'It's not like that. Don't believe everything you read in the papers.'

Chris sent him a knowing look. 'Oh, come on! All that time you two spend together, all those events you're always taking her to? You're not telling me you're not on for it?' He stared at Tierney's photograph again. 'No bloke in his right mind would say no to a bit of that!'

'*SHUT IT*!' Jake turned on them, grey eyes dark with anger. 'Before I do it for you!'

The others exchanged embarrassed looks, shocked into remembering Tierney was a colleague and friend. Glaring again, Jake grabbed the magazine and stormed out of the room.

Punching the lift button and waiting impatiently for it to arrive, he flicked through the glossy pages until he found the interview with Tierney, reading the comments with an incredulous face. It just didn't *sound* like her, and the more he read, the more convinced Jake was that Damien had coached Tierney, schooled her in what she could and couldn't say.

The girl was turning into a puppet.

Jake stalked into the lobby, which had just been given a Zen makeover. Little Japanese waterfalls whispered away in the background, and windchimes sang sadly each time the glass doors opened. Right now the place was swarming with photographers and even a few television cameras. Jake ducked and weaved between them to reach the other side of the room, passing small groups of employees huddled together, lounging on sofas, giggling and gaping.

And at the centre of it all was Tierney, posing for pictures, looking unbearably cute in tight blue jeans and a white T-shirt.

'What's going on?' Jake made his way over to Liz, who was perched on the edge of one of the larger fountains, trailing her fingers idly through the cool green water.

Liz sighed. 'Tierney's been voted Rear of the Year. Britain's Most Beautiful Bum.'

They watched as the photographers surrounded Tierney, edging closer all the time, flirting, one or two of them openly propositioning her. She responded to it all with an enticing smile.

Finally one of the men lowered his camera. 'Come on, then, let's see why you won!'

'Yeah, luv, *show us yer cheeky side . . .'*

Tierney hesitated, and Jake watched resentment flitting across her perfectly made-up face. He almost chuckled, recognising the stubborn set of her mouth. Then she glanced at Damien. The agent nodded.

Still Tierney stood there, hands on hips, face sullen. Damien sent her a stern look, and finally, smile now taut, Tierney gave the photographers what they wanted, turning round and bending over while they leered and took more pictures than they could possibly need of her shapely, denim-clad *derrière*.

'Oh, for fuck's sake . . .' Jake wasn't sure who he was angrier with: Tierney, Damien or the journalists. Noting that Liz looked equally unhappy, he touched her shoulder. 'You look less than overjoyed for her.'

'She's making a total arse of herself, excuse the bad pun!' As she glanced back at her friend, Liz's eyes darkened. 'I hardly recognise her any more. Not that I see her much, she's too busy *networking* . . . and you know what's going to happen next, don't you?'

Jake nodded. 'You think she's going to win *the Next Big Thing* vote?'

'Yep! I'd put money on it!'

In a few weeks the programme's viewers would vote for the Coolest Girl in the Country. The papers were obsessed with the idea, and every day they featured another contender. Tierney was a popular choice, especially since ***Sorted!***.

Wiping her now wet hands on her trousers, Liz smiled sheepishly. 'Soon she'll be too hip to be seen with us mere mortals!'

Catching the hurt in her voice, Jake squeezed her arm. He too had noticed something different about Tierney, but then he was hardly objective where she was concerned.

Ever since The Kiss, they'd both pretended nothing had changed, until they were dizzy from bending over backwards to be normal with each other. But it was no good, because now every event, party and opening they attended together was fraught with possibility.

Jake shook his head, frustrated. They were lurching towards something and couldn't apply the brakes, because neither he nor Tierney would admit there was anything *to* stop. And as he'd predicted, the press were now obsessed with them, shadowing their every move, pouncing on the slightest hint that they were either sleeping together, about to tie the knot and go public, or break off the affair *obviously* raging behind closed doors.

The papers analysed every photograph, even enlisting the help of experts in non-verbal communication to explain the nuances of how the couple stood together when posing for pictures. One tabloid brought in a graphologist to examine their handwriting, which caused much mirth, both Tierney and Jake screeching with laughter.

Jake sighed – in a way the papers were right. Because emotionally, he felt almost as if he *was* having an affair and cheating on his fiancée with this girl.

He loved Lisa.

He wanted Tierney.

Glancing over at her again, Jake experienced a sudden sense of loss. These days it seemed the closest contact he had with Tierney Marshall was staring at her face on a magazine cover.

*

Being invisible was easy.

Zoë had perfected the art way back, when her brother would come sidling out of his bedroom and into hers. She'd hear the chilly creak of his door opening slowly, and just sort of blank herself out. Cancel Zoë. Become invisible to herself, so she couldn't see or feel what was happening. She'd go limp, and he'd take his hand off her mouth, realising she wasn't going to scream, realising she wasn't going to do anything to stop him.

How could she? *She wasn't there.*

Then Zoë found she could disappear whenever she wanted, and after that, it was hard not to.

But the *real* thrill was learning she could make herself invisible to others, too.

Like now.

She was in a tiny newsagent's, her back to the shop as she gazed at the shelves of magazines with the glamorous, gorgeous women on the covers. Normally the shopowner was irritable with people who loitered without buying, but of course, he couldn't see Zoë.

So she'd been standing there, undisturbed, for a good twenty-five minutes. Outside it was a sunny day, the streets full of people all too busy to stop for ten seconds and buy the *Big Issue*. She could never decide which hurt more, the people who brushed past and wouldn't even look at her, or those who stopped to buy a magazine, with pity in their eyes and pleasure in their smiles because at least they were doing the Right Thing, even as they looked at her like she was the star attraction in some freak show.

It made Zoë mad. They thought their lives were light years away, but all they really had that she didn't was Luck.

So now, tired, she'd ducked in here to look at the women's mags. She'd flicked through about seven, and they all told her she could get whatever she wanted in life, if she wanted it badly enough. But then, Zoë slammed one back on to the rack, she wasn't exactly their target audience, was she now? Bored with their glib advice, she glanced at the men's section, staring at ***Sorted!*** for a good minute before realising who was on the cover. Frowning, Zoë picked up the thick, glossy magazine and blinked.

Tierney.

Quickly she opened it and flicked to the article, eyes widening as she read the interview. An icy wave of shock almost knocked her sideways as she got to the bit where Tierney talked about her role in the Eve's Brew campaign.

The world seemed to ***tilt***.

Zoë glanced round in a panic, realising she'd broken the rules – she was *feeling* again, and that meant she wasn't invisible any more! Sure enough, the store assistant was already watching her suspiciously. Stifling a sob, she dropped the magazine and fled from the shop, bolting out into the street and running blindly down a side road.

The one thought that had been keeping her going was that Tierney would help her, that Tierney would get in touch, eventually, and explain what had happened. Zoë reached into her pocket and took out a crumpled piece of paper with Vanita's phone number on. She'd looked at it umpteen times over the past few weeks, even getting as far as dialling the number before putting the phone down. She'd wanted to speak to Tierney, and only Tierney.

Now all she wanted to do to Tierney Marshall was smash that beautiful face in.

*

'That went well!' Damien beamed at his protégée as, yawning, Tierney sank on to one of the sofas. 'Have fun, doll?'

'Oh yeah, loved every minute of it! What do *you* reckon?' Tierney's voice oozed sarcasm as she popped a headache pill into her mouth, gulping it down with some mineral water. 'I mean, having my backside inspected by a room full of men; what more could a girl want?' Grimacing at the tablet's bitter taste, she frowned. 'Damien, do enlighten me. How exactly does this sort of stunt help me be taken seriously? I'm obviously missing something here.'

He patted her arm. 'We've been over this before, haven't we? Once you're firmly established in the public mind, you'll be free to pursue whatever you like!'

'Right now the only thing being firmly established is my rear end!' Tierney flopped back on the sofa, switching her smile back on as the photographers waved goodbye.

'I really don't see what the problem is.' Damien sounded bored. 'You can't say your column's not being taken seriously, can you?'

'Tell me about it . . .' Tierney wailed.

Her weekly column in *Dado*, 'Tierney's Trends', was

now required reading. Everything and anything Tierney recommended was guaranteed to take off. At first she'd been flattered, now she was frightened; it was scary, having this much influence, seeing how mindless people could be in their quest to be cool.

'So?' Damien stood up and looked at her impatiently. 'What's the matter? Why aren't you happy?'

'I am, of course I am . . . It's just – oh, I don't know . . .' Tierney smiled wanly. 'How will I know when I'm established enough?'

Damien's voice was soothing. 'Soon, soon.' Taking her hand, he pulled her to her feet. 'Now come on. Cheer up. We can't have you getting all stressed. Go home and relax.'

'I can't. I've got to get next week's column ready.'

Damien nodded. 'Okay, but after that, I want you to take it easy. The Eve's Brew campaign starts soon and I want you on top form for that. You know I'm right, don't you?'

Tierney smiled wearily. 'Of course you're right, Damien. You're always right.'

Suddenly she noticed that he was pulling on thick woollen jumpers and a bulky coat, even though it was ninety degrees in the shade. 'Damien, I'm sure I'll regret asking, but what are you doing?'

Buttoning the coat up to his chin, the agent smiled cheerfully. 'The Sahara'll be *way* hotter than this. I need to get used to running in those sorts of conditions. Figured this was the most sensible way.'

'Sensible . . . right . . .' Tierney watched Damien jogging out of the doors and into the street, wrapped from head to foot in winterwear.

She yawned again. She'd been out with Honey until the early hours at the opening of a new organic restaurant, and tonight, after she'd written her column, she was due at Sebastian Carmichael's party.

Things at Prophets Inc. were becoming frantic, for Tierney was now so well known that every client clamoured to work with her. Joel had given her several key accounts and Tierney was struggling to keep on top of them all, though thrilled at the challenges now being offered to her.

Barnaby and Julian still demanded a lot of her time and energy, constantly consulting her about their plans for Eve's Brew, about which everyone was becoming seriously excited. In addition, there was a continual round of parties and events she had to attend. Tierney frowned. Finally, she had to fit in interviews with the police, who were keen to talk to her about the West End Rapist. So far Tierney had spent around five hours sitting with a police artist, helping to put together a sketch of the attacker, still on the loose.

She shivered. Surely they'd catch him eventually? As far as anyone knew, he hadn't surfaced since her fist-fight with him in Oxford Street; or if he had assaulted anyone, the victim hadn't reported it. Occasionally Tierney had nightmares about the man, and eagerly scanned the newspapers, hoping to read that he'd been apprehended.

Now she yawned yet again. These days, she didn't have a minute to herself, but maybe that was just as well.

Because sometimes Tierney suspected if she stopped to think about things, she might just stop, period.

14

Constant Craving

Blondie Meets Barbarella!
We Give You – Space-Slut Chic!

declared the *Mail*'s fashion pages.

The PMS We Love – *Post Modern Slut*

screamed the *Mirror*'s style section.

Tierney Says TARTY is TRENDY . . .

announced Cosmo.

'Jesus, could these headlines *get* any worse?' Tierney shook her head in disbelief. It was a Sunday morning and she was lazing around, studying the papers. Following Felix Lightfoot's article on her, an array of women in white plastic dresses, shimmery silver underwear, crimson lipstick and giant hemp boots had appeared in every paper, women's glossy, and daytime show.

Tierney didn't know whether to laugh or cry.

Realising that the phone was ringing again, she padded into

the hall. The answer machine was clogged up with messages for her, all requests from reporters and researchers.

'Tierney, can you do two thousand words on the coolest clubs in London?'

'Tierney, we're doing a programme on the hippest homes in Britain – can you come on?'

'Tierney, would you do a piece on women in the year 2002, you know, usual sort of thing, what they'll be wearing, drinking, blahblahblah? Oh, and I need it by tomorrow afternoon – that's no problem, is it?'

She let out a shriek of frustration. Between work, public appearances, writing her column, and all the freelance journalism, she didn't have a minute to herself. In theory all the requests should go through Damien, but now Tierney was a regular on the celebrity circuit, people approached her directly. Not that her agent would have refused any of them.

But the final message was different, it was from Richard Midas, asking if Tierney would come to his offices for a meeting. The date he suggested was a good six weeks away, and Tierney scribbled it down in her diary, wondering what he was planning.

Glancing out of the window, she sighed. It was a miserable sort of day, the hot weather finally having broken. Now the rain was diving to the ground in warm, fat drops, while the sky was a watery, can't-be-bothered grey.

And though neither know it yet, Tierney and Jake are about to meet up.

Pacing the room, she feels restless, wants to *do* something, bored with reading about herself in the tabloids. According to them, she's dating the lead singer of Gits, considering a job offer from BSkyB, and about to star in a film with Hugh Grant.

It's all rubbish, of course, but written with such authority Tierney laughs. Total strangers believe themselves to be experts on her life. Amazing.

Now she quickly showers and dresses in jeans and a plain white T-shirt, leaving her face totally free of make-up. Her hair is still a pale, ivory blonde, but it's grown so she can scrunch it back. Today, decides Tierney, she's going to treat herself to something she's wanted to do for weeks. There's the Healing Arts Festival on in town, including a collection of crystals; perfect for a rainy Sunday.

Yes, decides Tierney happily, a crystal exhibition would be perfect for today.

'Hey, what you doing?' She smiled fondly at Andy as he walked slowly up the driveway. Then she frowned at his morose face. 'What's the matter?'

Seeing the folder he was carrying, she followed him back into the house. 'Is that from the travel agent's?'

'Yeah, the prats.'

'Why, what's gone wrong? I thought all the details were sorted?'

'I wanted to defer my trip, but they're saying I can't. Either I leave in five weeks, or I lose my place and my deposit.'

Now Tierney was uneasy. 'Why wouldn't you go? It's what you want to do more than anything!' she said slowly, sitting down as Andy switched the kettle on.

'Yeah, but you know, things are different now . . .' His voice trailed off as he saw her expression.

'Andy, please tell me I'm getting this wrong! Please tell me you're not thinking of cancelling your trip just because of Carin?'

'Not cancelling, just delaying.' He turned away, loading coffee into a mug and refusing to look at her.

'Same difference.' Getting up, Tierney took his hand. 'Look, tell me it's none of my business—'

'It's none of your business.' Andy smiled and kissed her. 'But thanks for caring.'

Realising she wasn't going to get through to him, Tierney felt helpless. 'I just hate to see you giving up on the dream of a lifetime for a relationship that probably won't even last! If you delay it once, you'll just go on delaying it, you know you will!'

'Why wouldn't we last?' Andy asked sharply.

Now it was Tierney's turn to avoid his eyes. 'You know what Carin's like . . .' she mumbled.

Coward, she told herself.

'Not any more. She's different now.' Andy poured his drink, face so trusting, smile so happy that Tierney couldn't bear it. She knew she should tell him about Gina, but she just could not find the words.

'And I want your word you won't mention to her that I'm thinking of changing my plans.' His face was fierce. 'I mean it, Tierney – give me your word!'

She wanted to run. This was *horrible*. Keeping secrets for both friends, watching one run rings around the other. Tierney wasn't sure who to be more angry with: Carin for being callous, or Andy for being so naive.

Muttering a promise, she hugged him again, tightly, then left the house quickly, before she said something she shouldn't.

Or should.

*

'Lisa, honey, honestly, I really don't mind *what* colour the name cards on the tables are!' Jake felt his fingers tightening around the phone and tried to hide his impatience.

'It might help if you'd show a preference!' Lisa was frustrated. 'Which typeface do we want them in? You *did* look at the samples I sent you, right?'

'They all look the same to me!' Jake didn't know whether to laugh or scream; this was all so *stupid*. But she needed him to make a decision. 'Okay, this is what I want, then: plain white cards, in capital letters, and you can choose the typeface. All right?' Silence. He heard her sigh.

'So you don't think the cards should be the same colour as the tablecloths, lilac?'

Jake gritted his teeth. 'Sure. Lilac is good. Lilac is perfect. Lilac it is.' He *loathed* lilac.

'But maybe that's too intense? Maybe the tablecloths should be white and the name cards lilac . . .'

'Fine, honey, fine. We can do that. So' – Jake crossed his fingers – 'are we agreed?'

'Oh, I don't *know* . . . and we haven't even started on the seating plan yet!'

Jake frowned. 'We spent two hours last week doing that! I refuse to waste any more time on who sits where – they'll sit where we put them!'

'Not *that* bit of the table plan! I'm talking about how it *looks*! What colour do we want it in?'

Jake decided he'd had enough; tactfully but firmly he changed topics. 'So, you need to give me the details of your flight so I can come meet you!' Lisa had finally managed to wangle a week off work to come and visit him.

She groaned. 'It fell through! One of the other reporters has broken her foot, so they need me! But they've said I can have a week off in August instead. I'm really sorry, you know how excited I was about coming over . . .'

'Yeah, me too.' Jake told himself he was disappointed. He must be, right?

Finally off the phone, he stared at the bulging folder in front of him, which contained all the paperwork connected to the wedding. The precious seating plans, travel brochures for the honeymoon, the present list.

Sheets and sheets and sheets of paper.

Minutiae and details.

Facts and figures.

Jake would be happy with a five-minute civil ceremony attended by close friends and family. Fat chance.

Going over to the window, he stared out at the rain-drenched day. He spent most Sundays doing what tourists do, taking in the sights he felt he ought to see while here. And he was diligent about it too. Today he'd been planning to check out Portobello Road, but what with the weather . . . Still, the Healing Arts Festival was on, and looked good; maybe he'd spot some trends in the health area to use on the programme.

Jake wonders what Tierney is doing today. How does she spend her weekends? He stares at the phone. How would she react if hers was to ring and it was him?

Just seven small digits to hit and he can speak to her.

Seven little numbers and he can hear her voice.

Tierney.

Seven seconds away.

Exasperated, Jake shakes his head, for here it is again, this constant, crazy, *craving*... It isn't that he thinks about Tierney in any sort of intense, focused way, it's just this low-key but constant craving to hear her voice, see her face. She flits into his mind on a regular basis. He can be doing something, anything, and suddenly there she is! Perched there in his imagination, smiling away at him. Jake will hear something amusing, and want to share it with her. Whenever he hears on the news that there's a train accident, or a motorway pile-up, Jake's first thought is always, instantly: *Is Tierney safe?*

He frowns. They aren't *friends*; he has plenty of female mates, and this isn't *that*.

Why, he grabs his wallet and opens the front door, isn't Tierney a friend? But he knows the answer: they aren't relaxed enough together, there's always that certain, strange tension threatening to break through. Jake flirts outrageously with every girl he knows, but not with Tierney. *Never* with Tierney.

Glancing at the phone again, he pauses, pulse jumping at the thought of speaking to her. Then he laughs at himself and slams the front door.

*

Tierney hurries through the rain-swept streets, listening to the wind screeching along beside her like an invisible, invincible train. Huge black rainclouds loom overhead, rearing up in the sky before racing forward again. People scurry past, clutching their coats, keys and children, cursing Bloody British Weather.

But Tierney is happy to be out, feeling the fresh, storm-charged air on her skin.

Not having to worry about how she looks is bliss.

Not having to smile is a gift.

Inside the exhibition halls she pauses. People are huddled in groups, studying leaflets and deciding what to do first, Feng Shui, Qui Gong, or Kirlian photography. Umbrellas slump on the floor in pools of water like tiny, shrivelled jellyfish, while soggy coats are bundled over arms and shoved in the sulky faces of silent cloakroom attendants. Tierney knows precisely where to go, heading for the wide grey steps which will take her up to Hall A.

*

Jake is standing in the lobby, pondering an array of pamphlets and notices, when he glances up. Walking briskly up the stairs at the other end of the lobby . . . isn't that?

Could it be?

Here, of all places?

Tierney.

He feels the shock of hope running through him like a sweet, swift current.

She isn't alone on the steps, she's surrounded by people, by young women of similar shape and size and colour. He can only see her from the back, but Jake chuckles, he would know this girl anywhere. The careless way her hair is tied back. The way her tan leather satchel is slung casually over her left shoulder. The jaunty sway of her hips as she walks quickly, as though scared whatever she's heading towards might vanish before she gets there.

Jake grins.

It is.

It's *her*.

Shoving the leaflets back on the small wooden table and not caring that most of them fall to the floor, he heads for the stairs, already knowing he's going to follow her. For Jake is curious: what is she doing here, on this wet, washed-out Sunday? He's a down-to-earth, pragmatic type of guy, he doesn't believe in karma, or kismet, and yet he has a sudden certainty that this, them both being here, is meaningful in some weird, wonderful way.

Mostly, Jake realises, he's just so *happy* to see her.

*

Tierney pauses just inside Hall A, and stares. Three entire rooms, full of crystals. Glimmering, shimmering crystals. Each hall contains five rows, and each row is one long glass-topped cabinet, stretching the width of the room. Slowly, she walks over to the first one and leans over, sighing with pleasure.

Deepest, darkest obsidian, black and heavy as the night. Chunks of mint-green malachite. Pale, pearly sheen of moonstone, like a blurred star. Glowing purple amethyst, the colour of the sky on a sultry summer evening. Warmest amber, flame encased in glass.

And a huge slab of her favourite, labradorite. Tierney's eyes widen. Leaning as far over the cabinet as possible, she gazes down at it, beaming. Ochra-red veins slipping this way and that through a blue that is grey, that is green, that is both and neither. It glitters and glistens where the light catches it, and closing her eyes, Tierney places her hands on the glass top, wishing she could reach right through it, imagining her skin against the hard, cool stone.

And that's how she's standing when Jake enters the room. He watches, fascinated, as she peers through the glass, head bowed, hands spread over the surface. He wishes he could see her face, but her back is to him.

After a few minutes, Tierney moves on, walking slowly along the length of the cabinet, sometimes going back, returning to the same spot maybe two or three, even four times, seemingly unable to tear herself away. And once, Jake could swear he hears her laughing softly.

She moves down the room to the next cabinet, without turning round; there are four more tables in this room and so Jake also starts looking at the crystals. Now he's really confused; this is how Tierney spends her spare time, looking at bits of *rock*?

Shrugging, he follows her, glancing at the crystals, then looking more closely, until before he knows it, he's seen four whole tables. The room is empty bar the two of them as silently, slowly, they move from case to case, Tierney oblivious to his presence, so enthralled is she by the crystals. Then she walks into the next hall without turning round.

Finally, at the end of the third hall, when she's seen all fifteen cabinets, she turns. Jake is still at the front of the room; she glances up, sees him, and they both stare.

No polite smile for an acquaintance.

No delighted rushing over to a friend.

None of that, and nothing like that.

'How long have you been . . . ? Tierney's voice trails off as she lets her bag slip to the ground.

Jake smiles wryly. 'Oh, about an hour.'

'And you didn't see me?' She raises an eyebrow in amusement. 'Might want to get that eyesight checked out.'

'I saw you,' he says simply.

'Then why didn't you—'

'Call out? Come over?' Jake shakes his head. 'Didn't want to disturb you. And besides, I was enjoying watching you.' He colours slightly. 'So, this is how you spend your weekends. I'm intrigued.'

Tierney sort of shuffles her feet, frowning. Jake knows he must be careful because he's shifting the boundaries on her. He hasn't planned on doing this, but somehow, it just seems like the natural thing.

The only thing, in fact.

She gives him a suspicious blue stare. 'Make a habit of stalking people, then? Only there are laws against that.'

Holding her gaze, he speaks quietly. 'Not people. You.'

She folds her arms. Unfolds them again. And Jake knows he is *this* close to walking over to her, slipping his arms round her waist, hugging her and never letting go. Not trusting himself, he turns, gestures at the door. 'Want to grab a drink?'

Tierney slings her bag over her shoulder and regards him quizzically, head tilted to one side. Something has changed, something is different.

She shrugs. 'Why not?'

In silence they head for the cafeteria.

As they both sit there stirring cups of weak tea, Jake realises they have never talked about anything remotely personal, not really. Tierney knows about Lisa, of course, but he doesn't know if she's involved with anyone, or what her own life plan is.

'Do you want to get married?' he asks abruptly.

She giggles. 'Can I finish my drink first?'

Instantly Jake feels his resolve crumbling. 'Cut it out!'

'Jesus, lighten up, will you? I was kidding!' Perplexed, Tierney stares at him before leaning down and peering under the table, then twisting in her seat and scanning the room.

'Where is it?' she demands.

'Where's what?' Jake is bewildered.

'Your sense of humour! God, I make one stupid joke and you're jumping down my throat!'

Jake blushes. Tierney's choice of wording has brought to mind a vivid image of the two of them together.

A fantastic, *forbidden* image.

Now guilt and desire flood through him, a Molotov cocktail of emotion, as he tries and fails to stop his eyes lingering on her pink, plump lips.

Tierney glances out of the window. 'So, Jake, you must be excited.' She smiles.

Jake tenses. *She knows*. 'What?' He feels his face flooding with colour again.

'About seeing Lisa – didn't you say she was coming over later this month? You must be really looking forward to it.'

Jake laughs with relief – she isn't reading his mind! Her remarks are totally, utterly, *wonderfully* innocent! It's just his own fucked-up imagination putting a slant on her comments where none exists.

'She isn't coming. Problems at work. Hopefully she'll be over in August.' Opening a packet of biscuits, he offers Tierney one. 'So . . . what about your love life? You never say much. What's the gossip?'

'Isn't any!' She munches on the shortbread. 'I'm not with anyone right now.'

Jake sees the sadness flickering in her eyes again, the way he does every so often. 'You look, I don't know, so pensive when you say that,' he remarks quietly.

Surprised by his perceptiveness, Tierney fidgets and looks down, frowning at the cracked Formica table. 'I was, well, I was with someone for a long time and now he's . . . he was . . . he's dead,' she says flatly. It feels strange telling Jake about Ben.

Stunned, Jake stares at her downcast face. 'I'm sorry.' He had no idea. Now he's scared to ask more, longing to, knowing he can't.

Tierney can see his reaction is genuine by the warmth of his grey eyes, and she is touched by his response; most people push for details and offer platitudes. He doesn't. Feeling a sudden, scary wave of affection for him, she stands up quickly, pulling on her coat before her face betrays her. 'Thanks for the tea. I should get going.'

Not wanting her to leave, Jake opens his mouth, ready to protest, then thinks better of it. 'Sure. But you still haven't told me about the crystals.'

'Nothing to tell. I wanted to see them.' Tierney shrugs lightly. 'That's all.'

Again Jake has that strange sense of being shut out; of rejection, because she won't say more.

Then she is smiling, raising a hand in farewell, before walking briskly out of the cafeteria, as Jake leans on the table, watching her. He wants to run after her, stop her leaving, as though there's something important he must say to her, something she needs to hear. Not merely important: *urgent*. He half gets up from the table, so overwhelming is the need to go chasing after Tierney.

Then Jake sits down again, checks his rowdy emotions.

She's just fun to be with.

That's all.

Just a sweet girl to spend time with on a rainy afternoon.

That's all.

And there's nothing to say.

Nothing at all.

*

Outside in the courtyard, Tierney leans weakly against the side of the building, fighting the panic tearing at her insides. She's still reeling from the way Matt betrayed her; she's not ready to care about anyone else. But Jake is different.

Jake is special.

Now she covers her face with trembling hands, feeling like an insect caught in a sink, in danger of being swept down the plughole, clinging on for dear life to the slippery side of the basin, feeling the momentum of the water pulling her down, sucking her into its gushing, rushing depths.

A whirling, swirling vortex of emotion for Jake.

She's drowning in feelings she doesn't want, for someone she can't have.

*

Angry with herself, Tierney marched through the forecourt and back out into the street. As she headed for the station her mobile started ringing.

'Tierney? *Fabulous* news!' Damien was shrieking down the phone, and Tierney stopped walking, bracing herself for whichever whacky idea he'd come up with now.

'What is it?'

'Just got a call from Rick Lesley –'

'The producer of *The Next Big Thing*?' Tierney frowned.

'The very same. He's got the results of the vote for the Coolest Girl in the Country, and guess what?'

Tierney froze. 'Damien, I didn't . . . ?'

'Tierney, you did!'

'But I just saw Jake, he didn't say any—'

'He doesn't know, no one does, Rick just called me as a favour before they issue a press release tomorrow.'

'*Oh-my-God!*' Tierney's scream was half horror and half excitement. 'But what does this *mean*?' she asked frantically.

'It means everything's playing out just as I planned.' He laughed. 'I've told the removal men to be at your place nine a.m. Tuesday morning. That okay?'

'What are you talking about?' Tierney frowned. What had she missed?

'You've won the flat! The coolest flat ever! Congrats!'

'But I don't want to move!' she wailed.

'Don't worry. You don't actually have to stay there if you don't want to, but you need to be seen living there, if only for a bit. Let's say for the next . . . six weeks! That's reasonable, isn't it?'

'I don't believe this!' Tierney suddenly found herself sitting on the pavement in the middle of the street.

'Now listen . . . in two weeks you're throwing a party at the new flat, to celebrate winning the competition and all. I'll sort the invites. It'll be great, you'll see, loads of media coverage.'

'But wouldn't it be better to have this party in a club or something?' Tierney queried, biting her fingernail.

'That's *so* last week!' Damien was horrified.

He continued rambling on while Tierney just sat there on the ground, hardly hearing a word.

She was the Coolest Girl in the Country.

Whether she wanted to be or not.

15

No Place Like Home

'It's got everything bar an electric fence and killer Dobermans prowling the parameters!' Tierney stepped up to the entrance of her new home for the retina-scan which was required before she could enter. The flat was in Primrose Hill, part of a tall, slender block with opaque-glass windows. The elaborate security system was apparently highly valued by the residents, all of whom were wealthy, famous or both.

Beside her, Carin dumped a box of Tierney's belongings on the floor and stared at the building. 'It looks like something out of that film, *Sliver* . . .'

She and Andy giggled as they crossed the plushly carpeted lobby, under the careful gaze of the concièrge, who sat before a row of video screens. Although he was watching Tierney and her friends, his gaze kept flicking back to the second screen, on which scantily clad women were working out in the spacious gym.

The lift was smooth and silent and they all waited impatiently for it to reach the third floor.

Moving out had been a strange experience, Tierney mused.

They'd talked a lot without actually saying anything.

Now she looked at them. 'Hey, don't look so miserable, I'll probably be back in a month!'

They smiled slightly and Tierney's own grin faded.

She had a strange feeling she wouldn't be going back to the house.

Perhaps it was for the best: she didn't feel comfortable there any more, which was sad. The constant strain of watching Carin pluck on Andy's heartstrings was getting to her, as was his willingness to let Carin do so. The pair had gone away together for a weekend earlier in the month, and it had been bliss for Tierney, having the place to herself. When they'd returned, Andy had looked like he was about ready to pop the question. Meanwhile, Gina was always there in the background: Tierney saw her meeting Carin from work sometimes, and it was obvious their relationship was still alive and kicking. Tierney had tried talking to Carin several times, and got nowhere. Partly it was her own fault, she knew, because her social life was so crammed she hardly had time to see her friends any more. She kept meaning to get together with them, yet never quite got round to it.

Now she opened the door to her new home, feeling excited and nervous at once. The flat was spacious, with two bedrooms, en suite bathroom, a large dining room, living room and a small balcony. Tierney stared; she felt like she knew this place inside out, having been part of the Prophets Inc. team that helped design it. But actually being here, that was something else.

Spicy, bright colours were in, so the main bedroom had blood-red walls, reminding Tierney of a fast-food joint. Grey was the coolest colour for furnishings, and the bed did indeed look like a slab of concrete. The main colour running through the flat, though, was green. The hallway was olive, the bathroom khaki, and the dining room took garden chic to the nth degree, since instead of carpet there was Astroturf.

In the living room, the sofas were hot pink, inflatable and huge, like miniature bouncy castles. As for the kitchen, it was a brilliant, glaring white and boasted the latest trend in technology – humancentric appliances.

The fridge, for instance, was Swedish and computerised, able to monitor its own contents and order new supplies over the internet. In a slim cupboard by the sink lived Cy2, a household robot popular in the States for its ability to perform simple tasks.

The bathroom was massive, designed to imitate the trendier health clubs in the States, with a row of shower cubicles each with frosted glass so that one could make out the outline of the person inside. The toilet itself was Japanese, and also humancentric; tiny sensors built into it monitored a person's temperature and other vital signs and a computerised voice would then announce the details.

Tierney frowned; at the time, helping to decide what should go into the flat, all of this had sounded cool.

Now she wasn't so sure.

'Oh, hey . . . great bathroom . . .' Carin joined her, nodding in approval.

'It's okay.' Tierney was glad of the chance to talk to her friend alone. 'Listen, I know you hate me asking about this, but what's going on with you and Andy? He seems to think it's serious. Is it?'

Carin looked edgy. 'Look, I won't hurt him. That's all you need to know. I'm not going to be rushed into a decision by you, Tier; it's my life.'

'But you *are* still seeing Gina?'

'Not much, but yes, now and then. It's called keeping your options open.'

'It's called being a two-timing bitch!' Tierney looked at her angrily. 'God, it was bad enough watching you do this to total strangers. It's doing my head in to see you messing Andy around!' Hand on the door, she looked coldly at her friend. 'You know something? I never thought I'd say this, but I'm glad I've moved out. At least I won't have to watch you in action any more – don't think I could stomach it!'

As Tierney stormed back into the hall, Damien popped his head round the front door. 'Greetings, earthlings!' He handed Tierney a stack of papers. 'Thought you'd like to see what the press are saying about you winning the competition!'

She chucked them on the floor, behind the door. 'Not just yet, I'm still getting used to all of this myself.'

Damien wandered round before stopping in the middle of the kitchen, a look of intense concentration on his face. 'Yes . . . I have a good feeling about this place . . .' He waved his arms around. 'Great energy flow . . . I suspect Primrose Hill is built over a ley line . . .'

'So the trains'll run on time . . . ?' Tierney grinned.

'Let's see this robot, then!' Andy came bounding into the room, followed by a subdued-looking Carin.

Damien gestured to a cupboard. 'It's voice activated.' He opened the door to reveal a tiny version of R2D2, metallic silver with a little round head, and two red lights for eyes.

'Watch. Good morning, Cy2.'

They all jumped as suddenly there was a whirring and a clicking, the robot's lights began flashing, and it suddenly lurched forward and ran over Tierney's foot.

'Er, well, it's certainly different, isn't it?' Andy linked his arm through Tierney's. 'Your flat-warming party should be good!'

'I'm sure I'll get used to it here,' she said firmly, trying to convince herself as well as them. Her smile was strained. 'No place like home . . .'

*

Nights were still the worst.

Zoë lay on top of the scratchy brown blanket, staring out of the tiny window beside her bed, watching the stars glimmering in the distance. She hated being at this hostel, hated having to sleep in a dorm with four other girls. Logically, she knew she was lucky to have a roof over her head and food on the table each morning, and during the day she coped fairly well.

But at night, she craved space. A room, all to herself, that's what she wanted. Staying at the hotel had made things worse, for she'd grown used to the privacy. A whole room, just for her. *Luxury*.

She didn't need the jacuzzi, or the state-of-the-art stereo system the room had also boasted, or the mini-bar. Those were all added extras that meant nothing to Zoë.

All she needed was that glorious, gorgeous *space*.

That was more than enough.

That was everything.

Now, back in this cramped, claustrophobic dorm, she felt trapped, her legs twitching with the desire just to *run*. Turning over, Zoë lay on her back, trying not to look at the walls. She could see them moving, ever so slightly, ever so slowly, closing in on her.

Now she was starting to feel panicky; always did, at night.

Over by the door Janey was having nightmares again, muttering feverishly, tossing and turning, calling out, crying over faces and places she never remembered the next morning. Zoë sighed; one of the other girls, Claudia, had nicked her pillow. Again. They were heading for a fight, she could feel it. Now her neck ached from having to lie flat. She didn't want to make an issue of it, though, because Claudia was a psycho.

Covering her ears to drown out Janey's wailing, Zoë thought back over her meeting with Vanita earlier that week. They'd gone to the same café she'd been to with Tierney, and it had been strange, sitting there plotting against the girl who'd seemed to offer her so much hope such a short time ago.

'I can't tell you what to do.' Vanita had smiled sympathetically. 'But I do know that if I was in your shoes, I'd want to teach Tierney a lesson.'

Miserably, Zoë had tried to pick up her teacup and failed because her hand was trembling too much. She hadn't stopped shaking since learning Tierney was going to do the Eve's Brew ad campaign. It was as though her body was still protesting at the unfairness of the situation.

'But how can I?' She'd looked angrily at the older woman.

'Who's going to listen to *me*?'

Vanita had paused. 'Lots of people, actually. If your timing's right.'

Then she'd outlined her plan, and Zoë's eyes had widened, because it was so simple it was inspired.

'You know what they say.' Vanita had seemed amused. 'Let the punishment fit the crime. You can make sure Tierney never does this to anyone, ever again. Wouldn't that feel good, Zoë? Wouldn't you feel proud of yourself? And everyone will know what you've gone through . . .'

Zoë had sat hunched over the table, eyes scanning the room as she watched other girls her age, sitting with their mates, lamenting their latest career/money/man crisis. She looked at Vanita. 'Where would I stay, though, if I came to London? It's not as easy as you make out . . .'

'It's exactly that easy.' Vanita had patted her hand. 'You silly girl. I'll get you a hotel room.'

And Zoë's heart did a little flip-flop.

A hotel room.

A whole room.

Just for her . . .

She had stared. 'Really? You don't mind doing that for me?'

'No.' Vanita had pictured Tierney's face. 'I don't mind at all.'

For a moment both women had been lost in their own daydreams. Vanita was imagining what Tierney would look like covered in bruises – because she was about to fall from a great height all right.

Zoë was picturing a room, a neat, nice room, empty apart from her. All that space . . . Stupid, she knew, to make a decision like this, just because of a room.

But she wanted it so *badly* . . .

'All right.' She had nodded. 'I'll do it. You just let me know when.'

'Good girl.' Vanita had sat back and lit a cigarette. 'You'll see. Tierney won't know what's hit her.'

16

Planet Cool

'Give me *strength . . .'* Tierney yelled as yet again she started sliding off the huge inflatable sofa towards the butt-shaped dent forming in the floor from her continual collisions with it. Clawing her way back up the slippery plastic, she clambered on to the cushions and collapsed, exhausted.

It was Saturday evening and she was trying to relax before her party, flicking through an article on her which had appeared in the *Guardian*'s media section earlier that week. Called 'Playing It Cool', it described Tierney's career to date, showing how her column had become cult reading and how the outfit she'd worn to Honey Trapp's première had started several new trends.

Easy Girl dresses had now been hailed as the Next Big Thing. Never mind that Tierney's fears were realised when the heating sensors on one of them malfunctioned and a hair-dresser from Hounslow brought new meaning to the phrase 'setting the town alight'. Hemp boots, meanwhile, were now the coolest kind of footwear, despite having to be sold with a special lotion, since the material was so scratchy people were breaking out in rashes.

Likewise, *Banshee* lipsticks had sold out, and across Britain blokes bolted in terror as their girlfriends' mouths went from pink to puce with alarming regularity. Chaos reigned until it transpired that not only oestrogen but also sugar triggered the colour change.

And everybody was watching Tierney, waiting to see what she'd wear next. After all, she reminded herself bitterly, she *was* the Coolest Girl in the Country. These days she couldn't throw on jeans and a T-shirt without it being seen as some kind of fashion statement. 'Tierney's Trends', her column in *Dado*, had been expanded to a double-page spread, elevated to holy status as letters poured in, asking for her advice on where to shop, eat, stay; what to wear, read and drink. She was Tierney Marshall, *Style-Seer*.

At work, Joel had set up a website for her 'followers', with details of what she wore each day to the office. Clients were clamouring to work with her, and everyone was falling over to get in her good books. Only the Valkyrie was behaving strangely, staying out of Tierney's way but sending her smug little smiles from time to time, as though she knew something Tierney didn't. Meanwhile, Julian and Barnaby were having orgasms over her popularity, impatient for the Eve's Brew ad campaign to start.

Job offers were multiplying by the minute, with *The Big Breakfast* and *The Next Big Thing* desperate to get her on board. As for sponsorship deals, well, she was spoilt for choice, and at this rate would never need to go shopping again. Damien was also fielding offers from literary agents wanting Tierney to write *The Girl's Guide To Cool.*

Now, feeling listless, she wandered around the flat. She couldn't get used to the silence after two years of Carin and Andy screaming and slamming doors. Yet again, she began rearranging the furniture, trying to make the place feel more like home, then stopped, throwing her hands up in despair.

This flat wasn't home. This flat was weird.

The supersophisticated Japanese toilet had stopped monitoring her temperature and vital signs, now cheerfully informing Tierney she was dead each time she used it, which was unnerving to say the least. The fridge had gone berserk, jamming on the letter A and ordering vast quantities of artichokes, anchovies and avocados while refusing to stock anything else. Tierney had started having a recurring nightmare in which she was buried alive beneath an Everest of asparagus spears. Glancing round, she sighed. The vomit-green walls were making her bilious, the inflatable sofas were giving her backache, the water bed made her seasick, and Cy2, the little robot, responded to all words rhyming with his name – Tierney couldn't say hi or 'bye to anyone without him zooming out of the cupboard and over her foot.

Feeling sorry for herself, she started tidying the flat properly; her guests would be here in about an hour and a half. Thank God she didn't have to cook – one of Damien's clients, a young Russian known as the Nearly Naked Chef for wearing only a skimpy apron while working, was coming over early to prepare dinner; he was even bringing the food. Vlad was the coolest thing in cuisine right now, and his show, *From Russia With Love*, was receiving rave reviews.

Tierney's agent had also organised the invite list, ensuring the right combination of journalists, celebs and friends. Now Tierney chuckled; she was going to play matchmaker and set Andy up with Honey Trapp. She might be too cowardly to tell him about Carin, but she could at least remind Andy he had options. And Honey was so terribly alone here in Britain . . . They even had something in common – a passionate interest in criminology!

'I'm a genius . . .' Tierney clapped her hands in delight. 'It's the perfect plan!'

Jake was also coming tonight. She hadn't seen him properly since their meeting at the crystal exhibition, and though it scared her to admit it, she missed him.

After a scalding-hot shower, she looked at the outfit she'd be wearing. Her latest sponsorship deal was with a company who believed ballet was the new rock 'n' roll; called En Point, they'd produced a range of delicate little dresses resembling tutus, and were paying a small fortune for Tierney to endorse them.

She twirled before the mirror. The dress was baby blue, with a low-cut bodice covered in white lace and nipped in sharply at the waist, while the skirt flared out around her hips in wispy layers. The shoes were shiny blue satin with tiny bows on them, just like ballet slippers. Tierney had tied her hair back in a loose chignon and giggled at her reflection. '*Swan Lake* here I come . . .' Although, she winced, the bodice was so flipping *tight* soon her face would be the same colour as the material.

The intercom buzzed. Pirouetting to the door, she threw it open to find Damien wearing a black and white tux and looking like an anorexic penguin. He gestured to the lanky man beside him. 'Tierney, meet Vlad, the Nearly Naked Chef!

Wait till his kit comes off – we're talking one *seriously* impressive utensil . . .'

Vlad was busy balancing several boxes, his face morose. Then he glanced up, black eyes widening until they were practically popping out of his head. *'Natasha!!! Bourgois moiz . . .'* Screaming in Russian, he pointed at Tierney, dropping the crates, which landed with a sickening crunch on Damien's toes.

'My fucking *foot*!!!' the agent screamed, face contorted with pain.

Suddenly Vlad lowered himself to the ground in a perfect *plié*; next thing Tierney knew he'd grabbed her by the waist and they were *arabesque*ing down the hall, the Russian whistling the 'Dance of the Suger Plum Fairy'.

'Either Nureyev here lets go of me, or I'll perform my own ***Nutcracker Suite*** – with my ***knee***!!!' Tierney scowled as the cook dipped her to the floor before swinging her between his legs and back on to her feet again.

Hopping round in circles, clutching his rapidly swelling foot, Damien groaned. 'Sod! I should have realised . . .'

'Realised *what*?' Tierney shot her agent a murderous look as she and Vlad galloped past again at breakneck speed. 'And who the hell is Natasha?'

'Natasha!!!' Vlad's eyes brimmed with tears. *'N-a-t-a-s-h-a-l-a . . .'*

Damien hobbled down the hall after them. 'Natasha is his childhood sweetheart and dance partner. She's with the Bolshoi and he's pining away, poor thing. Vlad trained with them as a teenager, he's into ballet bigtime. Expect your outfit's set him off.'

'You don't sayyyyyyyy . . .' Tierney hollered as Vlad swept her away in a demented *pas de deux*.

Apart from anything else, her tutu-type dress wasn't designed to withstand this sort of g-force. Tierney could feel her breasts preparing to make a break for freedom, the underwired bodice creaking in protest.

Meanwhile Vlad was squealing with euphoria, laughing like a hyena on acid. 'N-a-t-a-s-h-a-l-aaahahahahahahahaa . . .'

Abruptly he stopped, crushing her to his chest, holding her face in his hands, gazing lovingly into her eyes and twisting her head from side to side while muttering feverishly in Russian.

Her neck gave an ominous *click*.

'Damien . . . for God's sake, *do something* . . .' As she tried to prise Vlad's fingers from her face, Tierney realised she couldn't feel anything from her jaw downwards.

Limping over to them, Damien grabbed Vlad's hand and steered him back down the hall. Watching him *entrechat*ing his way round the kitchen, Tierney had a horrible feeling she was in for a long, long night . . .

*

She was right. By nine the flat was filling up and Tierney was exhausted. Her neck had locked at a right angle to the rest of her body, making her look like Quasimodo in a tutu, and sending her into spasms of pain every ten minutes. She could only stare straight ahead since it was agony to turn her head, which made talking to anyone impossible. She continued playing hostess, however, pasting a bright if deranged grin on her face, running around ensuring everyone had a drink, while collecting coats and bags to dump in the spare room.

Most of her time was spent ducking and weaving to avoid Vlad, now clad in nothing more than a minuscule white apron and big chef's hat, revealing pasty, dough-like skin and spindly limbs.

Tierney nudged Damien. 'My God – he looks like a genetically modified Chippendale . . .'

Hearing raised voices, she hurried into the hall. Sebastian Carmichael had arrived with a sylph-like girl called Desiree; he was using her for his next exhibition, and tonight had wrapped her up, mummy-like, in silver foil. As various guests passed her, their steps would slow as, glancing coyly at the metallic paper, they all spent a few minutes furtively preening and admiring their albeit distorted reflections.

Oblivious, Desiree gushed over what an 'honour' it was to work with Sebastian, who looked as if he wanted to whack a wad of foil over her hyperactive lips.

'Des, darling, do stop breathing so *quickly* – the foil'll rip! Can't you get *anything* right?'

Back in the living room, Tierney paused just inside the door. Cleopatra was embroiled in a heated debate with Felix Lightfoot over the 'message' Tierney's titanium coffee table was sending out.

'Look, it's *obvious* – it's only got three legs, making it unstable – a clear expression of post-millennium angst! How can you not *see* it?' she squealed.

Felix shook his head and the row raged on. Tierney decided not to tell them the table originally had four legs until she fell off the sofa and landed on it.

In the far corner of the room, Carin was busy flirting with the three curvacious brunettes who made up *Paprika!*, the coolest girl group around. Watching her from the opposite side of the room was Andy. He was standing in a small group of people, but Tierney could see he wasn't into the conversation, since his eyes were locked on Carin's face as she laughed at something one of the singers whispered to her.

It was with relief that Tierney watched Honey Trapp arrive, looking gorgeous in a strapless black dress, her long molasses-coloured hair streaming over tanned shoulders.

'About time!' Grabbing the bemused actress, Tierney dragged her forward. 'Andy, Honey. Honey, Andy. You guys have something in common – you're both into dead bodies! Isn't that *sweet*? So, talk!' Giving them a dazzling smile, Tierney retreated as they looked at each other in confusion. Finally Andy laughed. 'You're either into necrophilia or criminology . . . ?'

Honey swooned at his plummy English accent and Tierney, observing from a discreet distance, sighed with relief as the pair sat down, already chattering happily about their favourite serial killers.

Then she saw Carin's face. Her friend was leaning nonchalantly against the door, brown eyes narrowed as she sipped a glass of wine, watching Andy and Honey as they leaned towards each other, musing merrily as to which American mass murderer had killed more people – Charles Manson or Ted Bundy.

Carin emptied her glass, flicked back her hair, and made her way across the room to ward off this new, unexpected threat to her hold on Andy's heart.

'Don't!' Tierney grabbed her hand, forcing Carin to meet her eyes. 'You don't want him, not really. Why can't you just cut him loose? He means *nothing* to you!'

Carin shook her off, dark eyes glittering. 'I'm not ready to end things yet.'

'You're sleeping with Gina!' hissed Tierney. 'You can't have it both ways!'

'Says who?' Carin's face was flushed from the wine. 'Tierney, you don't understand. I have to do this, have to see which relationship burns out first. Maybe then I'll know what I really want, for once . . .'

'And never mind who gets hurt while you're sorting out your psyche, right?' Tierney snapped, disturbed by Carin's selfishness, and her own weakness in not warning Andy. She tried one last time. 'Carin, for Christ's sake, this has been going on for *months*! It's not fair!'

Carin wasn't even listening.

As she began pushing past, Tierney stopped her again, needing to understand. '*Why?* Why do you always *do* this?'

Carin's voice was bleak. 'Because I can.'

Tierney watched helplessly as her friend sank on to the sofa next to Andy, placing a hand on his leg. Honey's infectious laugh faltered, as, instantly, Andy's attention switched from her to Carin. After waiting a few minutes for Andy to turn to her again, the actress smiled politely and excused herself. Tierney saw the way her face slumped with disappointment as, behind her, Carin and Andy were already busy getting tongue-tied.

Tierney glared at Carin, but she didn't see. Well, her face tightened, by the end of tonight Andy would know the truth. Carin could choose who told him, but if *she* didn't do the right thing, Tierney would.

She should have done it from the start.

Suddenly there was a blood-curdling scream from the kitchen followed by a metallic crash. A second later the door burst open and Vlad came hurtling through it like he'd just been shot from a cannon, his tiny white apron working its way loose, his tall white hat perched jauntily on his head.

Glancing over his shoulder with a look of abject terror, the shivering chef gave another piercing shriek. 'Dybbuk!!! *Dybbuk!! Deveeeeel . . . AAAGHHH*!!!!'

Hot on his heels was Cy2, beeping gleefully, his red and blue lights flashing, his little round head rotating rapidly.

Wide-eyed and open-mouthed, everyone stared as the startled Slav legged it down the hall, baring his backside as he careered round the corner, the tiny robot racing after him in close pursuit. Finding himself trapped at the end of the hall, Vlad doubled back, and as he skidded past the gaping guests, the inevitable happened and the tiny apron floated to the ground.

'Goodness . . .' Cleopatra drawled. 'Usually a bloke's biggest feature is his ego . . . Tell me, Damien, does Vlad do private functions? Ages since I had a good Russian . . . so *filling* . . .'

Standing beside her, Carin giggled. 'Whole different ball game, aren't they? I'd give this one a job any day!'

'Join the queue, darling . . .' muttered Sebastian.

As the women cackled, Vlad let out an indignant yelp, replacing the apron with the hat before dashing back the way he'd come and hurling himself through the nearest door.

Damien ushered everyone back into the living room and Tierney snatched up the apron before hurrying after the distraught chef, eventually locating him in the spare bedroom, huddling under a pile of coats, while Cy2 spun round by the bed.

As she gently squeezed Vlad's shoulder he glanced up, tears spilling down his pale cheeks. '*Spacibo . . . Natashala . . . spacibo . . .*' he sobbed, burying his face in her cleavage.

Dismayed, Tierney watched as the fragile corset strained valiantly for a few moments before giving up and ripping clean down the middle.

Hearing an exclamation from the doorway, she turned to find Jake, coat in hand, glowering. She smiled weakly. 'Hi . . .' Sure someone was finally addressing him, Cy2 beeped joyfully and ran over Tierney's toes.

'Ow! You little sod.' She scowled, then realised how this must look to Jake: she was sprawled on the bed with a naked cook whose head was shoved down what remained of her bodice. She opened her mouth to explain, but Jake just glared in disgust and stormed out.

Throwing on a jumper and averting her gaze until Vlad secured the apron again, Tierney then marched him back into the kitchen where Damien was waiting. The Russian must have been ladling out the borscht when Cy2 scared him, because the gleaming white tiles were stained a vivid violet, mauve mush was dripping off the cooker, and a purple puddle was fast becoming a lake on the floor.

Tierney groaned. It looked like the set of a slasher movie.

'Damien, you've got to do something with this guy! He's doing my head in!'

The agent produced a big bottle of vodka. 'Needs must . . .'

Tierney grabbed it. 'Cheers. It's a start . . .' She knocked back a generous gulp while Damien looked on in alarm before wrestling the bottle out of her hands.

'Er, that's for Vlad . . .' He shoved it at the Russian, who pounced on it and scuttled off. Damien sighed. 'It's the only thing which calms him down. Last week he was on *Ready Steady Cook*, and he was in such a state I had to get him totally plastered! Thank God his accent's so heavy no one realised!' Damien frowned. 'Strange, actually, his food improves the more pissed he gets . . .'

'Oh, this is perfect – not!!! I've got a naked Russian Cook sobbing into my cleavage, a girl dressed in silver foil hiding under my bed, and my flat's full of people I don't even *like*!' Tierney looked at him earnestly. 'These people may be the Coolest crowd in London, but Damien, face it, they're all raving *fruitcakes*!'

*

Finally, at ten thirty, the food was ready. Judging by the riotous singing coming from the kitchen, the booze had done the trick and Vlad was happier. Tierney was pleased to see him smiling as he proudly laid out steaming bowls of hot red borscht on the table, alongside platters of blintzes, pancakes filled with rich, sweet cheese, and kasha, warm wheat cakes.

For twenty minutes there was silence as everyone munched happily, smiling and laughing as they broke into smaller groups. Filling her plate up for the third time and noting others heaping theirs with food as well, Tierney frowned. Every dish was delicious, but strangely similar. Then she realised why: Vlad had laced – make that *drowned* – all the food with vodka. No wonder everyone was giggling . . .

*

'You want me to *what*?' Putting down his plate, Jake stared at his agent.

Damien smiled. 'Rob and Jeremy want you for series three of *The Next Big Thing* – with Tierney Marshall as co-presenter! She's very keen, I've already run it past her. What do you say?'

Jake glanced round, locating Tierney in the hallway where she was talking to Honey Trapp, her face solemn. He felt like he was being torn in two. On the one hand, he'd love to stay in London and do the next series. But working with Tierney . . . Jake shook his head. He'd never get her out of his system. Realising Damien was waiting, he shrugged. 'Look, I'm not saying no . . . but I can't say yes either. It's not . . . well, let's just say it's not that easy.'

'Sure, you've got commitments back home, I understand, but the powers that be are reasonable. If what you want is for Lisa to come over, they're amenable to that. They know she's a journalist too, they'll find something for her.' Damien was enthusiastic. 'Focus groups love you, and with Tierney on board, the ratings will soar, you'll see! This could be good for you, *very* good . . .'

Turning away to hide his stricken expression, Jake gazed out of the window into the night. Was that what he wanted, to live with Lisa and work with Tierney? It was hard enough seeing her at parties and events, but if they were thrown together on a daily basis . . . Jake didn't trust himself as much as he used to, not since meeting this girl.

'So?' Damien was growing impatient. 'What d'you say? You'd be mad to pass this up!'

'I don't know. I need some time.' Jake felt trapped. Was

this Destiny giving him a shove in the right direction? Perhaps he and Tierney were *meant* to get together? He smiled wryly at his own flight of fancy. *Snap out of it*, he told himself sternly.

'Look, Damien, I mean it, I'm flattered. I'll think about it.' Jake frowned. 'That's the best I can do right now.'

'You do that.' Damien had seen Jake's pensive glance in Tierney's direction, and he wondered.

Seeing Carin slip out of the room, Tierney smiled at Honey and excused herself. This was her chance. 'Here goes nothing . . .' Taking a deep breath, she followed her friend into the brightly lit kitchen.

'Can we talk?' She put down her glass of wine, noting how her hand shook.

'Sure.' Carin turned to face her calmly.

'I can't do this any more. I mean it.' Tierney's eyes beseeched her friend. 'I know you're trying to work through something, but I have a really bad feeling. Andy's going to get burned and I can't just stand by and watch!' Though she'd promised herself she'd keep cool, Tierney was very aware of her voice trembling almost as much as her hands.

'So what are you saying?' Folding her arms, Carin looked her straight in the eye.

Tierney gulped. 'I'm saying . . .' Now her voice was more subdued. 'I'm saying that either you tell Andy . . . or I will.'

'Fine.' Carin shrugged, smiling slightly. 'Go on, then.'

Tierney felt her heart skip a beat. 'You're not *serious*? You'd actually let him hear it from me?'

'There's no problem here, except the one *you're* creating.' Carin looked bored with the whole subject. 'Why can't you just back off? It's none of your business!'

Tierney glared at her. 'He's my friend!'

'So am I – and I'm *asking* you just to let this go, and let me work it out. Which I will.'

'Yeah, sure.' Tierney's voice was scathing. 'Look, it's really very simple: either you tell Andy, or I will.'

'Tell me what?' Andy appeared in the doorway.

The two girls looked at each other.

Tierney took a deep breath. She'd rehearsed this moment countless times in her mind, prepared her script, covered all the angles. She was being cruel to be kind.

Concern for Andy mingled with resentment at Carin as she turned to him, clearing her throat nervously. 'Carin's got something she wants to tell you.' Her voice hardened so that she didn't even sound like herself. *'Don't you?'*

Giving her a dirty look, Carin brushed past her, taking Andy's hand, leading him out into the empty hall. Tierney watched them disappear into the spare room, wincing as the door slammed. She busied herself cleaning up, mopping up the borscht, stacking plates, listening to the laughter and chatter filtering through from the dining room. At least her guests seemed to be enjoying themselves.

Wandering back into the hall again, she found Honey Trapp being backed into a corner by Vlad. The actress stumbled backwards in a bid to escape and practically fell over Damien, who looked bemused.

By now totally fed up with the Russian, Tierney shoved him into the hall cupboard and locked the door. 'I'll let him out later,' she reassured Honey. 'The way I'm feeling, he's probably safer in there right now . . .'

'Tierney!' Damien looked round furtively. 'Honey Trapp, what star sign is she?'

'God knows!' Tierney frowned. 'Er, why?'

The agent looked sheepish. 'It's just, well, my horoscope said I was in for a "sweet surprise" this week. Venus is in my sun sign, good for relationships and so on . . .'

'Ah . . . I get it!' Grinning, Tierney grabbed his hand and dragged him over to where Honey was helping herself to more food. 'Honey, you were looking for a location for your next video, right? Well, Damien's going to the Sahara to run a marathon! Quirky, don't you think?'

The singer's face lit up. 'Sure is! Would make a stunning setting . . .'

Tierney left them chatting happily; at least *something* was going well.

Grabbing some more plates, she returned to the kitchen, switching on the dishwasher before falling into a chair, exhausted. Hearing the door open sharply, she turned to find Andy standing behind her, his face a sad, sickly white.

Tierney jumped up again, staring at him in alarm. He looked like a watered-down version of himself, as though all the colour had been sucked clean out of him. Even his normally bright blue eyes seemed to have faded to a dull grey.

Carin had told him.

'Andy, I'm so sorry.' Tierney reached for his hand but he recoiled.

'You knew . . .' Eyes narrowed. He looked at her as though he'd never really seen her before. Rage seemed to leak through every pore in his body, like steam hissing out of an iron.

'I wanted to tell you, that's why tonight I—'

'Tonight?' Andy's lips twisted in a bitter smile. 'Sod tonight! You've known for *weeks*, haven't you? *Haven't you?* I might have expected this from Carin – God, I was stupid to ever think I . . . that we . . .' His voice broke. 'But *you* . . .' His eyes flickered with hurt while Tierney groped mentally for the right words to say.

'Andy, please, I've been worried sick! I swear, I didn't know what to do, she kept—'

'I don't give a shit. I thought we were mates.' He turned to go, then paused. 'Oh, and by the way, I know all about you and Carin and your little fling.'

As Tierney paled, he looked her up and down in a visual smirk. 'Yeah, have to say, I was a bit surprised . . . wouldn't have thought it of you . . . not little Miss *Perfect* . . .'

Weak, Tierney leaned against the fridge. 'How did you . . . ?'

'I'd half guessed, and I asked her, weeks ago.' Hand on the door, Andy laughed, a horrible, hollow sound which seemed to hang there. 'You know what? You and Carin should get together again – *you deserve each other*!'

The door slammed and he was gone.

Tierney shivered. Nothing she tried worked out, so why bother any more? Her relationships were clearly all doomed, might as well face it.

Standing there alone in the kitchen, listening to her guests talking loudly, shrieking with vodka-induced merriment, Tierney shook her head. She was the Coolest Girl in the Country, and her flat was full of cool people, all here because of her and how popular she was, yet she'd never felt so alone in her life.

Realising she was in no fit state to face anyone, she hurried out of the kitchen, and down the dimly lit hallway to her room.

'Tierney! Wait up . . .' Jake was smiling tentatively. 'How's it going?'

She shrugged. 'Oh, you know. Hectic.'

'Damien told me you're doing the cover of *GQ*.' Without meaning to, Jake let disapproval slip into his voice and she caught it.

'Look, I know what you're going to say, Jake, so just save it. I'm tired of having to defend my choices to you.'

Not wanting another argument with her, Jake shrugged, staring moodily into space. It was the weirdest thing. Tierney was standing right there in front of him, yet he *missed* her.

He looked at her again. 'Haven't seen you much lately. What have you been up to?'

'Oh, you know.' Her smile was edgy. 'This and that.'

'Yeah, but what, exactly?' Jake demanded, determined to pin her down.

Tierney waved a hand dismissively. 'Seeing people. The usual.'

'Which people?' he persisted, aware he was pushing her and not caring.

'Friends.'

'Which friends?'

She glared. 'Someone really should have told you the Spanish Inquisition ended a while back! God, what is this, *Twenty Questions*? I wasn't aware I had to run my social diary past you for approval!'

Jake felt his concern for her being eclipsed by anger at her secrecy.

'I suppose that means you're still hanging around with Cleopatra and her coke-head friends?' he accused sharply.

'Right. That does it. I'm not going to stand here and be interrogated by you.' She turned and opened her bedroom door. 'Nice talking to you, Jake.' Her voice was icy. 'See ya 'round.' She shut the door on him.

Cursing, Jake retrieved his jacket from the hall cupboard and stalked out of the flat without even saying goodbye to anyone. Yeah, like he was really going to sign up for the next series of the programme when it meant working with *her*. And in that moment, he made his mind up: he was going to reject the offer, and go back to New York.

Slamming his car door and resting his head against the steering wheel, Jake nodded. He had to forget this girl. How hard could it be?

Then the Eve's Brew ad campaign started, and Jake realised it wouldn't be hard to forget Tierney Marshall.

It would be impossible.

17

The Next Big Thing

She was ***HUGE***.

Sixty feet tall, to be precise.

She appeared overnight, across the capital, and London didn't know what had hit it. Suddenly, there she was, on specially designed billboards set up outside pubs and clubs, on the forecourts at Euston, Waterloo and other stations; outside cinemas; along the sides of buses, in shopping centres. Billboards bigger than any posters or ads seen *ever*.

She was naked, a black and gold snake coiled possessively around one shoulder, draped over her breasts and other parts which had to be hidden. Her blue eyes were mischievous, one finger over her lips as she held out a bottle of Eve's Brew:

Ssh! *Don't tell Adam . . .*

More billboards appeared alongside the roads, causing mayhem. In these she wore a bra and knickers, bright green and shaped like fig leaves, while reclining in a lush garden, surrounded by fruit-laden trees, plus flowers of every colour and kind, and again she held out Eve's Brew with a seductive smile:

Turn over a new leaf:
try Eve's, and enter Paradise

Phase one of the Eve's Brew ad campaign had started; Tierney Marshall was now, literally, the Next Big Thing. And Britain was baffled.

No one knew quite what to make of the ads. In the nationals, pundits filled column after column analysing them. Were they intended to be taken seriously? Or were they a tongue-in-cheek parody of all the other ads using sex to sell? Surely, female writers argued uneasily, it was some sort of *statement*?

'This is "fuck-me feminism!"' wrote one reporter.

Others argued the campaign wasn't saying anything, but was just the logical extension of a trend seen in the marketing of everything from soap to shoes to stereos. But one thing was certain: the whole country was talking about Eve's Brew.

Religious leaders protested against the imagery used in the ads, writing to the papers, ranting and raving on radio, and accusing Tierney of degrading the Bible. Daytime chat shows held debates and phone-ins to discuss the billboards. In schools, magazines featuring Eve's Brew ads were banned, but supermarkets and off-licences were desperate to stock the drink.

And the focus of all the attention was Tierney. She was an icon. She was a tart. A blasphemer. A *babe*. Love her or hate her, *everyone* was talking about her.

Two weeks after the billboards went up, she made the cover of *Time*.

Within a month, Eve's Brew was the coolest drink in the country and not one bottle had been sold yet. And through it all, acting on Damien's instructions, Tierney stayed silent; just smiled and said nothing. Only at the official opening of Bar Eden and the launch of the drink, in one week's time, would she give a statement. Everyone wanted to know what she thought, and no one did. The debate raged on.

Barnaby and Julian breathed a sigh of relief and got plastered.

Damien sat back and watched as Marshall Mania took hold.

Tierney became a prisoner in her own home as the media went mad and mobbed her every time she left the flat. It got to the point where Damien had to hire a minder to ensure she wasn't injured by the hacks and fans who went crazy each time she appeared in public.

And Jake felt like he was going insane.

Now, sitting in his car with the roof off and stereo blaring, oblivious to the traffic gridlocked around him, he gazed at the billboard outside Selfridges, in honour of Tierney's tackling the West End Rapist there and her original claim to fame. In the brilliant sunshine the colours glared out at him, Tierney's eyes an intense, beautiful blue, her blonde hair gleaming.

She lay on a bed, a flimsy white sheet draped over her tanned body, her head resting in the lap of a gorgeous male model, her lips closed around a bottle of Eve's Brew, under the blurb:

Just Swallow . . . *It's heaven*

A crowd had formed around the poster, tourists gaping and snapping photos. Jake noted that the eyes of every driver he could see, male *and* female, were locked on the ad; the strategy was working like a dream. Women wanted to *be* Tierney, men just wanted her, period.

Jake thumped the steering wheel – *how* in God's name was he supposed to get her out of his system, when each time he got in the car and went anywhere, or opened a magazine, or turned on the television, there she was? Tierney Marshall, Next Big Thing and media babe *extraordinaire*. He'd been wishing he could see more of her, but *this* was crazy, a kind of slow, sweet torture, as though someone had reached inside his head, plucked out his fantasies, and plastered them across London for all to see.

Because there was no way of avoiding her. As part of his research for the programme, Jake had to study both men's and women's magazines. The other day he'd flicked through the latest issue of ***Sorted!*** to find a double-page spread for Eve's Brew, showing Tierney on a golden beach, a bottle of Eve's Brew bobbing through the water towards her as she sat there, face tilted towards the sun, lips parted in a dreamy smile, a palm tree throwing shade over her skimpily clad body while azure waves lapped gently against the shore. Jake tried not to notice the way the white bikini clung to her curves as he smiled at the caption:

Tempted? *It's a sin to resist . . .*

Jake couldn't even escape the ads when he took refuge at the gym he'd started attending three times a week. Walking in the other evening, he'd been confronted with a poster showing Tierney in a crisp white karate suit, hair pulled back, eyes sparkling: 'THE BEER WITH REAL *KICK*!!!'

Now he looked up to find the traffic moving again. One hand on the burning-hot steering wheel, he eased his foot down on the accelerator while snapping open the glove compartment, removing a white plastic folder. Inside were the details of his open ticket back to New York. One more programme to record and he was free. Getting out his mobile phone, he hesitated, glancing back at Tierney smiling down at him from the billboard.

It was just a physical attraction. Granted, an unusually intense one, but nothing more.

Dialling his travel agent, he booked a seat on a plane departing Heathrow three weeks after the opening of Bar Eden. He had to be here for that.

*

'Damien, I'm serious, I can't take much more of this!' Visibly wilting, Natalie collapsed at her desk. 'Those sodding phones have been going crazy all morning, and I think the fax machine's in danger of exploding! If I have to tell one more person that Tierney Marshall is booked solid for the next three months I am going to *scream*!!!!!!!!!'

Damien poured her a cup of Lemon and Lime Fizz herbal tea. 'Perhaps we'd better leave the answer machine on for a while,' he sighed. 'It is getting a bit much . . .'

'A *bit*?' Natalie stared at him. 'I've never seen anything like it!' She shook her head in disbelief. 'And was that *Playboy* on the phone just now? *Again?*'

'Sure was! They're offering an *obscene* amount of money for exclusive photos of Tierney baring all. As are the *Sun*. It's almost a shame we have to turn it down . . .'

Going back to his desk, he sat down and studied the array of magazines before him. This month alone, Tierney was on the covers of *Arena, Maxim* and *Esquire*.

He was uneasy.

The press were closing in; several contacts had warned Damien that editors were briefing their reporters to get the dirt on Tierney. Any way they could.

Gazing out of the window at two young girls playing with skipping ropes out in the street, he hoped that if and when the backlash began, Tierney could cope with it; you couldn't achieve this sort of exposure and not expect some fall-out. Damien sighed. Luckily, by the time the press *really* turned on the heat, *he* should be halfway across the Sahara . . .

*

'I swear, I'm addicted . . .' Vanita slid off Matt, curling up beside him on the rumpled bedsheets, and sighing as he leaned over on his side, planting a quick kiss on her lips before sauntering into the bathroom. She watched him, her smile faltering.

Matt was the *best*, no other guy came close. And just as she'd predicted, when he'd realised Tierney was out of his reach, it hadn't taken much arm-twisting for Vanita to get him back in her bed. But she felt sad things weren't the way they used to be, because sometimes she got the feeling Matt was thinking about Tierney, imagining Tierney, even while he was driving Vanita insane with pleasure.

In fact, she *knew* he was, because once he'd murmured the other girl's name.

Propping herself up on the pillows, she opened a drawer in her tiny bedside cabinet, and pulled out a diary, flicking through the pages and penning a red line through that day's date.

Six days until the opening of Bar Eden.

Six days until she taught Tierney Marshall a lesson she'd *never* forget.

Slamming the drawer shut again, she lay down, eyes narrowed as she went over everything in her mind for the hundredth time. Everything was in place. Zoë, still bruised and bemused, had been putty in her hands. Everything was set.

Vanita glanced up as Matt got back into bed beside her, his eyes distant.

But never mind, because soon the only thing he'd be feeling for Tierney Marshall was pity.

*

Tierney wasn't excited, she was *psyched*.

Even now, sprawled on her bed, trying to relax before getting ready to go clubbing with Honey, she couldn't keep still, her feet absently beating against the cushions as she flicked through the stack of glossy magazines scattered over the duvet. And in every one of the magazines, there she was. Every time she saw one of the Eve's Brew ads, every time someone recognised her, it felt like her ego was being hugged.

Even though, Tierney flopped over on to her back, she'd practically been under house arrest for the past week with the press camped out on the doorstep, determined to get some comment from her. But Damien was adamant: Tierney must say nothing. She would talk to the media only at the opening of Bar Eden, when a short press conference would be held.

She sat up, fidgeting again. She felt as though events were taking on a momentum of their own, speeding up, like she was hurtling headfirst towards something, something she'd been waiting for. It was nothing specific, just a general sense that things were *moving*.

When the phone rang she snatched it up, grinning. 'Eve speaking!'

'Tierney?' Carin sounded amused.

This was the first time they'd spoken since the flat-warming party, and Tierney felt awkward. 'Hiya. What's up?'

'Just thought I should let you know a few of your . . . *friends* from the press have started hanging around the office, asking questions about you.' Carin's laugh was tight. 'They've offered to buy my story.'

Confused, Tierney stared at the phone. 'Your story?'

'The story of what it was like living with the Next Big Thing. They want to know if I'll dish the dirt on you and Jake.' She sounded embarrassed. 'I told them to fuck off, obviously!'

Tierney shrugged. Nothing could get her down today. 'Cheers. So how much did they offer you?'

'A hundred thousand pounds. More, if I could tape you talking to or about Jake. For pictures, they'll double the amount.'

'Suppose I should be flattered . . .' Tierney laughed.

'You don't sound very worried!'

'No need to be.' She continued flicking through the magazines, cradling the phone against her left shoulder. 'They can't touch me. No one's going to tell them anything. Besides, there's nothing to tell.'

'Guess not.' Carin paused. 'A hack from the *Sunday Splash* tried to get Andy to talk. He almost hit the guy!' At the mention of his name, Carin's voice darkened. 'Anyway, Tier, you'd better warn your family, because those hacks are bound to try them next. They've even approached Matt.'

Tierney cursed.

'Don't panic. He told them where to go. I actually think he feels really bad over what he did to you.'

Not wanting to talk about Matt, Tierney sat up on the bed. 'How *is* Andy? I've called him a thousand times at work but he never takes my calls.'

Carin sighed. 'He's still not speaking to me. Apparently he's going to visit his brother this weekend; he's taken a few weeks off work. To be honest, I've hardly seen him since . . . you know. I think he's acting like a prat.'

'Yeah, well, you would. It's called Being In Love.' Tierney knew her voice was sharp but she didn't give a shit.

'Guess I walked into that one.' Carin sounded distracted. 'My mobile's ringing.'

'You'd better get it, then, hadn't you?' muttered Tierney, still angry.

'Talk to you soon . . .'

'Sure.'

Tierney hung up and stared at the phone, wondering if things would ever be the same again with her friends, and having a horrible feeling they wouldn't. She resolved to make sure she spoke to Andy before he went away. At first she'd been gutted that he was upset. Now she was angry that he was blaming her when she'd tried her best. Tierney scowled. As usual though, her best just hadn't been good enough.

*

'Excuse me, is this seat taken?'

Above the lively chatter filling the crowded pub, Andy realised someone was talking to him. The sarcastic retort died on his lips as, looking up, his eyes widened at the sight of the beautiful oriental girl waiting for his reply. 'No . . . go for it . . .' He watched as she sat down gracefully, putting her bag on the table between them.

'I'm meeting a friend, but she's late and I *hate* sitting in pubs alone!' Rolling her eyes, she gave him a self-deprecating smile. 'How silly is that, right?'

'No, no, not at all!' Andy felt his interest quickening. 'Let me buy you a drink?' he suggested, hopefully, feeling something other than anger and hurt for the first time in weeks.

Her smile was shy. 'Oh, that's so sweet! Thanks, I'd love one . . .'

She watched as Andy strode over to the crowded bar with a sudden spring in his step. As he leaned across to get the barman's attention, she quickly opened her bag, checking that the tiny tape recorder was working, before closing it again. Although the real dirt would come later, back at her place. Nothing like a bit of pillow-talk . . . Deftly she unbuttoned the top two buttons of her blouse and fluffed out her long raven hair.

She'd played a hunch and hung around this pub every weekend for five weeks, convinced that sooner or later, either

Tierney or one of her housemates would appear, would be drinking, would have their guard down. Glancing up, she caught Andy's eyes on her again.

Lian smiled warmly at him.

Gotcha . . .

18

Paradise Lost

Trying to tame her tattered nerves with a glass of white wine, Tierney glanced hopefully at her watch, then groaned. Still *ages* until the car arrived to take her to Bar Eden. Someone, somewhere, must have pressed a cosmic pause button. All day, the minutes had meandered along, in no hurry to get moving, while the seconds, selfish little sods, were positively dawdling.

It was now eight in the evening, and she had started getting ready at eight that morning, plastering mud from the Dead Sea, a seaweed wrap from Scotland, and moisturiser from Shiseido all over her body. 'God, glow any brighter and the only thing I'll be wearing's a lampshade!' she giggled. Still, all the preparation was worth it, because tonight was *her* night.

Pouring herself more wine, she gazed out of the kitchen window. The clouds were billowing into pink, tangerine and lime-green spirals and turrets, a fairy castle of colour just hanging there in the heavens. A tease of a breeze caressed her skin and Tierney smiled.

It was a perfect summer evening.

And it was going to *be* perfect.

The only thing denting her mood was the problem with Andy. Now she dialled his number, her old number, with a shaking hand, praying he'd answer. She felt almost sick with relief when after about fifteen rings he finally picked up.

'Andy, it's me.' She paused, half expecting him to slam the phone down. 'Andy, please *talk* to me!'

'Can't. Nothing to say.'

Tierney flinched at the coldness in his tone.

In the background she could hear faint voices, like they had a crossed line. Or was it an echo of all the conversations she and Andy had had over the years?

A ghost, trapped in the wire.

Faint and fading, like their friendship.

'Andy, *please*, I wouldn't hurt you for the world! I did my best, what more do you want? Blood?' Now Tierney was getting angry. 'For crying out loud, *I* haven't done anything wrong! Why are you *being* like this?'

'You should have told me.' Andy sounded petulant, and Tierney leaned over the sink, her head swimming with tension.

'I didn't know how. I kept hoping Carin would, and when I realised that wasn't going to happen . . . well, you know the rest.'

Andy sighed. 'It's not just that. It's everything. You and her, the fact that you two . . . I don't know, I feel weird.'

'But this is *me*!' Tierney gripped the phone, her eyes closed, wanting him to hear in her voice how much she missed him. It seemed impossible that things wouldn't get back to normal.

'I feel like I don't know you or Carin any more. Or maybe I never really knew you in the first place.' Andy sounded sad, and now Tierney could feel the friendship unravelling, the bonds between them dissolving.

'Don't say that. Look, can't we meet up? Maybe go for a drink? Talk ab—'

'I'm going to my brother's for a while. I need to get out of the house, away from Carin. I'll call when I get back.'

She bit her lip, nodding. There was no point in pushing him, he sounded so . . . *detached*. 'Andy, promise you'll get in touch? Soon?'

He paused. 'Yeah.'

''Bye.'

'Goodbye, Tierney.'

Tierney told herself things would work out.

And she'd keep telling herself that until she started believing it.

Wandering into the hall, she peered anxiously into the mirror. Her reflection stared back, then smiled slightly. She'd insisted on wearing a dress of her own choice, despite Damien having an apoplectic fit over her offending any of the many sponsors begging her to wear their clothes. Wills clashing and words colliding, he and Tierney had scowled at each other, but for once she'd stuck to her guns, because this was *her* night and she was going to feel good in what she wore.

So she'd chosen a favourite from way back. It was an azure-blue, long sheath dress which had a pretty, low neckline, and fell in a slinky, silky line to her sandals; the only jewellery she wore was a delicate silver chain round her left ankle, glimmering softly against her tanned skin.

It wasn't cool.

It wasn't trendy.

It was *perfect*.

Still not used to the silence of her new flat, Tierney switched on the television, turning the volume up to full; instantly, as if responding to her presence, an Eve's Brew ad appeared and she stared at it, mesmerised. How strange, to think that while she grew up and moved on, these images, these pictures and posters and billboards, would remain for ever young and lovely. Tierney had become obsessed with her looks, scrutinising her face and figure for lines and bags, sags and shadows, for the slightest hint that her body was about to do the dirty on her. Perhaps she'd become a female Dorian Gray, and hide a poster of herself away in the attic, let it carry the weight of the years so she could stay young.

Maybe the Coolest Girl in the Country never needed to grow old.

Outside, she heard a car pulling up and felt her pulse skitter. It was time to go. Jake would be waiting in the limo. As she double-locked the front door, Tierney tried to forget that he'd soon be returning to the States. She felt resentful of his life and his soon-to-be-wife, and angry with herself – for what right did she have to resent anything?

Carefully lifting the hem of her dress, she climbed into the car, avoiding Jake's eyes as he shut the magazine he'd been reading and stared at her, noting how the silky material clung to her curves.

Jake sighed. Having so little time left, being alone with her like this, he felt a mounting pressure to say something, and if he had the words, he would.

But, he smiled affectionately as he watched Tierney's solemn face, there was one thing he *could* say.

'You look beautiful.'

Startled, she looked up. 'Oh, thanks . . .'

Jake laughed. 'Don't look so surprised. If I've criticised the way you dress in the past, it was only because I knew you could look nicer. Like tonight.'

Tierney smoothed out an imaginary crease in the dress. Jake's being nice to her hurt like hell. 'So, when's your flight home?' She tried to sound casual.

'Three weeks today. I've just recorded the last programme in the series. Now it's over to you.' Jake fiddled with his watch strap.

She flashed him a carefree grin. 'If you're in London again, look me up. When you're a hotshot movie star, I can remind you of your humble origins on Channel Five, can't I?'

'Yeah, I'm sure you'd soon yank me back down to earth all right . . . and Tierney, ditto for you. If you're ever in New York, I mean.' He shrugged, almost shyly. 'I'd love to see you again. It's always good to touch base with old . . . friends.'

Friends . . .

A lasso of hurt was knotting around her heart, *tightening*, until Tierney could hardly breathe.

Jake saw her as a *friend.*

Suddenly that was the most hateful word in the world.

Sighing, Jake opened his magazine again, staring with unseeing eyes at the neat paragraphs of text. Tierney didn't care he was leaving soon. All she wanted was to get to the party and see the people she *really* cared about, her precious A-list friends and admirers.

Why couldn't he just accept he meant nothing to her?

And suddenly Jake was glad he was going home.

Because he couldn't do this, not any more.

This was just too hard.

*

'Get your hand *off* my leg . . .' Smiling briskly at her colleague, Lian removed his hand from her thigh and placed it firmly on the leather taxi seat between them. Giving her a drunken smile, he slipped his arm round her shoulders instead, and she elbowed him sharply in the ribs, wriggling around on the seat trying to put more space between them, difficult with six journalists squeezed into one cab.

After a late, long dinner, they'd all decided to go *en masse* to Bar Eden to cover its opening for their respective papers. It had seemed like a good idea at the time, but right now Lian wasn't so sure. What she needed was a bit of peace and quiet to think about her story . . . Trying to blank out the loud, booze-laden laughter of her peers, she watched the passing shop fronts and office windows gleaming in the pale evening sunlight.

She had a scoop, simple as that. Tierney Marshall swung both ways, and had slept with the girl she lived with, who herself then slept with Andy. Lian fought to keep a knowing smile from inching across her face.

She was the only journalist with this story.

For now.

Mentally, she gave herself a pat on the back for a job well done. It was easy, getting Andy to open up: he'd been so choked up with anger and hurt, all she'd had to do was ply him with drink and soon he was talking freely to this girl beside him in the pub, this girl who was so sweet, so sympathetic, so interested without being intrusive. By the time Lian had helped him stagger outside and into her car, she had half the story. The rest she'd pieced together back at her place. Not that she'd had to do much: Andy had been out so cold, his performance didn't even make it to Act One.

And the next morning he'd remembered nothing of what he'd done or divulged, asking anxiously what had gone on. She'd quietened him with a kiss and a compliment about his prowess between the sheets, and seeing his sleepy eyes widen with pleasure, Lian had felt the first twinge of guilt. It was always the way: she got caught up in the story, in the chase, and it was only later, sometimes much later, that she went from being a reporter to a person again.

Now, oblivious to the jostling and arguing of her colleagues, she sighed, face screwed up in concentration. The question was what to *do* with her scoop. Confronting Tierney with it at tonight's press conference would be by far the most dramatic thing . . . But then, she grimaced, her rivals would have a head start.

No, she decided, far better to sit on it, let Tierney have her moment of glory. The paper where she was currently working shifts could then run with it in a few days, just as Eve's Brew went on sale. The timing would be perfect; Lian could already see the headlines. She'd be offered a staff job, for sure.

'Yes, I agree.' Smiling, she turned to answer the woman opposite her. 'Tierney Marshall has done brilliantly, hasn't she?'

Enjoy it while you can, Golden Girl . . .

*

'If I do say so myself, I look *divine* . . .' Laughing, Vanita spun around before the full-length mirror in her bedroom, admiring the way the little white dress from Ghost flared out around her curvy hips. A few hours on a sunbed had turned her skin a rich, mahogany shade, and her hair, newly washed and cut, tumbled over her shoulders in glossy, dark waves.

Glancing at her watch, she tapped her fingers impatiently, before going over to the bed, opening her bag, and patting the shiny black video cassette inside. It had taken a lot of work, a bit of bribery, and a few favours called in, but she was pleased with her plan.

After tonight, she'd never have to worry about Tierney Marshall again.

*

As night slid through the sky, Bar Eden lit up like some unearthly sphere. Emerging from the lift, Tierney gazed around in awe at what was essentially one huge, rooftop garden on the top of a hotel. For a few minutes she watched Julian and Barnaby, immaculate in designer suits, their hair slicked back, both oozing charm as they greeted each new arrival with airy kisses, compliments tripping off their tongues. Tierney laughed; those two elevated glibness to an art form. Leaving them to it, she wandered off, looking around Bar Eden with widening eyes. She'd been here several times recently to help organise things, but had never seen it looking quite like this . . .

Over the opulent gardens stretching before her was a glass bubble now glistening faintly against the pitch-black sky. Hundreds of tiny candles flickered among the lush foliage, while the trees, tall and wispy like upright eyelashes, cast slender shadows over the moon-dappled grass.

Harps strummed softly in the background, and every now

and then Tierney caught a wistful cry from one of the pale pink flamingoes strolling around, looking disdainfully at the crowds of people milling around.

Opening a bottle of Eve's Brew, she giggled; all the waiters and waitresses were dressed in bras and briefs designed like fig leaves; exact replicas of the outfit she'd worn in the billboards.

Just past the elevators was a large, sunken stone circle, like a small amphitheatre, over which streamed a huge waterfall, tiny strobe lights around it turning the water into a liquid rainbow. Around the outside ran the main bar, which was actually a large, circular, tropical fish tank; guests leaned over the side, staring and pointing as the fish edged through the jade-green water, people laughing at their cute faces and coy manoeuvres.

Still admiring the waterfall, Tierney sauntered over to one of the many tables groaning under the weight of enough food to feed a small planet. Eyes widening at the baskets overflowing with every type of fruit imaginable, she popped a fat red cherry into her mouth; it was on the turn and tasted like wine, staining her lips a deep, blood red as she sucked out the juicy sweetness and reached eagerly for more.

And, she stared, there they were. The Cool Ones. The hippest actors, most sought-after stars, prestigious presenters, the movers and shakers of the media world. All looking gorgeous, like a swarm of multicoloured butterflies as they moved through the plush gardens, confidence surrounding them like an aura.

As Tierney continued looking around she noticed other details: little pathways leading down leafy corridors of trees; tiny flights of steps up to ornate stone benches where several couples were sitting and talking softly. Everyone was drinking Eve's Brew, exclaiming with pleasure at its sweet, smooth taste, the mead and raspberries giving it a rich, fruity flavour, while the cranberries added a slight tartness and made it extremely thirst-quenching.

'Tierney!' Damien hurried towards her. 'Child, why aren't you *mingling*?'

'Give me a chance!' Annoyed at him for breaking the mood, Tierney gestured at the gardens. 'I'm soaking up the atmosphere. Isn't this place stunning?'

Glancing at the sky, Damien made a face. 'All *I* know is that Mercury is retrograde this week! Lots of mistakes and misunderstandings . . . I don't like it, I don't like it at all!'

'Damien, there's something I've been meaning to say to you for a while . . .' Tierney smiled sweetly at her agent.

'No need to thank me, just get out there and network!network!network!'

'It wasn't that. It's just that, well' – Tierney shrugged – 'I reckon you've lost the plot. In fact, I'm not sure you ever had it in the first place!' Laughing at his bemused face, she waved and wandered off to enjoy the evening.

And everyone was watching her.

Smiling, Tierney drifted through the gardens, feeling like a fairytale princess holding court, leaving a trail of admiring hearts and envious glances in her wake.

Tonight, Tierney smiled, she *was* Eve.

The first, the only woman.

It was ludicrous, and tomorrow, she was sure, she'd be laughing at it, but tonight, that was how she felt.

And, she had to hand it to him: Damien's strategy of not

letting her make a statement about the ad campaign had worked, for while the whole country had been debating and discussing, arguing and insisting, she'd stayed silent. Now everyone was waiting to hear what she had to say. She'd been over her speech a hundred times, refining it until it was perfect.

Tierney couldn't wait.

*

In the middle of the main garden, Jake stood, hands jammed in his pockets, gazing up at yet another huge likeness of Tierney which everyone was staring at in awe. It was the ice sculpture, cool and clear and pure, glimmering under the pearly moonlight streaming over and through it.

He couldn't stop staring at it, struck by how the artist had captured the expression in Tierney's eyes, the slight tilt of her chin. The figure stood, one hand loosely at her side, the other holding a bottle of Eve's Brew, the lips parted in the lightest of smiles, waves of serrated ice forming the hair flowing over the shoulders.

Jake's smile turned bitter.

He'd probably get more warmth from this chunk of frozen water than he ever would from the girl whose likeness it bore.

Turning round again, he located Tierney, and watched her flitting from group to group, heard her laughter winding through the myriad voices, noting the flirty smiles she offered the various men vying for her attention. Under the soft lighting, the blue dress rippled over her body like water.

Jake took a deep breath, tried to clear his head. His pulse stung; it was beating too fast, too heavy, as he watched Tierney. His very blood seemed to ache with wanting her, and here, he glanced round, here in these gardens, there were so many nooks and crannies and corners where they could—

'*Jesus!*' He slammed his glass down angrily. Jake didn't know what was wrong with him tonight: maybe he'd just thought about her too much, for too long. But right this minute he felt like getting hold of Tierney, dragging her off into one of those corners, where no one would hear her cry out, and showing her exactly what she was doing to him, and *exactly* what he wanted from her . . .

He sighed. Three weeks until he returned home. Three weeks until this *madness* left him.

He grabbed that thought and clung on to it for the rest of the night.

*

Finally, at around eleven, Barnaby and Julian began ushering people over to a flight of stone steps near the ice sculpture, from where Tierney would make the speech officially opening Bar Eden and launching Eve's Brew. Damien had arranged for a giant video screen to be set up and for the launch to be broadcast live on Channel Five.

Nervously, Tierney waited while the screen flickered behind her. One of the technicians gave Barnaby the thumbs-up, and glancing round, she saw her own face looming large, and blushed. Standing there, looking out over the hundreds of people in front of her, with yet more scattered around the gardens, she felt her heart lurch. Everyone was silent, everything was still. All eyes were on her.

Tierney beamed. 'Welcome to Paradise! On behalf of everyone involved with Bar Eden and Eve's Brew, let me start by th—'

Something is wrong.

There is another voice, talking over hers, a woman's voice, loud and clear.

Irritated, Tierney glances up to silence the heckler, and is confronted by a crowd of puzzled faces. People are turning to each other, frowning and whispering. Some of them are pointing, looking past Tierney, and, keeping a bright smile on her face, she turns.

Her face is no longer on the screen.

Instead, there is . . . a street . . . people lying in dirty brown blankets. Coins glittering in cups. And still the woman's voice, talking about being homeless. Tierney gasps as the street scene fades and a face appears on the screen.

Zoë.

'I don't understand . . .' Tierney turns to Julian, who is standing nearby, pale-faced. The crowd is growing restless, murmuring more loudly as the words began registering. Tierney goes rigid as Zoë's voice, cool and commanding, tells the story of how Tierney Marshall, golden girl, gave her hope and then snatched the chance for herself. How she, Tierney, promised the world to an eighteen-year-old homeless girl, then betrayed her.

'*What . . . ?*' Tierney can't believe what she's hearing. She starts to protest, then stops, staring at the faces.

So many faces . . .

Stretched out before her, eyes narrowing in suspicion and shock, as they recognise the ring of authenticity in Zoë's words. Her limbs heavy and cold as stone, Tierney simply stands there, numbly, until the voice stops, the screen flickers, and there is silence.

Then, from the back of the crowd, movement. Zoë walks towards her, looking straight at her. Cameras start flashing. People begin talking again, nudging each other, asking each other if it's true, looking at Tierney with disdain.

Tierney watches Zoë; she is in a pale-pink dress, and in high heels, she's taller than Tierney remembers. Her sandy hair is now streaked with blonde, her huge golden eyes glittering with anger as she meets Tierney's stare. She looks like she should be on the catwalk.

Tierney blinks. Dazed, she glances over at Barnaby and Julian, both of whom look shellshocked. Already she can see Julian tugging on his friend's sleeve, whispering urgently, no doubt concocting some story. Slowly, Zoë approaches until she's standing beside Tierney on the top step, and for a moment they just look at each other.

Zoë shakes her head, eyes narrowed, voice so quiet that Tierney alone hears her. 'You *bitch* . . .'

She holds up a sheet of paper which Tierney recognises as the letter she herself wrote, officially offering her the Eve's Brew contract. A frantic glance tells her the screen is again reflecting what's happening. Not just the people here, but anyone and everyone watching will see this.

And the press are going *mad*.

Now the hacks swarm over to Tierney, grabbing and clutching, clinging on to her like leeches. Microphones assault her like fierce metal fists. Cameras flash in her face, turning the world around her into a white, glaring landscape. The voices merge into a sort of squawking which doesn't even sound human. And still, all the guests and staff just stand there, watching Tierney and Zoë, two beautiful girls staring at each other silently, one in shock, one in triumph, while the reporters scream out their questions, frantically elbowing each other out the way.

'Tierney, is it true?'

'Tierney, what do you say about these allegations?'

'Is it true you offered the job to this girl first?'

'When did you decide *you* should be Eve, Tierney?'

'Zoë, how did you feel when you found out who got the role of Eve?'

The words go round and round and round, running into each other, forming a verbal web and trapping Tierney inside. The world seems to consist of nothing but raw emotion and noise; a loud buzzing has started and it's a few moments before she realises it's coming from inside her head. Tierney knows she should do something, should be saying something, but she can't take it all in. This can't be happening.

'But I . . . I didn't *know* . . .' She grabs Zoë's arm, but the girl shakes her off and turns back to the journalists clustered around her.

And the cameras keep on flashing.

No one's listening to her, no one cares. And suddenly, standing there, Tierney realises it doesn't matter what she says. It actually doesn't matter, not one little bit, what's true or false, fair or fake.

All that matters is the story.

The press wanted dirt; now they've got it. And she, Tierney, is the scapegoat. Already she can see Barnaby and Julian trying to salvage their credibility, shaking their heads, denying all knowledge. Not everyone will believe them, and in the days that follow, the truth will come out, but right now, that doesn't matter. Because it's she, Tierney, the public knows and loves and trusts; it's her name on the line. And there's no such thing as objective reality, not any more, not in this world she's chosen to inhabit.

Trembling, Tierney tries to walk down the steps, pushing through the crowds of reporters who instantly swivel to pursue her, forming a corridor of hands. The guests step back to let her pass, and she tries not to notice how their faces have changed when they look at her.

The journalists are blocking her way, tugging on her arm, screaming and pushing and glaring. Lashing out at one of them, Tierney turns too quickly and stumbles; her left foot twists over sharply and she trips, pitches forward and ends up sprawled on the ground. She hears someone snickering.

Tierney's face is aflame as she scrambles to her feet. Within the space of ten minutes she's become a figure of ridicule. Public enemy number one. Staring straight ahead, she continues pushing her way through the pack of hacks still surrounding her.

One face catches her eye, one face smiling coldly.

Vanita.

Tierney stops. The icy tip of temper twists sharply inside her, and she brings her hand back and slaps the Valkyrie round the face. The journalists stare in glee, the guests gasp in shock, and the cameras carry on clicking.

'Happy now?' Shaking with rage, Tierney glares at Vanita, feeling pure, unadulterated hatred surging through her. *'I hope you rot in hell!'*

Vanita affects a look of mock innocence as she turns to the reporters who are recording all this with relish.

Feeling a warm hand on her shoulder, Tierney jumps. It's Jake. His face is grim, and for a moment she panics: he believes Zoë. Then his eyes soften. 'Come on, let's get out of here.'

Grasping her arm, he guides her towards the lifts, but angrily she shrugs him away. 'I don't need a minder!'

He looks at her calmly. 'No, but I think you need a friend.'

Now the journalists are frantic, snapping shot after shot of Jake ushering Tierney through the gardens, running after them, still shouting questions. Jake stares straight ahead as if they don't exist.

As they hurry past the fountain, Tierney glances at the bar, at the tiny tropical fish still darting in and out of the sea shrubbery. *She's no better off than them.* Like them, she lives in a world of glass, the glass of the omnipresent, omnipotent camera lens, of the media constantly monitoring, mirroring and manipulating her.

They pass the ice sculpture and Tierney stares; the clear, calm eyes seem to be gazing at her, a single droplet of water, like a tear, trickling down the icy face.

Jake is still pulling her quickly through the gardens, grasping her arm so tightly she winces.

As they reach the lift, Tierney turns round.

Paradise is in chaos.

The hacks scuttle round like gleeful children allowed up past their bedtime. The guests stand in groups, whispering and muttering and giggling, shaking their heads in righteous anger at what Tierney has done. Barnaby and Julian flap around, trying desperately to calm everything down.

And as she watches, Tierney sees something which almost makes her laugh. Zoë is left alone for a moment, and two men are sidling up to her from opposite sides. Matt Lucas, offering her a drink as he slips his arm gently round her shoulders, and Damien, pressing his business card into her hand.

A group of reporters come charging through the gardens towards them, and Jake grabs Tierney's hand. 'I don't like this. We have to get you out of here.'

He pushes her into the lift ahead of him, then slams his fist into the lift console and the elevator jerks down to the ground floor. Dazed, Tierney stands silently, not even moving when the doors slide open. Again Jake grasps her arm, half pulling, half pushing her out into the street and over to his car. But even as they get in, the reporters are leaving a second lift, their faces triumphant as they spy the couple pulling away from the kerb.

'Fuck!' Jake scowls as the hacks jump into a small blue car parked nearby.

Tierney doesn't even understand what's happening. They've watched her being publicly humiliated – what more do they want?

Jake's car is a little red Mazda, and it's fast, but the journalists are still right behind them, and Tierney stares at them in the rearview mirror. There are three men, all in their thirties, their eyes too bright, their car practically touching Jake's, they're so close. The men are all looking at Tierney, and she can see their lips moving, can see them smirking.

As Jake turns into a busy main road, he accelerates, and Tierney feels her chest tightening, her breathing becoming shallow. Ahead of them the traffic lights are just turning amber. Jake speeds through them and Tierney winces as the seatbelt bites into her shoulder.

She looks in the rearview mirror again, her lips parting in a silent scream. Behind them the journalists are determined to run the lights too, but amber is already turning to red, and another car, pulling out of a side road, goes slamming into the hacks.

The hack driving the car slumps forward on to the steering wheel, and as Tierney stares, the car starts spinning around, like a toy vehicle about to fall off the edge of a table. The other two reporters fling their hands in front of their faces, one almost managing to reach forward and grab the wheel, when the car leaps forward and is impaled on the metal crash barrier separating the two lanes of traffic.

Jake's car skids to a stop as he pulls on to the hard shoulder. The entire road seems to shimmer for a moment as Tierney unclasps the seatbelt with shaking fingers and gets out. Vaguely she's aware of Jake punching numbers into his mobile. Everything is silent but for this weird, whimpering sound, and it's a few moments before she realises it's her, sobbing. People are running forward to the reporters' car, which is twisted out of shape, a deformed hunk of metal sort of hovering just above the ground, bodies slumped, motionless, inside.

Further down the road, another car of hacks which has been following brakes sharply, more men Tierney recognises from Bar Eden now clambering out, all clutching mobile phones and cameras. They see their colleagues, trapped inside the wreck, and they see Tierney, and for a few moments they're visibly torn between the two. Tierney feels sick.

'Get back in the car!' Jake glares at her.

'*What?* We have to go over there and help, what are you talk—'

'I said, get back in the car!' Jake gets hold of her and forces her back in the car. 'I've called for an ambulance. Now we have to get you out of here. You're white as a sheet, look like you're about to pass out!' Getting back in himself, he slams the door, and before Tierney can even speak, they're moving again.

He's right, she realises, looking in the mirror. She is deathly pale, and she feels dizzy, her brain grappling with the events of the last half-hour.

Then Jake covers her hand with his.

And now Tierney has another problem.

Because he makes her feel safe, and that's dangerous.

19

The Sweetest Taboo

Tierney felt like she was running an emotional marathon, only each time she neared the finishing line, someone moved it. Her feelings were bruised and sore, aching like over-worked muscles, and she knew she couldn't take much more.

Closing her eyes, she leaned back against the cool leather headrest, the events of the last hour unfolding before her in glaring, garish colour: the reporter's head, flopping forward on to the wheel; the car, squashed flat; Bar Eden, all those faces, looking at her in confusion, and then suspicion. Even if people didn't believe she'd betrayed Zoë, doubt had been planted. The mud would stick.

Beside her, Jake stared straight ahead, hands clenched round the steering wheel, not looking at her, even once. Did he too believe the worst?

That she couldn't bear.

Above all, she was confused. Why had Zoë suddenly re-appeared?

And why was the girl angry with *her*?

Jake fiddled with the radio, trying to find a news

programme and get an update on the journalists' condition, but there was nothing, not yet. He focused on driving, scared by the intensity of his own responses. Seeing Tierney at the launch, standing there, so alone and helpless while chaos erupted around her, he'd felt something sort of *twist* inside. Taking her back to his flat was both the right and the wrong thing to do: it was right to look out for a friend; it was wrong to do so when he ached to put his arms round her, when he dreamed of kissing her, when he longed to . . . Swiftly Jake put the brakes on the slippery slope down which his imagination was careering. He had no right to think these things, to think about doing these things, with the girl sitting beside him. And no choice either.

'Tierney, we need to stop off at your flat. I'll dash in and grab some of your clothes. Okay?'

She nodded miserably, then slumped down in the seat, covering her face with her hands. 'Jake, those hacks . . . you don't think they're . . . I mean, they will be all right . . . ?'

'I don't know. I hope so. There'll be something on the news tonight, I'm sure of it.'

Half an hour later, Tierney's clothes collected, the car slid into a parking space outside Jake's house, and they sat there, looking straight ahead, both feeling awkward.

'I should go to a hotel.' Tierney spoke firmly.

'What, so someone who works there can tip off the press?' Jake looked at her earnestly. 'Look, it's fine. Stay here. I know how to handle the media, and when things have calmed down, you can go home. I really don't think you should be alone.'

'But I really thi—'

'Shut up!!!' Jake hit the steering wheel. His rugged face was stern, but she could see concern glinting in those grey eyes. 'Now, this is how it's going to be . . .'

Tierney listened while he outlined his plan for the next day, and soon she realised it made sense.

'Right, then.' Jake unfastened his seatbelt and turned the engine off. 'We're going inside, where you, young lady, are going to have a nice hot bath and relax.'

With that, he jumped out of the car, slamming the door firmly. This was how to play it – be a bossy older brother. Keep it bright and brisk and everything would be fine. In three weeks he'd be back in the States; all he had to do was play it cool until then, be a shoulder to cry on while Tierney needed one, no more and no less. Problem solved, Jake concluded, opening the front door and giving her a quick guided tour of the house.

'There are clean towels in the bathroom. I'm going to fix some food, should be ready in about an hour, okay?'

Outside the bathroom she paused, looking at him gravely for a moment before closing the door quietly. As Jake felt his imagination straining at the leash again, he prayed his will-power was in better shape.

*

Turning on the hot tap, Tierney poured in some ylang-ylang oil then lay back in the rapidly filling bath, the tiny bubbles fizzing and foaming like champagne over her skin. She sighed as the warm water gently licked her body, trickling over her thighs, tendrils of blonde hair snaking over her breasts and shoulders, clinging to her skin.

Her eyes felt heavy and, letting them close, she tipped her head back so her body was stretched taut in the bath, then relaxed again, sinking down, the waves lapping gently against her stomach, sliding over her hips. Lifting her hand, Tierney sprinkled water over her face; it felt like hot lips on her eyelids and cheeks, and a vivid image of Jake's mouth on hers made her blush; quickly, she sat up, shaking her head to clear it.

She was over-stressed, that was it. That was all.

With a sudden flare of anger, she realised that if she'd followed her intuition and refused to take part in the Eve's Brew ad campaign, none of this would have happened. But, as usual, she'd allowed herself to be swayed by what others wanted.

Feeling chilly, she lay back in the water again, and tried to cry, for if only she could release this anguish, maybe she'd feel better.

But nothing.

Two years with no tears, and still, nothing. Just this godawful restlessness now building, and a strange, steely anger flickering within her. She frowned; it was more than anger, it was *defiance*.

Tierney stared into space.

Pleasing others didn't work, did it?

Now it was time to please herself.

*

Jake wasn't the most domesticated of men, but he knew how to cook a few basic things. Pasta seemed like a safe bet, but would Tierney like that? Most of the women he knew back home were on bizarre diets precluding anything with wheat, sugar, flour, and a hundred other foods, so in the end Jake decided simply to ask.

Outside the bathroom he paused, ready to knock and call

out, when suddenly the door opened and there she stood, a white towel wrapped around her, fair hair pulled up in a mass of glistening ringlets and spirals.

Jake tried to tear his gaze away. 'Just wondered if you were hungry.'

'Always . . .' Tierney smiled. 'I'll throw on some clothes and come help you.'

'No need,' he said quickly, 'everything's under control.' He watched as she padded down the hall to the spare room. 'Is pasta all right with you?'

'Yeah, fine.' She vanished through the door and Jake cursed.

Yeah, sure everything was under control.

Everything but him.

*

In the spare room, Tierney opened her case and rummaged through the clothes inside, choosing a pair of snug blue jeans and a cream-coloured sweater with a low, rounded neckline. She couldn't face putting on make-up, so added a quick coat of clear lip-gloss, and apart from that left her face bare, her hair loose and tumbling over her shoulders.

'So what needs doing?' She wandered into the spacious kitchen to find Jake busy at the cooker.

He turned to greet her, eyes widening in appreciation. 'You look nice.'

'Thanks.' She watched as he stirred a large saucepan of spaghetti sauce.

'Want to try it, tell me if it needs anything?' he offered.

'Sure.' Tierney put her hand lightly on his to steady the spoon as she leaned forward.

'Ouch!' Jake yanked his wrist back – she'd given him an electric shock.

She blushed. 'It must have been the static from this jumper or something. Sorry.'

'I've heard of sparks flying, but this is ridiculous!' Jake's laugh was strained.

'Yeah, well, you know me, such a livewire . . .' Tierney countered weakly, and they both started doing other things.

I've got it bad . . . Jake busied himself putting plates out.

I'm in trouble . . . Tierney took the wine out of the fridge.

They began discussing the weather.

*

Despite Jake's worry, the dinner was delicious, though they were both too shaken to eat much. Several times Jake tried to talk about what had happened that night, but Tierney cut him off, and it was clear she was coping by blocking out her own feelings.

As they started on dessert, she glanced over at a picture of Lisa. 'How are the wedding plans coming along?'

Jake tipped his glass of wine to one side, frowning. 'I'm not sure. We . . . haven't spoken for a few days.' He looked up again. 'What sort of wedding do you want?'

Tierney thought for a moment, one elbow resting comfortably on the table. 'Me and my man on a beach somewhere hot! I told my parents when I was eleven I'd probably elope.' She shrugged. 'Everyone thought I'd grow out of the idea.'

'But you didn't?'

'No chance! The idea of a big, conventional wedding, all that fuss and planning and hassle . . . *ugh*!' She grimaced, wriggling around, and Jake chuckled. 'So what sort of day are you and Lisa planning?' Tierney looked at the photo again.

His grin was wry. 'A big conventional wedding!'

'Oh God, I'm sorry, I didn't mean . . .' She looked at him ruefully.

'Forget it. I agree with you. I could happily do without the fuss, but Lisa, well, she's more . . . traditional.'

Tierney frowned at the way his voice dipped suddenly, and Jake decided he should change the subject.

Getting up and starting to clear away the plates, he grinned. 'I'll tell you one thing I've become addicted to.'

'What?' Tierney followed him into the brightly lit kitchen.

'*EastEnders* – I've even taped tonight's episode! Can you believe it?' His face was so sheepish she giggled.

'Yes, because so have I!' Tierney smiled at him as they went into the living room and sat down on the sofa.

As she leaned forward to pick up the paper, Tierney's mane of fair hair swung forward, brushing lightly against Jake's shoulder. Instantly he tensed; it was as if he could feel it through his clothes; right there, soft and silky against his skin. He shifted in his seat, relieved when a moment later she sat back again.

While he rewound the video, Jake flicked to a news programme. Sure enough, there was a bulletin about the car crash, and they both sat very still, listening as the men's conditions were described as 'serious but stable'.

'Whatever *that* means . . .' muttered Jake, glancing at Tierney to find her staring forlornly into space. Quickly, he hit the remote control.

'Tierney, what happened to those reporters wasn't your

fault. And as for all that crap Zoë was coming out with, people will see it for what it is.' He placed a hand gently on her shoulder to comfort her and reinforce his words. 'You do know that, right?'

She attempted a small, plucky smile which almost broke his heart. 'I still feel guilty, though. I should have *known* something was wrong when Barnaby and Julian said Zoë had done a runner – she wouldn't have! I should have done more to try to find her! Why didn't I think about contacting The Big Issue?'

Her voice was brimming with bitterness as she drew her knees up to her chest and sat there hugging them tightly, looking like a child who had just woken from a nightmare.

'You're wrong.' Jake was adamant. 'You shouldn't beat yourself up over this. How were you to know they'd pull a stunt like that? You trusted them. They're the ones who should be feeling bad, not you!' He gave her a stern look. 'And I know you feel bad about Zoë, but don't. I have a feeling after tonight, her luck's going to change. She'll get snapped up by a modelling agency, you'll see. And Tierney, that's because of you, because you're the one who found her in the first place!'

Jake watched her anxiously as she sat there, huddled in the corner of the sofa, eyes downcast. She looked so fragile it broke his heart, and he couldn't help it, his hand just seemed to move of its own volition as, reaching out, he gently traced the delicate curve of her cheek.

Tierney sat there, scared to move, scared to chase away the moment. A moment, she realised now, they'd been slip-sliding their way into. A moment which had always been there, waiting for them to find it.

And again she could feel it, that rebellious little ache, starting up again as they sat there staring at each other. Now the restlessness was building again. Lust was tugging at her groin, there was a soft fluttering in her stomach. Tierney felt her eyelids grow heavy, felt her lips parting, and she saw Jake notice, his eyes darkening.

He snatched his hand back, noting the steady look in Tierney's eyes; she'd felt it too and she wasn't troubled, wasn't even surprised. Jake frowned; if he was crossing a line, then she was letting him. If he didn't get away from her now, he wouldn't be able to stop what they both knew was about to happen.

'I'm tired.' He got up and walked towards the kitchen. 'Think I'll go to bed. Do you need anything?'

She just looked at him. Jake met her stare; he wasn't going to insult her with a casual smile or superficial joke as though things were fine.

Things were *not* fine.

Things were not going to *be* fine.

'I'll see you in the morning.' Turning to leave the room, Jake tried not to look at the photograph of Lisa which stood there like an accusation over how he was feeling, and what, or rather who, he was wanting.

For a few minutes, Tierney sat on the sofa, confused. He was engaged. If he was the sort of man who would cheat, she didn't want him. She sighed. There it was again, that little thread of defiance, now circling her feelings, tightening around them, squeezing out all the *niceness*. She thumped a cushion.

Back in the spare bedroom she felt hot, ripping her top

and bra off and throwing on a thin white cotton T-shirt over her jeans. Kneeling on the bed, Tierney looked at the wall separating her from Jake. Now it felt like all the air was solidifying into a wall of heat settling over her as she lay on her back and stared at the ceiling.

She felt unbearably, unbelievably *charged*. Her body seemed full of static and light, as though she'd been swimming through pure electricity, and again, Tierney could feel the tears she couldn't cry hardening into this strange, seductive anger which was surely leading her astray.

She decided to go and get a drink.

On her way out of the room she slammed the door.

*

Jake tossed off his bedsheets and sat up, staring into the darkness. That was Tierney's door opening and then closing. Being with her this evening, he'd noticed something: when she was unhappy, so was he; he felt what she did, in some weird, wonderful kind of instant empathy. He frowned; when Lisa was troubled over something, he'd sit and talk it through with her. Apply logic and reason. Fix it. It was a purely intellectual response. He'd never even known the difference, until now.

And suddenly Jake laughed in delight – for the first time in *for ever*, he wasn't feeling that restlessness. The question he'd been asking himself all that time back in New York about what was missing; here in the room next to his, was the answer.

Tierney.

He'd missed her before he even knew her.

Sipping a glass of water, Tierney stared out of the kitchen window at the night sky, watching the light covering of mist suspended in the darkness like a shimmering cobweb.

'Can't sleep either?'

Slowly she turned. Jake walked into the room, fair hair dishevelled, wearing only a pair of black boxer shorts. Tierney smiled. 'I was thirsty.'

He joined her at the sink, trying not to stare at the T-shirt clinging to her full, high breasts, the way her dark nipples were pressing against the flimsy material. When he finally dragged his gaze back to her face again she was watching him.

'Sorry,' he muttered.

'Are you?' she asked lightly.

Jake's face tightened. 'No.'

She was still staring at him, and seeing the provocative curve of her lips, Jake tried to break the eye contact. 'Stop looking at me like that!' he flung at her.

Tierney raised an eyebrow. 'Like what?'

'You know.' Jake glared.

She put down the glass of water. 'Do I . . . ?'

'Oh, I think so . . .' Jake tensed as Tierney walked up to him, standing so close they were almost touching, looking at him through long, lush eyelashes, her voice soft.

'Why don't you tell me . . .'

'Keep this up and I'll do more than that!'

Tierney pouted. 'Promises, promises . . .'

And Jake's willpower fled.

Angrily, he pushed her back against the wall, his arms sliding around her slender waist, then she was reaching up, pulling his head down and kissing him even more intensely than he'd dreamed of. He slipped a hand up under the T-shirt, cupping her breasts, circling her hardening nipples with his thumb.

Tierney was pressing herself against him, her tongue exploring his mouth with such urgency Jake felt himself losing control, twining his hands through her long hair, grasping it tightly, tilting her head back and kissing her roughly as she clung to him, her hands slipping around and inside his boxer shorts.

Hating himself, Jake pushed her back roughly against the cupboard door again, snapping open the buttons of her jeans and pulling them down quickly, followed by the lacy wisp of her knickers. He ran a hand over the taut plane of her stomach, feeling her skin fluttering softly under his fingers. Tierney watched him silently, her face flushed, eyes dark gashes under heavy lids and the ebony curtain of her lashes.

Deftly Jake lifted her T-shirt, and she shrugged it off. As he stared, the chocolate-brown nipples hardened, and slowly, he traced the delicate line of her throat, feeling her pulse trembling at the base of her neck. Eyes still locked on hers, he reached out, taking one breast in his hand and leaning forward to kiss it, feeling the nipple stiffening even more as his tongue flicked over it, encircling it as Tierney's back arched, her eyes closing as he slipped his fingers between her legs, feeling them slicken as he touched her.

Fingers lingering over the smooth curve of her hip, Jake ran his hand over the high, tight buttocks before removing his boxer shorts and sliding into her, feeling her warm and slippery around him, heard her sharp intake of breath.

'More?' he teased.

Eyes still closed, she murmured something.

He smiled and guided himself in further, started fucking her slowly until she was moaning.

Jake started thrusting harder and Tierney writhed against the wall, crying out; he plunged deeper into her, then teased her, withdrawing slightly, slowing his rhythm, placing a hand over the flat of her stomach and feeling heat rippling under his touch again.

Her eyes were so dark they were almost black, her lips swollen, and she cried out again as Jake thrust deeper into her, faster and harder and *harder*, thrusting more violently until they were almost there, at heaven's edge.

She was moving with him, and then they both felt it, the air shattering around them like glass, the blood tearing through their veins, a great crashing tidal wave of bliss as he came inside her and Tierney shuddered, collapsing against him.

For a moment they stayed like that, then Tierney raised her head, eyes flitting over him as she gave him a cheeky grin. 'Reckon I've found the Next Big Thing . . .'

They never made it to the bedroom.

*

Guilt lunged at her like a punch to the stomach, and Tierney awoke a few hours later with a start, dazed, and disorientated in the dark. They'd ended up on the sofa; Jake was asleep beside her, his arm round her, a slight smile on his face. Sliding out of his embrace, Tierney padded back into the adjoining kitchen, quickly scooping up her clothes and putting them on before curling up in one of the chairs, shivering.

What in God's name had got *into* her?

You really need ***to ask****?* snapped her conscience, and Tierney covered her face with her hands, horrified by what she'd allowed, what she'd *encouraged* to happen.

She'd had sex with *Jake*.

Frantic, fierce, fantastic sex.

With *Jake.*

'*What's* happening *to me?*' Tierney whispered. In the space of one night, she'd become public enemy number one, and slept with a man she should have run a million miles from. Her body felt bloated with shame. Usually guilt lay lightly on the surface of her emotions, like oil floating on water, so careful was Tierney with other people's feelings. Oh, but she was feeling it now all right, and it was horrible, like all the light and life were leeching out of her, like she was filling up with night. Tierney pictured it, gallons of black, slimy, sticky guilt flowing through her system, clogging up her heart like emotional sewage. Maybe one day it would all come gushing out and choke her.

Now Tierney groaned; she'd been a fool, thinking she could enjoy the sex and not care about the consequences.

What if the press got hold of this story?

By tomorrow morning they'd surely be staking out Jake's house. One photograph of her here, that was all it would take; they'd *crucify* her. It would be the final nail in the coffin that was her career.

If the media ever got hold of this, Tierney knew she'd never be able to show her face in public again. And God only knew what it would do to Jake and his fiancée.

She couldn't let that happen.

Especially because to Jake she was probably just a last-minute fling before he walked down that aisle. Tierney winced. Uncurling from the chair, she headed for the spare bedroom again, swiftly repacking her tiny case and scribbling a frantic note which she left on the pillow beside Jake. Then she looked at him for a long moment before slipping out of the front door.

Outside she doesn't pause, just walks quickly, gripping her little case, staring straight ahead, fighting the urge to break into a run. Lately she can't shake this feeling, like something is gaining on her, something she can't escape.

She feels *hunted.*

Stopping in the middle of the street, Tierney realises something. She doesn't want to be the Coolest Girl in the Country, not any more. Not for another day, minute, or second. What she wants is the right to make mistakes, to have privacy. Not be judged, or copied, or watched.

Right now, being the Next Big Thing is the *last* thing she needs.

*

Jake was tired of Tierney using his heart for a punchbag. Sitting on the bed in the darkness, trying to work out how long ago she'd left, he stared at her hastily scribbled note, feeling sick with hurt. She was gone. Oh, she had her reasons, couldn't cope with what the press would say, and so on. But Jake could read between the lines: if she cared enough, she wouldn't give a shit about anything else. If she cared enough, she'd still be here.

Crumpling up the note, he lobbed it into the bin. This was obviously just a one-night stand for Tierney, and she hadn't wanted to hang around. She just wanted to get on with her life, and who was he to stop her?

For him it was different, though: one night with her, and everything that had gone before seemed like a game, one-dimensional. Lacking.

Jake walked over to the window, peering out into the darkness. This was it. The End. She didn't want him. Now he just had to get through the next few weeks before he could go home. Jake lay on his bed, staring at the ceiling for the rest of the night, telling himself he'd get over her.

One day.

20

Backlash

Would You Adam & Eve It?

Tierney Turns Out To Be Snake In The Grass

Columnist and Eve's Brew model Tierney Marshall remains in hiding after revelations that she stole the role of Eve from a homeless teenager. Guests at the beer's launch were shocked to learn that the Cool Hunter originally offered the job to 18-year-old Zoë Mason, after seeing her selling the Big Issue.

But once Ms Marshall achieved fame for tackling the West End Rapist, she persuaded the company behind the beer to use her instead for their high-profile campaign. This has led to numerous job offers for Ms Marshall, including a chance to present The Big Breakfast.

Zoë Mason said, 'One minute she was promising me the world, the next I was out in the cold. When I found out she was taking over the role, I was gutted'.

Following her surprise appearance at the Eve's Brew launch, Zoë Mason has been approached by Storm model agency and is now being tipped as the Next Big Thing on the catwalk.

> Tabloids are linking her name with the creative director of Prophets Inc., 28-year-old Matt Lucas, after the pair were seen leaving the launch party together. Mr Lucas was recently featured in Cosmopolitan magazine as one of London's twenty-five most eligible bachelors.
>
> Ms Marshall was unavailable for comment.

'Like hell I was!' Tierney slammed the paper down, knocking over a cup of tea and cursing. She'd spoken to the journalist for a good twenty minutes on the phone, but, as usual, her comments had been dropped. It made for better copy if she was the bad girl.

Since last week's fiasco at Bar Eden, she'd barricaded herself in her flat, trying to ignore the journalists hanging around outside hoping for a photograph or interview. Jake, Liz and other friends had phoned constantly, but she let the answer machine pick up their calls, too miserable and embarrassed to face anyone. The three reporters involved in the car crash were still on the critical list, and Tierney couldn't erase their petrified faces from her mind. She felt responsible, and couldn't convince herself otherwise.

And as she'd predicted, no one was interested in the truth about how she'd ended up as Eve. The truth? One big yawn. *Boring!* The story was just too juicy, and the papers were having a field day, every headline more crass than the last. Every tabloid and several broadsheets carried pictures from Bar Eden of Zoë and Tierney: two gorgeous girls glaring at each other.

'THE HOMELESS AND THE HEARTLESS', ran one caption.

'BLONDE AMBITION GONE BERSERK', declared another.

The *Sunday Splash*, owned by Richard Midas of all people, had run pictures of Tierney under the caption 'THE THREE FACES OF EVE'. The first showed her with an arm round Lucy Midas; the second was one of the more risqué men's magazine covers, and the third featured her slapping Vanita.

The article accused Tierney of conning the public and manipulating the media, which was so absurd it almost made her laugh. But it also called her 'volatile, violent, and vapid', which didn't.

Another down-market tabloid, again from the Midas stable, had shown a picture which caught Tierney glaring at Zoë, just after the teenager had called her a bitch. Above Tierney's picture the caption read: 'FROM COOLEST TO CRUELLEST – TIERNEY SHOWS HER TRUE COLOURS'.

Barnaby and Julian moved quickly, swearing that Tierney had persuaded them Zoë was unreliable and would do a runner, and that she herself was a better bet for the ad campaign. Reading their account of things sent Tierney into a tailspin; at one point, she smashed seven plates in an effort to get the rage out her system. It helped for about five seconds. The entire country was convinced she was a ruthless, wily bimbo; everyone thought they knew her, and it was the strangest feeling.

Controversy was clearly cool, however, since Eve's Brew was selling out. Barnaby and Julian were now planning a new product, this time a soft drink for the teenage market, and they wanted Zoë for the ad campaign. She'd also taken over the role of Eve, and new posters already featured her instead of Tierney.

She couldn't help smiling at the irony: everything was

playing out the way she'd predicted when she first found the teenager.

The only detail she hadn't foreseen was herself being an outcast.

Damien had called urgent meetings with all of Tierney's sponsors, at which he'd explained the situation so lucidly even she was impressed. Still several companies had pulled out, but ***Sorted!*** showed their support by promptly booking Tierney for the following month's cover. *Dado*, however, had temporarily suspended Tierney's column.

'You do understand, don't you, precious?' Cleopatra had phoned the day after the launch. 'It's just until, well, until things have calmed down a bit . . .'

'I understand perfectly,' Tierney said quietly.

Nothing was cool for ever.

Including her.

The job offers had all been withdrawn, such was the public anger towards her. At Prophets Inc., a few clients stuck by her, but Joel agreed she should take some time off, sort her head out. Tierney caught the relief in his voice when she said she'd need a month or more. She'd become a liability.

Now, hearing the phone ring, she snatched it up impatiently. 'Yes?'

'Have you seen today's papers?' Damien demanded.

'I've just started going through them, it's mostly the same stuff as yest—'

'You don't know what I'm talking about, do you, Tierney?'

'Apparently not.'

'Got the *Sunday Splash* there?'

'Hang on . . . should have . . .'

Perplexed, she sat cross-legged on the floor, flicking through the stack of newspapers she'd had delivered that morning.

'Got it!' She pulled it out from the bottom of the pile, glancing at the front page. Then she did a double-take, staring at the photograph and the teaser:

The Breast Is Yet To Come . . .
See p.3 for more

Beneath was a picture of Tierney.

Topless.

The image had been lifted from the internet and was a bit grainy, but everyone would recognise her. Inside the paper were more pictures, all showing her with breasts thrust forward, lips curving in a sexy smile, blonde hair tousled. No coercion or shyness, just a girl looking confident and in control.

Suddenly Tierney could have sworn she heard a gun firing nearby – must be the sound of her credibility being shot to pieces.

'Well?' Damien was impatient.

Mortified, Tierney let the paper slip from her trembling fingers. 'It was at the first ***Sorted!*** shoot! Alex, the photographer, wanted to take just a few topless shots and I let him! But he seemed so *nice*! I can't believe he'd *do* this!'

'He didn't. It was someone in the lab where he sent them to be processed, they recognised you, probably got a small fortune for the pictures. Happens all the time.'

Tierney groaned. This would ruin her. Damien had built her reputation partly on her anti-nudity stance and the fact that she was different; these pictures made her look like a liar and a hypocrite. They made her look cynical.

Suddenly she realised her agent was *laughing*.

'What in God's name's so funny?' She stared at the photos of herself, cursing her own naiveté.

'This is! We needed something to distract people from the whole Zoë débâcle, and this is it! It's *fab*!'

'Damien, you seem to forget: I'm supposed to be the only media babe who *doesn't* strip!'

'For money. You don't strip for money. Which is why we say that we decided to stick your photos on the internet, where everybody can enjoy them for free. You, my dear, turned down six-figure offers from *Playboy* and the *Sun*, in favour of the Web. That's our story.'

'But—'

'But nothing. We're going to use these topless shots as a gimmick – to illustrate that *you have nothing to hide – literally*! These pics are a statement that you're prepared to reveal all, about yourself, about what happened with Zoë, *everything*! I've already set up interviews with the *Mail*, *Mirror* and *Guardian* for the day after tomorrow. If I'm right, these photos could turn out to be the best thing that ever happened to you!'

'If . . .' Tierney pointed out, morosely.

Damien laughed again. 'Like I'm ever wrong!'

'But what's the point in me doing interviews when everyone believes Zoë?' Tierney was becoming frustrated.

'Because we're going to get her to change her story,' Damien replied calmly. 'Now look, I'm coming over, be with you in half an hour. And don't fret, there's a full moon in Aries this week!'

'Oh, well, no need to worry, then!' Tierney shot back dryly, but he'd already gone.

For a few moments she stood there, bemused. Things were only as real as the spin you could put on them. Nothing, it seemed, was inherently good or bad, right or wrong. Shaking her head to try and clear it, she resisted the urge to have a stiff drink.

*

When the doorbell rang, she didn't bother with the intercom, just buzzing Damien up. She quickly ran a brush through her unruly fair hair and slipped on a pair of shoes, but when she threw open the door, Tierney found Jake, Liz and Carin standing outside, all wearing sheepish smiles.

Carin held up a newspaper. 'We were worried about you.' Giving Tierney a stern look, she peered round the door. 'Aren't you going to invite us in, then?'

Tierney shrugged and moved back, refusing to meet Jake's eyes when he walked past. He'd called constantly since the launch, and left countless messages. Each time, Tierney just stared at the phone, longing to just pick it up and speak to him, never quite managing.

'So . . .' Carin waved a copy of the *Splash* in her friend's face. '*Nice* pics, Tier!'

Liz hugged Tierney. 'I've been so worried! Why haven't you been answering your phone, you daft mare?'

'Sorry. I wasn't in the mood for speaking to people.'

'We're not "people". We're friends.' Carin gave her a pointed look, a slight query in her tone, and Tierney felt a lump forming in her throat, wishing yet again she could cry. Maybe it was just as well she couldn't, for the way she was feeling this week, if she started, she might never stop.

Jake cleared his throat. 'I've been talking to Damien.'

'How nice for you,' Tierney muttered, tidying up the pile of papers, still not looking at him. Carin and Liz exchanged a look, then went over to the other side of the room, sitting down on the sofa and flicking through magazines.

Jake crouched down on the floor next to Tierney. 'Why are you being like this?'

'Like what?'

'So . . . cold.'

Tierney raised an eyebrow in mock surprise. 'Gee, I wonder!' Her voice shook. 'You've obviously forgotten the other night. Wish I could.'

'I've been calling you non-stop for a week!' Jake reminded her angrily. 'You're the one who refused to pick the phone up!'

'Good morning, mortals!' Damien swept into the room, Honey Trapp trotting along beside him. 'Tierney, be an angel, fix some drinks. I'm parched.'

Giving Jake a bitter look, Tierney disappeared into the kitchen with Liz.

After they'd all sat around making small talk for a few minutes, Damien turned to Tierney. 'Okay, here's the thing. This story about what you "did" to Zoë is just going to run and run. It's tabloid heaven, and they're not going to let it go. There's only one person who can set the record straight, and that's Zoë herself.'

Tierney scowled. 'Yeah, right, like she's really going to do that! She hates my guts!'

'Only because Barnaby and Julian have filled her head with all this rubbish. Poor kid doesn't know whether she's coming or going. She needed someone to blame when it all went wrong and you were the obvious person. You must speak to her face to face, make her understand that you're both victims in all this. We think going through Matt Lucas is your best bet, since those two are pretty tight. Jake's going to call him now, and try to set it up.'

The thought of going to Matt for anything made Tierney feel queasy.

'Come on, Tier!' Liz guessed the reason for her friend's hesitation. 'The guy owes you one.'

'I agree.' Jake looked sternly at Tierney. 'Don't worry, I know the whole story. I made Liz tell me; don't be angry with her. She's been worried sick about you.'

Tierney hugged her. 'I'm sorry, Lizzy. I haven't been much of a friend.'

'True. You've been pretty crap, actually.' Liz grinned. 'But I'll forgive you. Only if you agree to what Damien and Jake are suggesting, though.'

Tierney fidgeted. Matt was nothing to her now, and it was true, he did owe her. And she'd love the chance to see Zoë and set the record straight. Besides, what did she have to lose? Finally she looked up, her smile subdued. 'Okay. Let's do it.'

Damien clapped his hands. 'Excellent! Knew you'd see reason. Now, I've been thinking about these topless shots. What we have to do is tackle it head on. You have to show *real* front!' He cackled. 'Oh, but you already have!'

As Tierney glowered, Damien continued laughing merrily while Jake and the others exchanged uneasy looks.

The agent got up and began pacing. 'What we'll do is brazen it out. Make it a statement about you baring all. We'll whack up *huge* pictures of you, topless, in all the men's mags – that'll take the sting out of these tabloid photos and make it look as if you're in control.'

He grinned. 'Now for the really good news . . . It was difficult, given what's going on, and I've had to call in a few favours, but' – Damien looked modest – 'I've managed to get you a new sponsorship with the trendiest bra company on the market – Treasure Chest!'

'"With a price so low you don't have to dig deep in your pocket . . ."' The girls recited the slogan in unison.

Damien was practically skipping round the room now, euphoric at this latest scheme. 'It's *marvellous*!' He leaped over the coffee table. 'I love this!'

'I hate it!' With rising panic, Tierney noted the manic light in his eyes. 'You *are* joking?'

'Not at all! It's perfect!'

She shook her head. 'No way. I'm not doing it.'

Damien gave her a wounded look. 'Come on, you've already made one *boob* by posing for the photos – don't make another one and turn this down!' He screeched with mirth at his own joke while Honey, Jake, Carin and Liz watched nervously.

'I said no.' Tierney's voice was ominously quiet.

Damien was carried away with visions of her being the Next Big Thing in Bras, however. 'I *insist* you think about it!'

A glint had entered Tierney's eyes. *'I said no . . .'*

'Now now, I can see you're getting tetchy – let's not have a bust-up! Get it? *Bust*-up?' He wiped tears of laughter away. 'Oh, this is *killing* me!'

'And if it doesn't, I will . . .' she snapped.

'This deal could be good for you. Give your career a real *lift*!'

Damien collapsed into a chair, howling with hysteria.

Steam started rising from Tierney's head. Her friends were now trying to edge out of the room without being noticed.

Damien, however, was still oblivious. 'Look, I know all this bad publicity's getting on your tits—'

'*That's* it!!!' Tierney jumped up, eyes enormous in her pale face, mouth quivering. 'Now listen to me, you flaming *nutter* – I am not doing any bra sponsorship! *I am not doing any sponsorship, ever again!*'

Damien's smile was complacent. 'You don't mean that, you're just upset – you *can't* mean that . . .'

'I bloody well do!' Tierney was in full flow now. 'You're *mad*!!! Thanks to you, I live with a robot who's trying to maim me and a toilet which talks to me – *in Japanese*! You made me wear clothes that could have either killed me or got me arrested! And let's not forget the raving Russian you brought to my party and who gave us all alcohol poisoning! And now *this*? Well, forget it! I'm tired of it all! I'm tired of *you . . .*'

The silence that followed was painful.

'But I . . .' Damien's voice faltered. '*I* made you what you are today . . .'

'Yes – and look at me!' Tierney screamed. 'I never wanted to do Eve's Brew in the first place, but would you listen? No, you were too busy with your crackpot schemes! I never wanted to write for *Dado*, but did *you* care? No, you were too busy with your precious sodding sponsorships! You've turned me into a *joke* . . .'

Damien's smile was nervy. 'That'll die down, I told you. The public have a short memory. They'll forget—'

'But I won't!' Tierney yelled, blue eyes flashing with fury.

'If you'd stop being so stubborn and just listen to me about this bra deal—'

Tierney covered her ears, blocking out his words. 'That's *it*!' She marched over to the door and threw it open. '**YOU'RE FIRED!!!**'

No one knew where to look.

Damien's face was white as he stared at Tierney in disbelief, before muttering something about 'bloody Pisceans' and storming out. Honey Trapp shot Tierney a reproachful little look and hurried after him.

Tierney turned to her friends. 'And you can all fuck off as well! Today's entertainment is *over* . . .'

She stormed out of the room, and a few seconds later they heard her bedroom door slam shut.

21

Girl Talk

Tierney's Tantrum, as it became known, was out of character, and everyone knew it.

Her friends started to worry when, the next day, she changed her answer-machine message to 'I'm not coming to the phone so go away'. It was crystal clear from her tone that she meant it. She ignored their calls, and as far as anyone knew, the only contact she had with the outside world was when she snatched the papers from the postman each morning.

The press soon learned she and Damien had parted ways. The pundits pounced, filling countless columns with stories of how the most high-profile agent had lost his most high-profile client. Damien issued a statement citing 'artistic differences' as being behind the split, and the reporters gleefully filled in the blanks.

Damien fired Tierney because she was the wrong star sign and he was an eccentric.

Tierney fired Damien because she'd been poached by Matthew Freud.

Damien wanted to represent Zoë, and Tierney had forced him to choose.

Tierney was having a nervous breakdown because of what happened at Bar Eden.

She read the stories wearily. Then the *Sunday Splash* claimed she was simply following in the footsteps of numerous celebs and was tucked away at the Priory or somewhere similar, battling cocaine addiction/anorexia/depression. The press stopped hanging around outside Tierney's flat and started staking out every hospital and clinic in London, desperate for a glimpse of the Golden Girl gone wrong.

Scared of being recognised the second she stepped outside, Tierney became a prisoner in her own home, ordering everything she needed over the internet, spending her days drifting around the flat, peeping out of the window at the people scurrying past and leading normal lives. She felt like a shadow without a body. Each day she scanned the papers, telling herself not to bother but unable to resist. On reading the ridiculous rumours about herself she'd cringe; surely no one actually *believed* this garbage?

Just as the public had been fascinated by the Coolest Girl in the Country, they were even more obsessed with her fall from grace.

The topless shots were still on the internet, and Tierney was dismayed to discover that she now had her own website, where anyone who wanted to could see them. She was parodied in *Private Eye*, which started a spoof column, 'Adventures of an Überblonde'. The *Evening Standard* diary mentioned her frequently, and the *Sun* begged its readers to contact them with ideas as to what Tierney's next move should be.

'Abroad' was a popular one.

Finally Tierney picked up the phone after Liz left a message making it clear she was frantic with worry. Reluctantly, Tierney agreed that Liz could come round, and later that day, seeing her friend, Liz stared.

Tierney looked like an extra from *Day Of The Living Dead*. She wore no make-up, and her normally rosy cheeks were pale. Her once glossy hair was matted, plastered to her head in a mass of knots and tangles. She was dressed in faded black leggings with several holes in them, and a loose grey T-shirt. There were dark bruises beneath her eyes and her face was gaunt.

The flat was also in a terrible state. Chocolate wrappers littered every surface, spilling on to the floor. The curtains were still drawn, even though it was three in the afternoon. Dirty plates and cups were piled up in and around the sink, and the dishwasher was crammed full.

As they headed into the living room Liz tripped over something, and glancing down, saw Cy2's head, Tierney having dismantled the tiny robot, his various parts now scattered across the carpet.

Now Liz watched as her friend ripped open a family-sized packet of chocolate biscuits, smothered them with whipped cream, then practically swallowed them whole. 'Feeling peckish, are we?' she asked lightly.

'If you're going to hassle me, you can go away again.' Tierney rummaged around in the freezer for a tub of Häagen-Dazs.

'If I don't "hassle" you, who will?' Liz followed her into the kitchen as Tierney grabbed two bowls and spoons. 'Why don't you just use a ladle, you could get more on it?' she asked dryly as Tierney attacked the ice-cream.

'Why don't you leave me alone to enjoy this in peace?'

'Because I'm worried about you, we *all* are . . . Jake calls me every single day.'

'How sweet.' Tierney got up and switched on the kettle, hitting it so hard Liz winced.

'He calls to find out if I've heard from you, since you've ignored all his messages and refused to let him in when he's come round!' She shook her head. 'It's obvious the guy's crazy about you, what's your problem?'

Pouring half a packet of sugar into her mug, Tierney looked at her sadly. 'You don't know the half of it, Lizzy . . .'

Liz smiled placidly. 'But you get on so well!'

Tierney's stare was scathing. 'Like a house on fire – *most of the time I wish he was in one*!'

'Me thinks the lady doth protest too much!' quipped Liz. 'And eats too much as well! You really do look bloody awful, Tier!'

'So, thanks for coming round to cheer me up!' Tierney shot back sarcastically. 'Anyway, I've spent the last six months being obsessed with how I look. I deserve a break. And besides, maybe if I get really fat, no one will recognise me . . .' She continued stuffing her face while Liz watched helplessly.

'I know Jake would love to see you. He's going home soon, Tierney.' She saw something flicker in her friend's eyes. 'For crying out loud, I know you care about him! You can't just let him leave with things like this!'

'It's too late, don't you understand?' Tierney shook her

head, then poured out the story of what had been going on over the past few months: Jake's kissing her, all the tension, right up to and including the night of the launch.

Liz listened, sympathetically, relieved that Tierney was finally opening up again, and understanding her dilemma. 'I can't believe you just did a moonlight flit like that!' She was horrified when Tierney described how she'd bolted. 'My God, he must have thought you didn't give a damn!'

'What was I supposed to do, stay and enjoy a cosy little breakfast with the guy? Jesus, don't you get it? He's *engaged*!'

'All I see is that he can't win: if he'd rejected you, you'd be livid. Because he didn't, you're angry with him for cheating on his fiancée! Poor bloke's damned if he does, and damned if he doesn't!' She giggled. 'Talk about being stuck between a rock and a hard place . . .'

'How can you encourage me to fall for a guy who's getting married in, like, five minutes?' Tierney slammed her spoon down on the table.

'Because you're being too black and white – as usual! These things happen. He's engaged – not married! Technically, he's still *single*. Available. On For It. Up For Grabs.'

'I have no intention of grabbing Jake Sheridan! Or doing anything else with him, for that matter!' Tierney insisted.

'Been there, done that . . .' Liz grinned, then looked contrite. 'All I'm saying is that you're giving the guy mixed messages. Look, it's simple. Either you want him, or you don't. It's obvious he's got a thing for you.' She got up to make them each a mug of hot, sweet tea. 'Hey, isn't that . . .' She stared at the television screen.

Tierney frowned as Zoë appeared on the *Dick and Trudy*

Show. In silence the girls watched as, ignoring Dick's crass flirting, she discussed her modelling career and plans for the future.

'Oh please!' Liz grabbed the remote and hit the button. 'If I watch much more of that I'll *vomit*! It's so unfair: you're turning into a recluse while she's out there making millions! I could scream!'

Tierney shook her head. 'I'm happy for her. She deserves a break.'

In amazement Liz stared at her friend. 'We're talking about the girl who hijacked *your* night and who's been trashing you in the press ever since!'

Tierney shrugged. 'I can't be too angry with her. God knows she could do with a bit of luck.'

Liz nodded, her plump face subdued. 'I guess it's Barnaby and Julian who are really to blame.'

'And Vanita.'

Liz looked pained. 'Hate to tell you this, Tier, but she's taken over the Eve's Brew account, and she's working with Julian and Barnaby on launching that new soft drink, you know, the one using Zoë in the ad campaign.'

'Figures.' Tierney threw up her hands in despair. 'Fate usually waits until I'm down before kicking me in the teeth!'

There was silence for a few moments as Liz wondered how to broach the next subject. 'Look, I know you're not really in the mood for seeing people, but Honey and Carin are going out of their minds with worry. And I happen to think Damien was right: you should talk to Zoë, get this mess sorted out.' Seeing Tierney's stubborn expression, she spoke firmly. 'If not for your sake, then for Zoë's.'

'What's that supposed to mean?'

'It sounds like being let down by people is the story of her life. She thought you were her friend, she really trusted you, and now she's convinced you stabbed her in the back.' Liz leaned forward, willing Tierney to see reason. 'She deserves to know the truth. She *needs* to know! What, you want her to think the only people she can count on are Barnaby, Julian and Vanita?'

For the first time in weeks, Tierney thought about someone else. One of the reasons she was so depressed, she realised now, was because she hated Zoë thinking the worst of her, even if she thought it of herself for not looking harder for the girl when she'd first 'vanished'.

'But she'll never agree to see me!' Tierney wailed, reaching for some more ice-cream.

Impatiently, Liz pulled the tub away. 'She will if Honey and Matt ask her. She and Matt are pretty tight, and she got friendly with Honey through the celebrity network, same way you did, I guess. They're just waiting for the word from you. One phone call from me to Honey, today, and it's as good as done. We can all be there when you meet her, for moral support. You know, help break the tension. Come on, Tier, you can't carry on like this!'

Tierney bit her lip. 'I don't know . . .'

'Yes you do!' insisted Liz. 'You've still got a career, you just have to fight for it a bit! You're a brilliant Cool Hunter, your column was the best! I know it all got a bit out of hand, but that wasn't your fault! Second time round, you wouldn't make the same mistakes. I know you, Tierney, I know you want this . . .'

Finally, for the first time since she'd walked through the door, Liz saw a smile tugging at Tierney's wan face. Jumping up, she flew over to the phone, Tierney watching nervously while Liz held several hurried conversations before turning to her with a triumphant beam.

'It's all set. Honey and Zoë will be round in two hours, Carin's going to try and make it too. Right.' She surveyed the chaos surrounding them. 'That gives us just enough time to try and find the floor under all this crap! And Tierney, for God's sake, put on some make-up – you look *scary* . . .'

*

Two hours later, Tierney opened the door with a thudding heart. Instantly Honey Trapp threw her arms around her, shrieking. 'I've been so worried about you!' Beside her stood Carin and Zoë, face sullen, clearly there under duress.

'Er, Honey, Carin.' Liz grabbed their arms and began hauling them towards the kitchen. 'Why don't we go and fix some grub?'

Carin glanced back at Zoë and Tierney, standing glaring at each other. 'Now, girls' – she winked – 'remember the rules – slapping and hair-pulling is allowed, but *try* not to leave bruises . . .'

Tierney sat down, finding herself at a complete loss for words. There was so much she wanted to say, if only she could find the way in.

'I'm only here because Honey asked me as a favour,' Zoë announced, joining Tierney on the sofa and sitting as far away as possible. Because the plastic was so slippery, she found herself sliding back towards Tierney and ended up clinging on to the armrest for dear life in an effort to stay still. 'Honey seems to think I've got you all wrong.' Her voice was hard. 'Can't imagine why.'

'Zoë, I know how things look, but if you'll just hear me out—'

'Like you heard *me* out?' The younger girl turned on her furiously, and Tierney shrank back at the anger in her brilliant tawny eyes. 'I even came looking for you at your stupid office and you didn't have the decency to contact me! But then, why would you? *You were too busy nicking my fucking job!*'

Tierney was confused. 'You came to Prophets Inc.? No one told me . . .'

Rolling her eyes, Zoë sat back, one foot kicking the coffee table with a vengeance. 'I suppose now you're going to tell me Vanita didn't pass on my mess—'

'*Vanita?*' Tierney's eyes widened. 'You spoke to the Valkyrie?'

Zoë's lips twitched. 'The *what*?'

'It's a pet name,' Tierney explained, 'and Zoë, I *swear*, she didn't say a word about seeing you! All I knew was what Barnaby and Julian told me – that you'd done a runner! And idiot that I am, I believed them!'

'I thought that's what *you* told *them*, that I'd scarpered!' Bewildered, Zoë stared at her. 'Go on, then, I'm listening. Tell me what happened.'

Hesitantly, Tierney told her everything, starting with the day she tackled the West End Rapist, right through to being pressganged into doing the ad campaign.

Zoë sat quietly, her face darkening when she heard how Tierney had been manipulated. 'You know,' she looked thoughtful, 'Matt said that's probably how it happened. He said all along that you'd never cheat anyone out of a job. He's very fond of you.'

Tierney blushed. 'Yeah, well, there's a bit of water under the bridge . . .'

'I know. He told me everything.' Now it was Zoë's turn to colour. 'We're quite . . . close.'

Seeing the affection which warmed her gaze, Tierney smiled slightly. 'I'm glad. He deserves a second chance.'

Zoë's face was wry. 'So do you.' Suddenly she covered her face with her hands. 'Oh God, I feel *terrible*! All those awful things about you in the paper! You must hate me!'

'Don't be daft!' Tierney chuckled. 'I'm just glad you know what really happened!'

The two girls smiled shyly at each other.

'Doesn't seem right, though, does it?' Tierney mused. 'Barnaby and Julian lied to us both, and they're getting away with it . . .'

'Is it safe to come in?' Liz peered round the door, closely followed by Carin and Honey, all carrying soft drinks and plates of doorstep sandwiches.

Seeing that Tierney and Zoë looked relaxed, the other three grinned as they set down the food and curled up on the floor around the table.

'So,' Carin looked round expectantly, 'the question now is, how are we going to teach the Evil Ones a lesson?'

There was silence as the five girls sat munching and wracking their brains.

'Well, they always say fight fire with fire, don't they?' Tierney stretched out on the sofa, feeling better already. 'They lied to us both, and humiliated me in the press, but I don't see how we can do the same back . . .'

Zoë leaned forward. 'What we have to do is hit them where it hurts! And you know what they care about most?' She thumped the table, making everyone jump. '*Money!*'

A wisp of conversation floated through Tierney's mind as she recalled something Honey had once said about wanting to put money into something meaningful. She frowned as an idea began to take shape. 'How about this . . .' Hesitantly she outlined the idea, and the others grinned.

'I like it.' Carin nodded slowly. 'But it's not enough, not on its own. Even if we leak it to the press, it's still not . . . I don't know . . .'

Zoë let out a scream of excitement. 'We can go one better – we can do it *live*! Barnaby, Julian, Vanita and I are appearing on the last episode of *The Next Big Thing*, next week! It's perfect!'

Tierney nodded. 'As long as you realise, after this, they'll never work with you again, and I doubt they'll want you fronting their ad campaign.'

'Fine by me!' Zoë shrugged. 'I've got enough modelling work to last me for ages. Tell me exactly what you want me to do.'

'You'll need Jake's help,' pointed out Liz, glancing at Tierney anxiously.

'I'll talk to him.' Honey squeezed her hand and Tierney smiled gratefully. She couldn't handle that, not right now.

For the next hour they went over the plan, everyone chiming in with suggestions.

Finally, Tierney sat back and looked at her friends. 'It's good. If it works, we've got them.'

'No reason why it shouldn't.' Zoë looked mischievous. 'They won't be able to wriggle their way out of this one.'

As the others continued chatting enthusiastically, Tierney sighed. She wanted this to go well so badly it hurt. But more than that, she wanted Jake.

Right now, she didn't hold out much hope of getting either.

22

Faking It

'Liz, how many walls d'you reckon my flat has?' Tierney's face was earnest.

'Er, why . . . ?'

''Cause I need to do some *serious* climbing! God, I wish *The Next Big Thing* would hurry up and start! I'm a nervous wreck . . .'

The girls were with Matt and Carin, sprawled before the television and becoming more edgy by the moment, while Zoë and Jake were at the studio going over their plan. It was a simple scheme, and if it worked, revenge would be sweet. Any minute now Barnaby, Julian and Vanita would arrive for the interview, blissfully unaware of what was going on.

The intercom buzzed and Tierney jumped. 'Jesus, I'm so *jittery* . . .'

'You think *you're* bad.' Matt shook his head, grinning. 'You should have seen Zoë this morning. I thought I'd have to sedate her, poor thing.'

Tierney laughed. She'd seen the couple together and couldn't believe how protective Matt was of his new girlfriend. Tierney felt strange, watching them, seeing how Matt had changed. She sighed. Maybe he'd just met the right person.

She had too. She just couldn't tell him.

As she opened the door, Honey Trapp practically fell into the room, clutching a giant parcel wrapped in bright paper which she thrust into Tierney's hands. 'I come bearing gifts! It's from Damien. Have I missed the show?'

'No, it's adverts.' Tierney ripped open the present, gasping as the paper fell away to reveal an enormous picture of her in the original Eve's Brew outfit, the green fig-leaf bikini. Attached was a note: 'Tierney – sorry for not listening to you more. I have an identical picture and I'm putting it up at the office. Hope you like it. And hope I haven't lost my coolest client . . . ?'

She couldn't help smiling. 'I guess you and Damien will be at Jake's pool party?'

'You bet.' Honey squeezed her hand. 'You're definitely not coming? I wish you'd change your mind . . .'

To celebrate the last episode of *The Next Big Thing*, Jake had organised a party at his house for the crew, researchers and a crowd of friends. Tierney's mates had tried everything to persuade her, but she'd been adamant. She felt far too fragile and mildly agoraphobic, not having been anywhere for weeks now.

Now Honey looked sad. 'I won't see you for ages!'

'You're still going with Damien, then?' Tierney giggled. Honey was going to watch the desert marathon, and it made Tierney laugh, imagining the singer, with her immaculate make-up and designer dresses, traipsing through the Sahara.

'It's on!!!' yelled Carin, and they rushed over to the television, all grabbing each other's hands as the credits began rolling.

'Oh my God, look at them . . .' Liz gasped. There, in the studio Tierney remembered so well, was Jake, looking totally relaxed, while to his left, Zoë sat very still, eyes glittery with glee. Beside her, Barnaby, Julian and the Valkyrie all wore smug little smiles.

Jake grinned into the camera. 'It's been voted the hippest drink on the market, with an ad campaign that got the whole country talking. The profits have been like Halley's Comet, so way up high they've rarely been seen before! I'm referring – like you don't know! – to Eve's Brew. And joining me are the brains behind the beer – Barnaby Hamilton and Julian Parry. With them are their Consultant on Cool, Vanita Slater, and Zoë Mason, the new Eve's Brew girl. Julian, why don't you talk us through the past few months?'

So puffed up with pride it was amazing he didn't explode, Julian launched into a self-congratulatory monologue on how he and Barnaby had revolutionised the beer market. As he piled on the praise, Honey stuck her fingers down her throat and pretended to gag while the others watched in amazement. The man's arrogance was truly something.

Through clever questioning, Jake had Julian boasting freely about the incredible profits they'd made. Every few minutes the Valkyrie would chip in, leaning across Zoë and edging on to the screen, keen to remind everyone of her contribution.

'Which is non-existent!' Tierney shook a fist at the screen.

Finally Jake turned to Zoë. 'I'm sure viewers would love to hear how you're feeling about all this?'

Her smile was humble. 'I *must* thank Barnaby and Julian. They really do bring new meaning to the word "modesty". And trust me, they've done more to make Eve's Brew a success than you could ever imagine . . . more than I could ever tell you . . .'

Tierney chuckled at the double meanings.

Barnaby and Julian, still beaming, didn't twig.

Zoë continued quietly. 'For me, this project has been the most wonderful chance. I've gone from living on the streets to being offered a modelling contract. It's a dream.' She sighed. 'My one wish is to do something for other homeless teenagers. And now – thanks to Vanita, whose idea this was, and who has pledged the fee that would have gone to Prophets Inc. to the venture I'm about to announce, and thanks to the generosity of Barnaby and Julian in backing it – now *I can*!'

Vanita tensed. Smiles slipping slightly, Barnaby and Julian watched Zoë as she stared straight into the camera with an excited smile.

'I'm *delighted* to reveal that **fifty per cent** of the profits from Eve's Brew will be used to establish a series of regional shelters for the homeless across the UK! And they will be known under the umbrella name of Eve's House!'

Julian looked like he'd been shot.

Barnaby let out a screech of horror then quickly converted it into a cough.

The Valkyrie's fists clenched.

'Well, you heard it here first!' Jake took over smoothly. 'What a wonderful gesture – I'm sure everyone watching will agree it's a truly cool thing to do! Now, in part two of

The Next Big Thing, we'll be meeting the singing sensation of the year – Deadly Nightshade! Join us after the commercial break!'

He signalled the cameramen.

In the studio, the adverts began rolling on the tiny monitors just as pandemonium erupted.

'You *moron*!' Julian rounded on Vanita, who looked stunned. 'For fuck's sake, how could you come up with something so *stupid*?' His voice rose in anger. 'How *dare* you not consult me first?!' Face a violent red, he looked like he was about to choke the living daylights out of her with his bare hands.

Vanita scowled. 'You bloody berk – it's got nothing to do with *me*! Zoë, tell them! *Now* . . .' She looked daggers at the teenager, who simply smiled frostily.

Barnaby clutched the sides of his chair, face ashen, staring into space. 'Half the profits . . . *half* the profits . . . That's . . . that's . . . *that's a fortune* . . .' He turned to Zoë, his lower lip quivering. 'Why are you doing this?'

Unable to hide her anger any more Zoë's face went taut. 'You lied to me! And Tierney! *You screwed us!* Now you know how it feels . . .'

Suddenly Julian sprang out of his seat like a demented Zeberdee, jabbing a finger in Barnaby's face and glowering at Zoë. 'I said we should have paid her off!' he screamed, eyes rolling wildly. 'I *told* you the stupid bitch would cause trouble! But you wouldn't listen, would you? Oh no, all you cared about was getting Tierney *fucking* Marshall for your precious *fucking* ad campaign! Now look where it's got us! *We'll lose more than we made!* The whole sodding country just saw us pledge our profits for that stupid project – we can hardly turn round and say we're not doing it, can we? I can't believe I ever listened to you . . . you . . . you . . . *tosser*!!!' Clutching his head, he sank slowly to the floor and curled up in the foetal position, muttering feverishly about profit margins.

'Of all the . . . You wouldn't have anything if it wasn't for me! *I* was the brains behind this whole thing and you know it!' Barnaby spluttered, shaking his fist. 'You . . . you . . . *wanker*!!!'

As the two men began screaming hysterically, Zoë and Jake winked at each other.

The show was still on air.

*

At Tierney's, they were in convulsions.

Liz lay on her stomach, thumping the ground, tears of laughter streaming down her cheeks. Beside her, Honey was doubled over, holding her stomach, while Matt and Carin cried with mirth. Curled up on the sofa, gaze locked on Jake, Tierney was the only one not smiling. While the others continued screeching with hysteria, she got up and slipped away into her room, grabbing her keys. She had to get to the studio and see Jake.

She couldn't not.

*

Vanita was spitting venom as she faced Zoë. Barnaby and Julian had legged it out of the studio at high speed, still yelling at each other and threatening legal action against the television studio. Now the two women were alone in the corridor, Zoë backed up against the wall as the Valkyrie blocked her way.

'You little bitch . . .' Vanita's eyes were slits of black anger. 'If it wasn't for me you'd still be stuck out on the streets! You're going to regret this . . .'

'I don't think so. God, I've met some sad people in my life, but you . . .' Zoë shook her head in disgust.

Vanita's long, icy fingers closed over the teenager's wrist. Zoë flinched and the older woman's hold tightened. 'I should have left you to rot in that hostel. What, you think a few decent clothes and a bit of make-up mean you're *somebody*?' Her laughter was cold. 'I did a bit of research on you. Very interesting. What *will* people say when they find out about you and your brother? Getting your own flesh and blood charged with rape?' Her lip curled. 'You think what the media did to Tierney was bad? They'll tear *you* to bits. I'll make sure of that . . .'

Zoë shuddered. Visions of her face and name all over the papers filled her head until she felt like it would burst. She tried to blank herself out, but this time, for the first time, it didn't work. All she could hear was Vanita's taunting voice, going on and on, wheedling its way into her brain. She felt her hopes collapsing as she cowered against the wall. No matter what had happened to her, she'd somehow managed to hold things together.

But now Zoë had no fight left in her.

As she slumped against the wall, she seemed to shrink, to fold in on herself, and the Valkyrie watched in triumph as the girl wilted before her eyes.

'Leave her alone.'

The voice was soft but steely, and slowly, Vanita turned round. She let go of Zoë's hand and watched Tierney walk down the empty hallway towards them. Her face was pale but her eyes were hard, and Vanita frowned. This wasn't the ditzy, dizzy girl she was used to. Something was different.

'You know what, Vanita?' Tierney gave her a weary look. 'I'm *bored* with you. Really. Now, why don't you just turn round, walk down that corridor, and crawl back under your little stone. You've done more damage in the past few months than most people could manage in a lifetime.'

Vanita looked at her in amusement. 'Think you're so clever, don't you? Just because of that little stunt today.' She shrugged and started moving past Tierney, eyes flicking back to Zoë. 'I've got things to do. A story to tell.'

Zoë paled again.

Tierney shook her head and blocked Vanita's exit. 'You're not telling anyone anything. If you do, Zoë goes straight to the press and tells them about your role in hijacking the Eve's Brew launch. Yeah, that'd look good, wouldn't it? The way you used her to get back at me. Oh, and by the way' – she smiled – 'Matt told me all about how you poached Adonis from the Trend Factory.' Her delicate face hardened, the blue eyes steady. 'I mean it, Vanita. You say one word about Zoë, you do one thing to hurt her, you so much as *think* something bad about her, and I'll come after you.'

Now it was Vanita's turn to blanch. If the details about Adonis ever came out, she'd never work again in cool hunting, simple as that. She sent Tierney a vicious look. 'Don't threaten me—'

'Or you'll *what*?' Tierney threw back her head in laughter. 'You forget, I've already lost everything once! But you . . . now, you've still got a career to try and rescue, haven't you? Don't suppose Joel'll be too happy about the company's fee going towards Eve's House. Still, you can probably talk him round on that. But what you did to Adonis?' She shook her head. 'If that gets out, you'll never get another job, and you know it. So if I were you, I'd get out of here now, before I change my mind and decide to ruin you just for the hell of it. God knows it's what you deserve.'

Knowing she was beaten, Vanita scowled at Tierney before storming off down the hallway.

Tierney knew she should feel good, but she didn't. This wasn't her way. 'You all right?' She looked at Zoë anxiously.

The girl nodded but her face was chalky white.

'Come on, let's go and have a drink. Do you know where Jake is?'

'Yeah, he went home to get ready for this pool party.' Zoë seemed dazed, and Tierney took her arm and steered her gently down the corridor.

'Where's Matt?'

'I said I'd meet him at Jake's.' Zoë managed a wan smile.

Tierney nodded. She'd have to go to the party after all. She felt like if she didn't see Jake soon she'd burst.

*

Hearing the door above the shouts and squeals coming from the pool, Jake hurried back through the house, praying it was Tierney. He knew she'd been watching the programme and he couldn't wait to see her.

The second the show had ended, the switchboard was jammed with calls from the media. Now Jake dashed to the front door, smiling as he imagined Tierney's reaction to the programme. He was desperate to talk to her and tell her how he was feeling.

He threw open the door with a grin and almost fell over.

'*Lisa!!!* What are you doing here?'

His fiancée beamed. 'Told you I'd try to get a week off! And you'd mentioned this big farewell bash, so here I am . . .' Her smile slipped. 'You don't look very happy to see me . . .'

'Of course I am! I'm just surprised, that's all . . .' Hugging her, Jake closed his eyes, hating himself. Life must be laughing at him. This was some kind of divine retribution for sleeping with Tierney. Karma playing catch-up.

'You must be shattered.' He smoothed back a wisp of soft brown hair from Lisa's face. 'Do you want to rest for a bit? Can I fix you some food? Or—'

'Would you relax already!' Lisa gave him a quizzical smile as she looked round, admiring the spacious house. 'I'll just grab a shower, then I'll be down so you can introduce me to everyone!'

'Sure.' Jake kissed her, feeling like a traitor. 'Whatever you want.'

*

Arriving at Jake's house flanked on either side by Liz and Carin, Tierney shivered. She felt sick with nerves.

'Hey, it'll be all right, promise!' Liz rang the doorbell.

'Thank you, guys.' Tierney smiled gratefully at them. 'I feel a bit shaky, what with those topless pictures and everything. I swear, if anyone says anything, I'll smash their stupid face in!'

'Tier, cool it!' Carin opened the side gate. 'You'll be fine.'

Hearing shrieks and music coming from the garden, they hurried out to the pool area, set back from the house and surrounded by lush weeping willows.

The turquoise water glimmered in the late-summer sunlight, and Tierney smiled at seeing her colleagues from Prophets Inc. all splashing and squealing like children as they dived and jumped in and out of the pool. A long line of brightly coloured sun-loungers was arranged so that some were in the shade, several of the women stretched out on them, chatting and munching on ice-creams.

Tierney felt self-conscious, paranoid that everyone was watching her as she pulled off her dress to reveal a simple black swimming costume. Glancing up, she saw a few of the men looking her way and murmuring to each other. Instantly she felt her face burning but forced herself to meet their eyes with a haughty tilt of her chin. The men smirked, like schoolboys caught red-handed with magazines from the top shelf.

As Liz hurried over to the buffet table, Carin pulled Tierney to one side. 'I didn't get a chance to say anything before, but guess what? I phoned Andy's brother this morning!'

'Is he coming back?' Tierney's face brightened.

'Hardly. He's finally got his arse in gear and gone travelling in the Far East. Can you believe it?'

'No way! I never thought he would . . .' Tierney shook her head in disbelief.

'He'll be gone at least six months.' Carin smiled complacently. 'And by the time he gets back, he'll have forgotten he was even pissed off with us in the first place!'

'Hope you're right. What's happening with you and Gina?'

Carin shoved her shoes under the sun-lounger. 'She wants us to get a place together.'

'My God, don't tell me you're actually getting serious about someone!' Tierney looked at her friend sceptically.

'We'll see. I haven't said yes yet . . .' With an arch smile, Carin dived gracefully into the pool, surfacing near a cute girl in a bright yellow bikini.

Tierney sat down on a lounger, feeling glum. Everyone was pairing off: Matt and Zoë, Honey and Damien, Carin and Gina. The whole crowd was in couples.

Jake included.

She watched him saunter out of the house, his arm casually round the waist of a slender brunette in a bright green bikini. *Lisa.*

Tierney blanched. The couple mingled with the various cliques, everyone looking at the American girl with interest as Jake introduced her. Lisa was beautiful. Lisa looked friendly. *Nice.* Lisa didn't seem like someone who needed to worry that her boyfriend was being unfaithful. And it was obvious, from the way that she was gazing up at him, and clinging on to his arm, that she adored Jake.

Reality hit Tierney like a slap around the face. For the first time, she understood that she and Jake had only ever been a one-night stand. In some corner of her mind, she'd believed they were different. Now she felt like the biggest fool on the face of the earth.

He was just another bloke screwing around.

And she was just another bit on the side.

She wasn't *even* that.

'Tier!' Liz pulled the next-door seat over, sitting down and looking anxiously at her friend. 'I just found out who that girl with Jake is! You okay?'

'No.' Tierney shook her head, face pale. 'But I will be. Come on, let's go for a swim . . .'

Walking quickly to the edge of the pool, she jumped in with an excited shriek and joined in the boisterous game of water polo which had started.

She'd show Jake he meant nothing, if it killed her.

So for the next few hours, Tierney was the life and soul of the party. No one laughed more loudly, talked more quickly, flirted more frantically. She was on automatic pilot, just going through the motions, but no one would have guessed.

*

Watching Tierney out of the corner of his eye, Jake was miserable. Lisa was having a wonderful time, thrilled finally to be here in London and meeting all his friends and colleagues. She looked lovely, having cut her hair so it framed her face and showed off her large hazel eyes. As they wandered around, hands linked loosely, Jake watched people watching him. He was the man who had it all – gorgeous girl, good job to go back to, great looks. Everyone assumed he was delirious with happiness, and why the hell wouldn't they? He was grinning, his face radiant with happiness at his own good fortune.

Jake alone knew he was faking it.

*

'Peace offering?'

Tierney turned to find Damien holding out a plate of chocolate biscuits.

They grinned sheepishly at each other.

'Thanks for the picture.' Tierney shielded her eyes from the sun.

'I saw the programme.' Damien glanced over at Jake. 'You two make quite a team. Shame, you could have presented *The Next Big Thing* together, since their offer to you is back on the table.'

'Is it?' Tierney shrugged. 'I'll think about it.'

'Do. They're keen.' Damien paused. 'I think you and Jake will rather miss each other.'

'Like I'd miss an axe through my skull . . .' muttered Tierney as Damien gave her a knowing smile.

'He's Saggitarius, Tierney. Perfect for you.'

She looked at him sharply. 'You're mad.'

'And so are you.' Damien nodded. 'About him.'

'For crying out loud, the man's engaged!' Tierney glared at her agent in exasperation. 'He's getting married in a matter of weeks!'

'Maybe.' Damien grinned at her as he wandered off again. 'And maybe not . . .'

Tierney wandered into the spacious kitchen to get a cold drink. As she stood by the sliding glass doors, gazing out with unseeing eyes, she heard footsteps behind her and turned to find Lisa. Tierney felt her own lips tremble with the effort of returning the American girl's smile.

'Hi, you're Tierney, right? I recognise you from the photos of you and Jake.' Lisa smiled wryly. 'He sent me some of the stories about you two . . .'

'Oh . . . right.' Tierney laughed nervously. She was surprised, but why? Of course Jake would have told his fiancée he was being paired up with someone for publicity purposes.

'Yeah, must admit, I felt a bit weird about it all, you know . . .' Walking forward and setting her own glass down, Lisa looked directly at her. 'What with not seeing Jake for so long.' She hugged herself, face brightening. 'Silly, really, I mean, we're getting married in six weeks!' She held out her hand and Tierney stared at the beautiful engagement ring which sparkled in the sunlight. 'Gorgeous, isn't it?' Lisa beamed. 'I'm so excited I can hardly sleep at night!'

Tierney nodded. 'It's beautiful.' Her voice was hoarse. The message from Lisa was crystal clear. Possession was nine-tenths of the law; Jake was hers. She didn't know what Lisa guessed, suspected or feared. All she knew was she had to get out of there.

Saying a few swift goodbyes, she grabbed her things and walked back through the side gate, not even bothering to put on her shoes but padding barefoot into the street.

'Tierney, wait . . .' Jake hurried down the driveway after her.

'Jake, hi. Oh, listen, I meant to tell you, the show was great! Thanks again for your help.' Tierney put on sunglasses.

Jake looked at her carefully, trying to gauge her mood. 'Look, about Lisa, I want to explain—'

'No need. She's your fiancée, for God's sake, you don't owe me any explanations!' She laughed as if the mere idea was absurd.

Jake was obviously confused, leaning against the car with his arms folded, grey eyes subdued. 'But you and I . . . we—'

'Had a fling!' Tierney interrupted briskly. 'We're both adults. It's cool, honestly. Go back and enjoy your party.'

She reached past him and opened the car door. 'I'd better get a move on.'

Jake stared. *This* was to be their goodbye?

Casual, careless, quick.

'Have a safe flight back, Jake, and a *wonderful* wedding!' Tierney smiled and slammed the car door. Jake watched as she drove off, wishing she'd turn round, knowing she wouldn't. Then he sat down on the kerb, tracing a line on the ground with a spindly branch.

Without even realising it, he drew a heart.

And then a line clean through it.

*

Hitting the brakes, Tierney stopped in the next road, not caring she was parked slapbang in the middle of the street as she thumped the steering wheel in frustration, before covering her face with trembling hands.

A one-night stand. That was all she'd been.

*

Jake locked the front door behind the last guest, took the phone off the hook, and went into the kitchen to find Lisa. Though she must be dead on her feet after the flight, she'd kept up a lively banter all afternoon, chattering too brightly, her laughter tinged with panic. And no wonder. Jake had been there in body only since the moment Tierney had gone.

'Leave all that,' he told his fiancée now, as she began bustling around the kitchen.

She smiled briskly. 'I'll just stack the dishwa—'

'No.' Taking her hand, Jake sat her down at the table. He loathed himself for doing this to her, doing it here, doing it now when she'd flown all this way to be with him. In the past, he'd always condemned those who broke off commitments. Now he knew better. Now he knew the most detailed plans, the most eloquent promises, the best intentions in the world, couldn't hold a heart if that heart wasn't truly there in the first place.

Slowly, sadly, he began breaking Lisa's.

23

Midas Touch

'Chocolate *is* a girl's best friend . . .' Tierney opened the cupboard, skipping out of the way just in time as an avalanche of chocolate bars and biscuits came pouring out. If she couldn't have Jake, and obviously she couldn't, then she didn't want to have sex ever again.

Ergo, she needed chocolate. Lots of it.

'Celibate and fat, that'll be me.' Attacking a huge bar of Cadbury's Whole Nut, Tierney curled up on the sofa and watched the sun filtering over the horizon. She'd woken early, and her meeting with Richard Midas wasn't for a few hours. Mind you, it would take that long to decide what to wear. Although, she scowled, since she hated his guts and was going to tell him so, who cared how she looked?

Who cared about anything, when she couldn't be with Jake?

She'd spent the last two weeks phone-watching, itching to dial his number, jumping up to answer it, hoping so much it was him that it physically hurt. It never was. No doubt he was busy having a great time showing Lisa round London, Tierney reminded herself bitterly.

Now that everyone knew the truth about what had happened with Zoë, Tierney was being fêted by the media again. She and Damien had agreed that she'd give just one interview, with ***Sorted!***, the only publication to stand by her. The piece which ran was a sympathetic interview in which Tierney described the ordeal of recent weeks, and her comments were quoted widely in the tabloids.

The picture used was very different from the shot of Tierney which had graced the cover a few short months ago. This one showed her curled up on the windowseat in her flat, long hair now tumbling way past her shoulders, gazing pensively out of the window with a slight smile.

Sometimes Tierney would hold the two magazine issues side by side and study the two pictures. Neither of them told the whole story.

Cleopatra was keen to reinstate her column, but Tierney refused. She was still wary of the media – the publicity over Barnaby and Julian's duplicity had given the papers an excuse to rehash the Topless Tierney story again. Several papers, including the *Sunday Splash*, had run the photos, to her fury.

Now she smiled grimly. Giving Midas a piece of her mind was something she was looking forward to all right! The smile faded as she glanced at her watch again. In a few hours Jake would be on a plane, taking him home, out of her life for ever.

It was for the best.

'So why,' she asked herself sadly, 'does it feel so *bad* . . . ?'

*

Jake stared glumly at his suitcases. He was all packed and ready to go, the house neat and tidy, as though he'd never even been there. Only his heart was in a mess.

The last two weeks had been a nightmare. Lisa had freaked out when he'd told her he couldn't marry her, her initial reaction being to scream and throw things. Then she'd calmed down, sobbing for hours, begging him to 'see sense'.

In the end, realising that to give her no reason was cruel, Jake had reluctantly told her the truth, that he had feelings for someone else. After locking herself in the bathroom for three hours, Lisa had emerged, packed her bags, and moved into a hotel, catching a flight back to New York the next morning. Jake had called her every day for a week, but she'd refused to come to the phone, so in the end he'd written to her, after which she'd finally phoned. The conversation was strained and sad and they'd both been in tears by the end, but Jake knew he'd done the right thing.

He hadn't contacted Tierney. What was the point? She didn't want to know. He'd spent his last week in London wandering around like a lost soul, going to all the places he knew Tierney hung out, hoping he'd run into her. He'd even gone back to the crystal exhibition, and waited there for hours in the hope she'd show.

It felt lonely, being there without her.

Now, knowing he had to be on a plane in three hours, Jake suddenly realised he couldn't leave, not without seeing Tierney one last time. One last chance to make things right. He checked the time. He had to return the keys to the estate agent, meet with Damien to go over some last-minute problems with his contract from the network, and get to the airport. There was still time to see Tierney.

But first he had to find her.

*

Tierney slid down in the back of the cab, hiding her face behind a newspaper and praying the driver wouldn't recognise her. Dressed in jeans and a black T-shirt, with dark glasses on, she hoped she could go incognito. So far so good, but as the cab pulled up outside Midas plc and she was paying the driver, he gave her a wink and nodded at the paper.

'Keeping *abreast* of the news, are we, luv?' He cackled, and Tierney slammed the change into his hand before storming off.

Midas plc headquarters were in a huge glass building with gold girders running between the panels, glowing in the morning sunshine. Pushing through the revolving door, Tierney entered the palatial lobby, all in white marble shot through with gold veins. In the middle was a sculpture of a giant gold hand which, as she entered, suddenly swung forward so that it was pointing straight at her.

The lobby was very quiet, and Tierney was acutely aware of her heels clicking across the floor as she approached the receptionist, a woman who looked like she'd been liposuctioned to within an inch of her life.

'Please wear this while you're in the building.' The woman smiled, handing her a security pass in the form of a tiny gold hand which Tierney pinned to her top with a bemused smile. 'If you'd like to go up to the eleventh floor, someone will meet you.' The woman gestured to the lifts and Tierney scuttled off.

The elevator was also huge, with a sofa and mirror; as it slid smoothly upwards, Tierney jumped as a sudden blast of muzak came pumping out. 'Goldfinger.'

'What else?' she murmured, checking her reflection.

She emerged on the eleventh floor to find a leggy brunette with the voice of an android waiting patiently. 'If you'd like to come this way . . .' Tierney followed her down several plushly carpeted corridors and into a large, corner office.

'Tierney, how lovely to see you again.' Richard Midas got up from behind his desk. He was just as she remembered, his slate-grey hair now pulled back in a ponytail, and those mischievous blue eyes twinkling away in his craggy face. Smiling, he gestured to one of the dove-grey leather sofas either side of a low glass table laden with magazines. Sitting down, Tierney was relieved that the office appeared normal, having half expected it to be gold-plated.

Sitting down opposite, Midas smiled warmly again. 'Well, I expect you're wondering why I asked you to come here today?'

She looked at him coldly. 'To apologise, I presume.'

'Why?' He seemed perplexed. 'Have I done something to offend you?'

'No – you've done several things!' Opening her bag, Tierney removed a folder and shook it so that a heap of newspaper cuttings fell out.

'These are all articles on me, going back over the last few months. They are all highly insulting, and they are all from papers *you* own!' Tierney was practically frothing at the mouth by now, having spent the morning working herself up into a little storm cloud of anger. 'Talk about *ungrateful*! I save your granddaughter from God knows what, and how do you return the favour? By having your hacks trash me! *Constantly!* According to them, I'm a cross between Cynthia Payne and Lucretia bloody Borgia!'

She slapped the sofa, irked by the spark of pure amusement in his watchful blue eyes. 'I'm here to ask, no, to *demand*, that you make your journalists lay off! I want my life back!'

Comprehension settled over Midas's patrician features. 'You have been having rather a tough time lately . . .' He looked at her thoughtfully.

'"Rather tough"?' Tierney spluttered. 'Thanks to your dirt-shovelling hacks, my breasts are on display for every bloke in Britain! It's ridiculous!'

Midas spread his hands in a gesture of confusion. 'But my dear, what did you expect? You're a celebrity. Now answer me this: did someone force you to pose topless?'

Tierney blushed. 'No! But that's not the poi—'

'So what do you want me to do?' His voice was dry. 'Put a gag on my reporters? Tell them that every other celeb is fair game, but not you, not Tierney Marshall?'

'That's *exactly* what I want you to do!' Tierney glared at him. 'And frankly, I don't think it's too much to ask!'

'Even if I did that, what makes you think the other papers would leave you alone?'

'It would be a start. You own three of the biggest-selling, most intrusive tabloids. If you stop printing all these so-called scoops on me, the others might back off too! I've had enough, I can't take it any more . . .'

Sitting back, Midas regarded her through narrowed eyes. 'So that's it, then, Tierney? You've had your fling with fame, and now you want life to return to normal . . .' He sighed. 'I'm disappointed. I hoped you'd use your success for something a bit more worth while than wasting your time and mine by whingeing about what a hard life you're having.'

Her mouth fell open in shock. *'Excuse me?'*

Midas shrugged. 'You've allowed yourself to be linked with sex and booze, now you're upset the papers treat you accordingly. Okay, so they've got a few snaps of you in your birthday suit. Big deal. You shouldn't have posed for the pics in the first place. But you did, so now, *brazen it out*! Come on, show a bit of the guts that made you famous in the first place!' He laughed in amazement. 'My God, girl – you tackled a serial rapist without a second thought! What are a few stupid stories in the paper?'

His words punctured her balloon of anger. 'But I'm not being taken seriously . . .' she lamented, folding her arms and screwing her face up like a spoilt child.

Again Midas smiled in disbelief. 'And why should you be? What have you done to *make* anyone take you seriously? Come now, you've got what every girl your age dreams of: money in the bank, more clothes than you know what do to with, famous friends, and every bloke in the land fantasising about you! Hardly reasons to be depressed! I'd say for a twenty-five-year-old you've done rather well, actually . . .' Seeing her crestfallen expression, his voice softened. 'But it's not enough, is it, Tierney? You wanted something more, didn't you? Something *real* . . .'

Miserably, she nodded. 'It's . . . not how I imagined it, nothing's the way I thought it would be.'

His smile was kind. 'Things rarely are.'

'The crazy thing is' – Tierney winced, recalling how malleable she'd been – 'I never wanted to do the Eve's Brew campaign in the first place!'

Midas frowned. 'So why did you?'

Shrugging, she looked down at her hands; she'd started ripping the newspaper articles to bits without realising it, and now a little funeral pyre of paper was forming on the carpet.

'I don't know. It all seemed to make sense at the time.' In her head she could hear their voices: Barnaby, Julian, Damien, Alex, Matt, Vanita, Joel. She'd made the same mistakes with all of them. Looking up again, she groaned. '*Why* didn't I listen to my intuition? Whenever I ignore that, I end up in trouble!'

Midas nodded, pouring them both a glass of mineral water. 'The question is, what now? You can't just stop being a trend-setter and celeb. It doesn't work that way.'

Tierney flopped back against the sofa. He was right: she was stuck. She couldn't go back to the life she'd had before, because she wasn't the same person. And in the minds of most, she would always be Tierney Marshall, Coolest Girl in the Country, the girl who made Eve's Brew the hippest beer around, the girl who bared her breasts after swearing she never would.

From now on, whatever she did, the press would be there, watching, waiting. If she succeeded, they'd court her affections again, and if she failed, they'd gleefully report on that too.

Tierney felt trapped.

She'd confused success with fame.

She'd chased fame.

And now fame was going to chase her right back.

*

'I'll be coming over to New York next month, so we can sort everything else then . . .' Damien shook Jake's hand as they stood in the circular hallway at his offices. 'The network are really keen on you, though, you shouldn't have any problems.'

Jake managed a weak smile. In two hours he'd be on the plane, and he was running late, having spent all day looking for Tierney. Now he glanced at the wall; alongside the pictures of Damien's clients, there was now one of Tierney in her Eve's Brew costume, the fig-leaf bra and briefs clinging to her curves, her blue eyes seeming to stare right at Jake.

Watching him, Damien wondered what to do. He wasn't in the habit of playing Cupid, but maybe just this once . . .

Walking Jake to the door, he sighed. 'Strange bloke, that Richard Midas.'

'Is he?' asked Jake, absently.

'He is, rather. A few weeks ago, out of the blue, he suddenly contacted Tierney and asked her to meet with him, without saying why!' Damien bit back a chuckle as Jake tensed. 'She should be there around now, I imagine . . .'

'She's at Midas plc. Now?' A slow smile started across the American's face. 'Are you sure?'

'Yep! I've been there a few times actually. There's this little coffee shop just round the corner, very nice. Good for when one wants to just sit and . . . talk . . .'

At the door they stopped, Jake now beaming. 'Damien, I owe you one!'

The two men hugged self-consciously before Jake dashed to his rental car, glancing frantically at his watch.

*

Tierney stared into space while Midas watched with a slight smile. Finally she looked at him glumly. 'So what do I do now? Run around wearing a yashmak and dark wig for the rest of my life?'

He laughed. 'No. What you do is use your profile for something good. Something you can be proud of.'

'Like what, though?' Tierney demanded.

'Which brings us to the reason I asked you here today.' Getting up, Midas went over to his desk, taking out a plastic binder full of papers. 'Here you go. Take it away with you, look through it. Let me know what you think.'

'What is it?' Now Tierney was totally confused. She'd entered the office brimming with righteous indignation, all set for a blazing row, not a career guidance session!

Midas sat down again. 'Basically, ever since you rescued Lucy, I've wanted to do something to encourage others to show a bit of your guts. Something to make them feel they have to stand up and be counted when someone's in trouble. What I've put together is a *massive* public awareness campaign. The slogan I want to use, and this is where you come in, is: "It's cool to care." Will you front it? Everyone associates you with saving Lucy from the West End Rapist – this would be a chance for you to make a real difference. Plus, it wouldn't interfere with your other work. I've got the backing of several politicians who want to throw their weight behind this project.

'I've also been talking with one of the top advertising

agencies, and they're going to put together a special awareness film which will run on television and in cinemas, as well as on cable. This is going to be big. This is a chance for you to show everyone another side to the Coolest Girl in the Country.'

Tierney frowned. 'You mean, I should reinvent myself?'

'No, I mean *be yourself*!' He waited while she took a deep breath, walking over to the window, staring out with unseeing eyes. She felt like she was being given a second chance. A way through the chaos which had taken over her life.

'But aren't you worried people won't take this seriously, with me involved?' she challenged.

'Not really. I don't suppose you have any deep dark secrets about to be revealed in the papers!' He chuckled. 'There aren't any more salacious stories or photos of you about to appear, are there?'

'God, no! I can promise you that!' Tierney shuddered at the mere thought. Then she laughed; for the first time in *forever*, life was starting to make sense again.

'Okay, I'm in. Let's do it!'

They sealed it with a handshake.

*

Crossing the lobby, glancing again at the giant golden hand gleaming in the sunshine, Tierney smiled sadly. She could do with the Midas Touch when it came to love. She doubted she'd ever stop thinking about Jake – Jesus, she was even starting to see guys who looked just like him! Tierney shook her head as she emerged in the street and saw a bloke leaning against the wall who instantly reminded her of the American.

Then she realised it was him.

24

It's Not Right, But It's Okay

Jake grinned. 'About time! I've been here for ages. Just so you know, my plane leaves in an hour.'

'You'd better go get it, then, hadn't you?' reported Tierney, walking quickly past him. She knew what this was about. Jake wasn't a bastard, and he felt bad about Lisa being at the party. He was here to apologise. Calm his conscience. He wanted to go home with a clear mind and a free heart, and Tierney was a loose end which needed tying up.

Jake felt *sorry* for her.

Before he could speak she cut him off. 'Look, we both know that night was wrong. It was a mistake. There's nothing more to say.'

Stricken, Jake stared at her. He felt like a fool, rushing over here to declare his feelings. For Tierney, what had happened between them really *was* just a one-night stand, nothing more, nothing less.

'Well.' He shrugged 'Just wanted to see you and tell you . . . goodbye . . .'

Again he looked at her, praying he'd missed something,

that suddenly her face would soften and they'd connect again, but she just looked at him calmly.

For a moment, Jake debated telling Tierney about calling off the wedding. Then he stopped himself; no point in guilt-tripping her.

Pausing outside a tiny café, Tierney gave him a quick smile. 'Well, what can I say? Have a safe flight . . .'

'Goodbye, Tierney.'

A moment later and Jake was striding down the street; she stood watching until he'd merged into the crowds.

Pushing open the door to the café, Tierney was relieved to see an empty table near the back. The brasserie was small, with brightly coloured rugs scattered over the gleaming wooden floor. Pavarotti was singing in the background, but not loudly enough to disturb the line of middle-aged businessmen perched on stools before the window, like waxwork dummies with their closed faces and bland clothes. Tierney sat down. A couple were arguing at the next table. The waitress was yawning. A child was crying. Life going on as normal.

And she's fine. Truly she is. Orders a cappuccino. Smiles brightly at the waiter. Opens her newspaper. Thinks about the Midas project. Then Tierney realises something is wrong, because she isn't feeling. Anything.

She seems to have gone numb.

Can one, Tierney frowns, run out of emotion? Perhaps it is finite, and she has used all of hers up? Oblivious to the chattering all around her, she sits very still, resting her face on her hand, trying to think. Her brain is sulking, though, because she didn't tell Jake that she loves him.

How could she?

He isn't hers to love.

And then Tierney realises something, eyes widening in shock.

Her hand. It's wet.

She is crying.

Something tightly coiled within her is unwinding. Closing her eyes, Tierney touches her face as tears, like salty kisses, stream down her cheeks. Finally, the relief, finally, the release, as the little bullet of grief inside her starts melting, pain that is sweet and slow now unfolding.

Not caring that everyone is watching, Tierney puts her head in her hands, and gives in to it properly, her shoulders shaking as she lets out huge, shuddering sobs. And through the tears she smiles at this wonderful feeling of her emotions making themselves at home.

People are murmuring, not sure what to do. Someone shoves a serviette on to her table, but she ignores it, standing up on shaky legs and stumbling out of the café while everyone stares at this strange girl who is half crying, half laughing.

She jumps as a hand grabs her shoulder, and turning, she trips. But it's okay. He reaches out to steady her; he always has, Tierney realises.

'I don't know, bloody women!' Jake rolls his eyes in mock exasperation. 'Always blubbering over something! All right, what is it this time – no, don't tell me! You've broken a finger-nail! Lost your lipstick?'

'I thought you'd gone . . .' Tierney smiles shakily as more tears come out of hiding.

He laughs. 'You don't get rid of me that easily. Just thought I'd leave you on your own for a bit and see if that worked. If not, well' – his grey eyes are serious as he gently tilts her chin – 'I had a thousand more things to try, and then some.' He shrugs helplessly. 'I can't walk away from you, Tierney. Just can't.'

Suddenly she pushes him away, blue eyes wary. 'What about Lisa?' Face reddening. Tierney stares at the pavement. 'I slept with you knowing you were engaged. It's not the sort of thing I normally do, and I, well, I don't like myself much.'

'Ditto for me. But then, I don't normally fall in love with mad English girls.' Jake pauses. 'I called the wedding off. Lisa and I are finished.'

'You did?' Tierney gulps. 'You said . . . in love . . . ?'

'I didn't mean to lay that on you so soon, or so casually. But here goes . . . Tierney Marshall, I am In Love with you. And I love you.' His smile is wry. 'I know the difference now.' Reaching out, he grasps her hand. Tightly, as though scared she'll float away. 'You're the One. The only one.'

Snatching her hand back, she looks at him accusingly. 'But you said all this to Lisa once, didn't you? That's why your ring was on her finger! And look what happened – *you ended up in bed with me*!'

Frustrated, Jake takes her hand again, and this time he doesn't let her pull away. 'You're getting it all wrong! I never felt like this about Lisa, or anyone!' Mistrust is like a glass barrier between them. Jake pulls her closer. 'Listen to me: Lisa and I were always wrong, whether you were in the picture or not. That you were, it just clarified things. Tierney, you were a catalyst – you weren't the cause! It wasn't right for us to sleep together, but it was okay – *we're* okay, if you'll let us be! It wasn't right, but it's okay, it's *life* . . .'

Tierney bites her lip. She knows it's true, she just needed to hear it from Jake. Nervous, she starts hopping from foot to foot, babbling on about where they're headed, what they are. Jake smiles as she tries to pin them down in words, find a way through, find a level she's comfortable with.

'So, what now?' She looks at him expectantly, eye make-up smudged down one cheek, as she winds a lock of fair hair round her index finger.

'Well, let's see . . .' Jake frowns in mock concern. 'I've missed my plane, so I guess I'll stay here . . . there are three months before you start presenting *The Next Big Thing*. I wonder if they'd still want me as a co-presenter? Either way, we've got a few months, we could go touring round Europe . . . trend-spotting . . . crystal gazing . . . we could *get married* . . .'

Tierney stops hopping and shrieks. 'Yes!!!'

Laughing at the speed of her response, Jake kisses her. 'Don't you even want to pretend to think about it?' he teases.

'No need to!' Tierney winks. 'You and me, we're going to be the ***NEXT BIG THING*** !!!'

Epilogue

Everything in Lian screams at her to run with this story *now*.

It's steamy, it's sexy, it's a front-page splash.

She stares at her computer screen, flickering away like a mini electric storm in the middle of the darkened newsroom. The only sound is the Hoover humming out in the hallway as the night cleaner trudges up and down, Walkman jammed over her ears.

Strange, being here alone.

Strange, having this much power at her fingertips. Literally.

If Lian hits the 'send' button, the story will go shooting through cyberspace to her news editor.

Or she can press 'save', grant Tierney Marshall a reprieve. She's already kept the story under wraps for a while, after the car accident involving three of her colleagues when they chased Tierney and Jake. One of the men is paralysed from the waist down, and meanwhile Lian is paralysed with indecision.

Lian sighs. *To Send or Save*, this is the question . . .

Before her on the desk is the latest copy of ***Sorted!***. She gazes again at the article she's read so often she knows it off by heart. In the middle of the text is a picture of the Sahara, a sea of golden sand, brilliant-blue sky, she can practically feel the heat shimmering off the page. 'THE COOLEST WEDDING OF THE YEAR – *Saying "I do" in the Sahara, a triple marriage to remember . . .'* And in the middle of the sand, three couples, all clad in white robes, all beaming. Tierney Marshall and Jake Sheridan. Matt Lucas and Zoë Mason. Damien D'Ville and Honey Trapp.

Tierney Marshall and Jake Sheridan. The coolest couple around. Co-presenters of *The Next Big Thing*. She's part of a high-profile campaign to beat bystander apathy and thanks to the details she provided the police with, the West End Rapist was recognised by a member of the public, and finally arrested.

And Jake, he's in the middle of filming his first movie, not to mention having achieved heart-throb status.

Tierney Marshall and Jake Sheridan.

They're news.

Absently tapping a Biro against her cheek, Lian closes the magazine, gazing at the screen again, frowning as she notes a mistake or two. A smile tugs at her lips as she begins typing, fingers flying over the keyboard as she deletes an error, toys with some meanings, plays with some words.

Words. Delicious, dangerous *words* . . .

And what a story. She grins. The beauty of it is, with the information Andy provided, she doesn't even have to lie, not really. She simply types in the facts and then . . . *flirts* with them for a while. It's all and always down to the angle. The slant. The spin.

Now she clicks on the cursor, returns to the top of the page, and types in the headline she's settled on: 'GIRLS JUST WANNA HAVE FUN' . . . The subs might change it, but she hopes they won't, 'cause it would look good, over the photograph Vanita has given her, of Tierney and Carin sharing a drunken kiss at an old office party. Yeah, it's all here, the inside track on the fling between Tierney Marshall and her housemate, Carin Wheeler. And the fling between Carin and Andy. The tangled, tawdry, private life of the Golden Girl. The *dirt.*

Outside in the street, she hears car doors slamming, someone whistling. Laughter. Usually around now she'd be down the pub with her colleagues, gossiping about whoever the news editor had selected that day for ritual humiliation because they'd failed to live up to his exacting standards. People never understood that reporters were only ever as good as their last story.

If any of the others had this scoop, guilt wouldn't get a look-in. So why can't she do it? *Why can't she just kick her conscience to the kerb and* go *for it?*

Because, she reminds herself fiercely, she made a promise, way back when she was still running herself ragged on a grotty little local rag, that if she ever made the leap to the nationals, she wouldn't wreck lives just to get her by-line on the front page, that she wouldn't be like all the other sleaze merchants. She'd be different.

But all's fair in love, war, and work . . . right?

'You still here?' Steve Wallace, the news editor, comes strolling out of his corner office and leans his bulky frame against the table.

Swiftly, Lian hits the screensaver. 'Yeah, afraid so, just going over some notes . . .'

Steve nods, impressed. 'Sorry I haven't had much time to talk to you since you've been on board. How are you getting on?'

Smiling shyly at this sudden interest, Lian tucks a stray lock of shiny black hair behind her ear. 'It's great! I mean, it's a steep learning curve, after being on a regional, but getting all these shifts on a national, it's a dream!'

Steve chuckles at her enthusiasm. 'Glad to hear it. So, what have you got for me this week? Something juicy, I hope?'

'Well, actually I do have something . . . not sure if I can make it stand up in time for this week's paper . . . I should know by tomorrow, though . . .' Her voice trails off as, disappointed, he turns away, his voice detached.

'You'd better get me something if you want to be the Next Big Thing in journalism, hadn't you . . . ?' He glances again at her computer and leaves.

Lian hits the keyboard again and the story reappears. So, which is it to be? '**Send**' or '**Save**'?

Her hand hovers over the keyboard for a good minute before, with a wry smile, she finally decides, finger landing firmly on the button.